W9-CKK-038

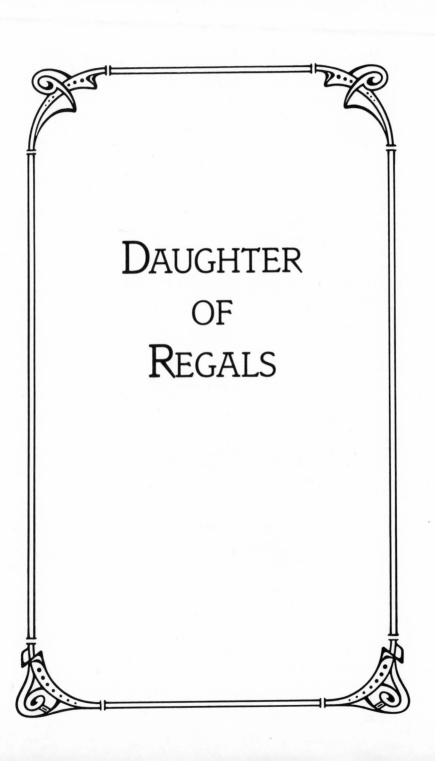

DAUGHTER
OF
REGALS

STEPHEN R. DONALDSON

DAUGHTER OF REGALS

AND OTHER TALES

A DEL REY BOOK

BALLANTINE BOOKS · NEW YORK

A Del Rey Book
Published by Ballantine Books

Copyright © 1984 by Stephen R. Donaldson

"The Conqueror Worm"—© 1983 by Stephen R. Donaldson
    First published in *The Dodd Mead Gallery of Horror*, 1983

"Unworthy of the Angel"—© 1983 by Stephen R. Donaldson
    First published in *Nine Visions*, Seabury Press, 1983

"Gilden-Fire"—© 1981 by Stephen R. Donaldson
    First published by Underwood Miller, 1981

"Animal Lover"—© 1978 by Random House, Inc.
    First published in *Stellar #4*, Del Rey Books, 1978

"Mythological Beast"—© 1978 by Mercury Press, Inc.
    First published in *The Magazine of Fantasy and Science Fiction*, January,
    1979

"The Lady in White"—© 1978 by Mercury Press, Inc.
    First published in *The Magazine of Fantasy and Science Fiction*, February,
    1978

All rights reserved under International and Pan-American Copyright Conventions.
Published in the United States by Ballantine Books, a division of Random House,
Inc., New York, and simultaneously in Canada by Random House of Canada
Limited, Toronto.

Manufactured in the United States of America

First Edition: April 1984

Library of Congress Cataloging in Publication Data

Donaldson, Stephen R.
    Daughter of regals and other tales.

    "A Del Rey book."
    1. Fantastic fiction, American.   I. Title.
PS3554.0469D3   1984   813'.54   83-9244
ISBN 0-345-31442-5

10   9   8   7   6   5   4   3   2   1

TO STEPHANIE—
WHO NEVER FAILS OF MAGIC.

CONTENTS

Introduction	ix
Daughter of Regals	1
Gilden-Fire	79
Mythological Beast	119
The Lady in White	141
Animal Lover	173
Unworthy of the Angel	235
The Conqueror Worm	271
Ser Visal's Tale	287

INTRODUCTION

I WISH I COULD CLAIM THAT THE STORIES IN THIS VOLUME were written as part of a continuing effort to conquer new literary territory. After six *Covenant* books, I'm fairly well established on my own ground; so some efforts in a different direction would be appropriate. In addition, the desire to extend oneself into new terrain—technically, thematically, imaginatively—is an admirable quality in a writer. And, in fact, I *am* ambitious along those lines. For that reason, I've always wanted to publish a collection of short stories. After all, the short story—and hence the short story collection—has several attractions rarely attributed to novels.

First, the short story is short—a fact which speaks for itself. Given the choice between a 15,000 word short story and a 1,000,000 word novel, few people will experience any doubt as to which is easier reading.

Second, in many circles the short story is regarded as a higher art form than the novel. A novel is to a short story as beer is to champagne. In a novel, the writer simply stands back and throws words at his subject until some of them stick—an ordeal from which the subject generally emerges spattered but unbowed. But in a short story the words, being so few, must be carefully placed on the subject (in the pockets, so to speak, or perhaps behind the ears) in order to have any impact at all. Thus the short story appears to demand more of both reader and writer. The reader must become adept at perceiving the writer's meaning as it peeps past the lapels of the subject—or the writer must become expert at tucking his intent here and there so that it still shows.

Third, a collection of short stories is attractive because it allows the writer to approach a wide range of subjects with a variety of disparate skills. For example, very few novels can discuss intelligently the moral implications of both genetic engineering and witchcraft. And a similar number can successfully combine the techniques of first- and third-person narration. But all that can be done in only two short stories. In a collection of, say, eight tales, a writer can even go so far as to tackle the same theme more than once without appearing either impoverished in imagination or destitute in seriousness.

Well, I'm no fool. I've *always* wanted to publish a collection of short stories.

Unfortunately, it hasn't been as easy as wanting for me.

One problem is that I have a one-track mind—and *Covenant* has been on the track for the better part of the past ten years. I don't regret this; the sheer intensity of digging into one subject for ten years was an experience not to be missed. But that degree of concentration has left me few opportunities for short stories. As a result, all the pieces in this volume (with the exception of "Gilden-Fire") were written either in the spring and summer of 1977, when the first *Chronicles of Thomas Covenant* were finished and the second were still in gestation, or in the summer and fall of 1982, after *The Second Chronicles* had achieved parturition. With only eight tales, I don't exactly qualify as a literary Marco Polo—but they're all I've had time for.

In addition, I seem constitutionally incapable of conceiving an exploration into any kind of *terra incognita* for its own sake. I'm a storyteller, not a literary pioneer. I don't write short stories to chart new facets of my prodigious-but-purely-speculative abilities. I work to teach myself whatever new skills are demanded by the stories I want to write. So I'm afraid that any new territory conquered in this collection has been overrun almost accidentally, as a half-unconscious side effect of other intentions.

Two of the stories here were written especially for this volume. The first, "Daughter of Regals," is a fairly straightforward novella of fantasy and intrigue with an untraditional conception of "magic." The second, "Ser Visal's Tale," uses a more traditional idea of magic in some unexpected ways.

As for the rest—

"Gilden-Fire" comes with its own sufficient introduction. I include it here for the sake of completeness.

"Mythological Beast," "The Lady in White," and "Animal Lover" were all produced in 1977. Behind its simpleminded telling, "Mythological Beast" is a quasi-sf story with a theme I happen to feel strongly about. "The Lady in White" is a more classic fantasy, complete with tests and unattainable love. By contrast, "Animal Lover" is ordinary sf action-adventure. But don't be misled: the undercurrents aren't accidental.

"Unworthy of the Angel" was produced for *Nine Visions*, an anthology billed as "religious fantasy." I mention this detail to explain why I permitted the story to be a bit more overt than usual. At the other extreme, "The Conqueror Worm" isn't precisely fantasy at all. It's a tale of "psychological horror" composed under the blandishments of its editor, Charles L. Grant. It contains some of the methods or apparatus of fantasy, but no magic.

In spite of their diversity—real or imagined—all these pieces have one thing in common: I wrote them because I fell in love with them. I'm too lazy to work this hard, except for love.

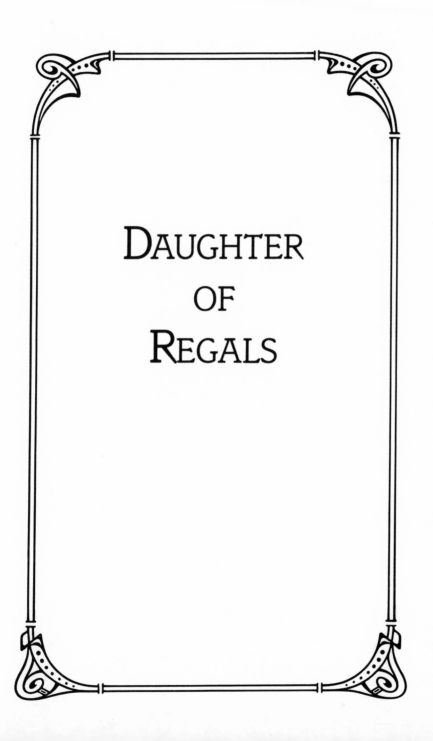

DAUGHTER
OF
REGALS

THROUGH A SMALL, NARROW WINDOW HIGH UP IN ONE wall of the manor's great ballroom, I watched the last of the lesser guests arrive. They were families of consequence, scions of made or inherited fortune, maidens like myself and otherwise, searching for excitement or marriageable partners. They were dressed and decked in all their splendor, as befitted people who attended any ball given at the manor of the Regals. But only the youngest and least cognizant among them came here simply to dance and dine under the chandeliers ablaze with candles. Most attended this night's festivities to witness the Ascension of a new Regal to the rule of the Three Kingdoms. Or—if the Ascension failed—to play whatever parts they chose for themselves in the collapse of the realm.

I was surprised to find that I did not wish myself among them. They were safer than I—and I was not blind to the value of safety. But I was willing to forego such luxuries for the sake of my chance. And—a point which frankly dismayed Mage Ryzel—I was willing to risk the realm along with myself.

He stood near me at another window, watching the arrivals as I did: the Mage Ryzel, my teacher, guardian, and guide—and for the past half year, since the death of my father, regent of the Three Kingdoms. He was a short man with a hogshead chest emphasized by the fit of his Mage's cassock, hands better suited to work at a smithy than to display at table, and a bald pate on which sweat gleamed at any provocation: not a prepossessing figure. But his worth showed in the keenness of his eyes, the blunt courage of his features—and in the crooked and rough-barked Scepter which he gripped at his side.

His Scepter was true Magic, a branch of the Ash which grew

3

high up in the forests of Lodan. Anyone with any education knew that the Ash was the only remaining Real Tree in the Three Kingdoms; and everyone who trusted or feared Ryzel wondered how an ordinary man, who was not Real himself, had contrived to claim a limb of the last Tree.

The Mages of the realm dealt in images of what was Real. These images had substance and effect; they could be shaped and controlled. Therefore they were powerful. But they were no more Real than simple wood or normal flesh-and-blood; true Magic could not be touched. Only the ancient Creatures were Real: the Cockatrice, Basilisk, and Gorgon, the Phoenix, Wyvern, and Banshee—only the Wood of the Ash—only the Fire buried in the mountains of Nabal—only the Wind which caressed or ruined the plains of Canna. Only the men who had founded and secured the line of the Regals, men who were somehow Creatures themselves, Magic men, the Basilisk-Regal and the Gorgon-Regal his son and the Phoenix-Regal my father. And only Mage Ryzel had a Magic Scepter.

He told no one how he had come by such a Scepter, or what uses it served. Secrecy helped secure his position. But I had the story from my father: the Phoenix-Regal himself had obtained that power for Ryzel when I was a young girl, in reward for the Mage's earlier regency.

As was to be expected in the Three Kingdoms, some had considered Ryzel a poor choice to stand as regent after the death of my father. After all, his detractors argued, did not the realm degenerate nearly to chaos during his previous regency, those awkward and perilous years between the failure of my grandmother and the Ascension of the Phoenix-Regal? Yet he was primarily resented because he was strong rather than because he was weak. In truth, no other man could have done what he did as regent for my father: he preserved some semblance of unity over the Three Kingdoms when every pressure of history and personality impelled them to warfare—preserved the realm despite my grandmother's failure of the Magic which alone had compelled the contending monarchs and factions to peace.

That failure had not been foreseen—the line of Regals was then too recent to have established precedents—and so the kings had taken scant advantage of it at first. With the Gorgon-Regal newly dead, no one had contested the Ascension of his daughter. And she had been a woman in middle life, her son just four years short of age. In her failure—and the realm's need—Ryzel had shown himself able to contain, if not quench, the hot struggle for power which followed. First he had demonstrated that my grandmother's son possessed the latent capacity for Magic which she had lacked, and then he had contrived to keep the youth alive and safe until my father grew old enough to attempt the Seat.

Then as now, it was Mage Ryzel who gave the line of Regals the chance to rule.

I was a young woman—this night was the eve of my twenty-first birthday—with no power and scant sources of hope. I was grateful to Ryzel from the bottom of my heart. But he had counseled me to flee rather than accept the hazard of my heritage, and I did not take his counsel. My father had warned me against him.

As indeed the Mage himself had warned me against everyone else. Below me, the influx of guests had ended to prepare for a more considerable arrival. Jeweled and lovely women were paraded by their escorts or admirers to stand against the warm wood of the walls. Families cleared the center of the ballroom, taking auspicious vantage points among the other spectators and leaving the polished tile of the floor to gleam its response to the bright chandeliers. Young gallants—some of them wearing rapiers in defiance of the etiquette which required that no weapons be brought to the manor of the Regals—posed themselves as advantageously as possible below the high windows and balconies. Then, when the doors and the hall were ready, the trumpeters blew a flourish; and my heart stirred because I dreamed of hearing such brave fanfares sounded for me. But this tantara was not mine: it belonged to the people who more than any others wished me dead—to the rulers of the Three Kingdoms.

As the doors rang open, the three entered together, unable to determine who among them should take precedence. On the right strode Count Thornden of Nabal, huge and bitter, and as shaggy as a wolf, with a wolf's manners and appetites. In the center, King Thone of Canna moved with more dignity: he was rotund, urbane, and malicious. And on his left came Queen Damia of Lodan, sylph-like and lambent in her unmatched finery, as well-known for beauty as for cunning. Into the silence of the assemblage they walked, commanding the respect of the guests. From my window, they appeared to catch and hold the light proudly. Variously and together, they seemed far more fit to manage the realm than I.

Behind them came their Mages, famous men in their own names: Cashon of Canna, Scour of Lodan, Brodwick of Nabal.

Any one of them would have attempted my life already if Ryzel had not stood by me since my father's passing, and if they had not secretly feared that I would yet prove myself a Creature, capable of holding the realm against them all.

The Ascension for which these festivities had been prepared would be the test. At midnight this night, I would rise to the Seat which the Basilisk-Regal had created for his line. Into that Seat had been set a piece of Stone, a Real span of slate on which nothing that was not also Real could rest its weight. If the Seat refused me, I would die at the hands of the forces arrayed against me—unless Ryzel contrived some means to save me. Perhaps I would be dead before dawn.

Ryzel believed that I would die. That was the source of his distress, the reason for the sweat on his pate. He believed that I would fail of Magic as my grandmother had failed. And I would not be rescued by the factors which had spared her life—by the surprise of her failure, and by the presence of her son.

Therefore the Mage had spent a good portion of the afternoon arguing with me in my private chambers. While I had pretended indecision concerning what I should wear to the feast and the ball and the Ascension, he had paced the rich rugs from wall to wall and rehearsed all his former efforts to dissuade me. Finally, he had protested, "Chrysalis, give it up!"

But I had only smiled at him. Not often did he call me by my given name.

"If the thought of death will not sway you," he continued, glowering, "think of the realm. Think of the price which your fathers have paid to achieve some measure of peace for this contentious land. It is not yourself alone that you risk. We must act now. *Now*, while we retain some leverage—while the thought that you may yet succeed still causes fear. Once your failure is assured, we will be left with nothing—neither fear nor doubt, coercion nor promise— by which we may secure your life. And the Three Kingdoms will run to war like mad beasts."

I was tempted to retort that his point had not escaped me. He and the Phoenix-Regal had taught me well to consider such questions. But I held to my purpose. Fingering the elaborate satin of gowns I did not mean to wear, I replied only, "Mage, do you recall why my father chose the name he did for his daughter?"

In response, Ryzel made a rude noise of exasperation.

Again, I smiled. Among other things, I loved him for his lack of ceremony. "He named me Chrysalis," I answered myself, "because he believed that in me something new would be born."

A thin hope, as I knew. But the Mage saw it as less. "Something new, forsooth!" he snorted. His Scepter thumped the old stone of the floor under the rugs. "Have we not labored for five years in vain to discover some ground for that hope? Oh, assuredly, your father was a Creature, not to be questioned. But in this he was misled or mistaken."

I turned from my wardrobe to challenge him; but he was too angry to relent. In truth, he appeared angrier than the case deserved. "My lady, we have tested you in every possible way. I have taught you all that lies within my grasp. You are not Magic. You have no capacity for Magic.

"It is *known* that the ability which makes a Mage is not born to everyone. And where that ability is born, it may be detected, be it active or latent. No surer test is required than that you are unable to place hand to my Scepter." That was true: my fingers simply would not hold the wood, no matter how I fought for grip. "Thus it is shown that you are not Real in yourself—not a Creature such as your fathers before you—*and* that you lack the blood or flesh which enable a Mage to treat with the Real. But we have not been content with one test. We have assayed every known trial. You fail them all."

"All but one," I murmured falsely. "I have not yet attempted my Ascension."

"My lady," he replied, "that is folly. The need of the realm does not forgive folly. Do you doubt that the crisis is upon us? You cannot. Your father did not rear you to be a fool. Count Thornden openly musters his forces into readiness for war. King Thone hides his harvests in secret storages, defying the command of the first Regal so that he may be prepared to starve both his foes and us. Queen Damia designs new ploys of every description. Uncertainty alone keeps these fine monarchs from our throats."

As he spoke, I sifted through my trays of jewelry and ornaments, holding baubles to the light and discarding them. But my apparent preoccupation only served to whet the Mage's anger. That was my intent: I wished him angrier and angrier—angry enough, perhaps, to betray his covert thoughts.

He did not, however, reveal anything of which I was ignorant. Grimly, he continued, "And that is not the full tale of the peril. Kodar and his rebels mount fiercer attacks with every passing season. They desire an end to all rulers, forsooth. Fools!" he growled. "They are blind to the fact that throughout history the Three Kingdoms have known no freedom from violence and bloodshed except through rulers—powers strong enough to impose peace."

I had no need to hear such lessons; but I let him go on while I sought the chink in his secrets.

"Canna has no wood. Lodan has no metals. Nabal has no food. This wild Kodar believes that each town—or each village—or each family—or perhaps each *individual*—will do well to fend alone. Does he credit that Canna will gift its harvests to all Lodan and Nabal? It will not; it never has. It will sell to the best buyer—the buyer of greatest resource. And how will such resources be obtained? Hungry towns and villages and families and individuals will attempt to wrest them from each other. Similarly Nabal with its mines and ores, Lodan with its great forests. Kodar seeks anarchy and ruin and names them freedom. The first Regal did not found his line in the realm because he sought power. He was a Creature and had no need for such trivialities. He brought the Three Kingdoms under his rule because he grew weary of their *butchery*."

And Mage Ryzel himself hated that butchery. I knew him well enough to be sure of that. Yet my father had warned me against him. And I had seen my father rise from his man-form into a Creature of wings and Real glory, almost too bright to be witnessed. I could not believe that he had lied to me in any way. Even Ryzel's long-proven fidelity was less to be trusted than the least word of the Phoenix-Regal.

My father was vivid to me, never far from my thoughts. Remembering the whetted keenness of his eyes—as blue as the sky—and the wry kindness of his smile, my throat ached for him. I could not bring him back. But he had promised me—had he not?—that I would follow him in splendor.

No. He had not. But his hopes had the force of promises for me. He had named me Chrysalis. And he had spoken to me often concerning Ascension.

A Regal is both human and Creature, he had said—*fully human and fully Real. This state is not easily attained. It may be reached in one way, by the touch of Stone to one whose very blood and flesh are latent Magic—not merely capable of Magic, but Magic itself. In that way, the first Regal found himself. And for that reason he built the Seat, so that his heirs might be transformed publicly and formally and the realm might acknowledge them.*

But this blood and flesh must be ready. It must be mature in its own way and touched by the influences it requires, or else it will not transform. His smile was bemused and dear. *It would have been well for the realm if I had Ascended when your grandmother failed. But the Magic latent in me was not ripe, and so for four years Mage Ryzel was needed to sustain the peace of the Three Kingdoms.*

Was it wrong that I saw a promise in such talk? No. How could I not? I was his daughter. And he and Ryzel had reared me to be what I was. I was full of memories and grief as I turned at last to face the Mage.

Softly, I replied, "All this is known to me. What is your counsel?"

My father had said of Ryzel, *He is the one true man in the Three Kingdoms. Never trust him.* Now for the first time I began to sense the import of that caution.

He mopped at the sweat on his pate; for a moment, his gaze avoided mine as though he were ashamed. Then he looked at me. Roughly, he said, "Propose marriage to Count Thornden."

I stared at him so that he would not see that I had considered this path for myself. From Thornden I might get a son. And a son might prove to be a Creature where I was not.

"Assuredly he is a beast," said Ryzel in haste—the haste of a man who liked none of his words or thoughts. "But even he will not dare harm to a wife who comes to him from the line of Regals. Some at least in the Three Kingdoms know the value of peace, and their loyalty will ensure your safety. Also their support will enable Thornden to master the realm. Already he is the strongest of the kings, and the boldest. If you name him your husband—and ruler in your stead—Canna and Lodan will be taken unprepared.

"He will be an ill monarch"—Ryzel grimaced—"but at the least he will hold the realm from war while we pray for the birth of another true Regal."

I measured his gaze and watched his soul squirm behind the dour facade of his face. Then, slowly, I said, "This is strange counsel, Mage. You presume much. Have you also presumed to suggest such a course to Count Thornden, without my word?"

At that, he stiffened. "My lady," he said, striving to match my tone, "you know that I have not. I am no fool. To be managed, the lord of Nabal must be surprised. He prides himself too much on his force of arms. Only surprise and uncertainty will bend him safely to your will."

"Then hear me, Mage Ryzel," I said as if I were the Regal in truth rather than merely in aspiration. "I say to you clearly that I count death a kinder resting place than Count Thornden's marriage-bed."

If he had allowed me time to soften, I would have added, So you see that I truly have no choice. But at once he swore at me as if I were a child—as if I had denied him something which he prized. And before I could protest, he said, "Then you have but one recourse. You must attempt the Seat now, before the coming of the kings. You must learn the truth of your heritage now. If you succeed, all other questions fail. And if you do not—" He shrugged abruptly. "Perhaps you will be able to flee for your life."

Now I let him see that I was not taken aback. That, too, I had considered. How not? From girlhood, I had dreamed repeatedly of Ascending the Seat—in public or in secret, according to the nature of the dream—and becoming Regal. The right to do so was the gift from my father which I most valued. And he had spoken so often of the transforming touch of Stone.

But I did not tell the Mage the truth—that I had already done as he advised.

The previous night in secret, I had entered the Ascension hall. Commanding the guards briefly from their posts, I had crossed the strange floor and mounted the marble steps to the Seat. But the Stone had refused the touch of my hands.

Yet I met Ryzel on his own ground without flinching, though in my heart I winced—betrayed by myself if not by him. "And if I fail and must flee," I asked, "will you accompany me?"

He lowered his head. His grip was hard on the wood of his Scepter. "No, my lady. I will remain where I am."

I took a moment to wonder what he might hope to gain from my flight—what dream of his my abdication might make possible—and also to let him observe that I wondered. Then I said simply, "My father commanded that I Ascend the Seat at midnight on the eve of my twenty-first birthday, under the light of the full moon. You have said that I am not Magic, and in all truth it would seem that I am not. Yet I would heed the plain word of any Creature. Still more will I obey the wishes of my father, the Phoenix-Regal. At midnight and not sooner I will attempt my Ascension, let come what may."

My regret that I had already disobeyed was fierce in me; and it held me to my purpose in the place of courage and confidence.

Ryzel's eyes were bleak as he saw that I would not be swayed. He began pacing again between the walls of my chamber while he mastered himself; and his bald head shone wetly in the light of the lamps. *The one true man in the Three Kingdoms.* I studied him as he moved, but did not know how to disentangle his fear for me from his fear for the realm. *Never trust him.* His helplessness did not sit well with him. Often I had believed that I would still be able to take my place as Regal and rule the Three Kingdoms even though I was not Magic—if only the Mage Ryzel would put forth his full power to support my claim. For what other purpose had my father given him his Scepter? But his talk of flight showed that my belief was vain. If I Ascended the Seat and failed, he might attempt to save my life—but he would not pretend me Regal.

In my turn, I would not trust my decisions to him.

And I gave him no glimpse of the pain my aloneness caused. I could not now afford to let him know how much I needed him.

By degrees, he regained his familiar gruff balance. Still shaking his head, he came to stand before me. "Soon the arrival of the guests will begin," he said as if my refusals had not trapped him among his bitter secrets. "My lady, what will you wear?"

That was very like him. Often he had told me that no detail of behavior, attitude, or appearance was irrelevant to the craft of rulers; and he had shown his belief by advising me on everything— how to bear myself at table, how much wine to drink, when and where to laugh. I was not surprised by his desire to know what I meant to wear. Beauty, like power, was vital to the position for which he had trained me.

I showed him my choice. Bypassing the wealth of beribboned and revealing and ornamental gowns which I had been given to mask my obvious shortcomings, I took from the wardrobe a simple white muslin dress, almost a shift, and held it for his inspection.

His exasperation came back with a snarl. "Paugh! Chrysalis," he rasped. "You are already the plainest woman in the Three Kingdoms. Do not seek to flaunt what you should disguise. You must at least appear that you are fit for Ascension."

There he hurt me. It was fortunate that I had been well-taught for self-command. With great care and coldness, I replied, "Mage, I will not conceal what I am."

Twisting his Scepter in his rough hands, he gave me a glare, then turned and strode from my chambers. But at the last he did not slam the door; he did not wish to give any public hint of his distress.

And when I joined him to watch the coming of the guests, his manner toward me had become the proper bearing of a Mage toward a woman who would soon Ascend to take her place among the Regals.

Below us, the three rulers entered together. Then they separated, moved with their Mages and courtiers to opposing places in the large hall—as far as they could be from each other. Count Thornden's retinue was unmistakably military in character, obviously armed. By contrast, King Thone had come accompanied by sophistication and gaiety—by style-setters and known wits of every description. But Queen Damia had surrounded herself with the most beautiful maids she could glean from the comely people of Lodan, showing by the way she outshone her entourage that her own loveliness was astonishing.

Doubtless that accounted for Count Thornden's loathing of her. Doubtless he had once made advances toward her, driven by one of his many outsize lusts—and she had laughed in his face. But the antipathy of these two altered nothing: the one thing I did not need to fear this night was that any two of the three rulers would league together against the third—or against me.

When the arrival was finished, the great doors were closed, and the musicians struck up a lively air of welcome. The sounds of talk began to rise toward my window. The rulers stirred where they stood without changing their positions; and the other guests flowed in conflicting directions around the walls, seeking safety, favorites, or excitement. Not raising his eyes from the scene, Mage Ryzel murmured, "It is time, my lady."

Is it, forsooth? I responded to myself. From the moment when I joined that gathering, my future would rest squarely in my open hands, exposed to every conceivable assault—and preserved by no power or beauty or love, but only by my own resources. An altogether fragile estate, as Ryzel had often deigned to inform me. Yet I had found that I did not envy those who were not in my place. When the Mage at last looked to me for my answer, I discovered myself able to smile.

"Time indeed," I said. "Let us go."

Glowering because he did not approve—perhaps of me, perhaps of himself—he turned and strode along the passage toward the head of the formal stair which stretched from this level down into the ballroom.

I followed at a little distance, so that I would not be seen from below before he had announced me.

His appearance cast an instant silence over the assemblage. The music stopped; all conversation ended; every eye was raised toward him. He was beyond question an unprepossessing figure, yet his influence was felt in every corner of the Three Kingdoms. And the Scepter he held would have compelled respect in the grasp of a child. He did not need to lift his voice to make himself heard down the length of the stair and across the expanse of the hall.

"Monarchs and Mages," he said in a dry, almost acerbic tone. "Lords and ladies. All true friends of the Regals—and of the realm. This is the night of Ascension, when old things become new. I give you the lady Chrysalis, daughter of the Phoenix-Regal and by his command heir to the rule of the Three Kingdoms."

A brave speech: one calculated to fan the doubts of my ill-wishers. It was not a flourish of trumpets, but it pleased me nonetheless. When Ryzel began to make his lone way down the long stair, I waited where I could not be seen in order to reinforce those doubts—waited until the Mage had descended into the ballroom, walked out into the center of the hall, and turned to present his Scepter toward my coming. Only then did I go to stand at the head of the stair.

The guests reacted with a sudden murmur—muffled expressions of surprise, approval, disapproval, perhaps of my person or dress, perhaps of myself. But it was quickly stilled. And in the silence I found that I could not say the words of welcome and confidence which I had prepared for the occasion. Hidden by white muslin, my knees were trembling; and I knew that my voice would betray me. Mutely, I remained motionless while I promised the memory of my father that I would not stumble as I descended the stair.

By no shift of his hands or flicker of his face did Ryzel express anything other than certainty. He almost seemed to dare the gathering to utter one breath of impatience. Grateful for that, I summoned my courage and started downward.

With such slow dignity as I could muster, I went to meet those who wished me dead.

When I saw that in fact I was not about to stumble, I smiled.

As I gained the foot of the stair, a man concealed at the rear of the crowd called, "Hail the coming Regal!" But no one seconded his shout.

Then Mage Ryzel's expression did change. Frowning dangerously, he lowered his Scepter, folded it to his chest, and began to clap applause for me.

At first tentatively, then with more strength, the guests echoed his welcome. Unsure as they were of me—and of their own future standing—the consequential people of the Three Kingdoms feared to insult me directly in Ryzel's presence.

As the applause faded, I looked to him, letting him see in my eyes that, whatever transpired later, much would be forgiven him for what he had done here. Then, before the assemblage, I said, "Mage, I thank you. The Phoenix-Regal held you to be the one true man in the Three Kingdoms. I am gladdened to learn that there are others like you here." I spoke brightly, so that no one would miss the threat I implied toward those who did not support me.

Bearing my smile and my plain white dress in the place of Magic, I moved to greet King Thone and his party, choosing him because he stood nearer to me than the other rulers.

Around the hall, another murmuring arose and subsided. Everyone wanted to hear what would pass between me and my principal enemies.

Thone considered himself a sophisticate, and he bowed over my hand in a courtly and suave manner, kissing the backs of my fingers—the only public display of homage which the Regals had ever required of the three rulers. Yet his eyes disturbed me as much as ever. They appeared milky, opaque, as though he were nearly blind. And their color concealed the character of his thoughts. As a result, the simple quality of his gaze seemed to give everything he said another meaning, a hidden intent.

Like several of his adherents, he wore at his side a slim sword as if it were merely decorative, a part of his apparel.

Nevertheless, I greeted him with an air of frankness, pretending that I had nothing to fear. And likewise I greeted his Mage, Cashon of Canna, though that man perplexed me. He was tall and straight; and until the passing of the Phoenix-Regal his repute had matched his stature, for both strength and probity—and perhaps also for a certain simplicity. Though his home was in Lodan—and though his arts would have been highly prized in Nabal, for the smelting and refining of ores—he contented himself with Canna, where the most arduous work asked of him was the clearing of stubbled fields, or perhaps the protection of frost-threatened orchards. This he did because he had wedded a woman of Canna. Doting on her extremely, he had set aside numerous opportunities to stand among the foremost folk of the realm. So I had been surprised—and Ryzel astonished—when Cashon had suddenly declared his allegiance to King Thone, displacing the monarch's lesser dependents. We had not thought that this Mage would have stomach for Thone's invidious pursuits.

He greeted me at his chosen lord's right hand and kept his gaze shrouded, hiding his thoughts. But he could not conceal the lines which marked his face. Some acid of sorrow or futility had cut into his visage, weakening his mouth, causing the flesh to sag from the line of his jaw. He had an aspect of secret suffering which both moved and alarmed me.

"My lord Thone," I said, still smiling, "I have not yet had opportunity to congratulate you on winning such a man as the Mage Cashon to your service. You are indeed fortunate."

"Thank you, my lady," Thone replied in a negligent tone, as if he were bored. "I have great need of him. He has made himself a master of Fire, as you know."

By this he meant, of course, that Cashon cast images of the Real flame that melted and flowed deep under the mountains of Nabal. There was much debate in the realm as to which form of magery was most powerful. The images of the great Creatures were certainly potent, but many argued that in practical application either Wind or Fire was the sovereign strength. No one comprehended the uses of Wood—no one except Ryzel, who said nothing on the subject— and Stone appeared too passive to be considered. King Thone's milky eyes gave the impression that he had offered me a hint which I was too obtuse to follow.

When I simply nodded, he changed his topic without discernible awkwardness or obvious relevance.

"Have you heard," he said in that same tone, "that Kodar and his rebels intend to commemorate this night with another attack? My spies are positive. They report that he means to put Lodan's largest warehouse to the torch. An entire season's timber will be lost." His fleshy lips smiled slightly. "Would it be wise, do you think, my lady, if I were to warn Queen Damia of her danger?"

"It would be useless, my lord of Canna," I replied. "I am certain that she has received the same report." Indeed, I suspected that every spy in the realm knew Kodar's plans and movements as well as Thone did.

"Have you observed," I went on, seeking to turn this king's hints and gambits another way, "that Kodar's many attacks are strangely ineffective? He challenges the Three Kingdoms often, but to little purpose. Word of his intent precedes him everywhere. Is it possible, do you think"—I mimed his tone as exactly as I could—"that his purpose against Lodan is a feint?"

His eyes revealed nothing; but one eyebrow twitched involuntarily. The storages of Canna were certainly as vulnerable as Queen Damia's warehouses.

Before he could reply, I bowed to him and moved away to give my greetings to Count Thornden. At the edge of my sight, I glimpsed Mage Ryzel. He looked like a man who frowned so that he would not smile.

But Count Thornden was more obviously a threat to me than either of the other rulers, and he demanded my full attention. He styled himself "Count" because he proclaimed that he would not be "King" until all the realm acknowledged him. But I considered that position to be the subtlest he had ever taken; he was not a subtle man. He stood head-and-shoulders over me and scowled as if I affronted him. When he spoke, his lips bared his teeth, which were as sharp and ragged as fangs. Pointedly, he refused to take my hand.

That insolence spread a stirring and stiffening of tension among the onlookers; but I ignored the lesser people who watched me, in hope or dread. Straightening my back, I met Thornden's stare. "My lord of Nabal," I said quietly, "I bid you welcome, though you offer me no good greeting. This night is the time of my Ascension, and many things will change. I suspect that before tomorrow's sun you will be content to name yourself King."

For a moment, I watched him grin at what he took to be my meaning. Then I had the satisfaction of seeing his brows knot as other possibilities disturbed his single-minded wits. His only retort was a growl deep in his throat.

For the sake of good manners—and good ruler-craft—I saluted Thornden's Mage as I had Thone's. Brodwick of Nabal was a shaggy lump of a man, large and misshaped, whose fawning was exceeded only by his known prowess. He appeared oddly dependent, perhaps because he shared appetites with Count Thornden which only the lord of Nabal could satisfy. Following his master's example, he refused my hand.

I dismissed the slight. Whatever motivations ruled Brodwick, he was still dangerous. Deliberately, I resumed my progress around the ballroom, nodding to those people who looked at me honestly, gauging those who did not—and moving toward the encounter I could not shun with Queen Damia.

Perhaps I had unconsciously left her to the last, hoping foolishly to avoid her altogether. In all truth, she daunted me—she and that quick ferret who served her, the Mage Scour. Perhaps I could have borne it that her loveliness and grace gave me the aspect of a scullion by comparison. Or that her finery would have made the grandest gown I might have worn appear frumpish and shabby. Or that even Ryzel was unable to speak of her without an undercurrent of longing in his voice. I envied such things, but they were not necessary to me. To those strengths, however, was added another which made my blood run cold in my chest because I was not equal to it. I could play games of implication and inference with King Thone and not lose my way. Count Thornden was obvious; therefore he could be thwarted. But Queen Damia's cunning ran far deeper than theirs—deeper and more dangerously. And I feared that I lacked the wit to fathom her. Certainly I lacked the experience to walk unscathed through the mazes she built for the bafflement of her antagonists.

In such matters, she was ably aided by Mage Scour. He served her, it was said, because she put her nearly limitless wealth at his disposal, enabling him to pursue his experiments and researches wherever he willed. And it was also said that he came here this night prepared by what he had learned to alter the entire order of the realm.

Ryzel had scoffed at that rumor, but in a way which conveyed uncertainty. The casting of images of what was Real was a known art, varying only according to the skill, dedication and inborn capacity of the Mage. But Magic itself remained a mystery, transcending that which was known, mortal, or tangible. And the rumors surrounding Scour claimed that he had gone beyond images of the Real into Magic itself.

I felt myself more a lost girl than a lady of state as I drew near to Queen Damia and her retinue.

Her smile was as brilliant as one of the chandeliers—so brilliant that it made me feel the fault of manners was mine rather than hers when she declined to accept my hand. But the gracious sound of her voice—as haunting as a flute—covered the social awkwardness of her refusal. "Lady," she said sweetly, "I have seen the portraits of your line which hang in the gallery of the manor. Surely no paint which is not itself Real can hope to portray the virility of the Regals. But the painting of your grandmother well becomes her—or so I have heard from those who knew the mother of the Phoenix-Regal. You are very like her. Your dress is so simple and charming, it displays you to perfection."

As she spoke, I found myself watching the movement of her décolletage as if I were a man. It was an effective sight; I was so taken by it that a moment passed before I grasped that I had been insulted in several ways at once.

"You flatter me, my lady," I replied, schooling myself to calmness so that I would not redden before the guests of the manor. "I have seen my grandmother's portrait often. She was altogether handsomer than I am." Then the success of my efforts gave me enough reassurance to return her compliment. "In any case, all beauty vanishes when Queen Damia appears."

A small quirk twitched the corner of her soft mouth; but whether it indicated pleasure or vexation, I could not tell. Yet my response sufficed to make her change her ground. "Lady," she said smoothly, "it ill becomes me to discuss the business of the Three Kingdoms upon such a festive occasion—but the need of my subjects compels me to speak. The next Regal simply must reexamine the pricing structure of Lodan woods against the ores and gems of Nabal and the foods of Canna. In particular, our mahogany is scarce, and growing scarcer. We must have a higher return for it, before we sink into poverty."

To follow her cost me an effort of will—and of haste. With the same words, she prepared for any outcome to my test. If my Ascension to the Seat succeeded, she would turn to me sweetly and say, "May we now discuss the price of Lodan mahogany, my lady?" And at the same time she contrived to suggest to all who heard us that the next Regal would be none other than Queen Damia herself.

I could not match her in such conversation. To escape her—and also to show her that I was not swayed—I attempted a laugh. To my ears, it sounded somewhat brittle. But perhaps it did not entirely fail.

"Surely you jest, my lady of Lodan. Your people will never know want while you have jewels to sell for their succor."

From the gathering, I heard a muffled exclamation, a low titter, whisperings of surprise or approbation. With that for victory, I turned away.

But I felt little victory. As I turned, I saw clearly Mage Scour's sharp face. He was grinning as if he had the taste of my downfall in his mouth.

To his credit, Ryzel allowed the monarch of Lodan no opportunity for riposte. He made an obscure, small gesture which the servants of the manor knew how to read; and at once a clear chime rang across the hush of the ballroom.

"My lords and ladies," he said casually, as though he were unaware of the conflicting currents around him, "friends and comrades, the feast is prepared. Will you accept the hospitality of the Phoenix-Regal's daughter at table?"

With an unruffled demeanor, he offered me his arm to lead me to the banquet hall. I gripped it harder than I intended while I continued to smile somewhat fixedly at the people who parted before us. Entering the passage which connected the ballroom and the banquet hall, he whispered softly to me, "Thus far, it is well enough. I will wager that even that proud Queen has been somewhat unsettled in her mind. Do not falter now."

Perhaps I could not trust him. But he was still my friend; and while his friendship lasted, I clung to it. In reply, I breathed, "Ryzel, do not leave me to dine alone with these predators."

"It is the custom," he said without turning his head. "I will regale the Mages while their masters feast. Do not fail of appetite. You must show no fear." A moment later, he added, "Perchance I will glean some hint of what has wedded Cashon to King Thone's side."

With that I had to be content.

At the doors of the hall, he dropped his arm. I walked without him ahead of the guests into the feasting-place of the Regals.

It was resplendent with light and warmth and music and savory aromas. In the great hearths fires blazed, not because they were needed, but because they were lovely and comforting. Long ranks of candelabra made the damask tablecloths and the rich plate gleam. Playing quietly in one corner, musicians embellished a sprightly air. The scent of the incensed candles gave each breath a tang. But this night such things provided me neither pleasure nor solace. As it was custom that Mage Ryzel would not attend me here, so also was it custom that I must take my feast uncompanioned—at a table set only for me and placed in full view of all the guests. The long tables had been arranged in a rough semicircle; but my seat rested on a low platform within the arms of the formation, solitary and exposed, so that all in the hall might study me as we ate.

A barbarous custom, I thought sourly. Yet I understood it. Always better—so my father had often told me—to rule by confidence of personality than by display of strength. And how better to show my enemies that I did not fear them, than by taking a calm meal alone in front of them?

Gripping what courage I had, I moved to my place and stood there while the three kings and their followers, the chief families and minor nobility of the realm, all my principal friends and foes found their proper seats. For a moment as I watched them, I fervidly wished myself a Gorgon as my great-grandfather had been, capable of turning to stone those who sought my ill. But then I shook the thought away; it did not become one who aspired to Ascension. The Gorgon-Regal had been a grim and fatal monarch—and yet there was no record that he had ever used his Magic to harm any of his subjects.

When all the guests were in their places, I made the short, formal speech expected of me, inviting the company to feast and happiness in the manor of the Regals. I was steadier now, and my voice betrayed no tremor. According to custom, I stood until the people around me had seated themselves. Then the steward clapped his hands for the servants, and I lowered myself gratefully to my chair.

At once, the feast appeared. Again according to custom, the steaming trays and chafing dishes, platters of meats and flagons of mulled wine and tureens of rich soup were brought first to me. And with them came a servant to act as my taster. He would taste for me; and I would taste for the guests; and so both caution and courtesy were satisfied.

But there I was somewhat surprised. The man who came to serve me was not my accustomed taster, an old retainer of the manor whom I had known and loved from girlhood. Rather he was a tall and excellently made fellow perhaps ten years older than I. I knew him little; but I had noticed him about the manor since the death of my father—indeed, I could not have failed to notice him, for his handsomeness was extreme, and it plucked at my heart in a way no man had ever done. His name was Wallin. Now, in the light of the candles and the aura of the music, he appeared more than handsome: he seemed to glow with perfection.

Looking at him, I thought that girls dreamed of such men. Women would be well advised to distrust them.

The blessing of my isolated seat and the music was that I could speak without being overheard. Softly, I said, "This is not your accustomed duty, Wallin."

"Your pardon, my lady." His composure was a match for his appearance. "Do not be displeased. Your taster was taken ill this evening—a slight indisposition, but enough to keep him from his feet." He smiled self-deprecatingly. "I begged for his place until the steward granted it to me so that I would desist."

"You have curious desires, Wallin," I said, studying him narrowly. In all truth, I distrusted him less than my attraction to him. "Why are you avid for such perilous duty? The task of taster is not altogether ceremonial here. There is a tradition of poison in the Three Kingdoms."

Speaking as quietly as I did, he replied, "My lady, your guests await their feast."

A glance showed me that he was right. Many of the men and women at their tables were watching me curiously. Others appeared restive. But I made a dismissive gesture. "Let them wait." It would serve to heighten their uncertainty. "You interest me."

"Then I must answer you frankly, my lady." His manner suggested diffidence, yet he was entirely unruffled. "It is said of the Regals that they take their mates from the common people rather than from the high families—or from the adherents of the three rulers. This is unquestionably wise, for it avoids any implication of favoritism or preference which might unsettle the realm." He glanced around us, assuring himself that there was no one within earshot. Then he concluded, "My lady, when you come to the choice of a mate, I wish to be considered. I serve you to gain your notice."

He astonished me. I was not the sort of woman whom handsome men found desirable—or any men at all, handsome or otherwise, in my experience. Somewhat bitterly, I responded, "Are you hungry for power, Wallin?"

"My lady"—his composure was extraordinary—"I am hungry for your person."

For an instant, I nearly laughed. But if I had laughed, I might also have wept. Without my will, he inspired a yearning in me to be loved rather than feared or hated; and the pain that I was not loved welled against my self-command. Mustering all the severity I possessed, I said, "You are bold. Perhaps you are too bold. Or your grasp of the risk you run is unclear. I have not yet proven myself Regal. If I fail, any man who dares ally himself with me will share my doom. In permitting such hazard to your life, I would demonstrate myself unworthy of the rule I seek." Then I relented a degree. Some weaknesses require utterance, or else they will seek admission in other ways. "You may be assured that you have gained my notice."

"With that I am content," he replied. But his eyes said candidly that he would not be content long.

He nonplussed me to such an extent that I felt gratitude when he went about his duties, enabling me to occupy myself with the first of my food—and to avoid meeting his gaze again. His attitude defied reason. Therefore I could not trust it—or him. And therefore the strength of my wish to defy reason appalled me.

Thus it was fortunate that I had no appetite for any of the food placed before me. I required a great concentration of will to sample each dish as if I were pleased by it; and that discipline schooled me to master myself in other ways. As the servants fanned away from me to the long tables, bearing rich fare and rare delicacies to the guests of the manor—not *my* guests, though Wallin had termed them so—I became better able to play my part with proper grace. Let those who studied me for signs of apprehension see what they willed.

Yet whenever I felt Queen Damia's gaze come toward me, I did not meet it. I was prepared to outface all the rest of the gathering if need be, alone or together. But I was not a match for Lodan's queen.

So the banquet passed. No toasts were proposed to me—a breach of good etiquette, but one easily forgiven, considering the vulnerability of those here who wished me well—and I offered none in return. Hostility and tension were covered by the gracious music, the plenty of the feast, the flow of superficial conversation and jests. And then the musicians set aside their instruments to make way for the minstrels.

The minstrels were perhaps the only people in the hall with nothing at hazard except their reputations. War provided them with material for songs; peace gave them opportunity to sing. As did this night, whatever the outcome of my Ascension. So they had come to the manor from around the Three Kingdoms, that they might establish or augment their fame, their standing in the guild. In consequence, their singing was exceptional.

Custom declared that the minstrel of the manor must perform first; and she regaled the guests with an eloquent and plainly spurious account of how the Basilisk-Regal had wooed and won the daughter of one of Canna's farmers, in defiance of the man's deathly opposition to all things Magic. Then came the turn of the minstrels of the three rulers. However, only two men stood forward—Count Thornden had no minstrel with him, either because he had none at all, or because he had not troubled to bring his singer here. King Thone's representative took precedence by virtue of his ranking in the minstrel's guild, and he delivered himself of an elaborate, courtly ballad, highly sophisticated in its manner but rather crude in its intent, which was to flatter the monarch of Canna. I felt no offense, however. I was willing to listen to him as long as possible. Even crude minstrelsy beguiled me as though it had power to hold back the future.

But Queen Damia's singer gave the banquet a song which caught in my throat. It was one I had not heard before, and it was at once passionate and poignant, fiery and grieving, as only the best songs can be. In brief, it described the slaying of the last Dragon by the Basilisk-Regal, my grandmother's grandfather.

That thought was frightening: Creature at war against Creature, kind-murder which bereft the world of something Real and therefore precious. In the known history of the realm, only the Mage-made images of the ancient Creatures fought and slew. The Magic beings themselves lived lives of their own, apart and untouched, ruled by interests and needs and commitments which took no account of that which was not Real. But Queen Damia's minstrel sang that the Basilisk-Regal went out to rid the realm of the last Dragon because that great, grim Creature had conceived a corrupt taste for unReal flesh and had begun to feed upon the folk of the Three Kingdoms. Thus for the sake of his chosen people the Basilisk-Regal was forced to take the blood of one of his own kind, and the stain of that death had marked his hands until his own passing. It had soaked into his flesh until at the last he was compelled to keep his hands covered because they had become too hideous to be looked upon by ordinary human eyes.

When the song faded from the hall, I found myself with tears on my face and a hot ache in my heart. It is only a song, I protested against myself. It has no power over you. Do not act the girl in front of your enemies. But to myself I responded, The last Dragon! Oh, father of Regals! The *last*! How did you bear it?

I paid no heed to the banqueters who watched me in my weakness, and I heard nothing of the songs sung by the remaining minstrels. I thought only of the fine Creatures which had filled my dreams from my earliest girlhoood—the fierce Wyvern and wild Banshee, the terrible Gorgon and subtle Cockatrice, the mystic Phoenix—of my dream that one day I would stand among them, a Creature myself. And of what the world had lost in the slaying of the last Dragon.

If the song were true.

At last I recollected myself enough to be firm: *if* the song were true. Mage Ryzel had told me all he knew of the history of Magic in the realm—and he had not spoken of any bloodshed among Creatures. And who had sung the song which had struck so deeply into my lone heart? Who, indeed, but the minstrel of Queen Damia?

Was this song some ploy of hers?

If it were, I could not fathom it. As in everything she did, her true intent lay hidden beneath a surface of immaculate innocence. Perhaps she mocked me—or perhaps warned. Whatever her purpose, I feared I had already fallen to the snare. But now I no longer sought to avoid her gaze; when she looked toward me, I let her see that there was a darkness in my eyes which she would be wise to interpret as cold rage.

Perhaps I should have made shift to prolong the banquet. Each new phase of the evening brought me closer to the time of my trial. But instead I wished for an escape from the masque of confidence I was required to perform. My smile felt brittle on my lips, and I had need for privacy in which to shore up my resolve. So when the minstrels had done I rose to my feet and thanked them formally. At this signal, the servants brought around brandies and richer wines to complete the meal; and the guests also rose to stretch their legs and mingle and talk while the ball itself was made ready.

But as I turned to leave the banquet hall, a servant came to inform me quietly that King Thone desired an audience with me alone before the ball.

I swore to myself because beyond question I could not afford to shirk such a request. Then I set aside my ache for respite and asked the servant to guide Canna's king to one of the private meeting-rooms near the banquet hall.

There were several of these rooms in the manor—places where the Regals might hold discreet conversation with kings and counselors and messengers—and it was surely known to half the ambitious connivers in the Three Kingdoms that these chambers were not in truth private. A ruler who sought to hold sway without bloodshed preserved his own secrets while at all times suggesting to his opponents that their secrets were not safe. Therefore some of the meeting-rooms were behung with tapestries behind which eavesdroppers might be concealed; others had listening slits cunningly hidden in the walls; still others possessed covert doors which might give sudden entrance at need to the guards of the manor.

For my audience with King Thone, I selected a chamber which displayed a brave weaving of the Ascension of the Phoenix-Regal. But I set no one behind the tapestry, neither Mage Ryzel nor any guard. Let King Thone believe himself overheard or not, as he chose; I had a need to show myself capable of facing him alone. And if Ryzel were indeed untrustworthy, I would do well to withhold as many secrets from him as possible.

Entering the room, I succumbed to my anxieties so far as to glance behind the tapestry for my own reassurance. Then I seated myself in the ornately carved chair reserved for the use of the Regals and awaited Thone's coming.

He arrived shortly, unaccompanied by any of his courtiers or dependents. Since I did not invite him to sit, he remained standing. To make him wait and wonder, I instructed the servant to bring a decanter of the Gorgon-Regal's choice brandy, and I did not speak to the monarch of Canna until after the brandy had come and the servant had departed again. Then, deliberately, I poured out one glass of the deep amber drink—for King Thone, not for myself— and said as obtusely as I could, "My lord, you asked an audience. Do you have some complaint? Does the hospitality of the manor displease you?"

He held his glass and gazed at it in silence for a moment. I had given it to him as a test, to see how he would choose between the courtesy of setting the brandy aside and the discourtesy of drinking when I did not. So my heart sank somewhat when he raised the glass to his mouth and sipped delicately.

His milky orbs betrayed nothing as he looked toward me at last; but his way of savoring the taste of the brandy hinted at other pleasures. "My lady," he said slowly, "the hospitality of the manor is without flaw, as ever. You do not believe that I would trouble you on such a pretext."

"What matters the pretext," I replied, seeking to unsettle him, "if it gives us opportunity to speak openly to each other?"

His gaze held me as if he were blind, proof against what I did. Still slowly, he said, "My lady, what do you wish to say to me?"

I gave him a smile to suggest any number of possibilities; but I answered only, "My lord of Canna, you requested this audience. I did not."

"My lady," he said at once, as if nothing lay hidden behind his words, "at such balls it is often done that the Mages of the realm give demonstration of their prowess. I ask permission for my Mage to entertain you."

He surprised me, but I did not show it. "Cashon?" I asked in mild curiosity. "You have termed him a master of Fire."

Thone's plump lips implied a smile.

"Then his demonstration will be hazardous in this crowded hall, among so many guests. Why do you wish him to display his skill here?"

"My lady, you are not Regal. You are merely aspirant. You would be wise to understand the significance of my Mage's power."

His tone made me stiffen. I knew now that I was being threatened, but I did not yet grasp the nature of the threat. Carefully, I responded, "It is undeniable that I am merely aspirant. But I am also the daughter of my father, the Phoenix-Regal. I need not risk harm to the guests of the manor in order to understand Cashon's magery—or the meaning of Fire."

He played his gambit well. His voice was that of a polite man who sought to disguise his boredom, and his eyes gave away nothing, as he said, "Perhaps if you better understood the uses of Fire, you would not risk the entire realm on a foolish attempt at Ascension. Perhaps if your eyes were opened, you would see that there are others better placed than yourself to assume the rule of the Three Kingdoms."

You dare? I wished to retort. You dare say such things to me? I will have you locked in irons and left in the coldest cell of the manor, and you will never threaten man or woman again. *That* power I still have while this evening lasts!

But I uttered none of those words. I kept my anger to myself. Instead, I said quietly, "You speak of yourself, my lord Thone. Please continue."

As if he had already won, he emptied his glass, then refilled it from the decanter. The faint twist of his mouth suggested that I was a fool not to share this excellent brandy.

"My lady"—now he did not trouble to conceal his sarcasm—"I had not thought you in need of such instruction. Mage Ryzel has taught you ill if you do not understand me. But I will be plain. Canna feeds the Three Kingdoms. Lodan and Nabal provide them with luxuries; Canna gives them life. And I am served body and soul by a Mage who has mastered Fire."

I did not let my gaze waver from the milky secret of his eyes. "That much is plain. Be plainer."

King Thone could not stifle a grin. "My lady, you are charming. This girlish innocence becomes you. But it does not render you fit for rule. However, you have commanded plainness, and while this evening lasts, you must be obeyed. Plainly, then, you must not attempt to Ascend the Seat of the Regals. Rather, you must give way to those better suited for rule. If you do not—I speak plainly at your command—if you set even one foot on the steps to that Seat, my Mage will unleash his Fire.

"Not upon the manor," he said promptly, as if I had questioned him. "Assuredly not. That would be hazardous, as you have said. No, he will set Fire upon the fields and crops of Canna. My secret storages will be spared, but Nabal and Lodan will starve. They will *starve*, my lady, until they see fit to cede their crowns to me."

Happily, he concluded, "You will find yourself unwilling to bring that much death upon the realm by defying me."

He made me tremble with shock and anger; but I did not show it. For an instant, I feared that I would. I had been trained and trained for such contests—but training was not experience, and I was not yet twenty-one, and until this night Mage Ryzel had always stood at my side. The peril to the realm, however, demanded better of me. Here the only question which signified was not whether I would later prove Regal, but rather whether I would be able to serve the realm now.

From my seat, I said softly, "You are bold, my lord. Apparently you care nothing that by these tactics you will make yourself the most hated man in the history of the Three Kingdoms. And apparently also," I continued so that he would not interrupt, "you have given careful thought to this path. Very good. Perhaps, my lord"—my courtesy was precise—"you will tell me how you intend to respond if I summon the guards of the manor and have you thrown without ceremony into the dungeon."

He stared through me as though I were trivial; but his mouth betrayed a smirk. "That would be ill advised," he replied. "My commands to my Mage have been explicit. If I do not shortly appear at the ball to restrain him, he will commence the razing of Canna."

"I see." I nodded once, stiffly, acknowledging his cleverness. "And if I imprison Cashon also, what then?"

"My lady," Thone said with elaborate patience, "I have told you that he is a master. And surely Ryzel has taught you that a Mage need not be free to wield his power. Neither distance nor dungeon can spare the realm from my will."

I paused for a moment, marshalling my thoughts. Thone's plotting depended upon Cashon—a man whose integrity and scruples had never been questioned. Yet the monarch of Canna was certain that Cashon would commit such massive wrong. The idea was appalling. Still I preserved my composure. Facing my antagonist squarely, I asked, "Would you truly commit that abomination, my lord of Canna?"

"My lady," he replied in his tone of patience, "do not insult me with doubt." His eyes concealed everything. "I mean to rule the Three Kingdoms, and you will not prevent me."

Waving my hand, I dismissed this assertion as if my ability to prevent him were sure. "And Cashon?" I inquired almost casually. "He has earned goodly reputation in the realm. Will he truly obey your atrocious commands?"

"You may rely upon it," said the king. I had not ruffled him.

"That is preposterous!" I snapped at once, probing hard for a point of weakness. "We speak of Cashon, my lord—not of Thornden's sycophant or Damia's ferret. He was not shaped in the same gutter which gave birth to your lordship. *Why* will he obey you?"

King Thone's response lacked the simple decency of anger. Pleased with himself, he said, "He will obey me because his wife and his three daughters are in my power. He knows not where they are— but he knows that I will have them slain if he fails me. And he fears that I will find other uses for them before they die. Do not doubt that he will obey me."

His wife and daughters? I wished to cry out. Are you so base?

And do you call yourself fit to rule? The nature of Thone's machinations horrified me; his revelation explained much.

But the sheer intensity of my outrage served as self-command.
"In that case," I said, my heart pounding, "perhaps you will be so
kind as to summon a servant." I indicated a bell-pull near him.

A slight faltering exposed him. Behind the veil of his gaze, I felt
him study me closely. But I offered him no reason, and my coun-
tenance told him nothing. Perhaps now he sensed his peril, yet he
had come too far to retreat. After a moment, he shrugged slightly
and gave a condescending tug to the bell.

When a servant answered, I said clearly, but without inflection,
"Request the Mage Cashon to attend us."

I was pleased to see that Thone now found he could not speak
again, in protest or in warning, without appearing foolish. To keep
himself still, he chewed upon his lower lip.

Cashon came to the chamber promptly. As he entered, his bearing
was wary. Now that I knew his plight, his pain and his fear were
unmistakable. Beneath its flesh, the courage which sustained his
face was being eaten away. In his life, he had given up much which
a Mage might find desirable for simple love of his wife—and it
was plain that he had never regretted the loss. But now she and
their daughters were threatened, and fear for them consumed him.
It ruled him. He did not look at me; the suffering in his eyes was
fixed on King Thone. His hands at his sides closed and unclosed
uselessly.

For his sake, I spoke as soon as the door had been closed behind
him.

"Mage," I said evenly, "this unscrupulous king has told me of
the means by which he thinks to make himself monarch of the
Three Kingdoms. You are the sword which he thinks to hold at my
throat. But my word is otherwise: I say to you that you need not
fear for your loved ones."

At that, Cashon's attention wrenched toward me.

Thone opened his mouth to speak, then closed it again, waiting
to hear what I would say.

"You are reputed a master of Fire, Mage," I continued. "Therefore King Thone seeks to compel you to his use. And therefore you
are able to defy him. Turn your Fire upon *him*, Mage"—now at
last I allowed my ire to rasp in my voice—"upon this heartless fop

who threatens thousands of innocent lives merely to serve his own ambition. Should you simply surround him with flame and let him feel its heat, he will reveal where your family is held to save himself pain. And he will go further. He will give you his written command for their release, so that you may free them this night."

That was my gambit for the protection of the realm. But I saw no hope leap up in Cashon's eyes; dread had dissolved all his strength. And the lord of Canna did not falter. His gaze did not shift from the Mage as he addressed me softly.

"You are a fool. Do you conceive that Cashon has not considered such threats for himself? But he knows that my men have been given command to first rape and then slay his wife and daughters, should harm of any kind come to me. If they hear any report that I have been hurt or defied, they will act. And I will never command any release.

"Look upon him." Cashon appeared to wither under Thone's scorn, so acid was the Mage's fear. "He counts himself fortunate that I will permit him to save his family by obeying me." Then Thone turned to me. "And I will achieve the same fate for you"— the calm of his demeanor broke into a shout—"if you do not submit to me *now*!"

My heart went out to Cashon in pity; but the safety of the realm hinged on him, and I could not afford to spare him. He had once been stronger; I gambled that he had not forgotten.

For the second time this night, I mustered a laugh. Smoothly, I rose from my chair. As I moved toward the door, I said, "Cashon, I leave him to you. You are a master. I trust you will do no harm to the manor. His command against your family will not be obeyed.

"Canna has not forgotten that he came to kingship through the suspected murder of his uncle—and that from the first moment of his rule all the laws and commands of the Kingdom were altered. When word of his death reaches those who hold your loved ones, they will not dare obedience for fear that they will lose favor with the next monarch." I threw my whole weight into the scales on Cashon's side. "And you will be the next monarch—should Thone fail to satisfy you here."

At the door, I paused to look again at the king of Canna and smile. "I trust you will enjoy the ball, my lord," I said in my sweetest way. Then I left the meeting-room and closed the door after me.

There my legs nearly failed me. Dismay at the risk I took made my head whirl with faintness. If Cashon did not take courage from my display of confidence—if he did not conquer his fear—! Hardly able to stand, I clung to the door and listened and did not breathe.

Through the panelled wood, I heard the first muffled roar of Cashon's magery—and King Thone's first shout of panic.

A servant nearby looked toward me in alarm. To calm her, I said, "Be not concerned." In an instant, my faintness became the light-headedness of relief. "King Thone and the Mage Cashon will resolve their differences well enough alone." I wanted to shout with jubilation. "And I wager that when King Thone emerges he will be unscathed. Leave them to themselves."

Turning in the direction of the ballroom, I walked away. For the first time, I felt that perhaps I was fit to become Regal over the Three Kingdoms.

A moment later, Ryzel appeared in the passage and came hastening toward me, barely able to hold his dignity back from running. "Chrysalis," he breathed urgently, "are you well? There is power at work in that chamber."

He was unusually sensitive to the vibrations which spread from any exertion or presence which touched upon the Real. Any magery or Magic anywhere in the manor was known to him instantly. By that means, among many others, he had determined that I was no Creature. Now as he approached his alarm was briefly plain in his face—concern for me, perhaps—or perhaps anxiety that something had transpired to undermine his own intentions. But when he saw that I was unharmed—and that I was grinning—he drew himself to a halt, stifled his haste. "My lady," he asked cautiously, "what has happened?"

Before I could consider my reply, the door of the meeting-room leaped open, letting the reek of brimstone wash into the passage; and Cashon came out, alive with energy and hope. In one hand, he gripped a scrap of paper. He waved it toward me, then sped in the opposite direction, running to gain his horse.

Firmly, I took Mage Ryzel's arm and turned him away from the aftersmell of Fire. Despite my inexperience, I knew that it would be unwise policy to humble King Thone further by forcing him to make his exit from the chamber before witnesses. Let him repair his appearance and attend the ball as he saw fit; the mere thought of how he had been weakened would give me hold enough over him.

To answer Ryzel, I said softly, "It would seem that Cashon is no longer bound to the lord of Canna." But I gave him no explanation. He had his own secrets; I would keep mine. Also—to be honest—I was young yet and did not wish to give him opportunity to chastise me either for the risk I had taken or for bragging.

My silence made him frown dourly, but he did not question it. Instead, he said, "Then I am no longer chagrined that I learned nothing of Cashon's circumstances to aid you."

As we walked, I asked, "Is it not the custom of Mages to talk at these rare gatherings?"

"It is," he replied. "But Cashon spoke no more than three words from first to last."

Something in his tone alerted me. In an instant, I set King Thone's defeat aside and turned my attention to the Mage. "If Cashon did not speak, who did?"

He mulled his answer for some time, chewing it around in his mouth as if he loathed the taste of it but feared to spit it out. Then, abruptly, he said, "Scour."

His dislike of Queen Damia's Mage was of long standing; but it did not account for his present vehemence. And my own apprehensions concerning the lady of Lodan were many. Carefully, I inquired, "And what did this Scour say?"

"My lady," Ryzel said, obscurely angered and unable or unwilling to say why, "he spoke nonsense—hints and jests to no purpose. He could not be silenced. His own cleverness was a source of vast amusement to him." The Mage snarled his vexation. "Only one thing did he say clearly: he revealed that at his request Queen Damia's minstrel would sing of the slaying of the last Dragon for your banquet."

The sudden tightening of my hand on his arm stopped him. His words brought the monarch of Lodan's unexplained subterfuge back to me. Almost involuntarily, I asked, "Is it true?"

He turned toward me at the doors to the ballroom. From beyond them came the sounds of musicians tuning their instruments. "That Scour requested that song for your banquet? I know not. Surely he wished me to believe it."

I met his questioning look squarely. "Is it true that the last

33

Dragon was slain by the Basilisk-Regal?"

He scowled as he studied me, trying to guess what was in my mind. "That tale is told," he said slowly. "Perhaps it is true. There are many who believe that one Dragon still lived in the world when the Basilisk-Regal's rule began—and that it was gone when his rule ended. But only one portion of the tale is known to be certain: for the last years of his reign, the Basilisk-Regal wore his hands covered."

Unwilling either to outface or to satisfy Ryzel's curiosity, I moved toward the doors. But as they were opened for me, I thought better of my silence. On the threshold of the ball, I turned back to the Mage and said, "Then his grief must have been as terrible as his crime."

A step or two ahead of him, I went forward to continue this night's festivities.

Most of the guests had preceded me. King Thone's retinue appeared somewhat unsettled by his absence; but Queen Damia presided over her portion of the ballroom in great state and glitter; Count Thornden and his attendants kept their backs to her as pointedly as possible; and around the hall moved those families, courtiers, eavesdroppers, and lovers of dancing or sport who were not restrained by allegiance or personal interest.

At my entrance the gathering was hushed. The musicians ceased their tuning; the rulers and their entourages looked toward me; after a last giggle or two, the more playful girls joined the general silence. For a moment, I gazed about me and tried to appear pleased. Taken together, these people were a gay and enchanting sight under the bright gleam of the chandeliers. They were comely and fashionable—and well-to-do. Indeed, hardly a person could be seen who did not display some form of wealth. Here was evidence that the realm had prospered mightily under the imposed peace of the Regals. The rule to which I aspired was manifestly worthy and admirable; yet all these gallant men and women bedecked in loveliness also served to remind me that I was the plainest woman in the Three Kingdoms, as Ryzel had said. For all my victory over King Thone, I was not the equal of the manor's guests.

Nevertheless, I played my part as I was able. Assuming a grace I did not possess, I advanced into the center of the ballroom and spread my arms in a gesture of welcome. "Please dance," I said clearly. "This is the night of my Ascension, and I wish all the realm happy."

At once, the musicians struck up a lively tune; and after a moment's hesitation the ball came to life. Commanding every opportunity for advantageous display, Queen Damia allowed herself to be swept into the arms of a fortunate swain and began to float around the floor. Quickly, other eager young men found themselves partners; dignified old noblemen and their wives made stately circles as they moved. From the corner of my eye, I saw King Thone enter the ballroom, unremarked amid the first swirl of dancing. To myself, I applauded the way he contrived to rejoin the festivities without calling attention to himself; and I noted that he had managed to change parts of his apparel, thus eliminating the marks of Cashon's persuasion. In a moment, he garnered a partner for himself—the wife of one of his dependents—and busied himself about the task of pretending that nothing had happened.

Even Mage Ryzel tucked his Scepter under his arm and took a woman to dance—a girl who gazed at him as if he were the highlight of her life. Thus he also played his part. Soon it appeared that only Count Thornden and I were not dancing. He remained aloof, too fierce for such pastimes. And I— Apparently there were no men in the room bold enough to approach me.

Stiffly, I turned to remove myself from the path of the dancers. My thought was to gain the edge of the whirl and there to watch and listen until I found my chance to slip away unobserved. I did not enjoy what I felt as I saw the youngest daughters of the least consequential families outshine me. But when I left my place in the center of the ballroom, I nearly collided with the servant Wallin.

He had exchanged his livery for a plain broadcloth coat, clean and well-fitting but neither formal nor festive—a garment which emphasized his extreme handsomeness by its very simplicity. He took advantage of my surprise by slipping one arm about my waist, grasping my hand, and pulling me into the music.

A servant. The same servant who had proclaimed a desire for my person. In my first confusion as he commandeered me, the only thing about him which was not surprising was the fact that he danced excellently. Whatever else he was, I did not take him for a man who would have placed himself in this position if he had lacked the appropriate graces.

For half a turn of the ballroom, I simply clung to him and let him lead me while I sought to clear my head. His physical nearness, the strength of his arms, the scent of him—half kitchen-sweat, half raw soap—all served to confound me. But then I caught Ryzel's eye as we danced past him, and his nod of approval brought me to myself. He conveyed the clear impression that he saw my dancing—and my partner—as a gambit I had prepared for the occasion, so that I would not appear foolish when no man freely asked my company. And the other guests who noticed me did so with curiosity, startlement, and speculation in their eyes, sharing Ryzel's assumption—or perhaps thinking that I had in fact chosen Wallin to be my husband.

The Mage gave me too much credit—and revealed that he had had no hand in Wallin's behavior. With an effort, I mastered my confusion. Leaning closer to Wallin, I said so that only he would hear me, "You are fond of risks."

"My lady?" I seemed to feel his voice through his broad chest.

"If the steward discovers that you have left your duties, you will lose them altogether. You are a servant, not the scion of some rich nobleman. Even men of goodly aspect and astonishing presumption must have work in order to eat."

He chuckled softly, almost intimately. "Tonight I do not covet either work or food, my lady."

"Then you are either a hero or a fool," I replied tartly, seeking an emotional distance from him. "Did you see Count Thornden's gaze upon us? Already he has marked you for death. King Thone surely will not wish you well. And Queen Damia—" Would not her blood seethe to see me dancing with a man who was handsomer than any who courted her? "You would be wiser to test your audacity upon her."

"Ah, my lady." His amusement seemed genuine; but his eyes were watchful as we circled. Watchful and brown, as soft as fine fur. "It would delight me to be able to thrill you with my courage. Unfortunately, I am in no such peril. I am merely a servant, beneath the notice of monarchs." Then he laughed outright—a little harshly, I thought. "Also, Count Thornden is a great lumbering ox and cannot run swiftly enough to catch me. None of King Thone's hirelings are manly enough to meet me with a sword. And as for the queen of Lodan"—he glanced in Damia's direction—"I have heard it said that Kodar the rebel has chosen her for his especial attention. While he occupies her, I will be secure, I think."

"And for more subtle dangers," I remarked, "such as poison or hired murder, you have no fear. You are a wonderment to me, Wallin. Where does such a man come from? And how does it chance that you are 'merely a servant'? I would be pleased to hear your life's tale as we dance."

For an instant, he looked at me sharply, and his arm about my waist tightened. More and more of the guests took sidelong notice of us as we followed the current of the dance. But whatever he saw in my face reassured him; his expression became at once playful and intent. "My lady, I am of common birth. Yet I have gleaned some education." His dancing showed that. "I am learned enough in the ways of the world to know that men do not seek to woo women by telling them tales of low parentage and menial labor. Romance requires of me a princely heritage in a far-off land—a throne temporarily lost—a life of high adventure—"

"No," I said; and the snap in my voice made him stop. I was on the verge of avowing to him that my Regal sires had all chosen their brides from the common people for reasons of policy—and for the additional reason that it was the common people whom the Regals loved, the common people who had suffered most from the constant warring of the Three Kingdoms. But I halted those words in time. Instead, I said, "If you truly wish to woo me"—if you are not toying with me—oh, if you are not toying with me!—"then you will speak of such things tomorrow, not tonight. Tonight I have no heart for them."

At once, he ceased dancing and gave me a formal bow. His face was closed; I could not read it. "My lady," he said quietly, "if you have any need that I may serve, call for me and I will come." Then he turned and left me, melting away into the gay swirl as discreetly as any servant.

I watched him go as if I were a mist-eyed maiden, but inwardly I hardened myself to the promise that I would not call for him— not this night. I could not afford to trust his inexplicable behavior; and if I failed at my Ascension, he would not deserve the consequences of aiding me.

Somehow, I found my way from the flow of the dance toward the wide stair to the upper levels. By the foot of the stair, a chair had been set for me on a low dais, so that I might preside over the ball in some comfort. There I seated myself, determined now to let any of the dancers who wished look at me and think what they willed.

Perhaps for those who had come to the ball simply because it was a ball, the time passed swiftly. For me it dragged past like a fettered thing. The musicians excelled themselves in variety and vivacity, the dancers glittered as if they were the jewels of the realm, bright and rich and enviable. At intervals, Mage Ryzel came to stand beside me; but we had little to say to each other. Diligently, he continued to play his part, so that all the gathering would know he was not at work elsewhere, laboring either to prevent my ruin or to preserve his own regency. And my exposed position required me at all costs to maintain my facade of surety. I could do nothing to satisfy my true need, which was to shore up my courage for the coming crisis. Blandly, I smiled and nodded and replied when I was addressed—all the while yearning for privacy and peace. I did not wish to die; still less did I wish to fail.

It happened, however, that when the evening was half gone Queen Damia grew weary of the ball and again took command of the occasion. During a pause between dances, she approached me, accompanied by Mage Scour. In a tone as gracious and lovely as her person, she said, "My lady, your guests must have some respite in which to refresh themselves, lest they lose their pleasure in dancing. If you will permit it, I will offer some small entertainment for their enjoyment."

Her voice and her suggestion chilled me. I feared her extremely. And—as ever—I was unable to fathom her intent. But I could hardly refuse her offer. The callowest youth in the ballroom would know how to interpret a denial.

I saw Ryzel shifting through the stilled assembly toward me. To temporize until he reached me, I replied, "You are most kind, my lady of Lodan. What entertainment do you propose?"

"A display of Magic," she answered as if every word were honey and wine. "Mage Scour has mastered an art which will amaze you— an art previously unknown in the Three Kingdoms."

At that, a murmur of surprise and excitement scattered around the ballroom.

Ryzel's eyes were wary as he met my glance; but I did not need his slight nod to choose my course. We had often discussed the rumor that Scour's research had borne remarkable fruit. That rumor, however, had always been empty of useful content, leaving us unable to gauge either its truth or its importance. An opportunity for answers was not to be missed.

Yet I feared it, as I feared Queen Damia herself. She did not mean me well.

My throat had gone dry. For a moment, I could not speak. A short distance away stood Count Thornden, glowering like a wolf while his Mage, Brodwick, whispered feverishly in his ear. Scour's grin made him resemble a ferret more than ever. King Thone's milky eyes showed nothing; but he had no Mage to support him now, and he held himself apart from most of the guests. Until this moment, I had not realized that my white muslin might become so uncomfortably warm. Surely the night was cooler than this?

Though every eye watched me as if my fears were written on my face, I waited until I was sure of my voice. Then I said as mildly as I was able, "A rare promise, good lady. Surely its fulfillment will be fascinating. Please give Mage Scour my permission."

At once, Scour let out a high, sharp bark of laughter and hurried away into the center of the ballroom.

Around him, the people moved toward the walls, making space for his display. Gallants and girls pressed for the best view, and behind the thick circle of spectators some of the less dignified guests stood on chairs. Mage Ryzel ascended a short way up the stair in order to see well. With a conscious effort, I refrained from gripping the arms of my seat; folding my hands in my lap, I schooled myself to appear calm.

Scour was a small, slight man, yet in his black cassock he appeared capable of wonders: dangerous. The silence of the ballroom was complete as he readied himself for his demonstration. He used no powders or periapts, made no mystic signs, drew no pentacles. Such village chicanery would have drawn nothing but mirth from the guests of the manor. These people knew that magery was internal, the result of personal aptitude and discipline rather than of flummery or show. Yet Scour contrived to make his simple preparations appear elaborate and meaningful, charged with power.

It was said that the blood of a distant Magic man or woman ran in some veins but not others, gifting some with the ability to touch upon the secret essence of the Real, leaving the rest normal and incapable. Whatever the explanation, Scour possessed something which I lacked. And I had been so thoroughly trained by Mage Ryzel—and to so little avail—that I needed only a moment to recognize that Scour was a true master.

Step by step, I watched him succeed where I had always failed.

First he closed his eyes and clasped his hands together before him. Such actions might be necessary or unnecessary, according to his gift for concentration. His mouth shaped complex words which had no sound—again an aid to concentration. Softly, then with more force, his left heel began to tap an unsteady rhythm against the floor. Another man might have done these same things and seemed merely preposterous. Queen Damia's Mage had the look of a man who would soon be strong enough to consume the very manor of the Regals.

Slowly, he separated his hands. Holding his arms rigid, he spread them wider and wider by small increments. Across the gap between his hands ran a palpable crackle of power. It was neither a clear bolt such as lightning nor a diffuse shimmer such as heat, but rather something of both. It shot streaks of red within the reach of his arms then green, then red again.

And as the colors crackled and flared, a shape coalesced within them.

I should have known what was coming. I had been given hints enough; a child could have read them. But the queen of Lodan had been too subtle for me from the first.

The shape took on depth and definition as it grew larger. Its lines became solid, etched upon the air. Moment by moment, its size increased. At first, it might have been a starling—then a pigeon—then a hawk. But it was no bird of any description. Passion flashed in its eyes, light glared along its scales. Gouts of fire burst from its nostrils.

As it beat its wings and rose above Scour's head, it was unmistakably a Dragon.

In response, cries of alarm and astonishment rang across the ballroom. Doors were flung open and banged shut as men and women snatched their children and fled. Some of the guests retreated to the walls to watch or cower; others cheered like Banshees.

It was small yet. But it continued to grow as it soared and flashed;

and the stretch of Scour's arms, the clench of his fists, the beat of his heel showed that he could make his Creature as large as he willed.

The sight of it wrung my heart with love and fear. I had risen to my feet as if in one mad instant I had thought that I might fly with it, forsaking my human flesh for wings. It was instantly precious to me—a thing of such beauty and necessity and passion, such transcending Reality and importance, such glory that for me the world would be forevermore pale without it.

And it was my doom.

Even as my truest nerves sang to the flight of the Dragon, I understood what I saw. Mage Scour had gone beyond all the known bounds of his art to make something Real—not an image but the thing itself. There was no Dragon in all the realm from which an image might have been cast. Scour might as easily have worked magery of me as of a Dragon which did not exist. He had created Reality, could summon or dismiss it as he willed. And thereby he had made himself mightier than any Magic or Mage or Regal in all the history of the Three Kingdoms.

Or else he had simply cast an image as any other Mage might— an image of a Dragon which had come secretly into being in the realm.

In a way, that was inconceivable. Knowledge of such a Creature would not have remained hidden; one Mage or another would have stumbled upon it, and the word of the wonder would have spread. But in another way the thought was altogether too conceivable: if some man or woman of Lodan—or Mage Scour—or Queen Damia herself—were a Creature such as the Regals had been? Capable of appearing human or Real at will? Then the knowledge might well have remained hidden, especially if the Magic had been latent until recently. That would explain all Queen Damia's ploys—her confidence, her choice of songs for her minstrel, Scour's talk at the Mages' dinner.

Whatever its meaning, however, the Dragon bearing itself majestically above Scour's head and snorting flame spelled an end for me. Any Mage capable of creating Reality was strong enough to take the realm for himself at whim. And a Creature hidden among Queen Damia's adherents—no, in the queen herself, for how could she appear so certain if one near her were stronger than herself and therefore a threat to her?—would be similarly potent.

Yet for that moment the sight alone contented me. Regardless of the outcome, I was blessed that such beauty had come to life before me and stretched out its wings. But others in the ballroom were less pleased. With a distant piece of my attention, I heard Count Thornden's harsh cursing—and his sudden silence. Scour's display was as much a threat to the lord of Nabal as to me. Now I realized that Thornden had been demanding a response from Brodwick. And Brodwick had begun—

A gust tugged at the hem of my dress. With a cry of grief or anger, I tore my gaze from the splendid wheel of the Dragon and saw Thornden's Mage summoning Wind.

More guests fled the ballroom, some shrieking; an image of true Wind was not a form of entertainment. But already their cries were scarcely audible through the mounting rush of air, the loud, flat thud of the Dragon's wing-beats, the furnace-sound of flame, the Creature's roar. People called Ryzel's name, demanding or imploring intercession. The chandeliers swung crazily against their chains; whole ranks of candles were blown out. Thornden barked hoarsely for more strength from Brodwick.

The Dragon was far from its full size, and Brodwick's exertion was likewise less than the blast of which he was known to be capable, the hurricane-force powerful enough to flatten villages, to scythe down forests. But within these walls his Wind had no free outlet. Rebounding from all sides, it made such chaos in the air that the Dragon's flight was disrupted: the Creature was unable to challenge its attacker.

Scour had been buffetted from his feet; he lay facedown on the floor, his cassock twisted about his rigid form. Yet he had not lost concentration. His fists pounded out their rhythm—and the Dragon continued to grow. Soon Brodwick would need a full gale to hold back the Creature.

An instant later, Count Thornden staggered forward. As strong as a tree, he kept himself erect under the force of the Wind. His huge hands gripped the hilt of a longsword—he must have snatched it from one of his attendants. Struggling step after step, he moved toward Scour.

If he slew Queen Damia's Mage, it would be a terrible crime. Before the coming dawn, he would find himself in open warfare with Lodan—and perhaps also with Canna, for no ruler could afford to let such murder pass unavenged. Even a Regal would not be able to prevent that conflict—except by depriving Thornden of his throne in punishment. And yet I grasped during the space of one heartbeat that Scour's death would save me.

I did not desire safety at the price of bloodshed. During that one moment, I tried to call Thornden back by simple strength of will.

Then I saw that his attention was not fixed on Scour. Whirling his blade, he aimed himself at the Dragon. He meant to throw the sword, meant to pierce the Creature's breast while it wrestled against Brodwick's Wind, unable to defend itself.

The sight tore a cry from me: "Ryzel!" But I could not hear myself through the roar of Wind and Dragon.

Yet the regent loved all Creatures as I did, and he did not withhold his hand. From him came a shout such as I had never heard before—the command of a Mage in full power.

"ENOUGH!"

Wrenching my gave toward him, I saw him upon the stair with his Scepter held high and his strength shining.

Without transition, the work of the other Mages disappeared. Between the close and open of a blink, both Scour's work and Brodwick's were snatched out of existence, dismissed.

The instant cessation of the blast pulled Count Thornden from his feet in reaction. Among the remaining onlookers, people stumbled against each other and fell. Of a sudden, there was no sound in the ballroom except muffled gasping and the high clink of the swinging chandeliers. Scour snatched up his head; Brodwick spun toward the stair.

For the first time, Ryzel had shown what could be done with a Scepter of true Wood. He had declared the best-kept of his secrets for all the plotters in the realm to witness: his branch of the Ash enabled him to undo magery.

Did it also enable him to unmake things which were Real?

Near me, Queen Damia continued smiling, but her smile appeared as stiff as a mask. King Thone stood motionless as if without Cashon's support or advice he feared to move. Unsteadily, Thornden regained his feet and began snarling curses.

Mage Ryzel lowered his Scepter, stamped his heel on the stair beside him. "*Enough*, I say!" He was fierce with anger. "A Dragon is a Creature, worthy of homage. Real Wind is among the first forces of the world. Such things should not be mocked by these petty conflicts. Are you not ashamed?"

"Paugh!" spat Thornden in retort. "Be ashamed yourself, Mage. Will you now pretend that you do not desire the rule of the realm for yourself?"

"I will pretend nothing to you, king of Nabal," Ryzel replied dangerously. "I am regent now, as I have been before. You know the truth of me. I will not accept warfare among the Three King-doms—neither here nor upon the realm."

He did not say that, if he had desired the rule for himself, he yet lacked means to take it. He had shown only that he could counter the actions of other Mages. The power to dismiss images was not the power to force others to his will. Such things did not need to be said; given time, even Count Thornden would understand them for himself.

The situation required me to speak, before Thornden provoked Ryzel further. Stepping away from my chair, I addressed the guests. I was relieved that my voice did not shake.

"My lords and ladies, we have all been astonished by what we have seen here. Wine and other refreshments will be brought to restore you." I knew that the steward would hear me—and would see that I was obeyed. "When we have recovered the spirit of the occasion—and when the chandeliers have been relit"—I glanced wryly up at the ranks of wind-snuffed candles and was rewarded with a scattering of nervous laughter—"the ball will be resumed.

"For the present, I will leave you a while. I must prepare myself for my coming test." Also I required time to think. My need to be alone with my thoughts was acute, so that I might try to find some grounds for hope.

Bowing to the assemblage, I moved to the foot of the stair and asked Ryzel, "Will you accompany me, Mage?"

"Gladly, my lady," he replied gruffly. He appeared grateful that I rescued him from a difficult circumstance. I took his arm, and together we ascended from the ballroom.

Behind us, the shrill rasp of Scour's voice rose suddenly. "Beware Mage! You tamper with that which you neither understand nor control."

Ryzel did not turn his head or hesitate on the stair, but his reply could be heard clearly from one end of the hall to the other. "I will always beware of you, Scour."

I felt a tremor of reaction start in the pit of my stomach and spread toward my limbs. So that I would not falter, I gripped his arm harder. He gave me a glance which might have been intended as reassurance or inquiry; but we did not speak until we had left the stair and traversed the passage to my private chambers.

There I stopped him. I did not mean to admit him again to my rooms—or to my thoughts—until this night was ended and all questions of trust had been answered. Yet some matters demanded discussion. Leaning against the door to steady my trembling, I studied his face and said, "Mage, you were able to dismiss Scour's Dragon. Therefore it was not Real."

He did not meet my gaze; his face appeared older than my conception of it. Dully, he said, "Only one who can make the Real can also dismiss it. Perhaps I succeeded only because the Reality of the Dragon was not yet complete."

"You do not credit that." I masked my fear with asperity. "If Queen Damia holds command of such Magic, why has she not simply proclaimed her power and demanded rule?"

He shrugged. "Perhaps Scour's discovery is recent and requires testing. Or perhaps his capacity to make and unmake a Creature is limited." Still he did not look to my face. "I am lost in this."

And you are afraid, I thought in response. Your plans are threatened. It may be that you seek to defend them by deflecting me from the alternative. Stiffly, I said, "No. If what you suggest is true, then I am altogether doomed. I will not waste belief on that which must slay me. Rather, I will concern myself with the casting of images.

"If Scour's Dragon is not Real, then there is indeed a true Dragon alive in the realm—a Creature such as the Regals were, capable of concealing itself in human form. Is that not true, Mage?"

He nodded without raising his head.

"Then who *is* this Dragon? Is it not Queen Damia herself? How otherwise would she dare what she has done?"

That brought Ryzel's eyes to mine. Fear or passion smoldered in his brown gaze. "No," he said as if I had offended his intelligence. "That is untrue. Damia is not such a fool, that she would play games when only direct action will avail her. There is some chicanery here. If she is a Creature, why has she not simply taken the realm for herself? No!" he repeated even more vehemently. "Her daring shows that the Dragon is neither someone she can control nor someone she need fear. Her caution demonstrates that she does not know who the Creature is whose image Scour casts."

It was a plausible explanation—so plausible that it nearly lifted my spirits. It implied that I might still have reason to hope and plan and strive. But I did not like the bleak hunger and dread in Ryzel's gaze; they suggested another logic entirely.

Abruptly, before I could find my way between the conflicting possibilities, he changed his direction. "My lady," he asked quietly—almost yearning, as if he wished to plead with me—"will you not tell me now how Thone and Cashon came to be parted from each other?"

He surprised me—and confirmed me in the path that I had chosen. If I had known of his power to dispel magery earlier, I would not have needed to outface King Thone. But Ryzel had kept his secret even from me. Carefully, I met his question with another.

"Before he died, the Phoenix-Regal spoke to me of you. He said, 'He is the one true man in the Three Kingdoms. Never trust him.' Mage, why did my father warn me against you?"

For an instant, his expression turned thunderous, and his jaws chewed iron as if he meant to drive a curse into my heart. But then, with a visible effort, he swallowed everything except his bitterness. "My lady, you must do as you deem best." His knuckles on his Scepter were white. "I have merely served the realm with my life— and you as well as I have been able. I do not pretend to interpret the whims of Regals."

Turning on his heel, he strode away from me.

He had always been my friend, and I would have called him back, but that I was unable to refute my own explanation for the apparently unnecessary indirection of Queen Damia's plotting. Her various ploys might be the caution of a woman who did not know the true source of Scour's Dragon. Or they might be the maneuvers of a woman who was still bargaining with Mage Ryzel for the rule of the Three Kingdoms.

In my heart, I did not accuse him of malice—or even of betrayal. His fidelity to the realm was beyond question. Yet he believed that my Ascension must fail. How then was he to prevent the Kingdoms from war? How, indeed, except by allying himself with one of the monarchs and settling the power there before the others could defend themselves?

Perhaps he was in all truth as true a man as my father had named him. But it was certain to me now that I could not trust him for myself.

So I went alone into my chambers; I closed and bolted the doors. Then I hugged my arms over my breasts and strove not to weep like a woman who feared for her life.

For a time, I was such a woman. Without Ryzel's support I was effectively powerless. And he had indeed been my friend. Every man or woman must place trust somewhere, and for years I had placed mine in him. In league with Damia against me? I would have felt great anger if I had been less afraid.

But then I thought of the Dragon Scour had evoked in the air of the ballroom; and I grew calmer. All Creatures were perilous, and among them a Dragon was surely one of the most fearsome. But the Real danger of that lovely strength made the more human risk of my plight seem small in contrast—wan and bearable. My life was a little thing to lose in a world where Dragons and Gorgons and Wyverns lived. And also—the thought came to me slowly— the restoration of any Dragon to the realm was a boon to the line of the Regals. If the Basilisk-Regal had in fact slain a Dragon, then that crime was now made less. My sires had less need for grief.

And while the identity or allegiance of the Creature remained hidden, I was not compelled to despair.

When I was steadier, I was able to think more clearly about what I suspected of Mage Ryzel.

I saw now that although my life was small my presumption had been large. For no other reason than that I was my father's daughter—and that he had named me Chrysalis in prophecy—I had been prepared to risk the realm itself on the test of my Ascension—the same realm for which the Basilisk-Regal had shed the blood of the last Dragon. But that willingness was indefensible; it was a girl's pride, not a woman's judgement. Ryzel was wiser: behind my back, he sought, not to deprive me of hope, but to keep the Three Kingdoms from war if I failed.

Though it pained me to do so, I resolved that I would accept whatever he did and be content. If I were truly the daughter of Regals—in spirit if not in Magic—then I could do no less, so that the innocent of the Three Kingdoms would not be lost in an abhorrent contest for power.

I wished sorely to be a woman of whom no Creature would be ashamed.

I had intended to remain in my rooms until midnight drew near, but after only a short time a servant came to my door and knocked. When I replied, she reported that Count Thornden desired a private audience with me.

My new calm did not extend quite so far; but the matter could not be shirked. While I held any hope for my life, I was required to walk the narrow line of my position, and so I could not afford to deny the lord of Nabal a hearing which I had earlier granted King Thone.

To the servant, I named a meeting-room in which a tapestry concealed a door through which guards might enter if I had need of them; but I did not immediately leave my chambers. I gave the guards a moment to be made ready—and myself an opportunity to insist that I was indeed brave enough for what lay ahead. Then I unbolted my doors and walked trembling to Count Thornden's audience.

I trembled because he was as large and unscrupulous and lacking in subtlety as a beast. And because I could not imagine what prompted him to request speech with me.

At the door, I nearly faltered. It was unattended—and should not have been. But I did not wish to betray my fear by refusing to meet the lord of Nabal until I was sure of my protections. Gripping my courage, I lifted the latch and went inward.

At once, a large hand caught my arm, flung me into the room. The back of the hand was dark with black hair, an its force impelled me against the table. Regals had often sat there with kings and counselors; and the peace of the realm had been preserved. I stumbled, and the edge of the table caught my ribs so that I gasped.

The room was lit with only two candles. Their flames capered across my vision as I fought to regain my balance, turn toward my attacker. I heard the door slam. At the edge of my sight, a massive chair seemed to leap from the table to wedge itself against the door. As I turned, a backhand blow took the side of my face with such force that I felt myself lift from my feet and sail toward the wall.

With my hands, I broke the impact; but it was strong enough to knock me to the floor.

While the room reeled and all my nerves burned with the pain in my face and chest, Count Thornden came looming over me.

Tall and bestial, he spat an obscene insult at me. Candlelight reflected in the sheen of sweat on his heavy forehead. I feared that he meant to kick me where I lay, yet I was slow to realize the danger. How does he dare this? I asked through the shock of my pain. Is he too stupid to fear my rescue by the guards of the manor?

But the door to the meeting-room had been unattended.

Glaring down at me, he snarled, "No, I will not do it. You are too plain and puny for any man's respect, *my lady*." In his mouth, that *my lady* was a worse insult than his obscenities. "And you have no Magic, *my lady*. Your Ascension will fail. I have been advised to offer you marriage—so that we may rule in alliance—but I will not demean myself by wedding such baggage."

"Fool," I panted up at him. Still I did not understand the danger. "Fool."

"Rather," he rasped, "I will render you unfit for any man or marriage. Then you will cleave to me in simple fear and desperation, because no other will have you, and my kingship will be accomplished at the cost of one small pleasure"—fury and hate were lurid in his eyes—"*my lady*."

I was rising to my feet, off-balance, unable to dodge him. In one swift movement, he grasped the white muslin at my shoulders and stripped it from me as if it were only gauze, as meaningless as my pretensions to the rule of the Three Kingdoms.

"Guards!" I shouted, recoiling from him. Or tried to shout; my voice was little more than a croak. "Guards!"

No guards came. The tapestries in the chamber hung unruffled by the opening or closing of any door which might have brought men with swords and pikes to my aid.

Count Thornden grinned his corrupt hunger at me. "Already I am king in effect if not in name. None who consider themselves your friends dare oppose me. You are lost, *my lady*."

Brutally, he grabbed at me.

I eluded him by diving under the table. I had none of the skills of a warrior, but I was well-trained at physical sports. Hone the body to sharpen the mind, Mage Ryzel had taught me. And he had betrayed me: no one else in the manor had authority to command the guards from their duty. I rolled under and past the table. There I flipped to my feet.

But then I did not run or cry out or seek to escape. Naked, I stood erect across from Thornden and faced him. Anger and pain and betrayal had taken me beyond fear. I had done Ryzel too much honor by thinking him in league with Queen Damia; doubtless he feared her too much to ally himself with her. Instead, he had chosen Thornden for his machinations—chosen to submit me to rape rather than accept the risks of my Ascension. The bones of my cheek flamed as if they had been splintered.

"Resist me!" Thornden snarled. "It increases the pleasure." He began to stalk me around the table.

With all my strength, I shouted, "NO!" and hammered both fists against the tabletop.

I was only a woman—and not especially strong. My blow did not so much as cause the candleflames to waver. Yet the sheer unexpectedness of it stopped him.

"You are a fool!" I snapped, not caring how my voice shook. "If you harm me further, the result will be *your* doom, not mine."

For the moment, I had surprised him into motionlessness. He took his pleasure from harming the weak and fearful; he was not prepared for me. And while it lasted I took advantage of his amazement.

"First, my lord of Nabal," I said in a snarl to match his, "let us agree that you dare not kill me. If you do so, you will forge an unbreakable alliance between Canna and Lodan against you. In the name of survival—as well as of ambition—they will have no choice but to do their uttermost together in an effort to punish my slayer."

I did not allow him time to claim—or even to think—that he was ready to fight any opposition in order to master the realm. Instead, I continued, "And if you dare not kill me, then you also dare not harm me. Look upon me, my lord of Nabal. *Look!*" I slapped the table again to startle him further. "I am indeed plain and puny. But do you think that I am also blind and deaf? My lord of Nabal, I am *aware* of my appearance. I understand the consequences of such plainness. You cannot render me unfit for any man or marriage; I have long since given up all hope of such things.

"Therefore it will cost me nothing to denounce you to Canna

and Lodan if you harm me. I will not be afraid or ashamed to proclaim the evil you have done me." If he had any more than half a wit in his head, he was able to see that I would not be afraid or ashamed. "The result will be the same as if you had slain me. In self-interest if not in justice, Canna and Lodan will join together to reave you of your crown so that I will be avenged."

His surprise was fading; but still I did not relent, did not allow him opportunity to think. I knew what his thoughts would be: they were written in the sweat and darkness of his face. He had reason to avoid anything which might ally Canna and Lodan against him. Why else had he given any credence to the counsel that he should offer me marriage?—why had he sought to rape rather than to murder me? But he also had reason to think that he might be strong enough to prevail even against the union of his foes—especially if Ryzel stood with him. I sought to deny his conclusions before he could reach them.

"And if you dare not murder me—and you dare not harm me— then you also dare not risk battle. Ryzel supports you now because you are the strongest of three. But if Canna and Lodan join against you, you will be the weaker of two, and so Ryzel will turn from you for the sake of the realm."

But in that I erred. Thornden's purpose was suddenly restored. His stance sharpened, a grin bared his teeth. Clearly, his hold upon Ryzel's support was surer than I had supposed, so the threats I had levelled against him collapsed, one after the other. As he saw them fall, he readied himself to spring.

Still I did not waver. I could not guess the truth between Ryzel and Thornden; but my ignorance only made my anger more certain.

"But if you are too much the fool," I said without pause, "to fear Ryzel's defection, then I will not speak of it. And if you are too much the fool to fear Queen Damia's Dragon, that also I will not discuss." Though Thornden's wits were dull, Brodwick's were as sharp as they were corrupt; and he had undoubtedly brought his lord to Ryzel's conclusion—that Damia's Dragon was an image of a Creature she could not identify, and that therefore it was not as dangerous as it appeared. "But are you also fool enough to ignore King Thone? Have you not observed that his Mage has left the manor?"

That shot—nearly blind though it was—went through Thorn-

den like a shock. He stiffened; his head jerked back, eyes widened.
I tasted a fierce relish for my gambit.

"My lord of Nabal, Cashon is a master of Fire. Without Brodwick to defend them, your armies are lost. Cashon will turn the
very ground beneath their feet to lava and death."

He could not know that I was lying. With a howl of rage, he
sprang toward the door, heaved the chair aside, burst from the
chamber. From the outer passage, I heard the pound of his running
and the echo of his loud roar:

"Brodwick!"

Relief and dismay and anger and fear rose in me as nausea. I
wanted to collapse into a chair and hug my belly to calm it. But I
did not. Unsteadily, I walked to the concealed door which should
have brought the guards to my aid.

When I thrust the tapestry aside, I found Mage Ryzel there.

His eyes were full of tears.

The sight nearly undid me. I was so shaken that I could hardly
hold back from going to him like a girl and putting myself into his
arms for comfort. At the same time, I yearned to flay his heart with
accusations and bitterness.

I did neither. I stood and stared at him and said nothing, letting
my nakedness speak for me.

He was unable or unwilling to meet my gaze. Slowly, he shambled
from his hiding place as if he had become unaccountably old in a
short time and crossed the room to the door. Bracing himself on
the frame as if all his bones hurt and his Scepter alone were not
enough to uphold him, he called hoarsely for any servant within
earshot to attend him.

Shortly, he was answered. His voice barely under control, he
told the servant to go to my private chambers and fetch a robe.
Then—still with that painful slowness—he closed the door and
turned back to face me.

"All I proposed to him," he said with a husky tremor, "was that
he ask your hand in marriage—or in alliance, if you would not
wed him. I conceived that Scour's Dragon would teach you your
peril so plainly that you would give up your reasonless pretensions."

"Oh, assuredly, good Mage," I replied at once, scathing him as
much as I was able. I only kept myself from tears by digging my
nails into the palms of my hands. "That was all you proposed. And

then you commanded the guards away, so that he would be free to act violence against me if he chose."

He nodded dumbly, unable to thrust words through the emotion in his throat.

"And when he sought to harm me, you did not intervene. He was certain that you would not."

Again, he nodded. I had never seen him appear so old and beaten.

"Mage," I said so that I would not rail against him further, "what is his hold upon you?"

At last, he looked into my eyes. His gaze was stark with despair. "My lady, I will show you."

But he did not move—and I did not speak again—until a knock announced the return of the servant. He opened the door only wide enough to receive one of my robes.

Without interest, I noted that the robe was of a heavy brocade which had been dyed to highlight the color of my eyes, so that I would appear more comely than I was. While I shrugged it over my shoulders and sashed it tightly, Ryzel averted his head in shame. Then, when I had signified my readiness, he held the door for me, and I preceded him from the meeting-room.

I desired haste; I needed movement, action, urgency to keep my distress from crying itself out into the friendless halls of the manor. But somehow I measured my pace to Ryzel's new slowness and did not lose my self-command. The death of my father had left me with little cause for hope and no love; but at least it had given me pride enough to comport myself as a woman rather than as a girl. Moving at Ryzel's speed, I let him guide me to the upper levels and out onto the parapets which overlooked the surrounding hills.

The night was cold, but I cared nothing for that. I had my robe and my anger for warmth. And I took no notice of the profuse scatter of the stars, though their shining was as brilliant and kingly as a crown in the keen air; they were no more Real than I was. I had eyes only for the moon. It was full with promise or benediction; and its place in the heavens showed me that little more than an hour remained before midnight.

The manor was neither castle nor keep, not built for battle; it had no siege-walls, no battlements from which it might be defended. The first Regal had designed it as a seat of peace—and as a sign to the Three Kingdoms that his power was not founded upon armies that might be beaten or walls that could be breached. In consequence, the Mage and I encountered no sentries or witnesses as we walked the parapets.

Still he had not spoken, and I had not questioned him. But after we had rounded one corner of the manor, he stopped abruptly. Leaning against the outer wall, he peered into the massed darkness of the hills. Sharply, he whispered, "There!" and pointed.

At first, I saw nothing. Then I discerned in the distance a small, yellow flicker of light—a traveler's lamp, perhaps, or a campfire.

"I see it," I murmured stiffly.

Moonlight caught the sweat on his bald head as he nodded. Without a word, he began walking once more.

Within ten paces he halted again, pointed—and again I saw a yellow flickering among the nearby hills.

Down the next stretch of the parapet, he showed me three more glimpses of light, and along the following section, two more— barely visible bits of flame at once as prosaic as torches and as suggestive as chimera. When we had completed a circuit of the manor, I had seen that we were surrounded at significant intervals by these uncertain lights.

Around me, the chill of the dark seemed to deepen. I knew from many strolls at night upon the parapets that the few villages among the hills were hidden in valleys, invisible. And in all truth these lights did not appear to be the lamps of travelers; I had not seen them moving—and in any case none of them lay on the roads which led to the manor.

Yet Ryzel did not speak. Hugging his Scepter to his chest, he stared in silence into the heart of the wide dark. I had resolved patience; but at last I could endure no more. "I have seen, Mage," I breathed tightly. "What have I seen?"

"Carelessness, my lady." His tone was distant and lorn. "Count Thornden is shrewd in his way, but not meticulous. You have seen the ill-muffled lights of his armies."

I held myself still and listened, though his words made my blood labor fearfully in my temples.

"He cannot believe that a woman will prove Regal, and so he lacks one fear which constrains both King Thone and Queen Damia. It was his intent to besiege the manor this night—to put it to the torch if necessary—in order to rid himself of all opposition at one stroke. You know that we have no defense; I was hard-pressed to persuade him to hold back his hand, at least until after midnight. Only the promise of my support brought him to hear me at all, and only my offer of an opportunity with you—or against you—caused him to agree that he would first allow me chance to give him the rule, before grasping it himself with bloodshed."

Therefore my lies about Cashon had turned Thornden aside from my harm. Only the Fire which Cashon might cast could hope to protect the manor from the forces of Nabal.

That I understood. I understood many things; my thoughts were as clear as the cold night. And yet inwardly I was stricken with treachery and loss, scarcely able to hold up my head. The presence of those armies surpassed me.

"You knew this," I whispered like weeping. So many men could not have moved among the hills to surround the manor without the knowledge of Ryzel's spies. "You knew this—and did not tell me."

The sense of betrayed hope filled my throat. Only dismay restrained me from shouting. "There was no need to fear these armies. Cashon would easily have been persuaded to aid us, if I had known to ask him. Thornden would not have dared his forces against Fire—not if he had known that you were able to silence Brodwick's Wind. All this could have been forestalled. If you had told me."

But now the chance was lost. Proud of my victory over King Thone—and ignorant—I had in effect sent Cashon from the manor, thus unbalancing the powers arrayed against me, tilting the scales in Thornden's favor. Now I could only pray that Queen Damia would be able to counter him.

That thought was gall to me. I grew sick from the mere suggestion of it.

Ryzel's presence at my side had become insufferable. Gripping my voice between my teeth, I said, "Leave me, Mage."

"My lady—" he began—and faltered. He was old and no longer knew how to reply to his own regret.

"Leave me," I repeated, as cold as the night. "I do not desire your company in my despair."

After a moment, he went. The door opened light across the parapet, then closed it away again. I was alone in the dark, and there was no solace for me anywhere.

If he had stayed, I would have howled at him, You were my friend! Of what value is the realm, if it may only be preserved by treachery?

But I knew the truth. My father had gauged the Mage accurately: he could not have been driven to such falsehood, except by one thing.

By the fact that I had no Magic.

From the moment of the Phoenix-Regal's death, all other considerations had paled beside the failure of my heritage. Born of a Creature—from a line of Creatures—I had nothing in common with them except yearning and love. Ryzel would have been steadfast in my service if he had held any hope at all for my Ascension.

I should have stopped trusting him much earlier. But he had told me so much, taught me so much, that I had not once wondered if he had indeed told or taught me everything. So I had been left to work my own doom in ignorance.

Above me, the moon entered its last hour before midnight. The end was drawing near. In me, the line of the Regals and all their works would fail. Because I did not wish to flee, I had nothing left to do with my life except approach the Seat as if it were an executioner's block.

Perhaps I would go to the Seat early, attempt my Ascension now, before midnight, so that my part in the ruin of the realm would not be protracted beyond bearing.

"My lady."

His voice startled me. He had not come through the door behind me—I had seen no light. And I had not heard his steps.

Handsome as a dream in the moonlight, Wallin stood before me.

I tried to say his name, but my heart pounded too heavily. Clasping my arms under my breasts, I turned my back so that he would not observe my struggle for self-command. Then, to ease my apparent rejection, I said as well as I could, "You are a man of surprises. How did you find me?"

"I am a servant." His tone conveyed a shrug. "It is an ill servant who remains unaware of the movements of his lady." Now I felt rather than heard him draw closer to me. He seemed to be standing within touch of my shoulder. "My lady," he continued gently, "you are grieved."

Somewhere in the course of the night, I had lost my defense against sympathy. Tears welled in my eyes. I was incapable of silence. "Wallin," I said in misery, "I am a dead woman. I have no Magic."

If he understood the implications of my admission—how could he not?—he paid them no heed. From the beginning, he had done and said things which I could not have expected from him; and now he did not fail to take me aback.

"My lady," he said in his tone of kindness, "some have claimed that your grandmother failed of Ascension because she was not virgin."

"That is foolish," I replied, as startled by his statement as by his sudden appearance. The Seat was a test of blood, a catalyst for latent Magic, not a measure of experience. "None have claimed that the Regals were virgin, either before or after they came into their power."

"Then, my lady"—he placed his hand firmly upon my shoulder and turned me so that I would look at him—"there can be no harm if you allow me to comfort you before the end."

The pressure of his kiss made the sore bones of my cheek burn; but I found in an instant that I welcomed that pain like a hungry woman, starving in the desert of her life. The smell and warmth and hardness of him filled my senses.

"Come," I said huskily when his embrace loosened. "Let us go to my chambers."

Taking his hand, I drew him with me back into the manor.

I had no reason to trust him. But everything trustworthy had been proven false, therefore it was not madness to place trust where none had been earned. And I was in such need—I cared for nothing now except that he should kiss me again and hold me during my last hour, so that I might die as a woman instead of as a girl.

In part because I wished to be circumspect—but chiefly because I did not want to be interrupted—I chose the back ways of the manor toward my chambers. As a result, we encountered some few servants busy about their last tasks, but no guests or revelers—and no one that I recognized as a minion of Ryzel's. During our passage, Wallin remained silent. But the clasp of his hand replied to mine;

and when I looked to him, his smile made his features appear dearer than any I had seen since the death of my father. I did not know how such eyes as his had come to gaze upon me with desire. Yet— by a Magic I had not felt before—their regard seemed to make me less plain to myself, leaving me grateful for that distant taste of a loveliness I did not possess.

But at the door to my chambers I hesitated, fearing that I had mistaken him, that I had been misled by my need—that at the last he would think better of himself and recant. Yet now his eyes were dark and avid, and the muscles at the corners of his jaw bunched passionately beneath the skin, so powerful were the emotions which drove him.

To my surprise, the sight of his intensity increased my hesitation. Suddenly, I found myself truly reluctant for him. I was reconsidering the danger he represented.

That he was dangerous was manifest. A harmless man would not have dared the things he had done this night. And how was it possible for a woman with my face to believe seriously in his desire for me? Deliberately, I placed my hand on his chest to restrain him from the door and said, "Wallin, you need not do this." Somehow, I contrived to smile as if I were not sorrowing. "Your life is too high a price for my consolation. I am content to think that perhaps you have cared for me a little. That is enough. Accept my gratitude and go to procure what safety you can for yourself."

Altogether, he was a surprise to me. At my words, his visage grew abruptly savage. Snatching my hand from his chest, he jerked me around, clamped his fingers over my mouth with my back gripped against his side so that I could not break free. His free hand wrenched open the door. "My lady," he panted as he impelled me inward, "you have not begun to grasp the things I care for."

Though I kicked at him with my heels, tore at his arm with my fingers, he held me helpless. In my chambers, he closed the door and bolted it. Then he lifted me from my feet and bore me to the bed.

Forcing my face against the coverlet, he knelt on my back to keep me still while he pulled free the sash of my robe. Deftly, as if he had done such things many times, he pinned my arms behind me and bound my wrists with the sash. Only then did he remove his weight so that I might roll over and breathe.

As I struggled up to sit on the edge of the bed, he stood before me with a long, wicked knife held comfortably in his right hand.

Pointing his blade at my throat, he gave me a grin of pure malice. "You may scream if you wish," he said casually, "but I advise against it. You can do nothing to save your life—or to prevent our success. But if you scream, we may be forced to shed more blood than we intend. Consider what you do clearly. It will be the innocent guards and servants of the manor who will die in your name, and the outcome will not be altered."

Feverishly, I tugged at my hands but could not free them. My life seemed to stick in my throat, choking me. I had been so easily mastered. And yet the simple shame of it—that I had been beguiled from my wits by nothing more than a handsome face and a bold promise—made me writhe for some escape, some means to strike back. As if I were uncowed, I glared at him and said, "You have lied and lied to me. It has been your purpose from the start to kill me. Why do you delay? What do you fear?"

He barked a short laugh without humor or pity. "I fear nothing. I have risen above fear. I wait only to share your dying with my companion—the one who will rule the realm for me—and will in turn be ruled by me."

Still straining at my bonds, I mustered sarcasm to my defense in the place of courage. "You dream high, Wallin. Servants are usually too wise for such ambition."

His smile was handsome and malign. "But I am no servant," he replied. His eyes glittered like bits of stone. "I am Kodar the rebel, and my dreams have always been high."

He astonished me—not in what he said (though it had surprised me entirely) but in that I believed him instantly. "Kodar?" I snapped, not doubting him, or what he would say, but seeking only to cover my dismay while he spoke. "Again you lie. It is known to half the realm that even now Kodar and his rebels prepare an assault upon Lodan."

He appeared to find a genuine pleasure in my belligerence. Softly, he stroked the side of my neck with his knife. "Of a certainty," he replied smugly. "It has required great cunning of me to ensure that every spy in the Three Kingdoms knows what my forces will do. But my end has been accomplished. While lesser men fight and die in my name, attracting all attention to themselves, my best aides and I have found employment here, disguised as servants. Unsuspected, we have placed ourselves in readiness for this night.

"My companion and I will slit your throat." The tip of his blade dug in until I winced. "Then we will summon the other monarchs to private audiences with you, and we will slit their throats." He made no attempt to hide his relish. "Then my men will fall upon the Mages and noblemen loyal to my enemies. Your Ryzel will not be spared. Before dawn, the rule of the realm will be ours. In truth, the rule will be mine, though my companion will assume that place." He considered himself clever in concealing the identity of his ally from me. "In that way," he said with a smirk, "my success will be as high as my dreams.

"Lest you misunderstand at all," he concluded, "let me assure you that I have never felt the slightest desire for you or your person. You are a savorless morsel at best, and I would not sully myself with you."

I heard him in silence. But if he thought that his insults would hurt me, he had misjudged his victim. His contempt only brought me back to clarity. To all appearances, my attention remained transfixed upon him; but within myself I was gone, seeking help and hope in places where he could not follow.

He looked at me narrowly. His excitement or his arrogance required the vindication of a response. "You would do well to speak," he said with velvet menace. "If you plead with me, perhaps I will spare you briefly."

I did not speak; I did not risk provoking him. I did not want to die. I wanted to learn who his confederate was.

A frown pinched the flesh between his brows. His desire to see me grovel was unmistakable. But before he could attempt to dismay me by other means, a faint knocking at the door interrupted him.

Nothing kindled in me at the sound. It was clearly a signal—a coded sequence of taps for Kodar's benefit, not mine. He cocked his head, at once gratified and vexed—gratified that his plans developed apace, vexed that he had no abject victim to show for his pains. Yet he did not hesitate; he had not come so far by giving spite precedence over ambition. Lithe and virile, he strode to the door and tapped a response.

When his question was answered, he unbolted the door and opened it, admitting Queen Damia to my chambers.

She appeared more radiant than ever. As Kodar sealed the door again, she flung her arms around his neck and kissed him as if she were insatiable for him. His ardor in return was everything a woman could have wished, yet she broke off their embrace before he was done with it. Her gaze turned to me, and her eyes were bright.

"Kodar, my love." She beamed. "You have done well. She considers herself defiant, but she will make an apt sacrifice nonetheless. I am pleased."

Watching her, I wondered if Kodar had noticed the subtle way in which she had already taken command of the room, reducing him from mastery to the status of one who obeyed.

But I did not understand why she had allied herself with him. For desire? Perhaps. It was conceivable in his case, but I did not think so. And if she had at her disposal the power of a Dragon— either Real or Mage-made—what need had she of him?

Kodar and his knife were several paces from me. I might be able to say a few words before I was silenced. Meeting her gaze alone as though I were capable of ignoring her companion, I said, "My lady of Lodan, this Kodar has advised me that I should not scream. But now that he has told me how he has betrayed his cause to serve you, and how he means to give you the rule of the Three Kingdoms by slaying all those who stand against you, I find I no longer comprehend why I should not. His plan will be foiled by any forewarning, however slight. With one cry, I will deprive you of all that he offers. Why then should I not—?"

Gripping his knife, Kodar started toward me. I snatched a breath, filled my lungs to call out with all my strength.

My threat meant nothing to him, yet Queen Damia stopped him. "Withhold a moment, Kodar." Her command was certain. "For the sake of blameless lives which would otherwise be lost, I will answer her."

This game was hers, and I was outplayed. But in the face of death I could do nothing but strive for life. My eyes held her as if Kodar had no significance between us, and I prayed that he had wit enough to understand her—and me.

"My lady," she said with demeaning courtesy, "you have not failed to reason that Mage Scour is not in truth able to create Magic. If he possessed that power, he would not suffer any other to rule him. Assuredly he would not suffer *me*." Her tone said plainly that

Scour was a man and would gladly have suffered anything for her sake. "Therefore his Dragon was but an image. And therefore it follows that there is a Creature in the realm that has remained hidden from all eyes."

She smiled gloriously. "All eyes but mine."

Kodar grinned at her. I wanted to curse him for the arrogance which blinded him to the queen's cunning; but I kept my gaze upon her and waited for her to continue.

"Lacking Ascension, his power has been latent," she went on, "but fortunately Mage Scour and I discovered it."

Doubtless that had indeed been fortunate for her.

"My lady, he is the reason you will not scream. Kodar and I pursue this plan against you because it will cost little bloodshed—and will enable us to assume rule swiftly. But if we are foiled in that, we will simply call upon the rebels concealed in the manor. They will assist the Dragon to the Seat, and he will take what we desire by greater violence. So you see," she said as though contradiction were impossible, "we cannot be defeated. You will accept your death quietly in order to spare a great many lives in the Three Kingdoms."

Perhaps I was too slow-witted for her. Perhaps I should have worked out much earlier what she wished me to understand. But at last I knew. I might have cried out in my anguish, had I not been too desperate for such weakness; she pushed me to the limit of what my sore heart could endure. That such beauty had come to such evil! I had no recourse but to prove myself equal to it or die.

"My lady," I said slowly, "you speak as if even a Dragon will be glad to serve you when you claim the rule. That is clever—to put a smiling face upon the fact that you will be merely a figurehead through which the Creature commands. If indeed he will not cast you off when he has gained his ends. You seek to distract me from the truth.

"But Kodar lacks so much wit. He has already vaunted himself outrageously before me. Your Dragon will teach him the worth of his arrogance.

"Unless the Creature is Kodar himself."

He was facing me now. He seemed deaf to insult. His face was alight, not with umbrage, but with a savage glee. He felt in himself the power of the coming transformation and was exalted.

But Queen Damia stood behind him and to one side. With his gaze upon me, he had no view of her. He did not see her smile broadly in my direction.

I did not take up her hint. Instead, I turned my attention to Kodar. Having failed to make him think better of his trust for Lodan's queen, I encouraged him to see my grave regard as a new deference. "My lord," I said quietly, "I do not understand." If I could have pulled my hands free at that moment, I would not have done so. They would have been of no help to me. "Possessing such strength, why have you troubled to mime rebellion?" I had no doubt now that the *lesser men* whose lives he spent to further his plans were the sincere ones, the honest rebels who believed—however wrongly—that the realm would be better without rulers. "Why do you persist in subterfuge now? And why do you accept the hand of this treacherous queen in your dealings? Why do you not declare yourself openly and claim what is yours by right? You require nothing but the touch of true Stone."

At once, I saw that he would not refuse to answer me. Where his Magic estate was concerned, pride outweighed judgment.

While Damia watched him with a loveliness which might have signified either adoration or scorn, he replied, "A hidden threat is stronger than a declared power. When first I conceived my intent to rule the realm, my nature was unknown to me. Therefore rebellion was the only path open. And now it is clear that I will be stronger if none know how I betray those who serve me. My queen will assume the throne—and an unknown Dragon will roam the Three Kingdoms, wreaking her will and its own—and my rebels will continue to strike where I choose, thinking that they still serve me. Stark fear and incomprehension will unman all resistance. The realm will be unified as no Regal has ever been able to master it, and every man and woman will tremble at my feet!"

His vision of sovereignty seemed to entrance him. But Queen Damia had no use for his transports. "Kodar, my love," she interposed, "this is pleasant—but the time flees before us." She was marvelously unafraid of him. "If the guests are called to the Ascension before we have dispatched Thone and Thornden, our opportunity will be lost. We must be at work. Will you accept the brave sacrifice of this daughter of Regals?"

He glanced down at his knife and smiled. "Gladly."

The unmistakable look of bloodshed on his face, he started toward me.

I had no time left. I had been meditating to the depths of my mind on what I must do in order to live—what must happen to save me. There was but one hope, and it was as scant as ever. But if I did not act upon it, I was lost.

Summoning every resource of will and passion and heritage, I sent out a silent cry of desperation and protest. Then I ducked under the knife and flipped forward, away from the bed.

I was hampered without the use of my hands; but I contrived to roll my feet under me and spring erect. Whirling around, I faced Kodar.

He charged after me. The knife swung. The unsashed brocade of my robe caught the blade, deflecting his thrust as I danced aside. Though my sandals were paltry as weapons, I swung my foot with all my strength against his knee. He answered with a grunt of pain.

Trusting that small hurt to slow him, I dove past his reach. He slashed at me and missed. Another flip and roll returned me to the bed. Nearly staggering for balance because I could not use my hands, I leaped onto the bed. From that position above him, I would be able to ward off his knife with my feet for a moment or two.

"Kill her, you fool!" Queen Damia hissed furiously.

A loud crash resounded through the chamber as the wood around the doorbolt splintered.

Another heavy blow burst both bolt and latch. The doors sprang inward and shivered against the walls.

Mage Ryzel strode into the room.

His bald head was flushed with exertion; but there was nothing weak or weary in the stamp of his feet, the stretch of his thick chest. His Scepter attacked the air; threats glared from his eyes.

My relief and jubilation at seeing him were so great that I nearly sagged to my knees—into Kodar's reach.

When he saw the knife, Ryzel stopped. "Wallin?" he demanded. "What means this?"

For a moment, Kodar's attention jerked from side to side as if he were a cornered animal. Damia appeared frozen by surprise or indecision. The four of us remained motionless, gauging the ramifications of Kodar's blade. Now Kodar would gain nothing by shouting for his rebels—not while Ryzel might fell him before help came. But the Mage was alone. Though he held his Scepter, its power would be useless against a knife. And he was no longer young. Would he be a match for the tall, strong rebel?

Kodar decided that the Mage would not. Turning his back to me, he advanced warily toward Ryzel.

Queen Damia stopped him without discernible effort. "You are timely come, Mage," she said calmly, defying anyone to credit that any threat or interruption could unsettle her. "This man is not Wallin the servant. He is Kodar the rebel. He means to slay both me and the lady Chrysalis. And when we are dead, he intends to treat King Thone and Count Thornden similarly. Then he will claim the rule—"

With a snarl, Kodar launched himself toward her, aiming his blade for the deep hollow of her decolletage.

He did not reach her. Though Ryzel was old, his hands were swift. One sure jab drove the end of his Scepter into the pit of Kodar's stomach. Kodar tumbled to the floor and groveled there, retching for breath.

"I thank you, good Mage," Queen Damia murmured as if she thought that she could sway Ryzel.

He did not waste a glance on her. When he was sure that Kodar would be unable to move for a few moments, he came to me and helped me down from the bed. Only the trembling of his hands as he undid my bonds betrayed his fear.

"My lady," he said grimly, "I felt power here. Therefore I came."

"That was Kodar," the queen answered. "He thinks himself a Creature." Her scorn for her confederate was evident. "Some small capacity for magery there is in him. But for the most part it remains stubbornly trivial."

I did not look at her; I did not wish her to see my reaction to this new demonstration of mendacity. Doubtless Scour had been clever in persuading Kodar to think himself a Dragon, so that his plans for rule would serve Damia's ends. Yet she betrayed him in his turn without compunction. I did not question that her purpose against me remained unaltered. My hands shook like Ryzel's as I took the sash from him and knotted it about my waist to close my robe.

From his place on the floor, Kodar gagged on gasps and curses.

"Mage," I said, controlling my voice as well as I was able, "Queen

Damia and her servant have done with me. Will you escort them to the Ascension hall?"

He opened his mouth to protest, then shut it again. The look in my eyes silenced him. Though his jaws chewed questions and fears, he bowed to me, then turned his attention to the monarch of Lodan and Kodar the rebel.

When he had plucked Kodar's knife from the floor and concealed it somewhere in the sleeve of his cassock, he bunched one heavy fist in the back of Kodar's coat and heaved him upright. Supporting Kodar with that grip, he said to Queen Damia, "My lady, will you accompany me?"

"Gladly," she replied. Wrapping her hands around his arm, she turned her back on me without farewell and clung intimately to him as they left my chambers. Still she treated me as if I signified nothing—and him as if she meant to seduce him before they gained the end of the passage.

Then I heard him shout a summons to the guards; and I had no more concern for him. On his own terms, at least, he was a match for Damia.

I needed time—and had none. Time to recover my courage from the close touch of death, time to think and to understand. Time to prepare myself for the attacks which would be directed against me in the Ascension hall. But no time remained. If I did not go now, I would risk missing the moment of midnight. More than once, my father had stressed the importance of midnight on the eve of my twenty-first birthday, when the moon would be full above the realm and I would attempt the Seat.

I was not concerned for my apparel; the robe I wore would do well enough for the occasion. But I went to my glass and expended a few moments with my hair, pinning it this way and that in an effort to give my appearance more grace if not more comeliness— striving by such small vanities to cover the hollow place which Kodar had opened in my heart. With a trace of rouge, I concealed the mark of Thornden's hand by matching its color upon my other cheek. However, I could not remove the memory of Kodar's kiss from my mouth. Schooling myself to steadiness, I gave up the attempt.

Alone and afraid and resolute, I left my chambers and went to meet my fate.

The hall in which the Seat of the Regals stood upon its pediment was at the far side of the manor. When I reached it, all the guests and personages of the realm had gathered there before me. I heard their excitement and anticipation in the hum of voices which issued from the open doors. And at the sound I nearly failed of courage. To meet King Thone alone did not seem to me a great matter. To stive for my life in private against Count Thornden and Queen Damia and Kodar had been necessary, inescapable. To bear the loss of Mage Ryzel's allegiance was a burden I could not avoid. But to risk failure and humiliation publicly, to prove unworthy of my heritage before the assembled lords and nobility of the Three Kingdoms — ah, that was another question entirely. I did not know how I would endure the shame.

While I remained hesitating outside the hall, Ryzel appeared in the passage and came toward me.

I believed that he meant to hinder or challenge me. There was a grimness in his face which spoke of anger and accusation. Therefore I prepared to rebuff him despite my gratitude. My fragile hold upon myself was not a thing which I could submit to the consideration of his uncertain loyalty.

He did not speak at once, however. Taking my arm, he steered me a few paces from the door, so that we would be unheard as well as unseen. And he did not meet my gaze as he asked, "Chrysalis, are you sure of what you do?"

That question I could answer honestly. "No," I said. "I am sure only that I must make the attempt."

The effort of will which brought his eyes to mine was plain in his visage. "Then trust me," he breathed, not in demand, but in appeal. "I have become a cause of shame to myself. I will support you to the limit of my strength."

With one touch, he drove home the linchpin of my resolve. And with that touch, all my thoughts concerning him turned. A moment earlier, I had determined that I would reject him, though he had saved my life. Now I made promise to myself that I would not risk him.

"The matter is mine to hold or let drop, Mage," I said, speaking at once in kindness and severity. "Whatever the outcome, the realm will have need of you. Do not intervene here. Only do as I command you — and stand aside. That will suffice for me."

His gaze sharpened; he regarded me as if he were unsure of what I had become. Then he turned his head aside, so that I would not see how he took my words. "As you will, my lady," he said. His frown was black and lost—the ire of a man who had been denied restitution for his faults. But I said nothing to ease him. Only by refusing his service could I hope to save him if I failed.

Because of his pain, I left him and moved toward the door. Midnight was drawing near, and I did not mean to miss it. The coming day would give time aplenty for regret or forgiveness, either in life or in death. Therefore I nearly did not hear the words he uttered after me:

"I have spoken with King Thone."

Almost I stopped to demand an explanation. His soft statement sent implications hosting at my back, dire and imprecise. Did he seek to warn me? Had he given himself new cause for shame? What role did he intend for the lord of Canna in my last crisis?

But I had no time, and I feared that if I halted now I would never move again. I had come to the last of my questions—to the one upon which all others depended. Though my stride faltered and my head flicked a glance backward, I continued on my way.

Unattended and unannounced, I entered the great Ascension hall, where the high Seat of the Regals stood empty.

The place had a stark majesty which consorted ill with the festive apparel and conflicting dreams of the gathered guests. The hall itself was round and domed, its ceiling beribbed and supported by the most massive timbers of Lodan. The light came from many wide, flaming censers, where the perfumed oils of Canna burned over the wrought metals of Nabal. Some sophisticates thought such things barbarous, but I considered them fit accompaniment for the grandeur of Creatures. Around the walls stood the spectators of my crisis in their anticipation. The floor had been formed of large but irregular slabs of basalt polished to a fine sheen and then cunningly fitted like the pieces of a puzzle, their cracks sealed with a white grout like tracery. It was said that these white lines across the basalt had a pattern which could only be discerned from the Seat. Some averred that the pattern was the image of a Basilisk, the first Regal; others, that the lines depicted the Creature which would be the last of its line, the end of the rule of Magic in the realm. But Ryzel had scoffed at such claims. He asserted bluntly that the floor of the hall was neither more nor less than a map of the Three Kingdoms.

And from the center of that floor rose the Seat.

Upon a stepped base of white marble—itself nearly as tall as I was—stood the heavy and rude-timbered frame which held the Stone. This frame was not properly a chair, had neither arms nor back; it had been built so that it might be approached from any side. But the frame itself was of no importance. All that mattered was the dull Stone of the Seat—the Magic slate to which nothing could be touched which was not also Magic. Upon occasion in the past, Ryzel had shown me that the Stone made no actual contact with the frame which supported it, but instead floated slightly among the members of ordinary wood that composed the Seat.

Upon that Stone I must place my hands or die.

Fully human and fully Real.

I had already made the attempt once and failed.

Count Thornden stood with Brodwick and his adherents not far from the door by which I entered the hall—and Mage Ryzel behind me, though he did not presume to move at my side. The lord of Nabal had taken his place because it was across the hall from Queen Damia and her entourage, Kodar among them, his arms pinned at his sides by two guards. But Thornden took the opportunity of my nearness to speak.

"You lied to me, girl," he growled, making no effort to conceal his anger. "My scouts report Cashon riding wildly away into Canna, with no other thought but flight." He seemed not to care how widely he was overheard. With a mounting tightness in my throat, I observed that he and all his men were now armed.

"I have sent out my orders," he continued. "You are lost."

I understood him. The heat of his scowl was plainer than his words. He meant that his armies had begun to march on the manor. I should not have attempted to provoke him. But I knew now that he had spurned Ryzel's support; and that thought gave my heart a lift of audacity. Also I was angered—though not surprised—that he and his men had come armed to my Ascension. So I turned on him a gaze which would have withered a wiser man, and I said, "No, my lord. The loss is yours. Until now, I have striven to spare you from the cost of your own folly."

I held his glare until I saw that at last it occurred to him to fear me. Then I swept past him with all the dignity which my slight form and uncomely face could convey.

Moving directly to the base of the Seat, I set myself before the three rulers.

Instantly, the murmurs of tension and curiosity and speculation in the hall were stilled. Every gaze and glance came to me. I had become the center of the night. Obliquely, I noticed how few nobles had brought their wives and children to witness my Ascension.

With Count Thornden and Queen Damia standing opposite each other, I expected to see King Thone somewhere equally distant from them both. But he was not; his party was beside Thornden's, so close that the two were almost intermingled. Thone's stance was turned toward the lord of Nabal rather than toward me.

A sizable number of Canna's courtiers had also procured weapons for themselves.

At once, I seemed to fall dizzy as a whirl of inferences passed through my head. Count Thornden had already set his forces into motion. Therefore he no longer cared for Ryzel's support. Or Ryzel had informed him that my Ascension must fail. And the Mage had spoken to King Thone. Deprived of Cashon's power, had Thone now been persuaded to cast his lot with Thornden as the lesser evil, so that Queen Damia would not gain ascendancy? The prospect affected me as if it were a form of vertigo.

But I had come too far for retreat—and was too close to fury. The truth I would disentangle if I lived. If I died, lies would lose their significance. Therefore I faced the assembled doubt and hope and hunger of the Three Kingdoms as though I could not be moved. And when I spoke, I did not quaver in any way.

"People of the realm," I said clearly, "the passing of the Phoenix-Regal has left a time of trial upon us all. The future of the peace which the Regals have wrought has been uncertain—and uncertainty breeds fear as surely as fear breeds violence. It is tempting to look upon those who are our foes and believe them evil, avid for our destruction. Therefore they must be slain, before they slay us. And no reason can put an end to this bloodshed, for how can we dare to set aside our fear when our enemies fear us and remain violent? For that reason do we need Regals. A Regal is a Creature and has no need or fear of us—and so is not driven to violence.

Rather, a Regal's power gives us peace, for it frees us from the fear of each other which compels us to war."

To one side, Count Thornden's men watched each other and him tensely. King Thone made a studious portrait of a fop immersed in the contemplation of his manicure. Queen Damia breathed deeply, but gave no other sign of her expectations. One ringed and immaculate hand rested on Mage Scour's shoulder. Kodar glared murderously at her, but she did not deign to notice it.

I was a plain woman, alone, and powerless; but my enemies had lost the capacity to make me afraid. "This night," I said as if I could hear the fanfare of trumpets which had never been sounded in my name, "I will put an end to uncertainty."

Thus I brought down upon my own head the crisis of my Ascension. Without hesitation or haste, I turned to the Seat and placed my feet upon the marble steps.

If I had spoken less clearly or appeared more frail, the rulers might have withheld their hands, awaiting the verdict of the Seat as both wisdom and caution urged them to do. But I had foiled each of them in turn, giving them cause to estimate me more highly. And I went to meet my Ascension as if there were no doubt of its outcome. In that way, I inspired them to risk themselves against me. If I succeeded, how could they believe that they would survive the punishment for their recent actions?

I knew that I was still some few moments early, that midnight had not quite come. But I had set my decision in motion at last. Better to hazard myself in advance of the time than to be made late by any delay or opposition.

Before I gained the second step toward the Seat, I heard Count Thornden's harsh command—and felt Wind begin to gather at my back.

Brodwick's image appeared to leap from nothingness to the force of a Banshee during the space between one heartbeat and another. And the hall erupted in a clangor of shouts and iron.

Involuntarily, I started to turn. A mistake: the mounting gale came upon me without my feet planted. Flame from all the censers gusted toward the timbers of the ceiling. I made a small pirouette like an autumn leaf in the air and fell to the basalt.

Somehow, I regained my feet—and lost them again. I stumbled heavily against the base of the Seat. The edge of the first step hit sharply across the center of my back. Wind pulled my robe away from my legs. I saw that both my knees were split and bleeding.

Then Brodwick's blast became so strong that I could hardly hold up my head. But I saw Kodar twist his arms from his surprised captors and break free. With a wrench, he sprang beyond them. His cry rose over the tumult:

"Kodar and freedom! To me, rebels!"

At once, all the doors burst open, letting a dozen men into the gale. They were dressed as servants; but they bore swords and pikes, and they fought the Wind toward Kodar's side.

He did not await them. With a single blow, he struck down one guard; he snatched a long dagger from the man's belt. Slashing that blade about him, he kept Damia's defenders back as he hurled himself toward the lady of Lodan.

Her hand on Scour's shoulder pushed the Mage away, out of Kodar's reach. So great was Scour's concentration that he simply pitched to the floor, unconscious of his own fall. Damia's smile did not waver as she met Kodar's assault.

One flick of her wrist and a gleam of metal stopped him. As his knees failed, the Wind seemed to take hold of him and lower him gently to the basalt, blood spurting from his cut throat.

In the air above them, Scour's Dragon appeared.

Leaping into existence, the image pounded its wings and struggled for size as though it were already hot upon the spoor of its prey. At first, it was too small to advance against the buffeting Wind which Brodwick hurled from across the hall. But Brodwick's force was focused on me, not upon the Creature, and Scour did not need his lady's blandishments to impell him. Surely he understood as all in the hall did that he could not afford to fail now, either to Thornden's Mage or to me. Lying as if he were as lifeless as Kodar, he put all his soul into his magery, and the Dragon let out a blast of flame which defied the Wind halfway to the spot where I cowered. The heat touched my sore cheek and was torn away. Laboring tremendously, the Dragon began to beat forward in the teeth of the gale.

I could not move. My limbs felt pinned and useless, as if my spine were broken. All Brodwick's exertion centered on me—and he was a master. I had known that this would happen—that my enemies would attack me here in all their fury—but I had not known that I would prove so weak. The simple effort to turn myself so that I might crawl up the steps surpassed my strength. The blood running from my knees appeared to carry my will away; the courage drained from me as from a cracked cistern. The Dragon was lovely and terrible; even the Wind seemed as beautiful as it was savage. I was no match for them. In all truth, I had no reason to move.

Mage Ryzel could have stilled both Wind and Dragon, but he did not. In the end, he betrayed me.

I had commanded him not to intervene.

And still I had not entirely understood that the iron clashing which punctuated the shouts and passion around me was the sound of swords.

Forcing my face into the Wind, away from the Dragon, I saw Count Thornden and his men fighting for their lives—and for Brodwick's protection—against the guards of the manor and King Thone's courtiers.

An awkward melee was in progress. Cudgeled by the gale, Thornden's men and Thone's and the rebels and guards hacked at each other in confusion. The lord of Nabal's party was large and heavily armed, but was hampered by the necessity of defending the Mage; it could not gain the advantage.

To my astonishment, I beheld King Thone deliberately block Count Thornden's path toward me. Thone's decorative blade could not withstand Thornden's huge sword; but the lord of Canna used his point so adeptly that Thornden was thwarted—prevented from charging forward to assail me personally.

I have spoken with King Thone.

Ryzel had not betrayed me. He had persuaded Thone to this defense—for what hope would remain to Canna now if Thornden was victorious. And the Mage had not stilled the rising magery because I had commanded him to withhold.

Perhaps after all I would be able to move. The life at issue was my own—but in the end it was not mine alone. It was also the life of the realm. While I remained in my weakness, blood was being shed; and that killing would give inevitable rise to the warfare which I abhorred as a matter of birthright. Surely I could at least move.

But when I had shifted myself so that my hands and cut knees were under me against the force of the Wind and the hammering approach of the Dragon, I understood that movement was not enough. If I held true, I might perhaps gain the top of the marble base—but beyond question I would be unable to stand erect in order to place my hands upon the Stone.

This state is not easily attained. It may be reached in one way, by the touch of Stone to one whose very blood and flesh are latent Magic. And I had already failed once.

I required help.

I demanded it as if it also were my birthright. In my extremity, I cried out through the battle and the blast and the roar:

"Ryzel! Your Scepter!"

Again, he obeyed. Without hesitation, the one true man in the Three Kingdoms flung his Scepter toward me.

The Wind bore it so that it sailed in a long arc to the base of the Seat. Bounding upon the steps, it struck like a whiplash against my side.

But I felt no pain; I was done with pain. Wildly, I slapped my arms around the Scepter and hugged it so that it would not slip away.

I had always failed in my efforts to grasp the rough-barked Wood. It was Real, not to be handled by ordinary flesh, yet it was simpler and less perilous than the Stone. The Stone could not be touched by anyone who was not Magic; but the Scepter required only the capacity for magery. Therefore Ryzel held a Scepter though he could not claim the Seat. And therefore I clung to the true Wood for my life.

Its nature transcended my own. Even with my arms about it, it seemed to ooze from me as if it were fluid rather than solid—a Scepter composed of a substance I could not comprehend. Brodwick's Wind cut across the hall, yowling like lost hope through my heart. And the Dragon—! Surely it was near to its full size now, its natural power and fury. All the air was fire and roaring. Those people who had not joined the melee either cowered against the walls or wrestled with the gale-kicked doors.

Yet I held the Scepter. Cupping one hand about its end, I kept it from slipping away. Then I began to crawl and squirm like a belabored mendicant up the steps.

The Wind was brutal to me, battering my head upon the marble, clogging my limbs, tearing my vision to shreds. In fear that I would lose my eyes, I kept my face turned from Thornden's Mage—turned toward the Creature beating like a holocaust against the blast to devour me. Its great jaws fountained flame in tremendous exhalations; heat slapped repeatedly at me, scorching my cheek, spreading black stains down the side of my robe. Only Brodwick's force as he strove to prove himself stronger than Scour preserved me from incineration.

But I did not fear the Dragon. It was a wonder in the world, and the sight of it gave me strength.

With that strength, my legs thrust me up the steps while my left arm crooked the Scepter and my right hand cupped its end.

Like water running impossibly upward, black char spread from step to step as the Dragon loomed over me, howling fire. The gale threatened to burst the ceiling of the hall from its timbers. Nails and pegs and weight could not hold; boards were stripped away into the outer dark. A new sound like a scream from many throats joined the turmoil. Only the Stone itself, immovable within its supports, kept the ordinary wood of the Seat from being swept away in kindling and splinters.

I had no time to gauge what I would do. The Creature inhaled, fearsome and savage; its next spewing of flame would roast me to the bone. A cry for my father wrung me, but I made no sound that I could hear as I took my last gamble.

Guiding the Scepter with my left arm, I thrust the Wood upward, forward—toward the Seat.

At midnight under the full moon on the eve of my twenty-first birthday, I touched the end of the Scepter to the Stone.

At once ponderous and instant, slow and swift, the shock of that contact began in my left elbow and right hand and spread through me, ripples of passion bringing flesh and muscle and bone to power. Ignited by this unprecedented connection of Stone and Wood and birthright, the blood which the Basilisk-Regal had shed came to life in me. All my weakness was swept away in wild glory. A roar came from me like a tantara—a challenge against every foe and traitor to the realm.

Bounding from the marble, I turned to my image with flame and claws and tore it from the air, heedless of Scour's screams. Then I flung myself toward Brodwick until his concentration melted to panic and he stretched himself groveling before me and his Wind was stilled.

Then I left the hall and went in bright joy and power out into the night.

Before dawn, when I had measured my wings and my fierce ecstasy across the deep sky—and almost as an afterthought had routed Thornden's armies among the hills—I returned to the manor and the hall and accepted the homage of the three rulers. Then I dismissed them, along with the rest of my guests. Servants bore away the injured for care, the dead for burial, but I did not leave the hall myself. Sitting upon the Seat in my human form, with my weight resting against the comfortable strength of the Stone, I spoke for some time alone with Mage Ryzel.

He was plainly astonished by what had transpired—and more than ever shamed by the things he had done in the name of his doubt. But he was a brave man and made no effort to excuse his mistakes—or to abase himself. Instead, he stood before me grasping his Scepter as he had formerly stood before the Phoenix-Regal, my father.

Gruffly, he said, "My lady, how is this done, that a woman of no great beauty gives a lesson of humbling to a man of no mean knowledge or strength, and the teaching provides him pleasure? You have become a source of pride to the realm."

I smiled upon him. My heart was at rest, and my gladness covered all the errors and betrayals of the night. If the three kings had known how little harm I intended toward them, their fear of me would have grown greater still. But to answer the Mage—and to exculpate him to himself—I attempted an explanation.

"The blood of the last Dragon had sunk deep into the flesh of the Regals. An extraordinary conjunction of powers was required to awaken it. Therefore when I was born, and my father saw that I had no Magic, he procured for you a limb of the Ash, so that it might aid the birth of something new in me—the restoration of the last Dragon to the world, and restitution for the ill deed which was forced upon the Basilisk-Regal."

"That much is evident," replied Ryzel. I was pleased that his manner toward me had changed so little. "But why did the Phoenix-Regal not tell me the purpose of my Scepter, so that I might aid you?"

"For two reasons." My father's dilemma now seemed plain to

me. "First, he was uncertain that the blood I had inherited had grown strong enough to be awakened. If it had not, then the one true hope of the realm was that you would betray me." The Mage began to protest, but I gestured him silent. "The Phoenix-Regal trusted that you would cobble together some manner of alliance after my failure—and that you would find means to preserve my life. There was his hope. If I lived long enough to wed and have a child, the blood of the slain Dragon would grow stronger yet and might be awakened in my child where it had failed in me. This hope he provided by holding secret the purpose of the Scepter.

"Second, he did not wish the blood awakened, however strong it might be, if I did not merit it enough to discover it for myself and prove worthy. He desired a test for me. If I lacked the need and the will and the passion to find my own way, then I would be a poor Regal, and the realm would be better served by my failure or flight. He sought to instill me with hope," I mused. It was curious that I did not resent the ordeal my father had required of me. Rather, I relished what he had done—and was grateful. "But for the sake of the realm he could not allow me to rise untested to power."

Ryzel absorbed this and nodded. But after a moment's thought he said, "You surpass me, my lady. I do not yet understand. If you grasped the Phoenix-Regal's intent so clearly—no, I will not ask why you did not speak of it to me. But why did you command me to stand aside? Had you permitted me to counter Scour and Brod- wick, your approach to the Seat would have been free."

There I laughed—not at his incomprehension, but at the idea that I had known what I was doing. I had learned that no path of hope existed for me but one; therefore it was hardly surprising that I had chosen that path. But I had not known what would happen. I had known only that I did not mean to fail. The things I knew now had come to me with the transformation of my blood, shedding light in many places where I had been ignorant.

That point, however, I left unexplained. Instead, I said, "No, Mage. Had you stilled Brodwick and Scour, our plight would have been unaltered. We would simply have had to strive against swords and pikes rather than against magery. Perhaps we would both have been slain. And also," I said, holding his gaze so that he would understand me, "I desired to spare your life. If I failed, the realm would have no other hope than you."

In response, he passed his hand over his eyes and bowed deeply. When he raised his head again, I thought he would say that he had not earned my concern for his life. But he pleased me by dismissing such questions. In his blunt way, he asked, "What will you do now, my lady? Some action must be taken to consolidate your hold upon the realm. And the treacheries of the three rulers merit retribution."

I wanted to laugh again for simple happiness; but I restrained myself. Calmly, I replied, "Mage, I believe I will commence a sizable conscription. I will claim all of Thornden's soldiery. I will demand every blackgard who serves Thone's machinations. And"—a grin of glee shaped my mouth—"I will call upon every eligible man within a day's ride of Damia's allure.

"These men I will set to work. Much hard labor requires to be done to unify the realm, so that it will be less an uneasy balance of kingdoms and more a secure nation."

Ryzel mulled what I was saying; but his eyes did not leave mine. Carefully, he asked, "What labor is that, my lady?"

I gave him my sweetest smile. "I am certain, Mage, that you will think of something."

After a moment, he smiled in return.

Outside the manor, dawn was breaking. When I had dismissed my Mage and counselor, I took on my other form and went out into the world to make the acquaintance of my fellow Creatures.

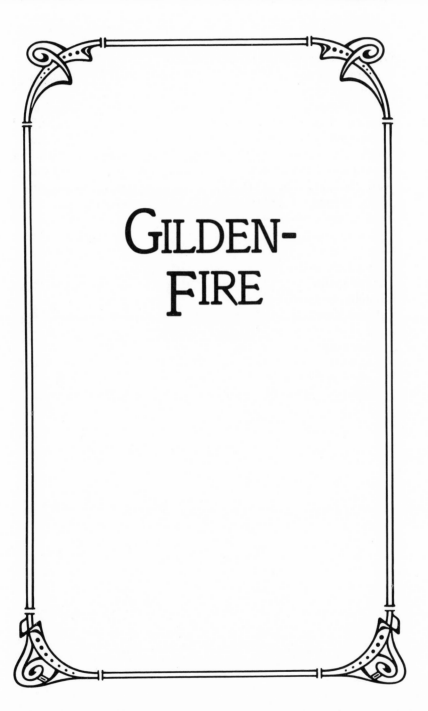

GILDEN-FIRE

FOREWORD

"GILDEN-FIRE" IS, IN ESSENCE, AN "OUT-TAKE" FROM *THE Illearth War*. For that reason, it is not a complete story. Rather, it describes an episode which occurred to Korik of the Bloodguard and his mission to Seareach during the early days of *The Illearth War*, after Thomas Covenant's summoning to the Land but before the commencement of the actual war. This material survived through two drafts of the manuscript, but is entirely absent from the published version of the book.

On that basis, I think it requires some explanation. As a general rule, I use my out-takes for wastepaper. But I've made an exception in this case for a variety of reasons.

Some of them have to do with why "Gilden-Fire" was taken out of *The Illearth War* in the first place. The version of the manuscript which originally crossed the desk of Lester del Rey at Ballantine Books was 916 pages long—roughly 261,000 words. That was manifestly too long. With much regret, Lester gave me to understand that I would have to cut 250 pages.

Well, I'm a notorious over-writer; and I was able to eliminate 100 pages simply by squeezing the prose with more than my usual ruthlessness. But after that I had to make a more difficult decision.

As it happened, the original version of *The Illearth War* was organized in four parts rather than the present three. Part II in that version dealt exclusively with Korik's mission to Seareach. It eventually provided me with the 150 pages of cuts I still needed, but not because I considered the material to be of secondary importance (I have little sympathy for anyone who considers the fate of the Unhomed, the fidelity of the Bloodguard, and the valor of the Lords to be of secondary importance). On the contrary, I was quite fond

of that whole section: I put my axe to the roots of my former Part
II for reasons of narrative logic.

From the beginning, that section had been a risky piece of writing.
In it, I had used Korik as my viewpoint character. For the first time
in the trilogy, I had stepped fully away from Thomas Covenant (or
from any direct link to the "real" world), and that proved to be a
mistake. It was crucial to the presentation of Covenant's character
that he had some good reasons for doubting the substantial "reality"
of the Land. But all his reasons were undercut when I employed
someone like Korik—a character with no bond, however oblique,
to Covenant's world—for a narrative center. (*The Illearth War*
does contain two chapters from Lord Mhoram's point of view. But
in both cases Mhoram is constantly in the company of either Covenant or Hile Troy. Korik's mission lacked even that connection to
the central assumptions on which *Lord Foul's Bane* and *The Illearth
War* were based.) In using Korik as I had, I had informed the reader
that the people of the Land were in fact, "real": I had uninten-
tionally denied the logic of Covenant's Unbelief. Which was already
too fragile for its own good.

Therefore I took the absolutely essential sections of that Part II
and recast them as reports which Runnik and Tull brought back
to Covenant and Troy—thus preserving the integrity of the narrative perspective from which the story was being viewed. And in
the process, I achieved the 150 pages of cuts I needed.

But all of "Gilden-Fire" was lost.

That does not exactly constitute high tragedy. Cutting is part of
writing; and narrative logic is more important than authorial fondness. My point is simply that "Gilden-Fire" was cut, not because
it was bad, but because it didn't fit well enough.

However, the question remains: if this material didn't fit *The
Illearth War*, why am I inflicting it upon the world now?

The main reason, I suppose, is my aforementioned fondness. I
like Korik, Hyrim, and Shetra, and have always grieved over the
exigency which required me to reduce their role in the story so
drastically. But, in addition, I've often felt that the moral dilemma
of the Bloodguard is somewhat obscure in the published version of
my books: too much of their background was eliminated when I
cut "Gilden-Fire." In fact, too much of the development of the
people who would eventually have to face the destruction of the

Unhomed was sacrificed. (How, for instance, can Lord Hyrim's achievements be fully understood when so little is known about him?) By publishing "Gilden-Fire," I'm trying to fill a subtle but real gap in *The Illearth War*.

Finally, I should say that I think the logic which originally required me to cut out this material no longer applies. Since it cannot stand on its own as an independent story, "Gilden-Fire" will surely not be read by anyone unfamiliar with *The Chronicles of Thomas Covenant the Unbeliever*. And those readers know that the question of whether or not the Land is ultimately "real" (whether or not a character like Korik is sufficiently "actual" to serve as a narrative viewpoint) no longer matters. In reality as in dreams, what matters is the answer we find in our hearts to the test of Despite. By publishing "Gilden-Fire," I hope to give more substance to the answers Korik, Hyrim, and Shetra found.

GILDEN—FIRE

AS SUNRISE ECHOED THE FIRE OF FAREWELL WHICH HIGH
Lord Elena had launched into the heavens from the watchtower of
Revelstone, Korik Bloodguard and his mission to Seareach wheeled
their Ranyhyn, tightened their resolve about them, and went running into the east.

With the new sun in his eyes, Korik could not see clearly. Yet
he moved comfortably to the rhythm of Brabha's strides, faced the
prospect ahead without a qualm. He had been riding Brabha for
nearly fifty years now, but his experience of Ranyhyn was far longer
than that: the great horses of Ra by the score had borne him in
turn, one after another as their individual lives ended and their
fidelity passed from generation to generation. He knew that the
Ranyhyn would not miss their footing. The terrain near Revelstone
was much-traveled and reliable; yet even in the cluttered rigor of
the Northron Climbs, or in the subtle deceptions of Sarangrave
Flat, the Ranyhyn would remain sure-footed. Their instincts were
founded on something more constant than the superficial details of
hills and plains. They bore Korik's mission down through the foothills of Revelstone as confidently as if the great horses were part
of the ground itself—a part made mobile and distinct by their
quicker life-pulse, but still sharing the same bone, the same ancestry,
so that no orphaning misstep or betrayal could occur between hoof
and earth.

Around Korik rode his companions, those who shared his mission to the Giants of Seareach: fourteen more Bloodguard and two
Lords, Hyrim son of Hoole and Shetra Verement-mate. The memory
of their parting from the people of Revelstone—Shetra's grief over
her separation from her un-Ranyhyn-chosen and self-doubting husband, Hyrim's argute attempts to probe the difference between what

the Bloodguard remembered and what they knew, Thomas Covenant's refusal to share this mission—was vivid to Korik. But more vivid still was the urgent need which gave cause to this journey. Summon or succor. A need so compulsory that it had been given into his hands, to the Bloodguard themselves, rather than to the Lords, so that if Hyrim and Shetra fell their defenders would go on.

For there had been a special timbre of exigency in Terrel's silent voice earlier that night as he had sent out his call to First Mark Morin:

—Summon the High Lord, Terrel had said, following a grim-eyed and haggard Lord Mhoram toward the Close. There is a peril upon the Giants of Seareach. He has seen it.

Lord Mhoram had seen it. Seer and oracle to the Council, he had described the death of the Unhomed stalking them across all the leagues between Revelstone and *Coercri*—a death no more distant than a score of days. When the High Lord and all the Council had gathered with him in the Close, he had told them what he had seen. His vision had left them gray with many kinds of dread.

In this Korik knew the Lords well. Without sleep or let, he had served the Council in all its manifestations for two millennia: he knew that the pain in Hyrim and Callindrill and Mhoram, the bitten hardness of Shetra and Verement, the wide alarm of the Lords Amatin, Loerya, and Trevor arose from concern for the life-loving Unhomed—a concern as deep as the ancient friendship and fealty between the Giants and the Land. But Korik also understood the other dreads. Corruption was mustering war against the Council; and that jeopardy had become so imminent that only scant days ago the High Lord had felt compelled to summon the Unbeliever from his unwilling world. In such a need, all the eyes of the Land naturally turned toward Seareach for assistance. And for three years there had been silence between the Giants and Revelstone.

A year of silence was not unusual. Therefore the first year had not been questioned; but the second gave birth to anxiety, and so messengers were dispatched to Seareach. None of them returned. In the third year, one Eoman was sent—and not seen again. Unwilling to hazard more of the Warward, the High Lord had then commanded the Lords Callindrill and Amatin to carry word of the Land's need eastward. But they had been turned back by Sarangrave

Flat; and still the silence endured. Thus the Council had already
known fear for the Giants as well as for themselves. Lord Mhoram's
vision gave that fear substance.

The High Lord did not hesitate to conceive aid for the Giants.
Summon or succor. But Corruption's hordes were believed to be
marching for the Land's ruin; and few warriors and little power
could be spared from the defense. So the mission was given to the
Bloodguard. Given by First Mark Morin to Korik by reason of his
rank and years, and by the High Lord to the Lords Hyrim and
Shetra: Hyrim son of Hoole, a corpulent, humorous, and untried
man with an avowed passion for all fleshly comforts and a silent
love of Giants; and Shetra Verement-mate, whose pain at her husband's self-doubt made her as bitter as the hawk she resembled. It
was a small force to hurl into the unknown path of Corruption's
malice. No Bloodguard required reminder that there were only two
roads to bear the Despiser westward: one to the south of Andelain,
then northward against Revelstone; the other to the north of Mount
Thunder, then westward through Grimmerdhore Forest. And Korik's way toward Seareach also lay through Grimmerdhore.

However, the road of Corruption's choice was uncertain; and
the Bloodguard did not pang themselves with uncertainties. Korik
and his people were not required by their Vow to know the unknown; they were required only to succeed or die. It was not in
that fashion that they had been taught doubt; the test of their service
was one of judgment rather than knowledge.

When Korik left the Close, he went without hesitation about the
task of selecting his comrades.

He had no qualm about his choices. The Bloodguard shared a
community of prowess and responsibility; and any individual mem-
ber of the community could be elected or replaced without causing
any falter in the service of the Vow. Yet he exercised care in his
decisions. Cerrin and Sill he included as a matter of course: they
had borne the direct care of Shetra and Hyrim since those Lords
had first joined the Council. Then he added Runnik and Pren because they were among the senior members of the two ancient
Haruchai clans, the *Ho-Aru* and *Nimishi*, that in the mountain
fastnesses of their home had warred together for generations until
the Bond which had united them. Similarly, he included five younger
Bloodguard from each clan, so that both would have a fair hand

in the mission. Among these was Tull, the youngest of the Bloodguard.

Some time ago, when Lord Mhoram had made his scouting
sojourn to the Spoiled Plains and Hotash Slay, and had been forced
to flee, the Bloodguard with him had fallen. In keeping with the
ritual of the Vow, the fallen had been Ranyhyn-borne to Guards
Gap and the Westron Mountains for burial in native grave-grounds,
and the *Haruchai* had sent new men to replace them. Tull was
among them. He was centuries younger than Korik; and though
the Vow bound him and straitened him and sustained him and kept
him from sleep, so that he was a Bloodguard like any other, still
he did not know the Giants as his older comrades did. For this
reason, Korik chose him. It would gratify Tull to see that the un-
flawed fealty of the Bloodguard was not unmatched: the Giants of
Seareach could also be trusted beyond any possibility of Corruption.

As he walked soundlessly through the halls of Revelstone, sending out his mental summons, Korik considered the advantages in
taking either Morril or Koral with him. They were the Bloodguard
who watched over the Lords Callindrill and Amatin. Morril and
Koral had accompanied those Lords when they had attempted to
reach the Giants and were driven back by some lurking power in
the Sarangrave. Both these Bloodguard had previous experience
with the dangers which faced the mission. But Korik had heard all
that Morril and Koral could tell concerning the danger, and they
had the right to remain with the Lords whom they had personally
warded.

The choosing completed, Korik went to the place where his
comrades would meet him—the one place in Revelstone reserved
for the Bloodguard. It was a dim uncompromising hall, with un-
rubbed walls and a rough raw floor on which no one but a Bloodguard would walk barefoot. The whole space was unfurnished and
unadorned, but it served them as it was. They needed only an open
space with a punishing floor and freedom from observation.

Korik did not have to wait long for his chosen comrades. They
came promptly, though without any appearance of hurry, for the
word of Mhoram's vision had gone out ahead of Korik's summons.
They had heard it in the mental talk of the *Haruchai*, in the orders
of the Lords, in the altered and quickened beat of Revelstone's
rhythms. But when Cerrin and Sill, Runnik and Pren, Tull and the

others gathered around him, Korik still took the time to speak to them. The mission which First Mark Morin had given him was special, perhaps higher than any other burden the Bloodguard would bear in this war. Their responsibility had always been to the Lords: they had Vowed to preserve the Lords while the Council went about its work. Rarely had any Bloodguard been given a command which was not part of his direct service. But the mission to the Giants had been entrusted to the *Haruchai*. Summon or succor. To meet this uncommon charge, Korik gathered his company about him for old rites.

—Faith, he greeted them.

—Fist and faith, they replied together.

—Hail, chosen brothers, Korik returned. The mission to the Giants of Seareach is in our hands. These are Bloodguard times. War marches. The end of the Giants' exile is near, as foretold by Damelon Giantfriend. Dour fist and unbroken faith prevail.

The Bloodguard answered in the words of the ancient *Haruchai* Vow:

—*Ha-man rual tayba-sah carab ho-eeal neeta par-raoul.* We are the Bloodguard, the keepers of the Vow—the keepers and the kept, sanctified beyond decline and the last evil of death. *Tan-Haruchai.* We accept.

—*Tan-Haruchail*, Korik said. Bowing to his comrades, he repeated the old warcry: Fist and faith!

They bowed in turn, stepped back so that there was a clear space around him. Then they began the trial of leadership, as prescribed by the rites he had invoked. One by one, they came forward to fight with him, to measure their strength against his.

Although he had been given the mission by the First Mark, Korik wanted to affirm his leadership among his company, so that in any future extremity no question of his right to command could arise. Therefore he fought for his leadership as he had once fought to be among the commanders of the army which had invaded the Land in the early years of High Lord Kevin son of Loric.

This trial came instinctively to the proud *Haruchai*, for they had been born to fighting in the same way that their forefathers had been born to it, and their forefathers before them, as the old tellers described. For them, it was not enough that they made their home in one of the most demanding places of the Earth. It was not enough that the fastnesses which they inhabited, the caves and crags, the ice-grottoes and crevasses and eyries, were snow-locked three seasons a year and in places perpetually clamped in blue glaciers—that simple survival from day to day, the preservation of the home-fires, and the tending of the goats and the bare gardening they did when in summer some of the valleys were free of snow and ice, took all the strength and fortitude which any people could ask of themselves—that blizzards and mountain winds and avalanches provided them with so much disaster that even the hardiest and most cunning of them could not look to have a long life. No, in addition the *Haruchai* were always at war.

Before the Bond, they had fought each other, battling *Ho-aru* against *Nimishi*, generation after generation, across cliffs and cols and scree and ravines, wherever they met. They were a hot people, strong-loined and prolific; but without food and shelter and warmth, children died at birth—and often the women died as well. Caught thus constantly between the need to replenish the people and the mortality of love, the clans strove to wrest every possible scrap of food or flicker of heat or shadow of shelter from each other, so that their wives and children might not die.

Yet in time a kind of understanding came to the *Ho-aru* and *Nimishi*. They saw that they fought a feud they could not win. First, the clans were too evenly matched for one side to retain for long any brief ascendance. And second, even victory offered no solution to the need, for a victorious family would quickly grow in size until it was as large as two; and then the lack of food and warmth and shelter would kill as before. So the leaders of the clans met and formed the Bond. Enmity was set aside, and hands were joined. From that time onward, *Ho-aru* and *Nimishi* warred together against their common need.

That need sent them eastward, out of the Westron Mountains, intending to conquer by might of fist the forms of sustenance their home did not provide, so that their wives and children would live. Korik had fought his way through a trial of leadership lasting an entire winter to gain a place—with Tuvor, Bannor, Morin, and Terrel—among the commanders of the army which had marched, a thousand strong, through Guards Gap and along the glacial purity of the Llurallin River, to wage war against the Land.

They passed without resistance across the region which was later to be named Kurash Plenethor, Stricken Stone, and Trothgard. Seeking battle, they were received by the inhabitants with quiet and fearless tolerance, were given without struggle all they demanded. These peaceful people had no use for war. Eventually, they even guided the *Haruchai* to Revelstone, where the Council of High Lord Kevin was still in its youth.

There began the stuff of which the Bloodguard Vow and the fealty between the Giants and the *Haruchai* were made.

Revelstone itself met the eyes of the invaders with a wonder such as they had never known. They understood mountains, cliffs, indomitable stone, and never in their warmest dreams had they conceived that gutrock could be made so welcoming, habitable, and extravagent. The great Giant-wrought Keep astonished them, inspired them with a fierce joy unmatched by anything except the sight of austere peaks majestically facing heavenward and the enfolding love of wives. And the more they looked, the more ecstatic Revelstone appeared. Half intuitively, they sensed the pattern, the commingling flow and rest of the balconies and coigns and windows and parapets, which the Giants had woven into the rock of the high south wall—perceived it dimly, and were enthralled. Here, amid warmth and lushness, fertility and food and sunlight, was a single rock home capacious enough to enclose the entire *Haruchai* people and hold them free of want forever. The suggestiveness of such luxuriance made the very crenellations of the battlements seem luminous, strangely lit by high mysteries and unquenchable possibilities.

In the rush of their unfamiliar passion, they swore an oath that they would conquer this Keep and make it their own. Without hesitation, one thousand unarmed *Haruchai* laid siege of Revelstone.

Their war-making did not go far. Almost at once, the great stone gates under the watchtower swung wide, and High Lord Kevin rode out to meet his besiegers. He was mounted on a grand Ranyhyn and accompanied by half his Council, one Eoman of the Warward, and a coterie of grinning Giants. Solemnly, Kevin listened while First Mark Tuvor delivered his terms of war; and some power of the Staff of Law enabled the High Lord to understand the *Haruchai* tongue. Then he declared so all the *Haruchai* might grasp his meaning that under no circumstances would he fight the invaders. He declined to make war; instead, he invited the five commanders into Revelstone to the hospitality of the Lords. And though they expected treachery, they accepted, because they were proud.

But there was no treachery. The great gates stood open for three days while the *Haruchai* commanders tasted the grandeur of Revelstone. They experienced the laughing genial power of the Giants who had made the Keep, received the confident offer of Kevin's Council to supply the *Haruchai* freely whatever they needed for as long as their need lasted. When the commanders returned to their army, they sat astride prancing Ranyhyn, which had come from the Plains of Ra at Kevin's call and had chosen to bear the *Haruchai*. Korik and his peers were of one mind. Something new was upon them, something beyond instinctive kinship with the Ranyhyn, beyond friendship and awe for the Giants, beyond even the fine entrancement of Revelstone itself. The *Haruchai* were fighters, accustomed to wrest what they required: they could not accept gifts without making meet return.

Therefore that night the army from the Westron Mountains gathered under the south wall of Revelstone. All the *Haruchai* joined their minds together and out of their common strength forged the metal of the Vow—unalloyed and unanswerable, accessible to no appeal or flaw, unambergrised by the promise of any uncorrupt end: a Vow like the infernal oath upon the river of death which binds even the gods. This they wrought out of the extremity and innocence of their hearts, to match the handiwork of the Giants and the mastery of the Lords. As they spoke the hot words—*Haman rual tayba-sah carab ho-eeal*—the ground seemed to grow hot and cognizant under their feet, as if the Earthpower were drawing near the surface to hear them. And when they brought their Vow around full circle, sealing it so that there was no escape, the rocks on which they stood thundered, and fire ran through them, sealing their bones to the promise they had made.

Thus it was done. Before dawn, the remainder of the army marched away toward Guards Gap and home. The five hundred *Haruchai* of the Vow went to Revelstone to become the Bloodguard, defenders of the Lords: the last preserving wall between Revelstone and any blot or stain.

Yet that was not all. Though now, on the eve of the mission to Seareach, Korik invoked the old trial of leadership to test his place in the company he had chosen—though the Vow he served was as always impeccable and binding—yet the history of the Bloodguard contained at least two other matters which each of them kept in account. The first of these came at once, the morning after the Vow was taken. When the *Haruchai* entered Revelstone and announced their purpose to the Council, High Lord Kevin was dismayed. Like the Lord Mhoram in the later age, Kevin was at times gifted or blighted with prescience; and he treated the Vow as if it proferred disaster. He insisted strangely that the *Haruchai* had maimed themselves. He strove to refuse the service, so much was he taken aback— and so little did he understand the fierce hearts of these people. But the Giants taught him to understand, and to accept.

The second matter arose from the last war, before Kevin chose to enact the Ritual of Desecration. When the High Lord knew in secret what he purposed, he set about saving as much of the Land as he could. He forewarned the Giants and the Ranyhyn, so that they might flee the coming havoc. And he ordered the Bloodguard away, into the safety of the mountains.

This was the question which now plagued the Bloodguard, taught them doubt, this question of judgment. They had obeyed the High Lord, and so survived the Desecration; but the Lords to whom they had sworn their service were lost. The Bloodguard had obeyed because they had never considered that Kevin might wish to thwart their Vow. Even now the fact felt inconceivable, threatening. They had trusted him, assumed that his orders were consonant with their intent. Now they knew otherwise. Kevin had prevented them from dying with him—or from opposing his dark purpose. He had betrayed them.

Now the Bloodguard knew how to doubt. And now their Vow had revealed an additional demand: to fulfill it, they must preserve the Lords from self-destruction.

Therefore Korik invoked the rites of leadership. He remembered his whole history—the Vow gave no relief from memory—and because of it he acted as he did. He raised hands which knew how to kill against his comrades.

He did not hold back his strength, or cover his blows, or in any other way fight less fiercely than he would have fought a foe of the Lords. There was no need for restraint: there were no frail or unskilled fighters among the Bloodguard; their devotion to the Vow kept their alertness keen and their thews strong. And the first tests were not long. Runnik and Pren were veterans of the Bloodguard, had measured their strength against his often enough to know him exactly. After a few swift passes, they acknowledged that he was the same warrior who had bested them before. And in deference to their example, the younger *Ho-aru* and *Nimishi* also contented themselves with fleet flurrying ripostes to demonstrate Korik's worthiness—and their own. Cerrin and Sill took longer, more because they respected the Lords they warded than because they desired to take away Korik's command. But he had been one of the original *Haruchai* commanders for good reason. Fighting with a speed which masked the precision of his movements, he showed Cerrin and Sill in turn that he remained one of the elite.

When they were satisfied, Korik encountered Tull.

He was gratified by the strength of Tull's mettle. In many ways, Tull was still an untried Bloodguard; and because of this, Korik attacked him relentlessly. But Tull quickly showed that over the generations the *Haruchai* had not been content with old skills: they had developed new counters and blows, new feints and angles of attack. In moments, Korik was pushed to his limits, and Tull seemed to have the upper hand. But Korik had experienced conflict against many different and versatile opponents. He learned swiftly. When an unusual feint caught him, knocked him back, he spun and twisted, avoided the fall which would have signaled his defeat. Then he met Tull with the same feint. The blow stretched Tull on the rough floor, and the trial was over.

Tull bounded to his feet, stood with the other Bloodguard facing Korik.

—Fist and faith, they said. We are the Bloodguard. *Tan-Haruchai.*

—*Tan-Haruchail*, Korik acknowledged. He bowed slightly to his comrades, and they followed him from the chamber. Among them, he was the only one whose pulse or breathing had quickened; but outwardly he revealed nothing of the trial of leadership.

When his company regained the main halls of Revelstone, they separated to gather supplies. For themselves they would carry nothing but raiment and long coils of *clingor*, the adhesive leather rope which had been introduced to the Land by the Giants. They bore no weapons. And, in part because of their Vow, they needed little food. As long as the hardy *aliantha* grew and ripened throughout the Land in all seasons, the Bloodguard required no other sustenance. But the Lords would need more equipage: food and drink, *lillianrill* rods for torches, some *graveling*, bedding, cookware, a few knives and other utensils. Such things the Bloodguard would carry on their backs, so that Shetra and Hyrim would not be wearied by packs. Korik left other resources to the Lords; he took care of the needs within his power.

Those which were not did not trouble him. He had no answer for Lord Shetra's dour dismay—though he had paid for centuries the cost of the yearning between a man and a woman—and so he stood aloof from it. He had no hand in the unvoiced fear which caused Lord Hyrim to ask Thomas Covenant's company in defiance of the High Lord's wishes; therefore he made no effort to sway or deny the Unbeliever. And he fended away all questions which ranged beyond the ambit of his certainty. Fist and faith. Succeed or die. Aided by the native flatness of his features, he bore himself as if he possessed no emotions which might be touched.

Yet he grieved for Shetra and respected Hyrim. He judged the Unbeliever coldly. And the arrival of the Ranyhyn, seventeen of the great horses of Ra with their starred foreheads and their strange responsive fidelity, thundering forward in the first hint of day in answer to his call—that pride and beauty was a hymn in his heart. He was *Haruchai* and Bloodguard. His people had shown in their Vow how extremely they could be touched.

Thus now there was a special note of reveling in him as Brabha bore him down out of the foothills of Lord's Keep into the lower plains, the easy farmlands which spread for leagues on all the eastern slopes. There he and his companions began to encounter brief villages—small clustered Stonedowns and an occasional Woodhelven in the old spread banyan trees which dotted this part of the plains, homes for the farmers and artisans who, despite their vital share in the life of Revelstone, preferred not to live in that massed habitation. In the dim dawn light, the riders slowed their pace to a more cautious trot, so that they ran no risk of trampling a groggy farmer or child. But when the sun rose fully, the Ranyhyn greeted it with glad nickering, as if they were welcoming an old dear friend, and stretched their strides again.

In the fresh day, the countryside shone as if it were oblivious to the looming threat of blood. Ripe wheat rippled like sheets of gold in some of the fields; and in others cut hay was stacked into high fragrant mowes. Over them, the air blew its autumn nip; the breeze carried the smells of the crops like a counterpoint to the morning enthusiasm of the birds. The farmland seemed to defy the spectre which haunted it. Korik knew better: he had seen land as fair as this helpless to withstand fire and trampling and the thick unhealthy drench of blood. But he did not forget, could never forget, the heartwrenching beauty which had in part brought the *Haruchai* to their Vow. It baffled expression, surpassed any language but its own. He understood the overflowing mood which caused Lord Hyrim to throw back his head and sing as if he were crowing:

> "Hail! Weal!
> Land and life!
> Pulse of power in tree and stone!
> Earth-heart-blood
> vital, vivid surge
> in pith and rock!
> Sun-warmth
> balm-bliss bless
> all air and sea and lung and life!
> Land's soul's beauty!
> Skyweir
> Earthroot
> weal!
> Hail!"

The song had a strange power to catch its hearers, as if it actively desired them to join it; and Lord Hyrim relished it. But Shetra did not smile or sing or even look toward Hyrim. She rode on grimly, as if the war were already upon her. This Korik also understood. He sat between them, comprehending and mute.

Thus they rode through the morning until the swift roaming gait of the Ranyhyn had placed most of the fields and villages behind them and the terrain began to give hints of its coming roughness. Lord Hyrim alternately sang and talked as if all the countryside were his enchanted audience; but Lord Shetra and the Bloodguard moved in their private silences.

Then toward noon they stopped beside a stream to give the Lords rest and the Ranyhyn chance to graze. Hyrim's awkward dismount confirmed an impression which had been growing on Korik: although the Lord had been freely chosen by the Ranyhyn, he was an unusually poor rider. Even an inexperienced person could sit safely on a Ranyhyn if he left himself in the horse's care. And Lord Hyrim was not inexperienced. Yet he rode with erratic jerks, as if repeatedly he lost his balance and nearly fell. His dismount was only half a matter of choice. Korik thought of the hard riding ahead and winced inwardly.

—He has always ridden thus, Sill answered. His balance is faulty. The tests of the Sword in the Loresraat almost defeated him, prevented him from Lordship.

—Yet the Ranyhyn selected him, Korik mused.

—Their judgment is sure.

—Yes, Korik replied after a moment. And his Ranyhyn knows the danger.

Nevertheless he felt anxiety. He wondered if the High Lord had known of Hyrim's deficiency as a rider. If she had, why had she chosen him? However, such questions were not within Korik's responsibility, and he recited his Vow to silence them. The mission would give him the measure of Lord Hyrim's fitness.

Hyrim himself was obviously aware of the problem. He limped ruefully away from the Ranyhyn and dropped flat on his stomach to drink from the stream. After a long draught, he pushed himself onto his back, spat a last mouthful of water over the grass, and groaned, "By the Seven! Is it only noon? Half of one day? Friend Korik, how long will we require to gain Seareach?"

Korik shrugged. "Perhaps less than a score of days—if we are not delayed."

"A score—? *Melenkurion!* Then let us pray that we are not delayed. A score of days"—he sat up with a huge show of difficulty—"will leave me eighteen in my grave."

"Then," said Shetra sourly, "we will be the first folk in life to hear a dead man complain for eighteen days."

At this, Lord Hyrim fell back to the grass, laughing gleefully. When his mirth had subsided, he rolled his eyes at Shetra and attempted to stand up smoothly, as if he were not sore and tired. But he could not do it: a spasm of strain broke across his face, and he started to laugh again, as if his own pretensions were the most innocent entertainment imaginable. Still chuckling, he limped away to a nearby *aliantha* and fed himself on the viridian berries of the gnarled bush, savoring their crisp tangy flavor and the rush of nourishment they gave him. Scrupulously, he observed the custom of the Land by scattering the seeds around him, so that new bushes might grow. Then with a flourish he indicated his readiness to ride on. In moments, the company was mounted again and cantering eastward.

As they traveled, they moved into sterner countryside, land which was only hospitable to people who knew how to husband it. And they met with fewer villages. By evening, they were beyond the range of Revelstone's immediate influence; and before the gloaming had thickened into darkness they had passed the last human habitation between that region and Grimmerdhore Forest. Yet they did not stop, though Lord Hyrim suggested the possibility with a genuine yearning in his voice. Korik kept the company riding in spite of Hyrim's groans. So they continued into the night, trusting the Ranyhyn to find their way. Moonrise was near when Lord Shetra said in a low, measured tone, "Now we must rest. We must have strength for the morrow and Grimmerdhore." Korik agreed: he did not miss the point of her glance toward Hyrim.

When his mount finally came to a halt, Lord Hyrim fell off as if he were already unconscious, moaning in his sleep.

—Is his pain severe? Korik asked Sill.

—No, Sill responded. He is unaccustomed. He will recover. But he will have difficulty in Grimmerdhore.

Korik nodded. He said farewell to Brabha for the night and began unwrapping the bundle on his back. The other Bloodguard followed his example; soon all the Ranyhyn had galloped away to feed and rest, and to keep a distant watch over the camp. When the *lillianrill* rods were unpacked, Lord Shetra used one to start a small campfire. With some of the supplies Korik had brought, she cooked a spare meal. While she ate, she watched Lord Hyrim as if she expected the smell of food to rouse him. But he remained face down on the grass, whimpering softly from time to time. Finally, she went to him and nudged him with her foot.

He shoved himself up sharply, clutched his staff as if he had been snatched out of sleep to face an attack. For a dazed instant, his lips trembled, and his eyes rolled widely. But when he gained his feet, he awoke enough to see where he was. The fear faded from his face, leaving it gray and weak. Heavily, he shambled to the fire, sat down, and ate what Shetra had left for him.

However, the food seemed to meet his needs. Soon he recovered enough cheerfulness to groan, "Sister Shetra, you are not a good cook."

When she made no reply, he stretched himself on his back by the fire, sighing plaintively, "Ah, agony!" For a time, he stared at the way the flames danced without consuming along the special wood of the *lillianrill*. Then he turned his face to the sky and said gruffly, "Friends, I had bethought me of fit revenge against those who gave to me this unendurable ride. Since noon, I have been full of dire promises—in place of food, I think. But now I am contrite. The fault is mine alone. I have been a fat thistle-brained fool from the moment the thought of the Loresraat and Lordship entered my head. Ah, what business had I to dream of Lords and Giants, of lore and bold undertakings? Better had I been punished severely and sent to tend sheep for the rest of my days, rather than permitted to follow mad fancies. But Hoole Gren-mate my father was a kind man, slow to chastise. Alas, his memory is poorly honored in my thick self. Were he to see me now, thus reduced to raw quivering flesh and strengthless bones by one single day astride the honor of a Ranyhyn, he would have shed great fat tears as a reproach to my overfed resourcelessness."

"Then let us rejoice in his absence," said Shetra distantly. "I do not like tears."

Hyrim took this up as if it were an argument. "That is well for you. You are brave of blood and limb—in every way enviably courageous. But I—do you hear the talk of the refectories in Revelstone? It is said there that my staff is warped—that when this staff was made for me by High Lord Osondrea, it felt the touch of my hand and bent itself in chagrin. By the Seven! I would be offended if only the talk were untrue. I weep at every opportunity."

He looked over at Shetra to see if he had produced any effect. But she appeared to be listening to some other voice, and she spoke as if to herself. "Am I?"

"Are you?" Hyrim inquired gently. But when she did not reply, he returned to his badinage. "Are you courageous?—is that your question? Sister Shetra, I assure you! I have proof positive. Who but a woman with bravery in her very marrow would consent to share such a mission with me?"

At this, Lord Shetra turned her bird-of-prey eyes toward Hyrim. "You mock me."

"Ah, no!" he protested at once. "Do not think it. You must learn to hear me in my own spirit. I seek only to warm the air between us."

"Better that you do not speak," she snapped. "I do not hear your desires. The wind of your words blows cold."

Instead of replying, Lord Hyrim gazed at her with the look of intent repose which came over the Lords when they melded their thoughts. She shook her head, refused him, climbed to her feet. But the next moment, she answered him barrenly, as if she were too full of dust to resist his question. "I have left behind a husband who believes I cannot love him. He believes he is inferior to me."

She cut off any response Hyrim might have made by stepping quickly to the fire. "We must not keep the wood alight more than necessary. Without a Hirebrand to tend them, the rods would decay slowly—and we will have greater need of them." As if she were in a hurry for darkness, she pulled the wood out of the fire and hummed a *lillianrill* command to extinguish it. Then she wrapped herself in a blanket and lay down on the grass a short distance from Lord Hyrim.

After a while, Korik asked Cerrin:

—Will her concern for Lord Verement weaken her?

—No, Cerrin replied flatly. She will fight for both.

Korik understood this assertion and accepted it. But he did not like it. It carried echoes of other losses and griefs—deprivations and hollow places which the *Haruchai* had not taken into account during their sole night of extravagance. Dourly, he posted his comrades in a wide circle around the camp. Then he stood with his arms folded on his chest, gazed warily out over the grasslands and the star-path of the moon, recited his Vow through the long watch. He could not forget any detail of the last night he had spent with his wife, whose bones were already ancient in the frozen fastness of her grave. The Vow sustained him, but it was not warm.

Still, it gave a rhythm to the sleepless night, and the time passed as a myriad other darknesses had passed—in ceaseless vigilance.

When the moon completed its worn traversal of the sky and fell into the west like a weary exhalation, Korik decided that soon he would awaken the Lords. However, a short time later Lord Hyrim struggled out of his blankets of his own accord. Even in the bare starlight, Korik saw that Hyrim was stiff and aching from the past day's ride. But the Lord suppressed the groans which twisted his face, and began to prepare breakfast.

The aroma he created revealed his talent for the work. Korik smelled strength and refreshment and delicacy in the steam of the broth Hyrim made—a savor Korik had not scented since the curious healing meal which High Lord Prothall had cooked after the battle of Soaring Woodhelven, when all the warriors and ur-Lord Covenant were sickened by the reek of blood and burned flesh. The food's subtle potency awakened Lord Shetra. She came close to the fire looking dull and pale, as if she had not slept well for many nights; but as she ate, Hyrim's work spread its beneficence through her, and she brightened. When she was done, she nodded to him, approving the food as if she were apologizing. He answered with a broad grin and an apothegm which he claimed he had learned from the Giants:

"Food is concentrated beauty—the sustaining power of the Land made savorable and ready for strength. A life without food is like a life without tales—deprived of splendor."

When he mounted to ride again, he managed to limit himself to one tight gasp of pain.

The Ranyhyn ran as if they were hurrying to rejoin the sun; and at daybreak the riders found that they were crossing short irregular hills covered with stiff gray grass. There was no sign of human life. The ground was arable, if not inviting; but no people had ever lived there. It was too close to Grimmerdhore. Though dark Grimmerdhore was among the least potent and most slumberous of the Forests, the surviving remnants of the One Forest which had formerly covered the whole Upper Land—and though since before the time of Lord Kevin there had been no Forestal in Grimmerdhore to sing the ancient trees to wakefulness and movement and vengeance— still people kept away from the severe woods. Many things lived in Grimmerdhore, and few of them were friendly. It was said— though Korik did not know the truth of it—that the *kresh*, the yellow wolves, had been born in Grimmerdhore.

Yet the Bloodguard did not waver in his determination to pass directly through the Forest. It would lengthen the journey by days to go around, either north or south. Still, he exercised added caution. As the company cantered into the new day, Korik sent one of his comrades wide of the company on each side, to increase the range of their wariness.

By midmorning, his caution was rewarded. Korik received a call from one of the ranging Bloodguard, who was out of sight behind a hill. He stopped the company and waited. When the caller came over the hill, he was accompanied by a woman mounted on a Revelstone mustang.

She was a brisk young Warhaft, and her Eoman was riding patrol along the western borders of Grimmerdhore. She asked for news of Revelstone, and when she heard of Lord Mhoram's vision, she requested permission to accompany the mission. But Lord Shetra ordered the Warhaft to remain at her scouting duty, then inquired about the condition of Grimmerdhore.

"Wolves," the Warhaft reported. "Not the yellow *kresh*. Gray and black wolves—nothing else. And few of them. Small packs raid outward, find nothing and return. We have avoided them so that they would not be wary of our scouting."

"No sign of the Grey Slayer?" Shetra pursued. "No scent of evil?"

"The Forest conceals much. But we have seen nothing—heard nothing."

The Warhaft and Shetra exchanged a few more details, and the Lord refused an offer of help for the crossing of Grimmerdhore. Then the mission started eastward again. As they left the Warhaft behind, Hyrim waved back at her and said as if he were lonely, "It may be that we will see no other people until we gain Seareach. I would have been glad for the company of her Eoman."

"They would slow us," Shetra returned without looking at him.

Korik sent two Bloodguard wide again. In this formation, he was confident of the company's readiness except on one point: Lord Hyrim's horsemanship. Since the previous day, Hyrim's scant control over his riding had deteriorated—the combined effect of rougher terrain and extreme soreness. Now at every jolt he clutched like a drowning man at the mane of the Ranyhyn; and between grasps he used his staff like a pole to steady himself.

—If he falls, I will catch him, Sill promised.

But Korik was not reassured.

—At full gallop in Grimmerdhore, he will be at hazard.

Sill stiffened, but could not deny Korik's point. He proposed constructing a harness for the Lord, then discarded the idea. The Bloodguard had no wish to affront the Ranyhyn that had chosen Hyrim; they preferred to carry the additional risk themselves. Korik drew calmness from his Vow and observed to his comrades that the question of Hyrim's riding would soon be answered.

Just before noon, the company swept over a ridge and came within sight of the Forest. The hills had hidden it until it was almost upon them. It loomed around them on the east and south as if they had surprised it in the act of trying to encircle them. But now that they had seen it, Grimmerdhore Forest stood up out of the grasslands like a fortress: its black trunks grew thickly together as if to form a wall; its gnarled limbs bristled like weapons; its shrouding dark green seemed to shelter lurking defenders. And over all the ground before and between the trees were brambles with barbed thorns as strong as iron. They interwove with each other tightly, to resist any penetration, and at their lowest they were taller than Korik.

The Ranyhyn stopped, unbidden. They were sensitive to the denying will of the Forest, though the trees had never held any enmity for them. The riders dismounted. Lord Hyrim stared at Grimmerdhore as if its mood confounded him; and Lord Shetra dropped to the grass, felt it with her hands, staring all the while at the trees—trying to read the Forest through the sensations in the ground. When Hyrim said, "Never have I seen Grimmerdhore so angry," she nodded slowly and replied, "Something has been done to it—something it does not like."

Korik was forced to agree. In the past, the ancient ire of the Forest, the hatred for people who cut and burned, had always been drowsier than this, more deeply submerged in the failing consciousness of the trees. Still, what he could see of Grimmerdhore did not look sentient enough to be active.

—Then the peril lies in what has been done to the Forest, said Tull, completing Korik's thought.

—Unless a Forestal has found his way here, Runnik suggested.

—No, Korik judged. Even a Forestal would require much time

to awaken Grimmerdhore. There is another danger within.

Gradually, the Lords began to resist the mood of the Forest. Hyrim started to prepare a meal—a large one, since he would not have the use of a cooking fire again until the company was past Grimmerdhore—and Shetra walked to the brambles to touch them with her fingertips and listen to the murmurings of the wind. When she returned, she had reached Korik's conclusion: there was not enough wakefulness in the timbre of the wood to account for Grimmerdhore's mood. Something else caused it.

"Not the wolves," said Hyrim, sampling his fare. "They have always been at home in the Forest. And they care for nothing but themselves—unless another power is there to master them. Another mystery I hope I will not be asked to unravel. Riding is challenge enough for me."

Shetra nodded absently, ate the food Hyrim gave her without paying it much attention.

In spite of their concern, the Lords did not delay. They ate promptly, then left the Bloodguard to pack their supplies and went together on foot to the edge of the brambles. There they raised their arms, held their staffs high, and gave the ritual appeal for sufferance to the woods:

"Hail, Grimmerdhore! Forest of the One Forest! Tree-home and root, and preserver of the life-sap of wood! Enemy of our enemies! Grimmerdhore, hail! We are the Lords—foes to your enemies, and learners of the *lillianrill* lore. We must pass through!

"Harken, Grimmerdhore! We hate the axe and flame which hurt you! Your enemies are our enemies. Never have we brought edge of axe or flame of fire to touch you—nor ever shall. Grimmerdhore, harken! Let us pass!"

They shouted the appeal loudly; but their cry was cut off, absorbed into silence, by the wall of the trees. Still they waited with their arms raised for a long moment, as if they expected an answer. But the dark anger of the Forest did not waver. When they returned to the company, Lord Shetra said squarely to Korik, "Grimmerdhore Forest has never harmed the Lords of its own will. What is your choice, Bloodguard? Shall we attempt passage?"

Korik suppressed the tonal lilt of his native tongue to speak the language of the Lords flatly, so that what he said was both a decision and a promise. "We will pass through."

With a silent nod, his comrades turned and called to the grazing Ranyhyn. Soon the company was mounted in formation, facing the Forest. Korik spoke quietly to Brabha, and the Ranyhyn started forward, walking directly at the fortifying brambles. When Brabha was close enough to nose the thorns, a narrow slit of path became visible before him.

In single file, the company walked into the shadowed demesne of Grimmerdhore.

The thorns plucked at them as they passed, but the Ranyhyn negotiated the path with such easy skill that even the long blue robes of the Lords suffered only small rents and snags. Yet the way was long and twisted, and Korik's senses quivered at the vulnerability of the company. If the brambles within the Forest were active, the riders were in grave danger. Korik sent a warning to the Bloodguard who rode nearest the Lords, and they braced themselves to jump to Hyrim's and Shetra's defense.

But none of the bushes moved; the low breeze carried no sound of awareness through the thorns. And then the brambles began to shrink and thin until they fell away like a sigh, leaving the riders in the hands of the Forest itself.

The air around them was thick and deep, almost audibly underlined with slumber; and it shifted faintly through the dim, mottled shadows like an uneasy rest, disturbed by dreams of damage and blood repayment. It smelled so heavily of moss and damp moldering soil and rot and growth that it was hard to breathe; it seemed to resist the lungs of the riders. And the crowded branches blocked out most of the sunlight; between occasional bright swaths of filtered lumination the trees seemed to brood in gloom, contemplating death.

But the quiet of Grimmerdhore was not as impenetrable as it had first appeared. From time to time, strange hoarse birds screeched forlornly. Black squirrels raced overhead. And frequently the Bloodguard heard frightened animals scuttling away from the company through the underbush.

Still, the way became easier. The woods spread out within the perimeter of the brambles. The path broadened as if the trees were guarding it less closely; and animal trails wove back and forth around it. As a result, the company was able to resume its formation, with the Lords and Korik riding on the path and the other Bloodguard moving through the trees around them. Here the Ranyhyn went more quickly, almost at a trot; and the company moved straight in toward the heart of Grimmerdhore.

They rode as if they were passing through a reverie—the shaded and somber musings of the Forest—until after dark. Except for Lord Hyrim's groans whenever he caught his balance, they traveled in silence, warding against something in the woods which might hear them. And even when he groaned, Hyrim gave no sign that he wished to stop or rest. He was caught up in Grimmerdhore's mood. But Korik finally halted the company. The darkest facets of the night seemed to flourish under the trees; and though the Ranyhyn were still able to make their way, the Bloodguard could not see well enough to avoid any ambush which might lie ahead. Yet he felt an odd reluctance when he gave the command to settle the company for the night in a small open glade. He did not like to remain at the mercy of the Forest.

In Grimmerdhore the night was proof against the swarms of fireflies that hovered and darted through the woods. They blinked and danced like beacons for the myriad denizens of the dark—they flew around in a brave enchanting display—but they were effectless, made nothing else visible. When the Lords went to sleep on a flat mossy rock, and the Bloodguard spread out over the glade to stand watch, their security was marred by the fireflies. Those lights stiffened the darkness, walled it up. They drew the attention of the Bloodguard, and so helped to conceal everything else. At last, Korik and his comrades were forced to watch with their eyes closed—to rely on hearing, and smell, and the touch of the ground under their bare feet.

The next morning at the first night-thinning of dawn they resumed their progress. At first, Lord Hyrim was inclined to talk, as if he wished to dispel the enshrouding gloom. For a pretext, he took his horsemanship: he claimed in defiance of his obvious difficulties that it had improved. On that and related subjects he rambled through the dawn as if the rest of the company were listening to him spellbound. But gradually his speech became frayed like his robe, and as the sun rose he faltered into silence. Despite the sunlight, Grimmerdhore's mood was darkening around them; and he could no longer pretend he did not feel it.

As they approached the heart of the Forest, they were drawing closer to the source of Grimmerdhore's inarticulate ire.

By noon, the mood of the Forest dominated everything. Even the familiar creatures of the woods had fallen into a silence of their own: no bird-calls, no chattering or scurrying, no noise of life lifted itself up against the prevailing dumb passion of the trees. Instead, something new came into the air—something musky and mephitic. It irritated Korik's nostrils like the smell of burning blood, made him want to jerk his head aside as if to avoid a blow. Lord Shetra barked softly, "Wolves!" and he knew that she was right. Their spoor hung in the air as if there were a great pack running just ahead of the Ranyhyn.

The smell troubled Brabha. He shook his mane, snorted angrily. But when Korik asked the old Ranyhyn if the wolves were nearby, Brabha indicated with a toss of his head that they were not. Then Korik urged the company ahead until it was moving as fast as Lord Hyrim's inept seat permitted.

Throughout the afternoon, they thrust constantly deeper into Grimmerdhore's distress. After a time, the reek of the wolves stopped growing, and as a result it lost some of its immediacy. But the mood of the trees suffered no such diminution. Rather, the company seemed to be riding into a deepening sea of emotion. Though the lingering consciousness of Grimmerdhore had been reduced to hebetude by time and the ancient slaughter of the One Forest, it was slowly taking heat, mounting toward outrage. In the evening, the breeze stiffened, lifted up the murmurous language of the trees and gave it a tone of execration—as if Grimmerdhore were struggling against slumber, against the inflexibility of wood and the chains of old time, to utter a root-deep hatred. When the riders stopped for the night, the darkness, and the smell of the wolves, and the strangled howl of the trees clung to them. And there were no fireflies.

Korik gauged that they were halfway through the Forest.

"But all in all," Lord Hyrim said in a tone of hollow cheer, "we have been fortunate. Grimmerdhore is dismayed in good sooth. Yet it is in my heart that this dismay is not the pain of the Despiser's presence. It is not his armies which lie before us, but rather some other instance of his malice."

"And by that we are made fortunate?" Shetra asked tightly.

"Of a surety." Hyrim tried to summon his wonted playfulness; but his tone failed. "We are but two Lords and fifteen Bloodguard. Against an army we are doomed. But perhaps we will suffice to flee this smaller ill."

In response, the stiff Lord glowered at him without speaking; but her heart was elsewhere.

She and Hyrim lay down, attempted to sleep. But the mood of the Forest grew, seemed now to gain virulence with each passing moment. Both Lords had given up rest and were on their feet staring into the dark with the Bloodguard when the first glimmer of light appeared north of them.

As they watched it, transfixed, the light became stronger and sharper, spread a hot orange glow through the trees. And with every brighter surge of the glow, the Forest increased its silent cry of horror, outrage.

"Fire!" Lord Shetra gritted fiercely. "By the Seven! A fire has been set. In Grimmerdhore!"

—Call the Ranyhyn, Korik commanded. Strike camp. Take formation. We must shun this peril.

Gasping, "*Melenkurion abatha!*" Lord Hyrim ran toward his mount. An instinctive energy possessed him, and he struggled without help onto the back of the Ranyhyn. Clutching his staff, knotting his other hand in the mane of the horse, he turned toward the fire.

Lord Shetra followed him in an instant. She vaulted onto her Ranyhyn, sprang forward, plunged through the underbrush after Hyrim.

—Halt them! Korik shouted. I will have no more Kevins. The mission must not fail!

He leaped astride Brabha and galloped after the Lords. But he saw through the firelit woods that he would not catch them in time. Shetra rode well; and the Ranyhyn bearing Hyrim displayed fine skill by keeping him in his seat.

Korik shouted after them, commanding them to stop with all the mettle of his personal strength.

Lord Hyrim made no response. He crashed through the woods as if he were oblivious to caution. But Lord Shetra wheeled her Ranyhyn at once. Immediately, Korik reached her side. Sill and Runnik flashed past in pursuit of Hyrim.

"The mission is in our hands," Korik snapped to Shetra. "We must flee this peril."

"And let Grimmerdhore burn?" she almost shrieked. "We would cease to be Lords!"

Slapping the Ranyhyn with her heels, she raced after Hyrim and his pursuers.

Korik followed her with the other Bloodguard. He demanded the best speed Brabha could manage through the trees. Ahead of him, Lord Hyrim crested the hill and dropped out of sight, dashing straight into the glow of the fire. But he was no longer alone. Sill had joined him, and Runnik was only one stride behind.

Moments later, Korik topped the hill with Shetra, Cerrin, and the other Bloodguard galloping beside him. Before them was a wide, almost treeless valley shaped like a bowl. The fire raged in its bottom, and around the conflagration capered a score of black forms.

Ur-viles.

They were burning a huge Gilden.

As the company charged down the hillside, Korik could hear the surrounding Forest's choked effort to scream.

He bent low over Brabha's neck, urged the Ranyhyn faster. Ahead, he picked out the loremaster of the ur-viles. It whirled its tapering iron stave and slapped power in a black liquid at the tree. At each new burst of fire, it slavered gleefully. But when it saw the approaching company, it barked a command at the other ur-viles. The whole group dropped its rapacious dance and sprinted away to the north.

Lord Hyrim ignored them. He went right to the fire, tumbled from the back of his mount. When he hit the ground, he fell, then rolled and bounced up again. Standing almost in the blaze, he held his staff over his head with both hands and began shouting words of power.

The next moment, Shetra rushed past him after the fleeing ur-viles. Like an angry hawk, she swooped across the bottom of the valley and started up the northern slope. Korik and the other Bloodguard hurried behind her as she closed on her prey.

At a sharp call from the loremaster, the ur-viles turned to fight. Instantly, they formed their close fighting wedge, with the loremaster at the point. In this formation, they could focus all their combined power through the loremaster's stave. As Lord Shetra attacked, the wedge lashed out at her. Her Ranyhyn jumped aside to avoid the loremaster's black thrust; and momentum carried her past the wedge.

Before the ur-viles could react, Korik sprang from Brabha's back. He dove over the loremaster, crashed like a battering-ram into the center of the wedge. Pren, Tull, and three more Bloodguard followed him; and their force scattered the ur-viles, breaking the concentration of the wedge.

But these attacks still left the loremaster untouched. While Shetra wheeled back to the battle, the loremaster threw power into the air with its stave and gave a raw barking cry like a signal. As he fought, Korik looked about him for hidden enemies.

Then Lord Shetra charged again. Holding her staff by one end, she chopped savagely at the loremaster. It caught her blow with its stave; but without the wedge behind it, it could not match her. With a hot blue burst of force, her staff split the iron stave. The loremaster fell, crushed by the backlash of the concussion.

During the blast, Korik received an urgent call from Sill. He completed his last blow, then left the remaining ur-viles to the abundant strength of his comrades and spun away to look around the valley.

Down at the bottom of the bowl, Lord Hyrim was laboring strenuously to save the Gilden. In a voice shrill with strain, he summoned the Earthpower to his aid. And he was making progress. In answer to his invocations, water bubbled up from the grass around the tree—already it was deep enough to touch his ankles—and the fire gradually sloughed away from the broad limbs, dropped down as if the tree were shrugging off a cloak of flame.

Still, the process was hard, slow. Hyrim sounded exhausted, and he had not subdued a quarter of the blaze.

But that was not the meaning of Sill's shout. After one brief glance at Hyrim, Korik saw the other peril.

There were wolves standing shoulder to shoulder around the entire rim of the valley.

They were poised and silent, gazing intently down into the bowl. Their eyes reflected the fire, so that the valley seemed ringed by a thousand red pairs of waiting fireflies. But even as Korik scanned them, took a rough estimate of their numbers, the leader of the pack threw back its head and gave a long high yipping howl.

Brabha returned a furious neigh, as if he were answering a challenge.

It affected the wolves like a tantara. At once, they broke into a hungry growl that pulsed in the air like the turmoil of seas. And they started down into the valley at a slow walk.

—A trap, Cerrin said. We have been snared.

Korik called to Lord Shetra, then bounded onto Brabha's back and pelted down the hillside toward the tree. The rest of the company followed him instantly. As he reached the fire, he ordered the Bloodguard into a defensive formation around him. To Lord Hyrim, he shouted, "Come!"

Hyrim did not turn his head. With sweat running down his cheeks and a wide intensity like obsession in his eyes, he kept working for the tree: he invoked water as if he were heaving it out of the ground by main force of will, vitalized the tree's resistance to flame, and now pulled at the fire itself, drawing it slowly, tongue by tongue, away from the branches. But through the slow beats of the *lillianrill* chant he wove for the Gilden, he hissed to Korik, "It must be saved!"

—This task consumes him, Sill said. He urges the mission to go without him.

—He will be slain, Korik snapped.

—Not while I live.

—You will not live long.

—That is the way with him, Sill shrugged silently.

Korik had no time to debate whether or not he should desert one Lord for the sake of the mission. He did not intend to make that choice. Summon or succor. Swiftly, he threw himself from Brabha, stepped in front of Hyrim. He could not allow the son of Hoole to commit suicide. Almost wincing at the way he was forced to violate his Vowed service to any Lord, he shouted into Hyrim's concentration, "Will you sacrifice the Giants for one tree?"

The Lord did not stop. His eyes reflected the fire with a ferocity Korik had never seen in him before. He seemed to be sweating passion as he panted, "The choice is not so simple!"

Korik reached out a hand to wrest Hyrim away from his mad purpose. But at that instant Shetra barked, "Korik, you forget yourself!" and cast her power like a shout to Hyrim's support. The sheer force of their combined exertion made Korik recoil a step.

The wolves were almost upon them; the bristling growl filled the air with the sound of fangs.

Briskly, Korik marshalled his comrades around him on their mounts. The Ranyhyn champed and snorted tensely, but held their positions against the slow advance of the wolves.

Together, the Lords gave a wild cry; and the light of Gilden-fire fell suddenly out of the night.

As darkness rushed back into the valley, Hyrim stumbled against Korik, nearly fell. Korik half threw the Lord to Sill, who boosted Hyrim up onto his mount.

Shouting the company into motion, Korik leaped for Brabha's back.

The next moment, the leading wolves attacked. But with a heave of their mighty muscles, the Ranyhyn started together toward the east. In close formation, they struck the springing wall of wolves— and the wall broke like a wave on a jutting fist of rock. The Ranyhyn surged through the pack, shedding wolves like water, striving to gain speed. At first their head-on charge threw the pack into confusion. But then the wolves chasing them came close enough to leap onto their backs. Pren and four other Bloodguard in the rear of the company were about to be engulfed.

Lord Shetra slowed her mount. Reacting instinctively, the Bloodguard parted behind her, let her drop back beside Pren. As the flood of wolves came toward her, she swung her staff at them. The blow knocked down the first beasts and set flame to them, so that they flared up like tinder. The following pack jumped aside from the sudden fire; the rush was momentarily broken.

In that respite, the Ranyhyn reached full stride. Plunging to keep away from the fangs, they labored up the slope. The pack raged at their heels; but they were Ranyhyn, swifter even than the yellow *kresh*. By the time they topped the valley's rim and thundered back into the closed woods, they were three strides ahead of the pack.

Then through the depths of Grimmerdhore the Ranyhyn raced the wolves. Korik could no longer see as well as the horses, so he abandoned to them all concern for the direction and safety of the run. Unchecked, they dodged deftly through the night as if they were riding the wind. But still the Forest hampered them, interfered with their running, prevented them from their best speed. And the wolves were not hampered. They swept along the ground easily, passed through the woods like a black tide. When they gave tongue to the chase, they did not break stride.

The gap between the pack and the company shrank and grew as Grimmerdhore thickened and thinned. Through one tight copse Pren and his clan-kin had to fend off wolves on both sides. But fortunately the terrain beyond was relatively open, and the Ranyhyn were able to restore the gap.

During it all—the dodging, the surging pace, the unevenness of the ground—Lord Hyrim clung to his seat. He was kept erect by the proud skill of his mount. And the other Ranyhyn aided him by choosing their ways so that his horse had the straightest path through the trees. When he observed this, Korik applauded silently, and his chest grew tight with admiration, in spite of the other demands on his attention.

Still the race went on. The Ranyhyn pounded through the Forest with growing abandon, discounting the safety of the company more and more for the sake of speed. As a result, the riders had to hold their seats when they were lashed by branches, wrenched from side to side while the horses evaded looming trunks. But the savage pursuit of the wolves did not abate. Clearly, the will which drove them was strong and compelling; and Korik guessed that a powerful band of ur-viles remained in Grimmerdhore—a force which used the wolves just as it had used the Gilden and the other ur-viles. But such thoughts were of no value now; the wolves were the immediate danger. Hundreds of ravenous throats howled; hundreds of jaws gaped and bit furiously, as if they were too eager to wait for the raw flesh of the company. The Ranyhyn gave their best speed— and the pack did not fall behind.

Korik was revolving desperate solutions in his mind when the company broke out into a broad open glade. Under the stars, he saw the ravine which cut through the center of the glade across the company's path. It was an old dry watercourse, deeply eroded before its source turned elsewhere. And it was far too wide for the wolves: they could not leap it. If the Ranyhyn could manage the jump, the company would gain precious time.

But when the wolves burst out of the woods, they broke into hard howls of triumph. In a few strides, Korik saw his danger: the ravine appeared to be too wide even for the Ranyhyn. For an instant, he hesitated. In his long years, he had heard the shrieking of horses far too often. He knew how the Ranyhyn would scream if they shattered their bones against the opposite wall of the ravine. But their night-sight was better than his; he could not make this decision for them. He silenced his fears, shouted to his comrades:

—Let the Ranyhyn choose! They will not err! But ward Lord Hyrim!

Then Runnik reached the ravine. His mount gathered itself, seemed for an instant to shrink, to coil in on its strength—and sprang. Already it was too late for the rest of the riders to stop; but Korik kept his eyes on Runnik, watched the leading Ranyhyn so that he would have an instant's warning of his fate—an instant in which to try to save himself for the sake of the mission. For the first time since the night when he had assumed his Vow, he left the Lords to their own fortunes. He expected Hyrim to fall. As old Brabha started into his own jump, the Lord wailed as if he were plunging from a precipice.

Then the Ranyhyn carrying Runnik touched down safely on the far side of the ravine. Beside him, Tull and another Bloodguard also landed with ground to spare, followed by Cerrin, Shetra, Korik, Hyrim, and Sill in a line together. Lord Hyrim flopped forward and back as if his mount were bucking; his wail stopped as if it had been broken off. But he did not lose his seat. Amid the wild yowling frustration of the wolves, the rest of the Bloodguard jumped the ravine. The Ranyhyn sprinted across the glade with clear ground at their heels.

Behind them, the wolves rushed on, caught in the grip of a demented passion. They piled into the dry watercourse, careless of what happened to them, and scrambled furiously up the far side. But Korik was confident of escape now. The company had almost reached the edge of the glade when the first wolf clawed its way out of the ravine. Korik leaned forward to say a word of praise in Brabha's back-bent ears.

Out of the corner of his eye, he saw Lord Hyrim tumble like a lifeless sack to the ground.

Korik shouted to the company. Immediately, the leaders peeled around to return to Hyrim as fast as possible. But Pren, the rearmost Bloodguard, saw Hyrim's fall in time to leap down from his own mount. In a few steps, he reached the motionless Lord. While Korik and the others were turning, Pren reported that Hyrim was un-conscious—stunned either by his fall or by the jolt of the jump over the ravine.

Wheeling Brabha, Korik gauged the distances. The wolves surged out of the ravine in great numbers now; they howled rabidly toward the men on the ground. The company would barely have time to snatch up Hyrim and take defensive positions around him before the pack struck.

But as Korik pulled his comrades into formation, Lord Shetra ordered him back. She had a plan of her own. Driving her mount straight for Hyrim, she called to Pren, "His staff! Hold it upright!"

Pren obeyed swiftly. He caught up Hyrim's staff from the grass, gripped it with one metal-shod end planted on the ground between him and the charging wolves.

As he did this, Shetra swung her Ranyhyn until she was running parallel to the line of the charge. When she flashed behind Pren, she cried, "*Melenkurion abatha!*" and dealt Hyrim's staff a ham-mering blow with her own.

A silent concussion shook the air: the ground seemed to heave momentarily under the hooves of the Ranyhyn. From Hyrim's staff a plane of power spread out on both sides, came like a wall between the wolves and the company across the whole eastern face of the glade. Seen through this barrier, the scrambling wolves appeared distorted, mad, wronged.

Then they smashed into the wall. In that instant, the area of impact flared like a sheet of blue lightning; and the wolves were thrown back. They charged it again as more of them reached it, hurled themselves against the rippling plane—howled and raved, assaulted the air. But wherever they hit the wall, it flared blue and cast them back. Soon they were crashing into it in such numbers that the whole plane across the length of the glade caught fire. Where the greatest weight of the pack pressed and fought against it, it scaled upward into dazzling brightness. Carefully, Shetra withdrew Hyrim's staff from the plane. It wavered as if it were about to break; but she sang to it softly, and it steadied, stood up firmly under the strain.

It was too much for the wolves. In a wild excess of passion and frustration, they began to attack each other—venting their driven rage on the nearest flesh until the whole place was consumed in a boiling melee.

Lord Shetra turned away as if the sight hurt her. She appeared suddenly weary; the exertion of commanding two staffs had drained her. Dully, she said to Korik, "We must go. If it is assailed again, my Word will not endure. And if there are ur-viles nearby, they will know how to counter it. I am too worn to speak another." Then she knelt to examine Hyrim.

In a moment, she ascertained that he had no broken bones, no internal bleeding, no concussion. She left him to Korik and Sill. Working rapidly, they placed Hyrim on the back of his Ranyhyn and lashed him there with *clingor* thongs. When he was secured, the Bloodguard sprang to their own mounts, and the company hurried away into the covered darkness of Grimmerdhore.

The Ranyhyn moved at a near gallop. Soon the intervening Forest quenched the tumult of the wolves, and the company was surrounded by a welcome silence. But still they ran; they did not stop or slow, even when Lord Hyrim returned groaning to consciousness. They left him alone until he was alert enough to free himself from the *clingor*. Then Lord Shetra explained to him shortly, in a tired voice, what had happened.

He took the news dumbly, nodded his comprehension of her words. Then he lay down on the Ranyhyn's neck as if he were hiding his head and clung there through the rest of the night.

At dawn, Korik called a halt beside a stream to water the horses and allow the Lords to eat a few treasure-berries. But after that they moved on again at a fast canter. Korik did not want to spend another night in Grimmerdhore; and he could feel Brabha's eagerness to break out of the dark woods.

The fatigue, the lack of rest, the unrelieved haste of their journey showed in both Lords: Hyrim's eyes, formerly so gay, had a gray angle of pain; and Shetra's lean face was lined and sharpened, as if some erosion had cut away the last softness of her features. But they endured. As time passed, they found deeper springs of strength to sustain them.

Korik should have been reassured. But he was not. The Lords had proven themselves equal to wolves and Grimmerdhore. But he had reason to know that what lay ahead would be worse.

MYTHOLOGICAL
BEAST

NORMAN WAS A PERFECTLY SAFE, PERFECTLY SANE MAN. He lived with his wife and son, who were both perfectly safe, perfectly sane, in a world that was perfectly sane, perfectly safe. It had been that way all his life. So when he woke up that morning, he felt as perfect as always. He had no inkling at all of the things that had already started to happen to him.

As usual, he woke up when he heard the signal from the biomitter cybernetically attached to his wrist; and as usual, the first thing he did was to press the stud which activated the biomitter's LED read-out. The display gleamed greenly for a moment on the small screen. As usual, it said, *You are OK*. There was nothing to be afraid of.

As usual, he had absolutely no idea what he would have done if it had said anything else.

His wife, Sally, was already up. Her signal came before his so that she would have time to use the bathroom and get breakfast started. That way there would be no unpleasant hurrying. He rolled out of bed promptly, and went to take his turn in the bathroom, so that he would not be late for work and his son, Enwell, would not be late for school.

Everything in the bathroom was the same as usual. Even though Sally had just used it, the vacuum-sink was spotless. And the toilet was as clean as new. He could not even detect his wife's warmth on the seat. Everything was perfectly safe, perfectly sane. His reflection in the mirror was the only thing that had changed.

The tight lump in the center of his forehead made no sense to him. He had never seen it before. Automatically, he checked his biomitter; but again it said, *You are OK*. That seemed true enough. He did not feel ill—and he was almost the only person he knew who knew what "ill" meant. The lump did not hurt in any way, but still he felt vaguely uneasy. He trusted the biomitter. It should have been able to tell him what was happening.

Carefully, he explored the lump. It was as hard as bone. In fact, it seemed to be part of his skull. It looked familiar; and he scanned back in his memory through some of the books he had read until he found what he wanted. His lump looked like the base of a horn, or perhaps the nub of a new antler. He had seen such things in books.

That made even less sense. His face wore an unusual frown as he finished in the bathroom. He returned to the bedroom to get dressed, and then went to the kitchen for breakfast.

Sally was just putting his food on the table—the same juice, cereal, and soyham that she always served him—a perfectly safe meal that would give him energy for the morning without letting him gain weight or become ill. He sat down to eat it as he always did. But when Sally sat down opposite him, he looked at her and said, "What's this thing on my forehead?"

His wife had a round bland face, and its lines had slowly become blurred over the years. She looked at his lump vaguely, but there was no recognition in her eyes. "Are you OK?" she said.

He touched the stud of his biomitter and showed her that he was OK.

Automatically, she checked her own biomitter and got the same answer. Then she looked at him again. This time, she, too, frowned. "It shouldn't be there," she said.

Enwell came into the kitchen, and Sally went to get his breakfast. Enwell was a growing boy. He watched the food come as if he were hungry, and then he began to eat quickly. He was eating too quickly, but Norman did not need to say anything. Enwell's biomitter gave a low hum and displayed in kind yellow letters, *Eat more slowly.* Enwell obeyed with a shrug.

Norman smiled at his son's obedience, then frowned again. He trusted his biomitter. It should be able to explain the lump on his forehead. Using the proper code, he tapped on the face of the display, *I need a doctor.* A doctor would know what was happening to him.

His biomitter replied, *You are OK.*

This did not surprise him. It was standard procedure—the bio-mitter was only doing its job by reassuring him. He tapped again,

I need a doctor. This time, the green letters said promptly, *Excused from work. Go to Medical Building room 218.*

Enwell's biomitter signaled that it was time for him to go to school. "Got to go," he mumbled as he left the table. If he saw the lump on his father's forehead, he did not think enough about it to say anything. Soon he had left the house. As usual, he was on time.

Norman rubbed his lump. The hard boney nub made him feel uneasy again. He resisted an urge to recheck his biomitter. When he had finished his breakfast, he said goodbye to Sally as he always did when he was going to work. Then he went out to the garage and got into his mobile.

After he had strapped himself in, he punched the address of the Medical Building into the console. He knew where the Medical Building was, not because he had ever been there before (in fact, no one he knew had ever been there), but because it was within sight of the National Library, where he worked. Once the address was locked in, his mobile left the garage smoothly on its balloon tires (a perfectly safe design), and slid easily into the perfectly sane flow of the traffic.

All the houses on this street were identical for a long way in either direction; and as usual Norman paid no attention to them. He did not need to watch the traffic, since his mobile took care of things like that. His seat was perfectly comfortable. He just relaxed in his safety straps and tried not to feel concerned about his lump until his mobile deposited him on the curb outside the Medical Building.

This building was much taller and longer than the National Library; but apart from that, the two were very much alike. Both were empty except for the people who worked there; and the people worked there because they needed jobs, not because there was any work that needed to be done. And both were similarly laid out inside. Norman had no trouble finding his way.

Room 218 was in the Iatrogenics Wing. In the outer office was a desk with a computer terminal very much like the one Norman used at the Library; and at the desk sat a young woman with yellow hair and confused eyes. When Norman entered her office, she stared at him as if he were sick. Her stare made him touch his lump and frown. But she was not staring at his forehead. After a moment, she said, "It's been so long—I've forgotten what to do."

"Maybe I should tell you my name," he said.

"That sounds right," she said. She sounded relieved. "Yes, I think that's right. Tell me your name."

He told her. She looked around the terminal, then pushed a button to engage some kind of program.

"Now what?" he said.

"I don't know," she said. She did not seem to like being so confused.

Norman did not know, either. But almost at once the door to the inner office opened. The woman shrugged, so Norman just walked through the doorway.

The inner office had been designed to be cozy; but something had gone wrong with its atmospherics, and now it was deep in dust. When Norman sat down in the only chair, he raised the dust, which made him cough.

"I'm Doctor Brett," a voice said. "You seem to have a cough."

The voice came from a console that faced the chair. Apparently, Doctor Brett was a computer who looked just like the Director of the National Library. Norman relaxed automatically. He naturally trusted a computer like that. "No," he said. "It's the dust."

"Ah, the dust," the computer said. "I'll make a note to have it removed." His voice sounded wise and old and very rusty. After a moment, he went on, "There must be something wrong with my scanners. You look healthy to me."

Norman said, "My biomitter says I'm OK."

"Well, then my scanners must be right. You're in perfect health. Why did you come?"

"I have a lump on my forehead."

"A lump?" Doctor Brett hummed. "It looks healthy to me. Are you sure it isn't natural?"

"Yes." For an instant, Norman felt unnaturally irritated. He touched the lump with his fingers. It was as hard as bone—no, harder, as hard as steel, magnacite. It was as hard as tung-diamonds. He began to wonder why he had bothered to come here.

"Of course, of course," the doctor said. "I've checked your records. You weren't born with it. What do you think it is?"

The question surprised Norman. "How should I know? I thought you were going to tell me."

"Of course," said the computer. "You can trust me. I'll tell you everything that's good for you. That's what I'm here for. You know that. The Director of the National Library speaks very highly of you. It's in your records."

The machine's voice made Norman's irritation evaporate. He trusted his biomitter. He trusted Doctor Brett. He settled himself in the chair to hear what his lump was. But even that amount of movement raised the dust. He sneezed twice.

Doctor Brett said, "You seem to have a cold."

"No," Norman said. "It's the dust."

"Ah, the dust," Doctor Brett said. "Thank you for coming."

"'Thank you for—'?" Norman was surprised. All at once, he felt very uneasy. He felt that he had to be careful. "Aren't you going to tell me what it is?"

"There's nothing to worry about," the doctor said. "You're perfectly healthy. It will go away in a couple of days. Thank you for coming."

The door was open. Norman stared at the computer. The Director did not act like this. He was confused, but he did not ask any more questions. Instead, he was careful. He said, "Thank you, Doctor," and walked out of the office. The door closed behind him.

The woman was still sitting at the outer desk. When she saw Norman, she beckoned to him. "Maybe you can help me," she said.

"Yes?" he said.

"I remember what I'm supposed to do now," she said. "After you see the Doctor, I'm supposed to get his instructions"—she tapped the console—"and make sure you understand them. But nobody's ever come here before. And when I got this job, I didn't tell them"—she looked away from Norman—"that I don't know how to read."

Norman knew what she meant. Of course, she could read her biomitter—everybody could do that. But except for that, reading was not taught anymore. Enwell certainly was not learning how to read in school. Reading was not needed anymore. Except for the people at the National Library, Norman was the only person he knew who could actually read. That was why no one ever came to use the Library.

But now he was being careful. He smiled to reassure the woman and walked around the desk to look at her console. She tapped the display to activate the readout.

At once, vivid red letters sprang across the screen. They said:

SECRET CONFIDENTIAL PRIVATE PERSONAL SECRET UNDER NO CIRCUMSTANCES REPEAT UNDER NO CIR-CUMSTANCES SHOW THIS DIAGNOSIS TO PATIENT OR REVEAL ITS CONTENTS....................................

Then there was a series of numbers that Norman did not understand. Then the letters said:

ABSOLUTE PRIORITY TRANSMIT AT ONCE TO GENERAL HOSPITAL EMERGENCY DIVISION REPEAT EMERGENCY DIVISION ABSOLUTE PRIORITY...........................

"Transmit," the woman said. "That means I'm supposed to send this to the Hospital." Her hand moved toward the buttons that would send the message.

Norman caught her wrist. "No," he said. "That isn't what it means. It means something else."

The woman said, "Oh."

The bright red letters said:

DIAGNOSIS..
PATIENT SUFFERING FROM MASSIVE GENETIC BREAK-DOWN OF INDETERMINATE ORIGIN COMPLETE RE-PEAT COMPLETE STRUCTURAL TRANSITION IN PROGRESS TRANSMUTATION IRREVERSIBLE.............
PROGNOSIS...
PATIENT WILL BECOME DANGEROUS HIMSELF AND WILL CAUSE FEAR IN OTHERS REPEAT WILL CAUSE FEAR TREATMENT ....
STUDY RECOMMENDED BUT DESTRUCTION IMPERA-TIVE REPEAT IMPERATIVE REPEAT IMPERATIVE EFFECT SOONEST...

"What did it say?" the woman said.

For a moment, Norman did not answer. His lump was as hard as a magnacite nail driven into his skull. Then he said, "It said I should get some rest. It said I've been working too hard. It said I should go to the Hospital if I don't feel better tomorrow." Before the woman could stop him, he pressed the buttons that erased the terminal's memory. The terminal was just like the one he used in the National Library, and he knew what to do. After erasing, he programmed the terminal to cancel everything that had happened today. Then he fed in a cancel program to wipe out everything in the terminal. He did not know what good that would do, but he did it anyway.

He expected the woman to try to stop him, but she did not. She had no idea what he was doing.

He was sweating, and his pulse was too fast. He was so uneasy that his stomach hurt. That had never happened to him before. He left the office without saying anything to the woman. His knees were trembling. As he walked down the corridor of the Iatrogenics Wing, his biomitter was saying in blue reassuring letters, *You will be OK. You will be OK.*

Apparently, his erasures were successful. In the next few days, nothing happened to him as a result of Doctor Brett's report. By the time he had returned home from the Medical Building, his read-out had regained its placid green, *You are OK.*

He did this deliberately. He did not feel OK. He felt uneasy, but he did not want his biomitter to send him to the General Hospital. So while his mobile drove him home he made an effort to seem OK. The touch of his lump gave him a strange reassurance, and after a while his pulse, blood pressure, respiration, and reflexes had become as steady as usual.

And at home everything seemed perfectly sane, perfectly safe. He woke up every morning at the signal of his biomitter, went to work at the signal of his biomitter, ate lunch at the signal of his biomitter. This was reassuring. It reassured him that his biomitter took such good care of him. Without it, he might have worked all day without lunch, reading, sorting the mountain of discarded books in the storeroom, feeding them into the Reference Computer. At times like that, his uneasiness went away. He went home again at the end of the day at the signal of his biomitter.

But at home his uneasiness returned. Something was happening inside him. Every morning, he saw in the mirror that his lump was growing. It was clearly a horn now—a pointed shaft as white as bone. It was full of strength. When it was more than four inches long, he tested it on the mirror. The mirror was made of glasteel so that it could never shatter and hurt anybody; but he scratched it easily with the tip of his horn. Scratching it took no effort at all.

And that was not the only change. The soles of his feet were growing harder, and his feet seemed to be getting shorter. They were starting to look like hooves.

Tufts of pure white hair as clean as the sky were sprouting from the backs of his calves and the back of his neck. Something that might have been a tail grew out of the small of his back.

But these things were not what made him uneasy. He was not uneasy because he was thinking that someone from the Hospital might come to destroy him. He was not thinking that at all. He was being careful; he did not let himself think anything that might make his biomitter call for help. No, he was uneasy because he could not understand what Sally and Enwell were doing about what was happening to him.

They were not doing anything. They were ignoring the changes in him as if he looked just the same as always.

To them everything was perfectly sane, perfectly safe.

First this made him uneasy. Then it made him angry. Something important was happening to him, and they did not even see it. Finally at breakfast one morning he became too irritated to be careful. Enwell's biomitter signaled that it was time for him to go to school. He mumbled, "Got to go," and left the table. Soon he had left the house. Norman watched his son go. Then he said to Sally, "Who taught him to do that?"

She did not look up from her soyham. "Do what?" she said.

"Go to school," he said. "Obey his biomitter. We never taught him to do that."

Sally's mouth was full. She waited until she swallowed. Then she said, "Everybody does it."

The way she said it made his muscles tighten. A line of sweat ran down his back. For an instant, he wanted to hit the table with his hand—hit it with the hard flat place on the palm of his hand. He felt sure he could break the table.

Then his biomitter signaled to him. Automatically, he left the table. He knew what to do; he always knew what to do when his biomitter signaled. He went out to the garage and got into his mobile. He strapped himself into the seat. He did not notice what he was doing until he saw that his hands had punched in the address of the General Hospital.

At once, he canceled the address, unstrapped himself and got out of the mobile. His heart was beating too fast. His biomitter was saying without being asked, *Go to the Hospital. You will be OK.* The letters were yellow.

His hands trembled, but he tapped onto the display, *I am OK.* Then he went back into the house.

Sally was cleaning the kitchen, as she always did after breakfast. She did not look at him.

"Sally," he said. "I want to talk to you. Something's happening to me."

"It's time to clean the kitchen," she said. "I heard the signal."

"Clean the kitchen later," he said. "I want to talk to you. Something's happening to me."

"I heard the signal," she said. "It's time to clean the kitchen now."

"Look at me," he said.

She did not look at him. Her hands were busy wiping scraps of soyham into the vacuum-sink, where they were sucked away.

"Look at me," he said. He took hold of her shoulders with his hands and made her face him. It was easy. He was strong. "Look at my forehead."

She did not look at him. Her face screwed up into tight knots and ridges. It turned red. Then she began to cry. She wailed and wailed, and her legs did not hold her up. When he let her go, she sank to the floor and folded up into a ball and wailed. Her biomitter said to her in blue, *You will be OK. You will be OK.* But she did not see it. She cried as if she were terrified.

Norman felt sick in his stomach, but his carefulness had come back. He left his wife and went back to the garage. He got into his mobile and punched in an address only ten houses away down the road. His mobile left the garage smoothly and eased itself into the perfectly sane flow of the traffic. When it parked at the address he had given it, he did not get out. He sat in his seat and watched his house.

Before long, an ambulance rolled up to it. Men in white coats went in. They came out carrying Sally in a stretcher. They loaded her carefully into the ambulance and drove away.

Because he did not know what else to do, he punched the address of the National Library into the console of his mobile and went to work. The careful part of him knew that he did not have much time. He knew (everyone knew) that his biomitter was his friend. But now he also knew that it would not be long before his biomitter betrayed him. The rebellion in his genes was becoming too strong. It could not stay secret much longer. And he still did not know what was happening to him. He wanted to use the time to find out, if he could. The Library was the best place for him to go.

But when he reached his desk with its computer console like the one in Doctor Brett's outer office, he did not know what to do. He had never done any research before. He did not know anyone who had ever done any research. His job was to sort books, to feed them into the Reference Computer. He did not even know what he was looking for.

Then he had an idea: he keyed his terminal into the Reference Computer and programmed it for autoscan. Then he tapped in his question, using the "personal information" code which was supposed to keep his question and answer from tieing up the general circuits of the Library and bothering the Director. He asked:

I HAVE HOOVES, A TAIL, WHITE HAIR, AND A HORN IN THE MIDDLE OF MY FOREHEAD. WHAT AM I?

After a short pause, the display ran numbers which told Norman his answer was coming from the 1976 *Encyclopedia Americana.* That Encyclopedia was a century out of date, but it was the most recent one in the Library. Apparently, people had not bothered to make Encyclopedias for a long time.

Then the display said:

ANSWER......UNICORN....................................
DATA FOLLOWS ....

His uneasiness suddenly became sharper. There was a sour taste in his mouth as he scanned the readout.

THE UNICORN IS A MYTHOLOGICAL BEAST USUALLY
DEPICTED AS A LARGE HORSE WITH A SINGLE HORN
ON ITS FOREHEAD ....

Sweat ran into his eyes. He missed a few lines while he blinked
to clear his sight.

IT REPRESENTED CHASTITY AND PURITY THOUGH IT
WOULD FIGHT SAVAGELY WHEN CORNERED IT COULD
BE TAMED BY A VIRGIN'S TOUCH IN SOME INTERPRE-
TATIONS THE UNICORN IS ASSOCIATED WITH THE
VIRGIN MARY IN OTHERS IT REPRESENTS CHRIST THE
REDEEMER ....

Then to his surprise the display showed him a picture of a unicorn. It was prancing high on its strong clean legs, its coat was as
pure as the stars, and its eyes shone. Its mane flew like the wind.
Its long white horn was as strong as the sun. At the sight, all his
uneasiness turned into joy. The unicorn was beautiful. It was beautiful. He was going to be beautiful. For a long time, he made the
display hold that picture, and he stared at it and stared at it.

But after his joy receded a little, and the display went blank, he
began to think. He felt that he was thinking for the first time in
his life. His thoughts were clear and necessary and quick.

He understood that he was in danger. He was in danger from
his biomitter. It was a hazard to him. It was only a small thing, a
metasensor that monitored his body for signs of illness; but it was
linked to the huge computers of the General Hospital, and when
his metabolism passed beyond the parameters of safety, sanity, his
biomitter would summon the men in white coats. For the first time
in his life, he felt curious about it. He felt that he needed to know
more about it.

Without hesitation, he tapped his question into the Reference
Computer, using his personal information code. He asked:
ORIGIN AND FUNCTION OF BIOMITTER?
The display ran numbers promptly, and began a readout.

WORLDWIDE VIOLENCE CRIME WAR INSANITY OF 20TH
CENTURY SHOWED HUMANS CAPABLE OF SELF-EXTER-
MINATION OPERATIVE CAUSE WAS FEAR REPEAT FEAR

RESEARCH DEMONSTRATED HUMANS WITHOUT FEAR
NONVIOLENT SANE..
POLICE EDUCATION PEACE TREATIES INADEQUATE TO
CONTROL FEAR OF INDIVIDUAL HUMANS BUT SANE IN-
DIVIDUAL HUMANS NOT PRONE TO VIOLENCE WAR
TREATIES POLICE WEAPONS UNNECESSARY IF INDIVID-
UAL IS NOT AFRAID..
TREATMENT ....
BIOMITTER MEDICOMPUTER NETWORK INITIATED FOR
ALL INDIVIDUALS MONITOR PHYSIOLOGICAL SIGNS OF
EMOTION STRESS ILLNESS CONDITIONED RESPONSES
INBRED TO CONTROL BEHAVIOR FEAR***CROSS
REFERENCE PAVLOV BEHAVIOR MODIFICATION SUB-
CONSCIOUS HYPNOTISM....................................
SUCCESS OF BIOMITTER PROGRAM DEMONSTRATES
FEAR DOES NOT EXIST WHERE CONTROL ORDER

Abruptly, the green letters flashed off the display, and the terminal began to readout a line of red.

DATA CANCEL REPEAT CANCEL ....
MATERIAL CLASSIFICATION RESTRICTED NOT AVAIL-
ABLE WITHOUT APPROVAL DIRECTOR NATIONAL LI-
BRARY FILE APPROVAL CODE BEFORE REACTIVATING
REFERENCE PROGRAM ....

Norman frowned around his horn. He was not sure what had
happened. Perhaps he had accidentally stumbled upon information
that was always restricted and had automatically triggered the Reference Computer's cancellation program. Or perhaps the Director
had just now succeeded in breaking his personal information code
and had found out what he was doing. If the interruption had been
automatic, he was still safe. But if the Director had been monitoring
him personally, he did not have much time. He needed to know.

He left his desk and went to the Director's office. The Director
looked very much like Doctor Brett. Norman believed that he could
break the Director with one kick of his hard foot. He knew what
to do. He said, "Director."

"Yes, Norman?" the Director said. His voice was warm and
wise, like Doctor Brett's. Norman did not trust him. "Are you OK?
Do you want to go home?"

"I am OK," Norman said. "I want to take out some books."

"'Take out some books'?" the Director said. "What do you mean?"

"I want to withdraw some books. I want to take them home with me."

"Very well," the Director said. "Take them with you. Take the rest of the day off. You need some rest."

"Thank you," Norman said. He was being careful. Now he had what he wanted. He knew that the Director had been watching him, knew that the Director had deliberately broken his personal information code. He knew that the Director had transmitted his information to the General Hospital and had been told that he, Norman, was dangerous. No one was allowed to take books out of the National Library. It was forbidden to withdraw books. Always. Even the Director could not override that rule, unless he had been given emergency programming.

Norman was no longer safe, but he did not hurry. He did not want the General Hospital to think that he was afraid. The men in white coats would chase him more quickly if they thought he was afraid of them. He walked calmly, as if he were perfectly safe, perfectly sane, to the stacks where the books were kept after they had been sorted and fed into the Reference Computer.

He did not try to be thorough or complete. His time was short. He took only the books he could carry, only the books he was sure he wanted. He took *The Mask, The Unicorn, and the Messiah;* the *Index to Fairy Tales, Myths, and Legends; Barbarous Knowledge;* the *Larousse Encyclopedia of Mythology; The Masks of God;* and *The Book of Imaginary Beings.* He would need these books when his transformation was complete. They would tell him what to do.

He did not try to find any others. He left the National Library, hugging the books to his broad chest like treasure.

The careful part of him expected to have trouble with his mobile; but he did not. It took him home exactly as it always did.

When he entered his house, he found that Sally had not been brought back. Enwell had not come home. He did not think that he would ever see them again. He was alone.

He took off his clothes because he knew that unicorns did not wear clothes. Then he sat down in the living room and started to read his books.

They did not make sense to him. He knew most of the words, but he could not seem to understand what they were saying. At first he was disappointed in himself. He was afraid that he might not make a very good unicorn. But then he realized the truth. The books did not make sense to him because he was not ready for them. His transformation was not complete yet. When it was, he would be able to understand the books. He bobbed his horn joyfully. Then, because he was careful, he spent the rest of the day memorizing as much as he could of the first book, *The Book of Imaginary Beings*. He wanted to protect himself in case his books were lost or damaged.

He was still memorizing after dark, and he was not tired. His horn filled him with strength. But then he began to hear a humming noise in the air. It was soft and soothing, and he could not tell how long it had been going on. It was coming from his biomitter. It found a place deep inside him that obeyed it. He lay down on the couch and went to sleep.

But it was not the kind of sleep he was used to. It was not calm and safe. Something in him resisted it, resisted the reassuring hum. His dreams were wild. His emotions were strong, and one of them was uneasiness. His uneasiness was so strong that it must have been fear. It made him open his eyes.

All the lights were on in the living room, and there were four men in white coats around him. Each of them carried a hypogun. All the hypoguns were pointed at him.

"Don't be afraid," one of the men said. "We won't hurt you. You're going to be all right. Everything is going to be OK."

Norman did not believe him. He saw that the men were gripping their hypoguns tightly. He saw that the men were afraid. They were afraid of him.

He flipped off the couch and jumped. His legs were immensely strong. His jump carried him over the heads of the men. As he passed, he kicked one of the men. Blood appeared on the man's forehead and spattered his coat, and he fell down and did not move.

The nearest man fired his hypogun. But Norman blocked the penetrating spray with the hard flat heel of his palm. His fingers curled into a hoof, and he hit the man in the chest. The man fell down.

The other two men were trying to run away. They were afraid of him. As they were running toward the door, Norman jumped after them and poked the nearest one with his horn. The man seemed to fly away from the horn. He crashed into the other man, and they both crashed against the door and fell down and did not move again. One of them had blood all over his back.

Norman's biomitter was blaring red: *You are ill. You are ill.*

The man Norman had punched was still alive, gasping for breath. His face was white with death, but he was able to tap a message into his biomitter. Norman could read his fingers: he was saying, *Seal the house. Keep him trapped. Bring nerve gas.*

Norman went to the man. "Why?" he said. "Why are you trying to kill me?"

The man looked at Norman. He was too close to dying to be afraid anymore. "You're dangerous," he said. He was panting, and blood came out of his mouth. "You're deadly."

"Why?" Norman said. "What's happening to me?"

"Transmutation," the man said. "Atavism. Psychic throwback. You're becoming something. Something that never existed."

"'Never existed'?" Norman said.

"You must've been buried," the man said. "In the subconscious. All this time. You never existed. People made you up. A long time ago. They believed in you. Because they needed to. Because they were afraid."

More blood came out of his mouth. "How could it happen?" he said. His voice was very weak. "We put fear to sleep. There is no more fear. No more violence. How could it happen?" Then he stopped breathing. But his eyes stayed open, staring at the things he did not understand.

Norman felt a deep sorrow. He did not like killing. A unicorn was not a killing beast. But he had had no choice: he had been cornered.

His biomitter was shouting, *You are ill.*

He did not intend to be cornered again. He raised his wrist and touched his biomitter with the tip of his horn. Pieces of metal were torn away, and bright blood ran down his arm.

After that, he did not delay. He took a slipcover from the couch and used it as a sack to carry his books. Then he went to the door and tried to leave his house.

The door did not open. It was locked with heavy steel bolts that he had never seen before. They must have been built into the house. Apparently, the men in white coats, or the medicomputers, were prepared for everything.

They were not prepared for a unicorn. He attacked the door with his horn. His horn was as hard as steel, as hard as magnacite. It was as hard as tung-diamonds. The door burst open, and he went out into the night.

Then he saw more ambulances coming down the road. Ambulances were converging on his house from both directions. He did not know where to run. So he galloped across the street and burst in the door of the house opposite his. The house belonged to his friend, Barto. He went to his friend for help.

But when Barto and his wife and his two daughters saw Norman, their faces filled with fear. The daughters began to wail like sirens. Barto and his wife fell to the floor and folded up into balls.

Norman broke down the back door and ran out into the service lane between the rows of houses.

He traveled the lane for miles. After the sorrow at his friend's fear came a great joy at his strength and swiftness. He was stronger than the men in white coats, faster than ambulances. And he had nothing else to be wary of. The medicomputers could not chase him themselves. With his biomitter gone, they could not even tell where he was. And they had no weapons with which to fight him except men in white coats and ambulances. He was free and strong and exhilarated for the first time in his life.

When daylight came, he climbed up onto the roofs of the houses. He felt safe there, and when he was ready to rest he slept there alone, facing the sky.

He spent days like that—traveling the city, reading his books and committing them to memory—waiting for his transformation to be complete. When he needed food, he raided grocery stores to get it, though the terror of the people he met filled him with sorrow. Gradually his food-need changed, so he did not go to the grocery stores anymore. He pranced in the parks at night and cropped the grass and the flowers and ran nickering among the trees.

And his transformation continued. His mane and tail grew thick and exuberant. His face lengthened, and his teeth became stronger.

His feet became hooves, and the horny part of his hands grew. White hair the color of moonlight spread across his body and limbs, formed flaring tufts at the backs of his ankles and wrists. His horn grew long and clean and perfectly pointed.

His joints changed also and began to flex in new ways. For a time, this gave him some pain; but soon it became natural to him. He was turning into a unicorn. He was becoming beautiful. At times, there did not seem to be enough room in his heart for the joy the change gave him.

Yet he did not leave the city. He did not leave the people who were afraid of him, though their fear gave him pangs of a loneliness he had never felt before. He was waiting for something. There was something in him that was not complete.

At first, he believed that he was simply waiting for the end of his transformation. But gradually he came to understand that his waiting was a kind of search. He was alone—and unicorns were not meant to be alone, not like this. He was searching the city to see if he could find other people like him, people who were changing.

At last one night he came in sight of the huge high structure of the General Hospital. He had been brought there by his search. If there were other people like him, they might have been captured by the men in white coats. They might be prisoners in the Emergency Division of the Hospital. They might be lying helpless while the medicomputers studied them, plotting their destruction.

His nostrils flared angrily at the thought. He stamped his foreleg. He knew what he had to do. He put his sack of books in a place of safety. Then he lowered his head and charged down the road to attack the General Hospital.

He broke down the front doors with his horn and pounded into the corridors. People fled from him in terror. Men and women grabbed hypoguns and tried to fire at him; but he flicked them with the power of his horn, and they fell down. He rampaged on in search of the Emergency Division.

The General Hospital was designed just like the Medical Building and the National Library. He was able to find his way without trouble. Soon he was among the many rooms of the Emergency Division. He kicked open the doors, checked the rooms, checked room after room. They were full of patients. The Emergency Division was a busy place. He had not expected to find that so many people were ill and dangerous. But none of them were what he was looking for. They were not being transformed. They were dying from physical or mental sickness. If any people like him had been brought here, they had already been destroyed.

Red rage filled his heart. He charged on through the halls.

Then suddenly he came to the great room where the medicomputers lived. Rank on rank, they stood before him. Their displays glared evilly at him, and their voices shouted. He heard several of them shout together, "Absolute emergency! Atmospheric control, activate all nerve gas! Saturation gassing, all floors!"

They were trying to kill him. They were going to kill everybody in the Hospital.

The medicomputers were made of magnacite and plasmium. Their circuits were fireproof. But they were not proof against the power of his horn. When he attacked them, they began to burn in white fire, as incandescent as the sun.

He could hear gas hissing into the air. He took a deep breath and ran.

The gas was hissing into all the corridors of the Hospital. Patients began to die. Men and women in white coats began to die. Norman began to think that he would not be able to get out of the Hospital before he had to breathe.

A moment later, the fire in the medicomputers ignited the gas. The gas burned. Oxygen tanks began to explode. Dispensaries went up in flames. The fire extinguishers could not stop the intense heat of burning magnacite and plasmium. When the cylinders of nerve gas burst, they had enough force to shatter the floors and walls.

Norman flashed through the doors and galloped into the road leaving the General Hospital raging behind him like a furnace.

He breathed the night air deep into his chest and skittered to a stop on the far side of the road to shake the sparks out of his mane. Then he turned to watch the Hospital burn.

At first he was alone in the road. The people who lived nearby did not come to watch the blaze. They were afraid of it. They did not try to help the people who escaped the flames.

But then he saw a young girl come out from between the houses. She went into the road to look at the fire.

Norman pranced over to her. He reared in front of her.

She did not run away.

She had a lump on her forehead like the base of a horn or the nub of a new antler. There was a smile on her lips, as if she were looking at something beautiful.

And there was no fear in her eyes at all.

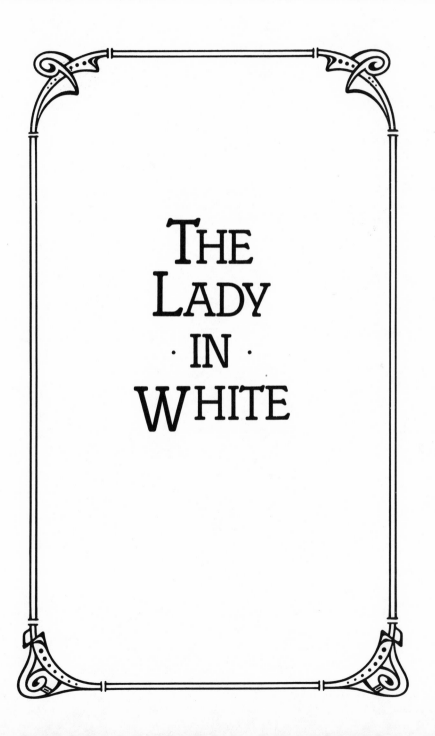

THE
LADY
· IN ·
WHITE

I AM A SENSIBLE MAN. I HAVE BEEN BLACKSMITH, WHEEL-wright and ironmonger for this village for seven years; and I have not seen the need to believe in magic, no matter what that loon, mad Festil my brother, says. I have not had need of magic. I am a man who does what he wills without such things—without such nonsense, I might once have said. This village is small, it's true, but not so small that Mardik the blacksmith does not stand as tall as any man here, fletcher or stonemason or vintner. I have all the work I choose to do, and my asking is fair because I have no need to ask for more. There is no woman here, widow or maid, who scorns the touch of my hands, though it's true my hands have the grime of the smithy in them and are not like to look clean again. Men listen when I speak; and if they do not hear me well, they can hear my fist well enough, and better than most. For my sake they treat mad Festil with respect.

Yet that respect is less than his dessert. Loon that he is, he is wise in his way, though the village does not see it. He is younger than I, and less of stature by a span of my hand; but when he smiles the look in his face is stronger than fists, and many are the angers he has brought to an end by gazing upon them with his blind eyes. For this I esteem him more than our village can understand. And for one thing more. Mad Festil my brother came to me when I was in need, brought close to death by the magic of the Lady in White.

Magic I call it, lacking another name for the thing I do not understand. Fools speak of magic with glib tongues that have no knowledge; they seek a respect that they cannot win with their own hands. Children prate of magic when they have taken fright in the Deep Forest. Well, the Deep Forest is strange, it's true. The trees are tall beyond tallness, and the gloom under them is cunning, and men lose their way easily. Our village sits with its back to the mighty trees like a man known for bravery; but oftimes tales are heard of things which befall those who venture into the Deep Forest; and in storms even the priests gaze upon that tall darkness with fear. And fools, too, are not always what they seem.

But fools and children speak only of what they hear from others, who themselves only speak of what they hear from others. Even the priests can put no face to their fear without consulting Scripture. I am neither fool nor child. I am not a priest, to shudder at tales of Lucifer. I am Mardik the blacksmith, wheelwright and iron-monger; and I make what I will, do what I will, have what I will. I fear not Satan nor storms nor black trees.

I speak only of what I have seen with my own eyes; and I was not struck blind by what I saw, as Festil was. I have kissed the lips of the thing I do not understand and have been left to die in the vastness of the Deep Forest.

I say I do not believe in magic; and I hold to what I say. Mayhap for a time I became ill in my mind. Mayhap all unknowing I ate of the mushroom of madness which grows at night under the ferns far in the Deep Forest. Mayhap many things, none of them magical. I do not say them because I cannot say them and be sure. This I do say: for a time under the spell of the Lady in White, I had need of a thing that was not in me; and because I had it not, I was left to die. If that thing has another name than magic, mad Festil knows it, not I. He smiles it to himself in his blindness and does not speak.

He was fey from his earliest youth, like a boy who knew that when he became a man he would lose his sight. My remembering of him goes back to the sound of his voice in the darkness of our loftroom. Though sleep was upon me, he would remain awake, sitting upright in the straw bed we shared, speaking of things that were exciting to him—of dragons and quests and arcane endeavors, things mysterious and wonderful. He spoke of them as if they were present to him in the darkness; and the power of his speaking kept me awake as well. I cuffed him more than once, it's true, to make him silent; but more often I listened and let him speak and laughed to myself.

At times when the excitement was strong, he would say, "Do you believe in magic, my brother? Do you not believe in magic?"

Then I would laugh aloud. And if the excitement was very strong, he would become stubborn. "Surely," he would say, "surely you believe that there is some witchery in the Deep Forest?" Then I would say, "A tree is a tree, and paths are few. It does not need magic to explain how fools and children lose their way. And if they come back to the village with strange tales to excuse their fear and foolishness, that also does not need magic." And then if he pressed me further, I would cuff him and go to sleep.

For this reason, I did not esteem Festil my brother as we grew to manhood. And for other reasons, also. I have no wife because I have no need of wife. No woman scorns me, and I take what I will. It pleases me to live my life without the bonds of a wife. But Festil has no wife because no woman in the village, be she ripe and maidenly enough to make a man grind his teeth—no woman pleases him. I believe he is a virgin to this day.

And when our father the blacksmith before me died, I did not learn to esteem my brother more. He was a dreamer and a loon and understood less than nothing of the workings of the smithy. So all the labor came to me, and until I grew strong enough to bear it I did not take pleasure in it.

Also his speaking of our father's death was worse than anile. Our father died from the kick of a horse whose hooves he was trimming. A placid plowbeast that never gave its master a moment's trouble suddenly conceived a desire to see the color of our father's brains. To this Festil cried, "Bewitchment!" He took a dagger and spent long hours in the Deep Forest, seeking to find and slay the caster of the spell. But I looked upon the beast when it grew calm again, and found that our father's trimming blade had slipped in his hands, and had cut the frog of the hoof. Bewitchment, forsooth! I saw no need to treat mad Festil with respect.

Yet he was my brother, kind and gentle, and willing in his way to help me at the forge, though it's true his help was often less than a help. And at times he fought the fools in the village for my sake when he would not fight for his own. I grew to be glad of his company and tolerant of his talk. And I knew that a matter to be taken seriously had arisen when he came to me and said that he had seen the Lady in White.

"The Lady in White!" he said softly, and his eyes shone, and his face was full of light. I would have laughed to see any other man act such a calf. But this was Festil my brother, who had not so much as touched his lips to the breasts of any woman but his mother. And in past days I had heard talk of this Lady in White—as who had not? The men who had seen her had told their tales until no ear in the village was empty of their prattle. For three nights now, every tankard of ale I took at the Red Horse was flavored with talk of the Lady in white. I cannot say that I was partial to the taste.

Fimm the fruiterer had seen her, with Forin his son, who was almost a man. Forin had gone senseless with love, said Fimm, and had crept away from his father in the night to follow the road taken by the Lady—into the Deep Forest, said Fimm. For two nights now Forin had not returned, and no one in the village had seen him.

"Well, lads are wild," said I, "and a Lady in white is as good a cure for wildness as any. He will return when she has taught him to be some little tamer."

But nay—Fimm would not agree. And Pandeler the weaver was of the same mind, though Pandeler does not take kindly to nonsense. He himself had seen the Lady in White. She had come to his shop to buy his finest samite, and there his two sons, the twins Paoul and Pendit, had seen her. They had come to blows over her—they who were as close to each other as two fingers on the same fist—and Paoul had gone away in search of her, followed soon afterward by Pendit, though they were both of them under the banns to be married to the ripe young daughters of Swonsil the fletcher.

Yet that was not the greatest wonder of it, said Pandeler. Neither of his sons had been seen in the village for two days—but that also was not the greatest wonder. Nay, the wonder was that Pandeler himself had near arisen in the black night and followed his sons into the Deep Forest, hoping to find the Lady in White before them. He had only refrained, he said, because he was too old to make a fool of himself in love—and because if the truth were known it would be that he was altogether fond of Megan his wife.

"What is she like, then," I said, "this Lady in White?" It was in my mind that any woman able to lead Pandeler the weaver by the nose would be worth a look or twain.

But he gave no answer. His eyes gazed into his tankard, and if he saw the Lady in white there he did not say what he saw.

Then other men spoke. If all the tales were true, this Lady had already consumed some half dozen of our young men; and no one of us knew a thing of her but that she came to the village from the Deep Forest and that when she left she took herself back into the Deep Forest.

Well, I thought of all this often in my smithy—and not with displeasure, it's true. If our young men were fool enough to lose themselves in the Deep Forest—why, soon the village would be full of maidens in need of consolation. And who better to console them than Mardik the blacksmith?

But that look in Festil my brother's face stood the matter on other ground. When he came to me and said that he had seen the Lady in White, I put down my hammer and considered him seriously. Then I took a step to bring myself close to him and said, "It's come to that, has it? When will you be after her?"

"Now!" he said gladly. It pleased him to think that I understood his desire. "I only came to tell you before I left."

"You are wiser than you think, my brother," said I. And because I am not a man who hesitates when he has made his decision, I swung my fist at once and hit mad Festil a blow that stretched him on the dirt of the smithy. "I have no wish to lose my only brother," I said, though it's true he was not like to hear me. Then I bore him sleeping to our hut and put him in his bed and contrived a way to bolt his door. When I was sure of him, I went back to my forge.

But I was wrong. The blood of our father flows in him as well after all, and he is stronger than he seems. When I returned home at midday, I found him gone. He had been able to break the wallboard that held my bolt in place. Without doubt, he was on his way into the Deep Forest.

I went after him. What else could I do? He was a dreamer and a loon, and he knew more of witches than of smithing. But he was my brother, and no other could take his place. Pausing only to slip my hunting knife into the top of my boot, I left the house at a run. It was my hope to catch him before he managed to lose himself altogether.

I ran to the stables and threw a saddle onto Leadenfoot, the gray nag that draws my wagon when I go to do work at the outlying farms. Leadenfoot is no swiftling—what need has a blacksmith's wagon for swiftness?—but when I strike him hard he is faster than my legs. And he fears nothing, because he lacks the sense for fear—which is also an advantage in a blacksmith's nag. So he heeded the argument of my quirt and did not shy as many horses do when I sent him running down the old road into the Deep Forest.

That road is the only way which enters the Forest; and all the talkers at the Red Horse had agreed that when the Lady in White left the village she walked this road. It began as a wagon-track as good as any, but it has long been disused and no longer goes to any place, though surely once it did in times so long past that they have been forgotten by all the village. Now only mad priests claim knowledge of the place where the old road goes. They say it goes to Hell.

Hell, forsooth! I have no use for such talk. Yet in its way Hell is as good a name for the Deep Forest as any. As I ran Leadenfoot along the road at his best speed, the trees and the brush were so thick that I could see nothing through them, though the sun was bright overhead; and birds answered the sound of Leadenfoot's shoes with cries like scorn. I called out for Festil, but the woods took my voice and gave back no reply.

In a league or two the road grew narrower. Grass grew across it, then flowers and brush. Fallen limbs cluttered the way, and the black trees leaned inward. Leadenfoot made it clear to me that he would not run any more, though I hit him more than I am proud to admit. And nowhere did I see any sign of Festil.

How had he eluded me? I had not left him alone more than half the morning, and he had been sleeping soundly when I had bolted his door. He could not have awakened immediately. He could not have broken the wallboard without effort and time. He could not have outrun me. Yet he was gone. The Deep Forest had swallowed him as completely as the jaws of death.

Railing against him for a fool and a dreamer, I left Leadenfoot and searched ahead on foot. Shouting, cursing, searching, I followed the road until it became a path, and the path became a trail, and the trail vanished. Almost I lost my way for good and all. When I found it again, I had no choice but to return the way I had come. All about me, the birds of the Deep Forest cried like derision.

At the place where I had left Leadenfoot, I found him gone also. This day everything was doomed to betray me. At first, I feared that the senseless nag had broken his reins and wandered away off the road. But then I found his shoemarks leading back down the road toward the village. I followed as best I could; and now there was a fear in me that darkness would come upon me before I could escape these fell trees.

But in the gloom of sunset, I gained a sight of Leadenfoot, walking slowly along the road with a rider upon his back.

I ran to catch the nag and jerked the reins, pulling the rider to the ground. Mad Festil.

"Mardik," he said. "Mardik my brother." There was joy in his voice, and there was joy in his face and all his movements as he rose to his feet and clasped me in his arms that were as certain as truth. And yet he was blind. His eyes were gone in a white glaze, and I did not need the noon sun to see that there was no sight in them.

I held him with all the strength of my anger and pain. "What has she done to you?" I said.

But my grip gave him no hurt. "I have seen her," he said.

"You are blind!" I cried at him, seeking to turn aside the joy in his face.

"Yet I have seen her," he said. "I have seen her, Mardik my brother. I have entered her cottage and have won through its great wonders to the greatest wonder of all. I have seen the Lady in White in all her beauty."

"She has blinded you!" I shouted.

"No," he said. "It is only that my eyes have been filled by her beauty, and there is no other thing bright enough to outshine her."

Then I found that I could not answer his joy; and after a moment I gave it up. I did not say to him that he was mad—that there was no cottage, no place of wonder, no Lady who could blind him with her beauty unless she had seduced him to eat the mushroom of madness and had done him harm by choice. I stored these things up amid the anger in my heart, but I did not speak them. I put Festil onto Leadenfoot's back and mounted behind him; and together we rode out of the Deep Forest in the last dusk.

That night, with mad Festil sleeping the sleep of bliss in our hut, I went to the Red Horse as was my custom. I said nothing of my brother's folly—or of his blindness. I listened rather, sifting through the talk about me for some new word of the Lady in White. But no word was said, and at last I spoke my thought aloud. I asked if any of the young men who had followed the Lady into the Deep Forest had returned.

The older men were silent, and the younger did not speak; but in his own time Pandeler the weaver bestirred himself and said, "Pendit. Pendit my son has returned. Alone."

I saw there in his face that he believed his other son Paoul dead. Yet I asked him despite his grief, "And what says Pendit? How does he tell his tale?"

With head bowed, Pendeler said, "He tells nothing. No word has he spoken. He sits as I sit now and does not speak." And in the firelight of the hearth it was plain for all to see that there were tears on the face of Pandeler the weaver, who was as brave a man as any in the village.

Then I returned to our hut. Festil my brother slept with a smile on his mouth, but I did not sleep. My heart was full of retribution, and there was no rest in me.

The next morning, I spoke with Festil concerning the Lady in white and the Deep Forest, though it's true that all the speaking was mine, for he would say nothing of what had happened to him. Only he said, "My words would have no meaning to you." And he smiled his joy, wishing to content me with that answer.

But when I asked him how he had come to be riding Leadenfoot out of the Deep Forest, he did reply. "When I had seen her," he said, "I was no longer in her cottage. I was in the dell that cups her cottage as a setting cups its gem, and Leadenfoot was there. I heard him cropping grass near at hand. He came to me when I spoke his name, and I mounted him and let him bear me away. For that I must ask your pardon, my brother. I knew not that you had ridden him in search of me. I believed that the Lady in White had brought him for me, in consideration of my blindness." Then he laughed. "As in truth she did, Mardik my brother—though you scowl and mutter to yourself at the thought. You are the means she chose to bring Leadenfoot to me."

The means she chose, forsooth! He spoke of magic again, though he did not use the word. And yet in one way he had the right of the matter, despite his blindness. My scowl was heavy on my face, and I was muttering as I mutter now. Therefore I swore at him, though I knew it would give him pain. "May Heaven damn me," I said, "if ever again I serve any whim of hers." Then I left him and went to the smithy to bespeak my anger with hammer and anvil. For a time the fire of my forge was no hotter than my intent against this Lady in White.

But all my angers and intents were changed in an instant when a soft voice reached me through the clamor of my pounding. I turned and found the Lady herself there before me.

She bore in her hands a black old pot which had worn through the bottom, and in her soft voice she asked me to mend it for her. But I did not look at the pot and gave no thought to what she asked. I was consumed utterly by the sight and sound of her.

Her form was robed all in whitest samite, and her head was crowned as if in bronze by a wealth of red-yellow hair that fell unbound to her shoulders, and her eyes were like the heavens of the night, star-bright and fathomless, and her voice was the music that makes men laugh or weep, according to their courage. Her lips were full for kisses but not too full for loveliness, and her breasts made themselves known through her robe like the need for love, and her skin had that alabaster softness that cries out to be caressed. Altogether, she struck me so full with desire that I would have taken her there in the dirt of the smithy and counted the act for treasure. But her gaze had the power to withhold me. She placed her pot in my hands with a smile and turned slowly and walked away. Her robe clung cunningly to the sway of her hips, and I did nothing but stare openly after her like the veriest calf.

But I am not a man who hesitates; and when she had left my sight among the huts on her way back to the old road and the Deep Forest, I did not hesitate. I banked the fires of my forge, closed my smithy, and went home. There in my room I bathed myself, though I do not bathe often, it's true; and when I had removed some of the grime of smithing from my limbs, I donned my Easter garments, the bold-stitched tunic and the brown pants with leather leggings which the widow Anuell had made for me. Thus I readied myself to depart.

But when I turned from my preparations, I found Festil before me. He was laughing—not the laughter of derision, but the laughter of joy. "A bath, Mardik!" he said. "You have seen her."

"I have seen her," I said.

"Ah, Mardik my brother," he said, and he groped his blind way to me to embrace me, "I wish you well. You are a good man. It is a test she gives you now. If you do not falter or fail, she will fulfill your heart's desire."

"That is as it may be," I answered. But in my own heart I said, Then I will not falter or fail, and you will not be blind long, Festil my brother. I returned his embrace briefly. Soon I had left our hut, and the village was behind me. I was walking along the old road into the Deep Forest, and there was an unwonted eagerness in my stride.

Striken with desire as I was, however, I did not altogether lose sense. I took careful note of the passing trees on my way, finding landmarks for myself and searching for any path by which the Lady in White might have left the road. I discovered none, no sign that any Lady lived near this track, no sign that any Lady however white had ever walked this way. In a league or two, my heart began to misgive me. Yet in time I learned that I had not missed my goal. For when I neared the place where I had tethered Leadenfoot the day before, I came upon a branching in the road.

A branching, I say, though I do not hope to be believed. I will swear to any man who asks it that no branching was there when I came this way in search of Festil. But that is not needed. It is plain to all who dare travel that road that there is no branching now. Yet I found a branching, that is sure. If I had not, then none of the things that followed could have taken place.

In my surprise, I walked along this other road and shortly came to the dell and the cottage of which Festil my brother had spoken. And he had spoken rightly: safe and sunlit among the gloom of the trees was a hollow rich with flowers, soft with greensward; and cupped in the hollow was a small stone cottage. Its walls had been whitewashed until they gleamed in the sun, and all the wood of its frames and roof had been painted red. White curtains of finest lace showed in the windows, and beneath the windows lay beds of columbine and peony. Faint white smoke rose from the chimney, showing to my keen desire that the Lady was within.

I went with heart pounding to the red door; and there I paused as if I, Mardik the blacksmith, were unsure of himself, so great and confused were my lust and my anger.

But then I recollected myself, put aside my unseemly hesitation. With my strong hand I knocked at the door, and there was both confidence and courtesy in the way I summoned the Lady in white.

The door opened, swung inward, though I saw no one, heard no one.

Then in truth began the thing for which I have no other name but magic. Many things in the world are strange, and magic is not needed to explain them. But in this thing I am beyond all my reckoning, and I know no explanation other than that I became ill in my mind, or ate of the mushroom of madness, or by some other means lost myself. But Festil my brother, who is wise in his way, says that I am neither mad nor ill; and I must believe him when I cannot believe the thing of which I speak. He was there before me, and this thing named magic cost him his sight.

But magic or no, I have chosen to speak, and I will speak. My word is known and trusted, and no man in the village dares call me liar or fool, though at times I seem a fool to myself, it's true. This, then, is the thing that befell me.

As the door opened, I stepped inward, into the cottage, so that no effort could be made to deny me admittance. Within, the air seemed somewhat dark to my sun-accustomed eyes, and for a moment I was not certain that I saw what I saw. But beyond question I did see it, just as it was. Behind me through the doorway was the sunlight and the green grass of the dell that cupped the cottage. But before me was no cottage-room, no cozy hearth and small kitchen: I stood in a huge high hall like the forecourt of an immense keep.

The ceiling was almost lost to sight above me, but even so I could see that its beams were as thick as the thickest trees of the Deep Forest. The floorspace before me was all of polished gray stone, and it was large enough to hold a dozen cottages such as the one I had just entered. A stone's throw to my left, a stairway as wide as a road came down into the hall from levels above mine. And an equal distance to my right, a hearth deep enough to hold my smithy entire blazed with logs too great for any man to lift. The light came from this fire, and from tall windows high in the wall behind me. And all about these prodigious stone walls hung banners like battle-pennons.

Two of these held something familiar to me. Woven large in the center of one was the weft-mark of Paoul son of Pandeler the weaver. And displayed across the other was a great bright apple. At this I ground my teeth, for it was known in all the village that Forin son of Fimm the fruiterer took pride in his apples.

Now in truth there was no hesitation in me, though this high castle-hall sorely baffled all my reckoning. My hands ached to entwine themselves in the bronzen hair of the Lady, and my mouth was tight with kisses or curses. When my eyes were fully accustomed to the keeplight, I espied an arched entryway opposite me. It had the aspect of an entrance into the less public parts of this castle; and I strode toward it at once. As I moved, the air thronged with the echo of my bootsteps.

Surprised as I was by the strangeness of this place, and by the meaning of the pennons about the walls, I had at first failed to note a small table standing in the very center of the hall. But as I neared it, I considered it closely. It was ornately gilt-worked; and it stood between me and the arched entryway as if it had been placed there for some purpose. When I came to it, I saw that on it lay a silver tray like a serving dish, polished until it reflected the walls and ceiling without flaw. All its workmanship was excellent; but I saw no reason for its presence there, and so I stepped aside to pass around the table toward the far entryway.

At my next step, I struck full against the outer door of the cottage. Of a sudden there was sunlight on my back, and my eyes were blurred by the brightness of the whitewashed walls. The dell lay about me as fragrant as if I had not left it to enter that place of witchery, and the red door was closed in my face.

Then for a time I stood motionless, as still as Leadenfoot when the fit comes upon him and he stops to consider the depth of his own stupidity. It seemed to me that the mere taking of air into my lungs required great resolve, that the beating of my heart required deliberate choice, so unutterable was my astonishment. But then I perceived the foolishness of my stance and took hold of myself. Though the act gave me a pang akin to fear, I lifted my hand and knocked at the door again.

There was no answer. As my surprise turned to ire, I knocked at the door, pounded at it; but there was no answer. I shook mightily on the handle, kicked at the door, heaved against it with my shoulder. There was no answer and no opening. The door withstood me as if it were stone.

Then I ran cursing around the cottage and strove to gain entrance another way. But there was no other door. And I could not break any window, neither with fist nor with stone.

At last it was the thought of the Lady in White that checked me. I seemed to feel her within her walls, laughing like the scornful birds of the Deep Forest. So I bit my anger into silence, and I turned on my heel, and I strode away from the cottage and the dell without a backward glance. And through my teeth I muttered to her in a voice that only I could hear, "Very well, my fine Lady. Believe that you have beaten me if you will. You will learn that you scorn me at your peril."

But when I regained the old road, I ran and ran on my way back to the village, wearying my unwonted fury until I became master of myself once again.

When I returned to our hut, I found Festil my brother sitting in wait for me on the stoop. Hearing my approach, he said, "Mardik?" And I replied, "Festil."

"Did you—?" he said.

"I failed," I said. I had become myself again and was not afraid to speak the truth.

For a moment, I saw a strange pain in my brother's face; but then the gaze of his blindness brightened, and he said, "Mardik my brother, did you take the Lady a gift?"

"A gift?" said I.

Then Festil laughed at my surprise. "A gift!" he said. "What manner of suitor are you, that you do not take a gift to the Lady of your heart?"

"A gift, forsooth!" I said. "I am not accustomed to need gifts to win my way." But then I reflected that mad Festil my brother, loon and dreamer though he was, had had more success than I with the Lady in white. "Well, a gift, then," I said. Considering his blindness and his happy smile, I asked, "And what was your gift?"

His laugh became the mischievous laugh of a boy. "I stole a white rose from the arbor of the priests," he said.

Stole a rose? Aye, verily, that had the touch of mad Festil upon it. But I am not like him. I am Mardik the blacksmith, wheelwright and ironmonger. I had no need to steal roses. Therefore I slept confident that night, planning how I would make my gift.

Dawn found me in my smithy, with the music of the anvil in my heart. The blade of a discarded plowshare I put into the forge, and I worked the bellows until the iron was as white as sunfire. Then I doubled the blade over and hammered it flat while the smithy ran with bright sparks as the impurities were stricken away. Then I tempered it in the trough and put it in the forge again and worked the bellows so that the fire roared. Again I doubled it, hammered it flat, tempered it. Again I placed it in the forge. And when I had doubled it once again, hammered it to the shape I desired, and tempered it, I had formed a knife blade that no hand in the village could break.

To the blade I attached a handle of ox-horn; and then I gave the knife a keen edge on the great grindstone made by our father in his prime, when Festil and I were young. And all the while I worked, my heart sang its song, using the name of the Lady in White for melody.

My task was done before the passing of midday. With the new blade gleaming in my hand, I determined at once to assay that cottage of bewitchment without awaiting a new day. I returned to our hut to take food. I spoke pleasantly with Festil my brother, who listened to my voice with both gladness and concern in his face, as if the hazards of the Lady were as great as the rewards. But when I sought to learn more from him concerning the "test," he turned his head away and would not speak.

Well, I felt that I had no need of further counsel. He had told me of the gift, and that was enough. I put the new knife in my belt and went just as I was, begrimed and proud from the smithy, to visit again the dell and the cottage of the Lady in White.

On my way between the dark and forbidding tree-walls of the Deep Forest, my confidence was weakened by a kind of dread—a fear that the branching of the road would be gone or lost. But it was not: it lay where I had left it, and it led me again to the dell of flowers and grass and the cottage of white walls and red wood.

At the door I paused, took the blade from my belt and held it before me. "Now, then, my fine Lady," I muttered softly, "let us see if any man in the village can match such a gift as this." With the butt of the knife, I rapped on the door.

Again the door swung inward. And again I saw no one, heard no one.

I entered at once and found myself once more in that huge high hall, castle-forecourt spacious enough to hold a dozen such cottages. But now I did not waste my time in wonder. Though the image of the Lady in white filled my very bones with desire—and though the pennons of the dead (young men consumed by whatever hunger drove that cruel and irrefusable woman) did not fail to raise my anger—still I had not lost all sense. I knew my time was short. If I were to fail another test, I meant to do so and be gone from this place before day's end. No man would choose to travel the Deep Forest at night.

So I strode without delay across that long stone floor toward the table in the center of the hall. The light was dimmer than it had been the previous day—the afternoon sun did not shine into those high windows—and this dimness seemed to fortify the echoes, so that the sound of my feet marched all about me like a multitude as I approached the table. But I did not hesitate. Nor did I trouble myself to make any speech of gift-giving. I held up the knife so that any hidden eyes might see it. Then I placed it on the silver tray.

There was no response from the castle. No voices hailed my gift, and the Lady in White did not appear. I stood there before the table for a moment, allowing her time for whatever answer seemed fit to her. But when none came, I took my resolve in both hands and stepped around the table toward the arched entryway at the far end of the hall. Almost I winced, half expecting to find myself in the dell once more with the cottage door shut in my face.

But I did not. Instead, another thing came upon me—a thing far worse than any unexplained vanishing of hall and locking of cottage door.

Before I had gone five paces past the table, I heard a scream that turned the strength in my limbs to chaff. It rent the air. It echoed, echoed, about my head like the howling of the damned. A gust of chill wind near extinguished the blaze in the hearth, and some cloud covered the sun, so that the verges of the hall were filled with night. I spun where I was, searching through the gloom for the inhuman throat which had made that scream.

It was repeated, and repeated. And then the creature that made it came down the broad stairs from the upper levels—came running with murder in its face and a great broadsword upraised in its foul hands, shrieking for my blood.

It was fiend-loathsome and ghoul-terrible, a thing of slime and scales and fury. Red flame ran from its eyes. In the dimness, its broadsword had the blue sheen of lightning. Its jaws were stretched to rend and kill, and it ran as if it lived for no other purpose than to hack my heart out from between my ribs for food.

The fear of it unmanned me. Even now, looking back on things that are past, I am not shamed to say that I was lost in terror—so much lost that I was unable to take the knife from my boot to defend myself. The creature screamed as it charged, and I screamed also.

Then I was lying on the greensward of the dell, and the afternoon sunlight was slanting through the treetops to glint in my eyes. The cottage stood near at hand, but the door was closed, and the windows had a look of abandonment. Only the curling of smoke from the chimney showed that the Lady in White was yet within, untouched by any desire or anger of mine.

Stricken and humbled, I left the dell and returned to the old road. As the sun drew near to setting, I went back through the Deep Forest toward the village.

But there was another thing in me beyond the humbling, and I came to know it soon. For while I was still within the bounds of the Forest, with the hand of the coming night upon me, I met a man upon the road. When we drew near enough to know each other, I saw that he was Creet the stonemason. He stood tall in the village; and it's true that his head overtopped mine, though mayhap he was not as strong as I. We were somewhat friends, for like me he had done much wooing but no marrying—and somewhat wary one of another, for we had only measured our strength together once, and there had been no clear issue to that striving. But I gave no thought to such things now. For Creet the stonemason was walking into the Deep Forest at dusk, and there was a spring of eagerness in his step.

Seeing him, the other thing in me was roused; and I shifted my path to bar his way. "Go back, mason," said I. "She is not for you."

"I have seen her," he replied without hesitation. "How can I go back? Mayhap you have failed to win her, blacksmith. Creet the stonemason will not."

"You speak in ignorance, Creet," said I. "She has slain men of this village. That *I* have seen."

"Men!" he scoffed. "Paoul and Forin? They were boys, not men." Clearly, he did not doubt himself. He placed a hand on my chest to push me from his way.

But I am Mardik the blacksmith, and I also can act without hesitation when I choose. I shrugged aside his hand and struck him with all my strength.

Then for a time we fought together there in the old road and the Deep Forest. Night came upon us, but we did not heed it. We struck one another, clinched, fell, arose to strike and clinch and fall again. Creet was mighty in his way, and his desire for the Lady in White was strong beyond bearing. But the other thing in me had raised its head: it was a thing of iron, a thing not to be turned aside by failure or fear or stonemasons. After a time, I struck Creet down, so that he lay senseless before me in the road.

Thus I chose my way—the way that brought me near to dying in the end, lost in the maze of the Deep Forest. From the moment that I struck down Creet the stonemason, I gave no more thought to humbling or fear. I was Mardik the blacksmith, wheelwright and ironmonger. I was accustomed to have my will and did not mean to lose it at the hand of any Lady, however strange. I lifted Creet and stretched him across my shoulders and bore him with me and did not allow his weight to trouble me. So I became the first man in my lifetime to find his way out of the Deep Forest in darkness.

I bore my burden direct to the Red Horse, where many of the men in the village were gathered, as was their custom in the evening. Giving no heed to their surprise, I thrust open the door, bore Creet into the aleroom, and dropped him there on a table among the tankards. He groaned in his slumber; but to him, also, I gave no heed.

"Hear me well," I said to the silence about me. "I am Mardik the blacksmith, and if Creet cannot stand against me then no man in this village can hope otherwise. Now I say this: the Lady in White is mine. From this moment forth, no other man will follow her. If your sons see her, lock them in their rooms and stand guard at the door. If your brothers behold her, bind them hand and foot. If your friends are taken with the sight of her, restrain them with shackles of iron. And if you wish to go to her—why, then, tell your wives or your maidens or your mothers to club you senseless. For the Lady in White kills whom she does not keep. And I will be no more gentle to those who dare cross my way. The Lady in White is mine!"

Still there was silence for a moment in the aleroom. Then Pandeler the weaver rose to his feet and met my gaze with his grief for Paoul his son. "Will you kill her, then, Mardik the blacksmith?" he said.

"Pandeler," I said, "I will do with her whatever seems good to me."

I would have gone on to say that whatever I did no more young men of the village would lose their lives; but before I could speak, another man came forward to face me, and I saw that he was Gruel the mad priest. His habit was all of black, and his long gray beard trembled with passion, and his boney hands clung to the silver crucifix which hung about his neck. "She is the bride of Satan!" he said, fixing me with his wild eye. "Your soul will roast in Hell!"

"God's blood!" I roared in answer. "Then it will be my soul that roasts, and not the souls of innocent calves who cannot so much as say aye or nay to their own mothers!" Then I left the aleroom and flung shut the door of the Red Horse so that the boards cracked.

Returning homeward, I found our hut all in darkness; and for a moment there was a fear in me that Festil had gone again into the Deep Forest. But then I recalled that Festil my brother had no need of light. I entered the hut and found him in his bed, awake in the night. When I opened his door, he said, "Mardik," knowing me without doubt, for in the darkness he was no more blind than I.

"Festil," I said. "Again I failed."

"It was very fearsome," he said; and in his voice I heard two things that surprised me—sorrow and a wish to console me. "Do not reproach yourself."

"Festil," I said again. My own voice was stern. There was a great need in me for the knowledge he could give. "What is that creature?"

"A test, my brother," he said softly. "Only a test."

"A test," I echoed. Then I said, "A test you did not fail."

After a moment, he breathed, "Aye." And again there was sorrow in his voice—sorrow for me.

"How?" I demanded. My need for knowledge was great.

"I—" he began, then fell silent. But I waited grimly for him; and after a time he brought himself to speak. "I knelt before the creature," he said, and he was whispering, "and I said, 'Work your will, demon. I do not fear you, for I love your Lady, and you cannot harm my heart.' And then the creature was gone, and I remained." But then of a sudden his voice became stronger, and he cried out, "Mardik, you must not ask these things! It is wrong of me to speak of them. It is not a kindness to you—or to the Lady. You must meet each test in your own way, else all that you endure will have no purpose."

"Do not fear, Festil my brother," I said. "I will meet that creature in my own way, be it beast or demon." That was a promise I made to myself and to the fear which the creature had given me. "Yet I must ask you to tell me of the other tests."

"I must not!" he protested.

"Yet I must ask," I said again. "Festil, young men are slain in that cottage, and it needs but little to make even old men follow the Lady to their graves. I cannot prevent their deaths if I cannot gain my way to speak with her."

"Is that your reason?" he asked; and now the sorrow was thick and heavy in his voice. "Is that why you will return to her?"

Then I answered openly because I could not lie to that sound in my brother's voice. "For that reason, and for the reason of your blindness. But if I lacked such reasons, yet I would go, for I desire the Lady in White with a desire that consumes me."

Still he was silent; but I knew now that he would tell me all he could without false kindness. And at last he said softly, "There is a woman. You must find some answer to her need. And then there is a door." Beyond that he could not speak.

But it sufficed for me. The thing I feared was a multitude of those screaming creatures; but now I knew there was but one. Therefore I was confident. Surely I could satisfy one woman. And as to the door—why, one door does not daunt me. I thanked Festil for his help and left him there in the darkness and spent the night planning for the day to come.

And in the dawn I left to carry out my will. I took a satchel of food with me, for I did not mean to return to the village until I had won or lost, and if I failed a test I would perforce remain in the dell until the next day to try again. Bearing the satchel on my shoulder, I went to Leadenfoot and lead him from the stables to my smithy, where I harnessed him to my wagon. Then into the wagon I placed all that I might need—hammers, an anvil, nails, chisels, rope, a small forge of my own making, an urn of banked coals for fire, a saddle and bridle for Leadenfoot, awls, a saw, shears, tongs, an axe, wood and charcoal—everything that need or whim suggested to me. And to all this I added a pitchfork—a stout implement with tempered tines which I had made especial for a doughty farmer who broke other pitchforks the way some men break axe-hafts. Then I was ready. I climbed up to the wagonbench, took the reins, released the brake, and went out through the village toward the old road and the Deep Forest.

I did not depart unnoticed, though the hour was yet early. My wagon does not roll quietly—it is well known that wheelwrights and blacksmiths do not tend their wagons as well as other men—and the squeal of the singletrees told all within earshot of my passing. Families came from their huts to see me go. But they did not speak, and I did not speak, and soon I was beyond them among the verges of the woods.

The Deep Forest was dim in the early light, and the noise of my wagon roused huge flocks of birds that cried out in anger at my intrusion. But I was content with their outrage. They were creatures of this dense and brooding wood; but I was not. I was Mardik the blacksmith, and I was on my way to teach the Lady in White the meaning of my desire. If the ravens of doom had come to bark about my ears, I would not have been dismayed.

Also I was patient. My wagon was slow, and Leadenfoot had no love for this work; but the pace did not dishearten me. There was a long day before me, and I did not doubt that the Lady would be waiting.

And yet in all my preparation and all my confidence, there was one thought that disquieted me. Festil my brother had gone to the dell and the cottage armed with naught but one white rose—and yet he had contrived to surpass me in the testing. "Aye, and for reward he lost his sight," I answered my doubt. It was not my intent to become another blind man.

Thus it was that I came forewarned and forearmed to the branching of the old road late in the sunlight of morning and took it to the grassy and beflowered dell that cupped the witch-work cottage of the Lady in White.

There I tethered Leadenfoot, allowing him to crop the grass as he chose, and set about readying myself to approach the red door. From my satchel I removed the food, storing it under the wagon-bench. Then into the satchel I placed all the tools and implements that were most like to be of use—rope, hammer, chisels, awls, nails, saw, shears, tongs. With that load heavy on my shoulder, I took the pitchfork in my right hand, hefted it a time or twain to be certain of its balance. I did not delay; I am not a man who hesitates. I addressed that safe-seeming red door and knocked at it with the haft of the pitchfork.

For the third time, it opened inward to my knock. And for the third time, I saw no one within, heard no one approach or depart.

I entered warily, alert for the creature of flame and fury. But all within that strange door was as I had seen it twice before. The stone hall stretched before me like the forecourt of an immense keep, far dwarfing the cottage that seemed to contain it. The huge logs in the great hearth burned brightly, and the sunlight slanted through the high windows. The pennons of the dead hung from the walls—but if they hung in derision of foolhardiness or in tribute to valor I did not know. And there in the center of the floor stood the small gilt-work table with the silver tray.

I strode warily through echoes to the table; and when I gained it I saw on the tray the knife that I had made—my gift. Mayhap the Lady in White had declined to accept it. Or mayhap it had been left there as a sign that the way beyond the table was open for me. This I did not know also. But I did not delay to make the trial. I settled the satchel upon my shoulder, clenched the haft of the pitchfork, and stepped around the table.

So I learned that my gift had not been refused, for I did not find myself without the cottage with the door locked against me. At once, my wariness grew keener. I walked on toward the arched entryway at the far end of the hall, but I walked slowly. I believe I did not breathe, so strong was my caution and my waiting.

And then it came again, the scream that rent the air and echoed in the dim hall and chilled my blood in the warmest places of my heart. A cold wind blew, and the air became full of shadows. And the creature that made the screaming came down the wide stairs from the upper levels with its broadsword upraised and its eyes aflame with murder.

I dropped my satchel, turned to face the demon.

Again it filled me with fear, and again it would have not shamed me to say that I had been unmanned. But I had found the thing of iron within me now, and I was prepared.

As the creature ran screaming across the floor toward my throat, I swung with all my strength, hurling the pitchfork like a handful of spears.

The tines bit the chest of the creature and sank deep. Such was the force of my throw that the creature was stricken backward, despite its speed. Its broadsword fell in a clatter against the stone, and the creature itself lay writhing for a moment on the floor, plucking weakly at the metal in its chest. Then on an instant it seemed to me that the creature was not a demon at all, but rather a woman in a white robe. And then the creature was gone, vanished utterly, taking broadsword and pitchfork with it. I was left alone in the great hall, with the logs that no man could lift ablaze in the hearth.

"God's blood!" muttered I to myself. But swiftly I shook off the wonder. I had not come so far to be unmanned by wonder. I lifted my satchel, and walked away toward the arched entryway; and my stride was the stride of Mardik the blacksmith, strong and sure.

But beyond that arch matters were not so certain. The entryway led to halls and chambers of great complication, and there were many passages and doors that I might choose. All were various, some spare and others sumptuous, and all had the appearance of habitation, as if the lordly people of this castle had left it only briefly and would return; but all were made of gray stone and told me nothing of the Lady in White. For a time, I wandered hither and thither, making no progress. When I came upon one of the high windows, I could see by the sun that midday was passing.

Then in vexation I stopped where I was and gave thought to my situation. I was in need of direction. But in this amazed place, east and west, inward and outward had no meaning. Therefore I must either climb or descend. And because that fell creature with the broadsword had come from the upper levels, I chose to go downward. Then at last I was able to advance, for there were many stairways, and many of them went down into the depths of this prodigious keep.

So I descended, stair beyond stair; and the air became dark about me. Torches burned in sconces in the walls to light the passages—burned and did not appear to be consumed—but they were few and the halls were many. Therefore I took one of the torches, a brand the length of my arm, and bore it with me; and so I was able to continue my descent.

Then of a sudden I came upon a chamber bright-lit and spacious, its walls behung with rich tapestries depicting I knew not what heraldic or sorcerous legends. And there in the center stood a low couch. And there on the couch lay a woman in black.

She turned her head toward me as I entered; but at first my eyes were unaccustomed to the brightness, and I could not see her well. "Ah, man!" she hailed me, and her voice was the voice of a woman in need. "Rescuer! I beg of you—redeem me from my distress!"

"What is your need, woman?" said I, seeking to clear my sight. But I knew already the name of her need. I had heard that need often before in the voices of women, and I saw no harm in it. I was prepared to answer it, for the sake of the Lady in White and her testing.

"Ah, man!" she said to me in pleading, "I am loveless and alone. Life is a long misery, and there is no joy for me, for I am scorned and reviled everywhere. Help me, O man! for surely I can endure no more."

That had an unsavory sound to it; but still I was undaunted. I moved closer to her, blinking against the brightness.

But then my sight cleared, and I saw her. She was hideous. Her raiment was not a black robe, but rather leper's rags, and her hands were gnarled and reft with leprosy. I saw them well, for she extended them toward me beseechingly. They were marked with running sores, as her arms were marked, and her face, also. Her hair hung in vile snatches from her head, and many teeth were gone from her gums, and the flesh of her face had been misshapen by illness, so that it seemed to be made all of bruises and scabs. Gazing upon her, I could not say which of them had become the greater, my loathing or my pity—for I was sickened by the sight of her, it's true; and yet the deepness of her misery wrung my heart.

But Festil had said, "You must find some answer to her need." And verily, this was a test to pale all testing of gifts and demon-creatures. Again she cried out, "Help me, O man, I beg of you! Ease my hurt." Now I knew not what answer Festil my brother had given this leprous crone; but some answer he had given, that was certain, for he had not failed this test. And I knew of no answer but one—no answer but one that could stand against this piteous and abhorrent distress. Therefore I bethought me of the Lady in White, and with her image I spurred myself until my hands ached to feel her throat between them. Then I stepped forward to stand beside the couch.

The woman's hands reached pleading for mine; but I stooped, and drew the knife from my boot and thrust it through her heart with one blow of my fist.

Then on an instant it seemed to me that her face softened, and her hair grew thick and bronzen, and her lips became full, and her rags were whitest samite. And then she was gone, vanished as utterly as the demon-creature, and there was neither knife nor couch with me in the chamber.

Then my anger came upon me again, and I vowed in my heart that the Lady in White would answer me for this. In my anger I did not delay. There was only one other doorway to this chamber. Taking up my satchel, I went out that way swiftly, hoping to come upon the Lady before she had prepared another and more foul test.

But that way led only to a lightless passage; and the passage led only to a stout wooden door that was shut. No Lady was there. And no woman, though mayhap she was as swift as a deer, could have run the length of that passage to open and close that door before I entered the passage behind her. Yet did I not doubt that I had come to the proper place: for there was light beyond that stout door, light shining through the edges of the lintel and the space along the floor. And across the light a figure moved within the room from time to time, casting shadows that I could see.

Therefore I did not question how the Lady in White had come to be beyond that door. Indeed it's true that in that place no swift-ness or startlement seemed strange to me. Desire and anger burned in me like iron from the forge, and I gave no thought to matters that any sensible man might misdoubt. I went forward with the sole intent of entering the room beyond the door.

I knocked; but there was no answer. I called out as courteously as I could. Still there was no answer. Soon it became clear to me that there would be no answer. The figure casting the shadows gave no heed to my presence.

At first, I was filled by a need to shout and rage; but I mastered it. Without doubt, this door was the door of which Festil had spoken—another test. A simple enough thing in itself, after the fear and loathing of the tests I had overcome. Yet for a moment I was daunted; I was unsure of my reply to this test.

My unsureness came from my belief that I knew what Festil's reply had been. No doubt he had announced himself here and then had simply set himself to wait, possessing his soul in patience until the figure within the room deigned to take notice of him. And in this cottage I had come to understand that Festil my brother was not unwise. Loon and dreamer though he was, he had within him a thing that met this testing better than I.

But I was Mardik the blacksmith, not Festil the dreamer; and after my meeting with the leprous woman there was no patience in me. I set down my satchel of tools and turned myself to a consideration of the door itself.

It was made of heavy timbers, ironbound and studded. Its hinges were set to open inward, and I could see through the crack along the lintel that it was held in place by a massive bolt which no strength of mine could break or bend. My first thought was to slip the blade of my saw through the crack to sever the bolt; but I did not, fearing that the figure within the room would not permit me to work unhindered. Therefore I turned to the hinges, and there I saw my way clear before me.

There were but two hinges, though they were of thick black iron; and they were secured, high and low in the door, each by but one heavy bolt through the wood. "Aye, verily, my fine Lady," I muttered to myself. "Does all your testing come to this?" For I was Mardik the ironmonger and knew beyond doubt that those two bolts could not stand against me.

In truth the iron of them was old beyond age, and they were no fair test for me. With chisel and hammer I sheared the head from the upper bolt in two blows. And in three the lower bolt failed before me.

Then using the chisel I pried the wood toward me until the door slipped from its frame. Here I had need of strength, for the timbers were heavy; but strength I had, and my chisel did not bend. And then light streamed into the passage, and the door was open.

Snatching up my satchel, I entered quickly and found myself in a large chamber like an alchemist's laboratory. Worktables stood everywhere, and on them were vials and flasks of crystal, small fires that burned without smoke, many-colored powders and medicines, and strange apparatus with a look of witchery about them. There was no source that I could discover to the light. Rather, the very air of the chamber seemed to shine.

And standing at one of the worktables across the room from me was the Lady in White.

She was as radiant as my brightest rememberings, as beautiful as the heavens. Her eyes shone starlike and fathomless, and her hair flamed in bronzen glory, and the whiteness of her robe was pure beyond bearing. At the sight of her, both my desire and my anger became as nothing for a moment, so great was the spell of wonder cast on me by her loveliness.

But she regarded me with something akin to curiosity in her gaze, and something akin to humor on her lips; and this regarding made her human to me. The hot iron in me awoke. I cast wonder aside and went toward the Lady in White to take her.

Yet I stopped again at once in astonishment. For at my approach the Lady turned to me and shrugged her shoulders; and with that simple gesture her white robe fell from her, and her bronzen hair fell from her, and her loveliness fell from her and was gone. In her place stood a tall man clad all in gray. His shoulders were stooped and his beard long; and on his grizzled hair he wore a pointed hat such as wizards wear. Curiosity and humor were there in his face; but there also were scorn and anger.

"Very well, Mardik," he said to my astonishment. "You have won your way to me. What is your desire?"

But I could not have told him my desire. There was a hand of confusion upon me, and I could not have uttered the name of my desire, even to myself. I stared at the wizard like a calf and muttered the broken pieces of thoughts until at last I found the words to say, "Where is the Lady?"

"There is no Lady," he said without hesitation.

"No Lady?" I said. "No Lady?" And then a great shame came

upon me, for I had shed blood for the sake of that Lady; and my anger broke from me in a roar. "Then what was the purpose?"

The wizard shrugged a shrug of scorn. "To disguise myself," he said. "I have work before me, and to work my work I have need betimes for things from the village. Therefore I disguise myself, so that I will not be known for what I am. I have no wish to be prevented from my work by callow fools, importuning me for spells to make their cows fruitful and incantations to make their maidens avid, enchantments to speed childbirth and fend off old age."

"Then you are a fool!" I cried, for I was full of rage. "To disguise yourself you clothe yourself in a form that draws men here to die!—a form that no man can refuse in his desire!"

"Mayhap," said the wizard. But he gave no explanation. He turned from me as if he had no more use for me—as if he had tested me in the crucible and found me to be impure, base metal. And he said, "Nothing that your heart desires exists at all."

Thus he took the measure of my worth and discarded me.

For there was no laboratory about me and no wizard before me. I stood on grass in the dell, and the air was dim with evening. The last light of the sun made the white walls of the cottage gleam strangely. All the windows of the cottage were dark, as if that place were no habitation for man or woman; and there was no smoke arising from the chimney.

And the Lady in White stood before me.

"Ah, Mardik," she said gently, "be comforted," and her voice was a music that made my heart cry out within me. "My magic is strait and perilous, but it is not unkind." Gently her arms came about my neck; and when her lips touched mine, all my desire and my anger melted, and I became helpless to meet or deny her kiss.

Then she was gone. The Lady in White was gone. The cottage was gone. Leadenfoot and my wagon were gone. The dell was gone. Even the branching which had brought me here from the old road was gone. The sun itself was gone, and I was left alone in the night and the Deep Forest.

Then I wandered the woods in misery for a time, reft and lorn. I was lost beyond all finding of my way, and there was no strength in me. My death was near at hand. I wandered among the inquiries of owls and flitted through madness like the flocking of bats and stumbled until I became an easy prey for any beast that might hunger for me. Lost there beyond help, it seemed to me that death was a good thing withal, comfortable and a relief from pain.

Yet when I sought the ground and slept for a time and thought to die, I did not die. I was roused by hands upon my shoulders; and when I looked up in the moonlight I saw blind Festil my brother bending over me.

"Mardik," he said, "my brother," and there was weeping in his voice.

"Festil," I said. "Ah, how did you find me?"

"I followed the trail of your need, my brother," said Festil. "I have traveled this way before you and know it well."

Then weeping came upon me also, and I said, "My brother, I have failed you. For the wizard asked me to name my desire, and I did not ask him to restore your sight."

"Ah, Mardik!" he said; and now I heard laughter and joy through his sorrow. "Do you truly not understand the reason for my blindness? My brother, it is a thing of choice for me and in no way ill. For I also was asked to name my desire, and to this I gave answer, 'It is my desire to gaze solely upon the Lady in White to the end of my days, adoring her beauty.' That desire was granted to me. For her image is always before me, and my eyes behold no other thing."

Then my heart wept. Ah, Festil my brother! You are a loon and a dreamer, and you are a wiser man than I. But I did not speak aloud. I arose from the ground; and mad Festil took my arm and guided me despite his blindness and brought me without mishap to the old road. There I found Leadenfoot awaiting me in patience or stupidity, my wagon with him. Together Festil and I climbed up to the wagonbench, and I released the brake and took the reins in my hands; and together we made our way out of the Deep Forest.

From that day to this, I have seen no evidence of magic and have had no need of it. I am Mardik the blacksmith, and I stand as tall as any man in the village, though it's true some muttered darkly about me for a time until I silenced them. I do what I will, and none can say me nay. For my sake they treat mad Festil with respect.

And yet I am not what I was. There is a lack in me that ale cannot quench, and work and women cannot fill. For I have failed the testing of the Lady in White in my way, and that is a failure not to be forgotten or redeemed. There was a thing that I needed, and it was not in me.

The Lady in White, I say, though I do not expect to be believed. I have thought long and painfully of all that has befallen me and have concluded that the wizard was like the demon-creature and the leprous crone—another test. By means of testing, the Lady in White sought to winnow men, seeking one worthy of her love. This I believe, though Festil gives it no answer but his smile and his joy. Well, smile, then, Festil my brother. You have won your heart's desire, though it has made you blind. But I failed the tests of the Lady; verily, I failed them all and knew it not. But this, also, I do not utter aloud.

In truth, we do not speak much of the matter. Betimes Pendit the son of Pandeler comes to our hut in the evening, and we three who have endured the ordeal of the cottage sit together in the darkness, where Festil's eyes are as good as any, and better than most. But we do not speak of what we have endured. Rather Festil spins dreams for us in the night, and we share them as best we may, loving him because he sees the thing that we do not.

Her old pot I keep in the name of remembrance, though without mending it is of little use.

There are some who say that we have been blighted, that we have become old and withered of soul before our time. But we are not blighted, Festil and I. For he has gained his heart's desire, and I—why, I am Mardik the blacksmith, wheelwright and ironmonger; and despite all my failures I have been given a gift worthy of treasuring, for I have been kissed by the Lady in White.

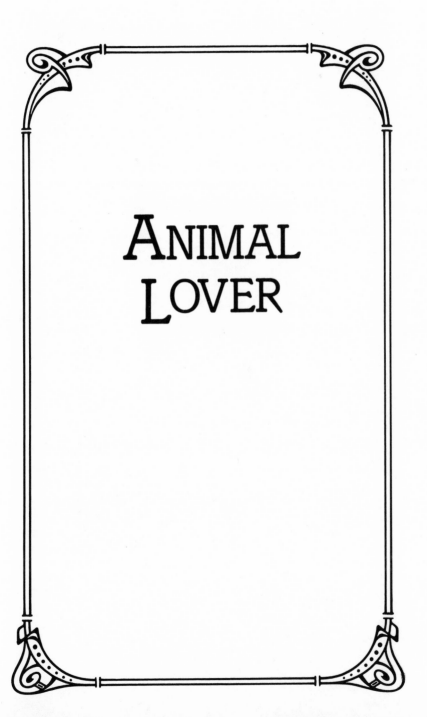

ANIMAL
LOVER

1

I WAS STANDING IN FRONT OF ELIZABETH'S CAGE WHEN the hum behind my right ear told me Inspector Morganstark wanted to see me. I was a little surprised, but I didn't show it. I was trained not to show it. I tongued one of the small switches set against my back teeth and said, "I copy. Be there in half an hour." I had to talk out loud if I wanted the receivers and tape decks back at the Bureau to hear me. The transceiver implanted in my mastoid process wasn't sensitive enough to pick up my voice if I whispered (or else the monitors would've spent a hell of a lot of time just listening to me breathe and swallow). But I was the only one in the area, so I didn't have to worry about being overheard.

After I acknowledged the Inspector's call, I stayed in front of Elizabeth's cage for a few more minutes. It wasn't that I had any objection to being called in, even though this was supposed to be my day off. And it certainly wasn't that I was having a particularly good time where I was. I don't like zoos. Not that this wasn't a nice place—for people, anyway. There were clean walks and drinking fountains, and plenty of signs describing the animals. But for the animals...

Well, take Elizabeth, for example. When I brought her in a couple months ago, she was the prettiest cougar I'd ever seen. She had those intense eyes only real hunters have, a delicate face, and her whiskers were absolutely magnificent. But now her eyes were dull, didn't seem to focus on anything. Her pacing was spongy instead of tight; sometimes she even scraped her toes because she didn't lift her feet high enough. And her whiskers had been trimmed short by the zoo keepers—probably because some great cats in zoos keep trying to push their faces between the bars, and some bastards who go to zoos like to pull whiskers, just to show how brave they are.

In that cage, Elizabeth was just another shabby animal going to waste.

That raises the questions of why I put her there in the first place. Well, what else could I do? Leave her to starve when she was a cub? Turn her over to the breeders after I found her, so she could grow up and go through the same thing that killed her mother? Raise her in my apartment until she got so big and feisty she might tear my throat out? Let her go somewhere—with her not knowing how to hunt for food, and the people in the area likely to go after her with demolition grenades?

No, the zoo was the only choice I had. I didn't like it much.

Back when I was a kid, I used to say that someday I was going to be rich enough to build a real zoo. The kind of zoo they had thirty or forty years ago, where the animals lived in what they called a "natural habitat." But by now I know I'm not going to be rich. And all those good old zoos are gone. They were turned into hunting preserves when the demand for "sport" got high enough. These days, the only animals that find their ways into zoos at all are the ones that are too broken to be hunters—or the ones that are just naturally harmless. With exceptions like Elizabeth every once in a while.

I suppose the reason I didn't leave right away was the same reason I visited Elizabeth in the first place—and Emily and John, too. I was hoping she'd give some sign that she recognized me. Fat chance. She was a cougar—she wasn't sentimental enough to be grateful. Anyway, zoos aren't exactly conducive to sentimentality in animals of prey. Even Emily, the coyote, had finally forgotten me. (And John, the bald eagle, was too stupid for sentiment. He looked like he'd already forgotten everything he'd ever known.) No, I was the only sentimental one of the bunch. It made me late getting to the Bureau.

But I wasn't thinking about that when I arrived. I was thinking about my work. A trip to the zoo always makes me notice certain things about the duty room where all the Special Agents and Inspectors in our Division have their desks. Here we were in the year 2011—men had walked on Mars, microwave stations were being built to transmit solar power, marijuana and car racing were so important they were subsidized by the government—but the rooms where men and women like me did their paperwork still looked like the squadrooms I'd seen in old movies when I was a kid.

There were no windows. The dust and butts in the corners were so old they were starting to fossilize. The desks (all of them littered with paper that seemed to have fallen from the ceiling) were so close together we could smell each other working, sweating because we were tired of doing reports, or because we were sick of the fact that we never seemed to make a dent in the crime rate, or because we were afraid. Or because we were different. It was like one big cage. Even the ID clipped to the lapel of my jacket, identifying me as *Special Agent Sam Browne*, looked more like a zoo label than anything else.

I hadn't worked there long, as years go, but already I was glad every time Inspector Morganstark sent me out in the field. About the only difference the past forty years had made in the atmosphere of the Bureau was that everything was grimmer now. Special Agents didn't work on trivial crimes like prostitution, gambling, missing persons, because they were too busy with kidnapping, terrorism, murder, gang warfare. And they worked alone, because there weren't enough of us to go around.

The real changes were hidden. The room next door was even bigger than this one, and it was full to the ceiling with computer banks and programers. And in the room next to that were the transmitters and tape decks that monitored Agents in the field. Because the Special Agents had been altered, too.

But philosophy (or physiology, depending on the point of view) is like sentiment, and I was already late. Before I had even reached my desk, the Inspector spotted me from across the room and shouted, "Browne!" He didn't sound in any mood to be kept waiting, so I just ignored all the new paper on my desk and went into his office.

I closed the door and stood waiting for him to decide whether he wanted to chew me out or not. Not that I had any particular objection to being chewed out. I liked Inspector Morganstark, even when he was mad at me. He was a sawed-off man with a receding hairline, and during his years in the Bureau his eyes had turned bleak and tired. He always looked harassed—and probably he was. He was the only Inspector in the Division who was sometimes human enough, or stubborn enough, anyway, to ignore the computers. He played his hunches sometimes, and sometimes his hunches got him in trouble. I liked him for that. It was worth being roasted once in a while to work for him.

He was sitting with his elbows on his desk, clutching a file with both hands as if it was trying to get away from him. It was a pretty thin file, by Bureau standards—it's hard to shut computers off once they get started. He didn't look up at me, which is usually a bad sign; but his expression wasn't angry. It was "something-about-this-isn't-right-and-I-don't-like-it." All of a sudden, I wanted that case. So I took a chance and sat down in front of his desk. Trying to show off my self-confidence—of which I didn't have a hell of a lot. After two years as a Special Agent, I was still the rookie under Inspector Morganstark. So far he'd never given me anything to do that wasn't basically routine.

After a minute, he put down the file and looked at me. His eyes weren't angry, either. They were worried. He clamped his hands behind his head and leaned back in his chair. Then he said, "You were at the zoo?"

That was another reason I liked him. He took my pets seriously. Made me feel less like a piece of equipment. "Yes," I said. For the sake of looking competent, I didn't smile.

"How many have you got there now?"

"Three. I took Elizabeth in a couple months ago."

"How's she doing?"

I shrugged. "Fair. It never takes them very long to lose spirit— once they're caged up."

His eyes studied me a minute longer. Then he said, "That's why I want you for this assignment. You know about animals. You know about hunting. You won't jump to the wrong conclusions."

Well, I was no hunter but I knew what he meant. I was familiar with hunting preserves. That was where I got John and Emily and Elizabeth. Sort of a hobby. Whenever I get a chance (like when I'm on leave), I go to preserves. I pay my way in like anybody else— take my chances like anybody else. But I don't have any guns, and I'm not trying to kill anything. I'm hunting for cubs like Elizabeth— young that are left to die when their mothers are shot or trapped. When I find them, I smuggle them out of the preserves, and raise them myself as long as I can, and then give them to the zoo.

Sometimes I don't find them in time. And sometimes when I find them they've already been crippled by careless shots or traps. Them I kill. Like I say, I'm sentimental.

But I didn't know what the Inspector meant about jumping to the wrong conclusions. I put a question on my face and waited, until he said, "Ever hear of the Sharon's Point Hunting Preserve?"

"No. But there are a lot of preserves. Next to car racing, hunting preserves are the most popular—"

He cut me off. He sat forward and poked the file accusingly with one finger. "People get killed there."

I didn't say anything to that. People get killed at all hunting preserves. That's what they're for. Since crime became the top-priority problem in this country about twenty years ago, the government has spent a lot of money on it. A *lot* of money. On "law enforcement" and prisons, of course. On drugs like marijuana that pacify people. But also on every conceivable way of giving people some kind of noncriminal outlet for their hostility.

Racing, for instance. With government subsidies, there isn't a man or woman in the country so poor they can't afford to get in a hot car and slam it around a track. The important thing, according to the social scientists, is to give people a chance to do something violent at the risk of their lives. Both violence and risk have to be real for catharsis to take place. With all the population and economic pressure people are under, they have to have some way to let off steam. Keep them from becoming criminals out of simple boredom and frustration and perversity.

So we have hunting preserves. Wilderness areas are sealed off and stocked with all manner of dangerous beasts and then hunters are turned loose in them—alone, of course—to kill everything they can while trying to stay alive. Everyone who has a yen to see the warm blood run can take a rifle and go pit himself, or at least his firepower, against various assortments of great cats, wolves, wilde-beests, grizzly bears, whatever.

It's almost as popular as racing. People like the illusion of "kill or be killed." They slaughter animals as fast as the breeders can supply them. (Some people use poisoned darts and dumdum bullets. Some people even try to sneak lasers into the preserves, but that is strictly not allowed. Private citizens are strictly not allowed to have lasers at all.) It's all very therapeutic. And it's all very messy. Slow deaths and crippling outnumber clean kills twenty to one, and not enough hunters get killed to suit me. But I suppose it's better than war. At least we aren't trying to do the same thing to the Chinese.

The Inspector said, "You're thinking, 'Hooray for the lions and tigers.'"

I shrugged again. "Sharon's Point must be popular."

"I wouldn't know," he said acidly. "They don't get Federal money, so they don't have to file preserve-use figures. All I get is death certificates." This time, he touched the file with his fingertips as if it were delicate or dangerous. "Since Sharon's Point opened, twenty months ago, forty-five people have been killed."

Involuntarily, I said, "Sonofabitch!" Which probably didn't make me sound a whole lot more competent. But I was surprised. Forty-five! I knew of perserves that hadn't lost forty-five people in five years. Most hunters don't like to be in all *that* much danger.

"It's getting worse, too," Inspector Morganstark went on. "Ten in the first ten months. Fifteen in the next five. Twenty in the last five."

"They're very popular," I muttered.

"Which is strange," he said, "since they don't advertise."

"You mean they rely on word-of-mouth?" That implied several things, but the first one that occurred to me was, "What have they got that's so special?"

"You mean besides forty-five dead?" the Inspector growled. "They get more complaints than any other preserve in the country." That didn't seem to make sense, but he explained it. "Complaints from the families. They don't get the bodies back."

Well, that was special—sort of. I'd never heard of a preserve that didn't send the bodies to the next of kin. "What happens to them?"

"Cremated. At Sharon's Point. The complaints say that spouses have to sign a release before the hunters can go there. A custom some of the spouses don't like. But what they really don't like is that their husbands or wives are cremated right away. The spouses don't even get to see the bodies. All they get is notification and a death certificate." He looked at me sharply. "This is not against the law. All the releases were signed in advance."

I thought for a minute, then said something noncommittal. "What kind of hunters were they?"

The Inspector frowned bleakly. "The best. Most of them shouldn't be dead." He took a readout from the file and tossed it across the desk at me. "Take a look."

The readout was a computer summary of the forty-five dead. All were wealthy, but only 26.67% had acquired their money themselves. 73.33% had inherited it or married it. 82.2% had bright financial futures. 91.1% were experienced hunters, and of those 65.9% had reputations of being exceptionally skilled. 84.4% had traveled extensively around the world in search of "game"—the more dangerous the better.

"Maybe the animals are experienced too," I said.

The Inspector didn't laugh. I went on reading.

At the bottom of the sheet was an interesting piece of information: 75.56% of the people on this list had known at least five other people on the list; 0.00% had known none of the others.

I handed the readout back to Inspector Morganstark. "Word-of-mouth for sure. It's like a club." Something important was going on at the Sharon's Point Hunting Preserve, and I wanted to know what it was. Trying to sound casual, I asked, "What does the computer recommend?"

He looked at the ceiling. "It says to forget the whole thing. That damn machine can't even understand why I bother to ask it questions about this. No law broken. Death rate irrelevant. I asked for a secondary recommendation, and it suggested I talk to some other computer."

I watched him carefully. "But you're not going to forget it."

He threw up his hands. "Me forget it? Do I look like a man who has that much common sense? You know perfectly well I'm not going to forget it."

"Why not?"

It seemed like a reasonable question to me, but the Inspector waved it aside. "In fact," he went on in a steadier tone, "I'm assigning it to you. I want you out there tomorrow."

I started to say something, but he stopped me. He was looking straight at me, and I knew he was going to tell me something that was important to him. "I'm giving it to you," he said, "because I'm worried about you. Not because you're a rookie and this case is trivial. It is not trivial. I can feel it—right here." He put his hand over the bulge of his skull behind his right ear, as if his hunches came from the transceiver in his mastoid process. Then he sighed. "That's part of it, I suppose. I know you won't go off the deep end on this, if I'm wrong. Just because people are getting killed, you won't go all righteous on me and try to get Sharon's Point shut down. You won't make up charges against them just because their death rate is too high. You'll be cheering for the animals.

"But on top of that," he went on so I didn't have a chance to interrupt, "I want you to do this because I think you need it. I don't have to tell you you're not comfortable being a Special Agent. You're not comfortable with all that fancy equipment we put in you. All the adjustment tests indicate a deep-seated reluctance to accept yourself. You need a case that'll let you find out what you can do."

"Inspector," I said carefully, "I'm a big boy now. I'm here of my own free will. You're not sending me out on this just because you want me to adjust. Why don't you tell me why you've decided to ignore the computer?"

He was watching me like I'd just suggested some kind of un-natural act. But I knew that look. It meant he was angry about something, and he was about to admit it to both of us for the first time. Abruptly, he picked up the file and shoved it at me in disgust. "The last person on that list of dead is Nick Kolcsz. He was a Special Agent."

A Special Agent. That told me something, but not enough. I didn't know Kolcsz. He must have had money, but I wanted more than that. I gave the Inspector's temper another nudge. "What was he doing there?"

He jumped to his feet to make shouting easier. "How the hell should I know?" Like all good men in the Bureau, he took the death of an Agent personally. "He was on leave! His goddamn transceiver was off!" Then with a jerk he sat down again. After a minute, all his anger was gone and he was just tired. "I presume he went there for the hunting, just like the rest of them. You know as well as I do we don't monitor Agents on leave. Even Agents need privacy once in a while. We didn't even know he was dead until his wife filed a complaint because they didn't let her see his body.

"Never mind the security leak—all that metal in his ashes. What

scares me"—now there was something like fear in his bleak eyes—
"is that we hadn't turned off his power pack. We never do that—
not just for a leave. He should have been safe. Wild elephants
shouldn't have been able to hurt him."

I knew what he meant. Nick Kolcsz was a cyborg. Like me.
Whatever killed him was more dangerous than that.

2

Well, yes—a cyborg. But it isn't everything it's cracked up to
be. People these days make the mistake of thinking Special Agents
are "super" somehow. This comes from the old movies, where
cyborgs were always super-fast and super-strong. They were loaded
with weaponry. They had built-in computers to do things like think
for them. They were slightly more human than robots.

Maybe someday. Right now no one has the technology for that
kind of thing. I mean the medical technology. For lots of reasons,
medicine hasn't made much progress in the last twenty years. What
with all the population trouble we have, the science of "saving
lives" doesn't seem as valuable as it used to. And then there were
the genetic riots of 1989, which ended up shutting down whole
research centers.

No, what I have in the way of equipment is a transceiver in the
mastoid process behind my right ear, so that I'm always in contact
with the Bureau; thin, practically weightless plastene struts along
my legs and arms and spine, so I'm pretty hard to cripple (in theory,
anyway); and a nuclear power pack implanted in my chest so its
shielding protects my heart as well. The power pack runs my transceiver. It also runs the hypersonic blaster built into the palm of my
left hand.

This has its disadvantages. I can hardly flex the first knuckles
of that hand, so the hand itself doesn't have a whole lot it can do.
And the blaster is covered by a latex membrane (looks just like
skin) that burns away every time I use it, so I always have to carry
replacements. But there are advantages, too—sort of. I can kill
people at twenty-five meters, and stun them at fifty. I can tear holes
in concrete walls, if I can get close enough.

That was what the Inspector was talking about when he said I hadn't adjusted. I can't get used to the fact that I can kill my friends just by pushing my tongue against one of my back teeth in a certain way. So I tend not to have very many friends.

Anyway, being a cyborg wasn't much comfort on this assignment. That was all I had going for me—exactly the same equipment that hadn't saved Nick Kolcsz. And he'd had something I didn't have—something that also hadn't saved him. He'd known what he was getting into. He'd been an experienced hunter, and he'd known three other people on that list of dead. (He must've known some of the survivors, too. Or known of them through friends. How else could he have known the place was dangerous?) Maybe that was why he went to Sharon's Point—to do some private research to find out what happened to those dead hunters.

Unfortunately, that didn't give me the option of going to one of his friends and asking what Kolcsz had known. The people who benefit (if that's the right word) from an exclusive arrangement don't have much reason to trust outsiders (like me). And they certainly weren't going to reveal knowing about anything illegal to a Special Agent. That would hurt themselves as well as Sharon's Point.

But I didn't like the idea of facing whatever killed Kolcsz without more data. So I started to do some digging.

I got information of a sort by checking out the Preserve's registration, but it didn't help much. Registration meant only that the Federal inspector had approved Sharon's Point's equipment. And inspection only covers two things: fencing and medical facilities.

Every hunting preserve is required to insure that its animals can't get loose, and to staff a small clinic to treat injured customers (never mind the crippled animals). The inspector verified that Sharon's Point had these things. Its perimeter (roughly 133 km.) was appropriately fenced. Its facilities included a very well equipped surgery and dispensary; and a veterinary hospital (which surprised me); *and* a cremator—supposedly for getting rid of animals too badly wounded to be treated.

Other information was slim. The preserve itself contained about 1,100 square km. of forests, swamps, hills, meadows. It was owned and run by a man named Fritz Ushre. Its staff consisted of one surgeon (a Dr. Avid Paracels) and a half dozen handlers for the animals.

But one item was conspicuously absent: the name of the breeder.

Most hunting preserves get their animals by contract with one of three or four big breeding firms. Sharon's Point's registration didn't name one. It didn't name any source for its animals at all, which made me think maybe the people who went hunting there weren't hunting animals.

People hunting people? That's as illegal as hell. But it might explain the high death rate. Mere lions and baboons (even rabid baboons in packs) don't kill forty-five hunters at an exclusive preserve in twenty months. I was beginning to understand why the Inspector was willing to defy the computer on this assignment.

I went to the programers and got a readout on the death certificates. All had been signed by "Avid Paracels, M.D." All specified "normal" hunting-preserve causes of death (the usual combinations of injury and exposure, in addition to outright killing), but the type of animal involved was never identified.

That bothered me. This time I had the computers read out everything they had on Fritz Ushre and Avid Paracels.

Ushre's file was small. Things like age, marital status, blood type aside, it contained only a sketchy résumé of his past employment. Twenty years of perfectly acceptable work as an engineer in various electronics firms. Then he inherited some land. He promptly quit his job, and two years later he opened up Sharon's Point. Now (according to his bank statements) he was in the process of getting rich. That told me just about nothing. I already knew Sharon's Point was popular.

But the file on Avid Paracels, Ph.D., M.D., F.A.C.S., was something else. It was full of stuff. Apparently at one time Dr. Paracels had held a high security clearance because of some research he was doing, so the Bureau had studied him down to his toenails. That produced reams of data, most of it pointless, but it didn't take me long to find the real goodies. After which (as my mother used to say) I could've been knocked over with a shovel. Avid Paracels was one of the victims of the genetic riots of 1989.

This is basically what happened. In 1989 one of the newspapers broke the story that a team of biologists (including the distinguished Avid Paracels) working under a massive Federal grant had achieved a major breakthrough in what they called "recombinant DNA research"—"genetic engineering," to ignorant sods like me. They'd mastered the techniques of raising animals with altered genes. Now they were beginning to experiment with human embryos. Their goal, according to the newspaper, was to attempt "minor improvements" in the human being—"cat" eyes, for instance, or prehensile toes.

So what happened? Riots is what happened. Which in itself wasn't unusual. By 1989, crime and whatnot, social unrest of all kinds, had already become the biggest single threat to the country, but the government still hadn't faced up to the problem. So riots and other types of violence used to start up for any reason at all: higher fuel prices, higher food costs, higher rents. In other words (according to the social scientists), the level of general public aggression had reached crisis proportions. Nobody had any acceptable outlets for anger, so whenever poeple were able to identify a grievance they went bananas.

That newspaper article triggered the great granddaddy of all riots. There was a lot of screaming about "the sanctity of human life," but I suppose the main thing was that the idea of a "superior human being" was pretty threatening to most people. So scientists and Congressmen were attacked in the streets. Three government buildings were wrecked (including a post office—God knows why). Seven apartment complexes were wrecked. One hundred thirty-seven stores were looted and wrecked. The recombinant DNA research program was wrecked. And a handful of careers went down the drain. Because this riot was too big to be put down. The cops (Special Agents) would have had to kill too many people. So the President himself set about appeasing the rioters—which led, naturally enough, to our present policy of trying to appease violence itself.

Avid Paracels was one of the men who went down the drain. I guess he was lucky not to lose his medical license. He certainly never got the chance to do any more research.

Well, that didn't prove anything, but it sure made me curious. People who lose high positions have been known to become somewhat vague about matters of legality. So that gave me a place to start when I went to Sharon's Point. Maybe if I was lucky I could even get out of pretending to go hunting in the preserve itself.

So I was feeling like I knew what I was doing (which probably should've told me I was in trouble already) when I left the duty room to go arrange for transportation and money. But it didn't last. Along the way I got one of those hot flashes, like an inspiration or a premonition. So when I was done with Accounting I went back to the computers and asked for a readout on any unsolved crimes in the area around Sharon's Point. The answer gave my so-called self-confidence a jolt.

Sharon's Point was only 80 km. from the Procureton Arsenal, where a lot of old munitions (mostly from the '60s and '70s) were stored. Two years ago, someone had broken into Procureton (God knows how) and helped himself to a few odds and ends—like fifty M-16 rifles (along with five thousand loaded clips), a hundred .22 Magnum automatic handguns (and another five thousand clips), five hundred hand grenades, and more than five hundred antipersonnel mines of various types. Enough to supply a good-sized street mob.

Which made no sense at all. Any street mob these days—or terrorist organization, or heist gang, for that matter—that tried to use obsolete weaponry like M-16s would get cut to shreds in minutes by cops using laser cannons. And who else would want the damn stuff?

I didn't believe I was going to find any animals at Sharon's Point at all. Just hunters picking one another off.

Before I went home, I spent an hour down in the range, practicing with my blaster. Just to be sure it worked.

The next morning early I went to Supply and got myself some "rich" clothes, along with a bunch of hunting gear. Then I went to Weapons and checked out an old Winchester .30–06 carbine that looked to me like the kind of rifle a "true" (eccentric) sportsman might use—takes a degree of skill, and fires plain old lead slugs instead of hypodarts or fragmentation bullets—sort of a way of giving the "game" a chance. After that I checked the tape decks to be sure they had me on active status. Then I went to Sharon's Point.

I took the chute from D.C. to St. Louis (actually, it's an electrostatic shuttle, but it's called "the chute" because the early designs reminded some romantic of the old logging chutes in the Northwest), but after that I had to rent a car. Which was appropriate, since I was supposed to be rich. Only the rich can afford cars these days—and Special Agents on assignment (fuel prices being what they are, the only time most people see the inside of a car is at a subsidized track). But I didn't enjoy it much. Never mind that I'm not much of a driver (I haven't exactly had a lot of practice). It was raining like hades in St. Louis, and I had to drive 300 km. through the back hills of Missouri as if I was swimming. That slowed me down so much I didn't get near Sharon's Point until after dark.

I stopped for the night at the village of Sharon's Point, which was about 5 km. shy of the preserve. It was a dismal little town, too far from anywhere to have anything going for it. But it did have one motel. When I splashed my way through the rain and mud and went dripping into the lobby, I found that one motel was doing very well for itself. It was as plush as any motel I'd ever seen. And expensive. The receptionist didn't even blush when she told me the place cost a thousand dollars a night.

So it was obvious this motel didn't get its business from local people and tourists. Probably it catered to the hunters who came to and went from the preserve. *I* might've blushed if I hadn't come prepared to handle situations like this. I had a special credit card Accounting had given me. Made me look rich without saying anything about where I got my money. I checked in as if I did this kind of thing every day. The receptionist sent my stuff to my room, and I went into the bar.

Hoping there might be another hunter or two around. But except for the bartender the place was empty. So I perched myself on one of the barstools and tried to find out if the bartender liked to talk.

He did. I guess he didn't get a lot of opportunity. Probably people who didn't mind paying a thosand dollars a night for a room didn't turn up too often. Once he got started, I didn't think I would be able to stop him from telling me everything he knew.

Which wasn't a whole lot more than I already knew—about the preserve, anyway. The people who went there had money. They threw their weight around. They liked to drink—before and after hunting. But maybe half of them didn't stop by to celebrate on their way home. After a while I asked him what kind of trophies the ones that did stop by got.

"Funny thing about that," he said. "They don't bring anything back. Don't even talk about what they got. I used to do some hunting when I was a kid, and I never met a hunter who didn't like to show off what he shot. I've seen grown men act like God Almighty when they dinged a rabbit. But not here. 'Course"—he smiled— "I never went hunting in a place as pricey as Sharon's Point."

But I wasn't thinking about the money. I was thinking about forty-five bodies. That was something even rich hunters wouldn't brag about. Probably those trophies had bullet holes in them.

3

I promised myself I was going to find out about those "trophies." One way or another. It wasn't that I was feeling confident. Right then I don't think I even knew what confidence was. No, it was that confidence didn't matter any more. I couldn't afford to worry about it. This case was too serious.

When I was sure I was the only guest, I gave up the idea of getting any more information that night. There was no cure for it—I was going to have to go up to the preserve and bluff my way along until I got the answers I needed. Not a comforting thought. When I went to bed, I spent a long time listening to the rain before I fell asleep.

In the morning it was still raining, but that didn't seem like a good enough reason to postpone what I had to do. So I spent a while in the bathroom, running the shower to cover the sound of my voice while I talked to the tape decks in the Bureau (via microwave relays in St. Louis, Indianapolis, Pittsburgh, and God knows where else). Then I had breakfast, and went and got soaked running through the rain out to my car.

The drive to the preserve was slow because of the rain. The road wound up and down hills between walls of dark trees that seemed to be crouching there, waiting for me, but I didn't see anything else until my car began picking its way up a long slope toward the outbuildings of Sharon's Point.

They sat below the crest of a long transverse ridge that blocked everything beyond it from sight. Right ahead of me was a large squat complex; that was probably where the offices and medical facilities were. To the right was a long building like a barracks that probably housed the animal handlers. On the left was the landing area. Three doughnut-shaped open-cockpit hovercraft stood there. (Most hunting preserves used hovercraft for jobs like inspecting the fences and looking for missing hunters.) They were covered by styrene sheets against the rain.

And behind all this, stretching along the ridge like the promise of something deadly, was the fence. It looked gray and bitter against the black clouds and the rain. The chain steel was at least five meters high, curved inward and viciously barbed along the top to keep certain kinds of animals from being able to climb out. But it didn't make me feel safe. Whatever was in there had killed forty-five people. Five meters of fence was either inadequate or irrelevant.

More for my own benefit than for Inspector Morganstark's, I said into my transceiver, "Relinquish all hope, ye who enter here." Then I drove up to the squat building, parked as close as I could get to a door marked OFFICE, and ran through the rain as if I couldn't wait to take on Sharon's Point single-handedly.

I rushed into the office, pulled the door shut behind me—and almost fell on my face. Pain as keen as steel went through my head like a drill from somewhere behind my right ear. For an instant I was blind and deaf with pain, and my knees were bending under me.

It was coming from my mastoid process.

Some kind of power feedback in my transceiver.

It felt like one of the monitors back at the Bureau was trying to kill me.

I knew that wasn't it; but right then I didn't care what it was. I tongued the switch to cut off transmission. And, shoving out one leg, caught myself with a jerk just before I fell.

It was over. The pain disappeared. Just like that.

I was woozy with relief. There was a ringing in my ears that made it hard for me to keep my balance. Seconds passed before I could focus well enough to look around. Not think—just look.

I was in a bare office, a place with no frills, not even any curtains on the windows to keep out the dankness of the rain. I was almost in reach of a long counter.

Behind the counter stood a man. He was tall and fat—not overweight-fat, but bloated-fat, as if he was stuffing himself to feed some grotesque appetite. He had the face of a boar, the cunning and malicious eyes of a boar, and he was looking at me as if he was trying to decide where to use his tusks. But his voice was suave and kind. "Are you all right?" he asked. "What happened?"

With a lurch, my brain started working again.

Power feedback. Something had caused a feedback in my transceiver. Must've been some kind of electronic jamming device. The government used jammers for security—a way of screening secret meetings. To protect against people like me.

Sharon's Point was using a security screen.

What were they trying to hide?

But that was secondary. I had a more immediate problem. The fat man had been watching me when the jammer hit. He'd seen my reaction. He would know I had a transceiver in my skull. Unless I did something about it. Fast.

He hadn't even blinked. "What happened?"

I was sweating. My hands were trembling. But I looked him straight in the eye and said, "It'll pass. I'll be all right in a minute."

Nothing could've been kinder than the way he asked, "What is the matter?"

"Just a spasm," I said straight at him. "Comes and goes. Brain tumor. Inoperable. I'll be dead in six months. That's why I'm here."

"Ah," he said without moving. "That is why you are here." His pudgy hands were folded and resting on his gut. "I understand." If he was suspicious of me, he didn't let it ruffle his composure. "I understand perfectly."

"I don't like hospitals," I said sternly, just to show him I was back in control of myself.

"Naturally not," he assented. "You have come to the right place, Mr. . . . ?"

"Browne," I said. "Sam Browne."

"Mr. Browne." He filed my name away with a nod. Gave me the uncomfortable impression he was never going to forget it. "We have what you want here." For the first time, I saw him blink. Then he said, "How did you hear of us, Mr. Browne?"

I was prepared for that. I mentioned a couple names off the Preserve's list of dead, and followed them up by saying squarely, "You must be Ushre."

He nodded again. "I am Fritz Ushre." He said it the same way he might've said, "I am the President of the United States." Nothing diffident about him.

Trying to match him, I said, "Tell me about it."

His boar eyes didn't waver, but he didn't answer me directly. Instead, he said, "Mr. Browne, we generally ask our patrons for payment in advance. Our standard fee is for a week's hunting. Forty thousand dollars."

I certainly did admire his composure. He was better at it than I was. I felt my face react before I could stop it. Forty—! Well, so much for acting like I was rich. It was all I could do to keep from cursing myself out loud.

"We run a costly operation," he said. He was as smooth as stainless steel. "Our facilities are the best. And we breed our own animals. That way, we are able to maintain the quality of what we offer. But for that reason we are required to have veterinary as well as medical facilities. Since we receive no Federal money—and submit to no Federal inspections"—he couldn't have sounded less like he was threatening me—"we cannot afford to be wasteful."

He might've gone on—not apologizing, just tactfully getting rid of me—but I cut him off. "Better be worth it," I said with all the toughness I could manage. "I didn't get where I am throwing my money away." At the same time, I took out my credit card and set it down with a snap on the counter.

"Your satisfaction is guaranteed." Ushre inspected my card briefly, then asked, "Will one week suffice, Mr. Browne?"

"For a start."

"I understand," he said as if he understood me completely. Then he turned away for a minute while he ran my card through his accounting computer. The ac-computer verified my credit due and printed out a receipt that Ushre presented to me for validation. After I'd pressed my thumbprint onto the identiplate, he returned my card and filed the receipt in the ac-computer.

In the meantime, I did some glancing around, trying nonchalantly (I hoped I looked nonchalant) to spot the jammer. But I didn't find it. In fact, as an investigator I was getting nowhere fast. If I didn't start finding things out soon, I was going to have real trouble explaining that forty-thousand-dollar bill to Accounting. Not to mention staying alive.

So when Ushre turned back to me, I said, "I don't want to start in the rain. I'll come back tomorrow. But while I'm here I want to look at your facilities." It wasn't much, but it was the best I could do without giving away that I really didn't know those two dead men I'd mentioned. I was supposed to know what I was doing; I couldn't very well just ask him right out what kind of animals he had. Or didn't have.

Ushre put a sheaf of papers down on the counter in front of me, and said again, "I understand." The way he said things like that was beginning to make my scalp itch. "Once you have completed these forms, I will ask Dr. Paracels to show you around."

I said, "Fine," and started to fill out the forms. I didn't worry too much about what I was signing. Except for the one that had to do with cremating my body, they were pretty much standard releases—so that Sharon's Point wouldn't be liable for anything that might happen to me. The disposal-of-the-body form I read more carefully than the others, but it didn't tell me anything I didn't already know. And by the time I was done, Dr. Avid Paracels had come into the office.

I studied him as Ushre introduced us. I would've been interested to meet him any time, but right then I was particularly keen. I knew more about him than I did about Ushre—which meant that for me he was the key to Sharon's Point.

He was tall and gaunt—next to Ushre he was outright emaciated. Scrawny and stooped, as if the better part of him had been chipped away by a long series of personal catastrophies. And he looked a good bit more than thirty years older than I was. His face was gray, like the face of a man with a terminal disease, and the skin stretched from his cheekbones to his jaw as if it was too small for his skull. His eyes were hidden most of the time beneath his thick, ragged eyebrows, but when I caught a glimpse of them they looked as dead as plastene. I would've thought he was a cadaver if he wasn't standing up and wearing a white coat. If he hadn't licked his lips once when he first saw me. Just the tip of his tongue circled his lips that once—not like he was hungry, but instead like he was wondering in an abstract way whether I might turn out to be tasty. Something about that little pink gesture in that gray face made me feel cold all of a sudden. For a second I felt like I knew what he was really thinking. He was wondering how he was going to be able to use me. And how I was going to die. Maybe not in that order.

"Dr. Paracels," I said. I was wondering if he or Ushre knew there was sweat running down the small of my back.

"I won't show you where we do our breeding," he said in a petulant way that surprised me, "or my animal hospital." The whine in his voice sounded almost deliberate, like he was trying to sound pathetic.

"We never show our patrons those facilities," Ushre added

smoothly. "There is an element of surprise in what we offer." He blinked again. The rareness of that movement emphasized the cunning and malice of his eyes. "We believe that it improves the sport. Most of our patrons agree."

"But you can see my clinic," Paracels added impatiently. "This way." He didn't wait for me. He turned around and went out the inner door of the office.

Ushre's eyes never left my face. "A brilliant surgeon, Dr. Paracels. We are fortunate to have him."

I shrugged. The way I was feeling right then, there didn't seem to be anything else I could do. Then I went after the good doctor.

That door opened into a wide corridor running through the complex. I caught a glimpse of Paracels going through a set of double doors at the end of the corridor, but there were other doors along the hall, and they were tempting. They might lead me to Ushre's records—and Ushre's records might tell me what I needed to know about Sharon's Point. But this was no time for taking risks. I couldn't very well tell Ushre when he caught me that I'd blundered onto his records by mistake—assuming I even found them. So I went straight to the double doors and pushed my way into the surgery.

The registration inspector was right: Sharon's Point was very well equipped. There were several examination and treatment rooms (including x-ray, oxygen, and ophthalmological equipment), a half dozen beds, a pharmacy that looked more than adequate (maybe a lot more than adequate), and an operating theater that reminded me of the place where I was made into a cyborg.

That was where I caught up with Paracels. In his whining voice (was he really that full of self-pity?), he described the main features of the place. He assumed I'd want to know how he could do effective surgery alone there, and that was what he told me.

Well, his equipment was certainly compact and flexible, but what really interested me was that he had a surgical laser. (I didn't ask him if he had a license for it. His license was hanging right there on the wall.) That wasn't common at all, especially in a small clinic like this. A surgical laser is very specialized equipment. These days they're used for things like eye surgery and lobotomies. And making cyborgs. But a while back (twenty-two years) they were used in genetic engineering.

The whole idea made my skin crawl. There was something menacing about it. As innocently as I could, I asked Paracels the nastiest question I could think of. "Do you save any lives here, Doctor?"

That was all it took to make him stop whining. All at once he was so bitter I half-expected him to begin foaming at the mouth. "What're you," he spat, "some kind of bleeding heart? The men who come here know they might get killed. I do everything for them that any doctor could do. You think I have all this stuff just for the hell of it?"

I was surprised to find I believed him. I believed he did everything he could to save every life that ended up on his operating table. He was a doctor, wasn't he? If he was killing people, he was doing it some other way.

4

Well, maybe I was being naive. I didn't know yet. But I figured I'd already learned everything Paracels and Ushre were likely to tell me of their own free will. I told them I'd be back bright and early the next morning, and then I left.

The rain was easing, so I didn't get too wet on the way back to my car, but that didn't make me feel any better. There was no doubt about it: I was outclassed. Ushre and Paracels had given away practically nothing. They'd come up with neat plausible stories to cover strange things like their vet hospital and their independence from the usual animal breeders. In fact, they'd explained away everything except their policy of cremating their dead hunters—and that was something I couldn't challenge them on without showing off my ignorance. Maybe they had even spotted me for what I was. And I'd gotten nothing out of them except a cold sweat. I had an unfamiliar itch to use my blaster; I wanted to raze that whole building, clinic and all. When I reactivated my transmitter, I felt like telling Inspector Morganstark to pull me off the case and send in someone who knew what he was doing.

But I didn't. Instead, I acted just like a good Special Agent is supposed to. I spent the drive back to town talking to the tape decks, telling them the whole story. If nothing else, I'd accomplished something by finding out Sharon's Point ran a security screen. That would tell the Inspector his hunch was right.

I didn't have any doubt his hunch was right. Something stank at that preserve. In different ways, Ushre and Paracels reminded me of maneaters. They had acquired a taste for blood. Human blood. In the back of my head a loud voice was shouting that Sharon's Point used genetically altered people for "game." No wonder Paracels looked so sick. The M.D. in him was dying of outrage.

So I didn't tell Inspector Morganstark to pull me off the case. I did what I was supposed to do. I went back to the motel and spent the afternoon acting like a rich man who was eager to go hunting. I turned in early after supper, to get plenty of rest. I asked the desk to call me at 6 A.M. With the shower running, I told the tape decks what I was going to do.

When midnight came, and the sky blew clear for the first time in two days, I climbed out a window and went back to the preserve on foot.

I wasn't exactly loaded down with equipment. I left my .30–06 and all my rich-hunter gear back at the motel. But I figured I didn't need it. After all, I was a cyborg. Besides, I had a needle flash and a small set of electromagnetic lock-picks and jimmies. I had a good sense of direction. I wasn't afraid of the dark.

And I had my personal good-luck piece. It was an old Gerber hunting knife that used to be my father's. It was balanced for throwing (which I was better at than using a rifle anyway), and its edges near the hilt were serrated, so it was good for cutting things like rope. I'd taken it with me on all my visits to hunting preserves, and once or twice it had kept me alive. It was what I used when I had to kill some poor animal crippled by a trap or a bad shot. Now I wore it hidden under my clothes at the small of my back. Made me feel a little more self-confident.

I was on my way to try to sneak a look at a few things. Like Paracels's vet hospital and breeding pens. And Ushre's records. I really didn't want to just walk into the preserve in the morning and find out what I was up against the hard way. Better to take my chances in the dark.

I reached the preserve in about an hour and hunched down in the brush beside the road to plan what I was going to do. All the lights in the barracks and office complex were out, but there was a bright pink freon bulb burning next to the landing area and the hovercraft. I was tempted to put it out, just to make myself feel safer. But I figured that would be like announcing to Sharon's Point I was there, so I left it alone.

The barracks I decided to leave alone, too. Maybe that wasn't where the handlers lived—maybe that was where Paracels kept his animals. But if it was living quarters, I was going to look pretty silly when I got caught breaking in there. Better not to take that chance.

So I concentrated on the office building. Using the shadow of the barracks for cover, I crept around until I was in back of the complex, between it and the fence. There, about where I figured the vet facilities ought to be, I found a door that suited me. I wanted to look at that clinic. No matter what Ushre said, it sounded to me like a grand place to engineer "game." I tongued off my transmitter so I wouldn't run into that jammer again and set about trying to open the door without setting off any alarms.

One of my picks opened the lock easily enough. But I didn't crack the door more than a few cm. In the light of my needle flash, the corridor beyond looked harmless enough, but I didn't trust it. I took a lock-pick and retuned it to react to magnetic-field scanners (the most common security system these days). Then I slipped it through the crack of the door. If it met a scanner field, I'd feel resistance in the air—before I tripped the alarm (in theory, anyway).

Isn't technology wonderful (said the cyborg)? My pick didn't meet any resistance. After a minute or two of deep breathing, I opened the door enough to step into the complex. Then I closed it behind me and leaned against it.

I checked the corridor with my flash, but didn't learn anything except that I had several doors to choose from. Holding the pick in front of me like some kind of magic wand, I started to move, half expecting the pick to start bucking in my hand and all hell to break loose.

But it didn't. I got to the first door and opened it. And found floor-cleaning equipment—electrostatic sweepers and whatnot. The night was cool—the building was cool—but I was sweating.

The next door was a linen closet. The next was a bathroom.

I gritted my teeth, trying to keep from talking out loud. Telling the tape decks what I was doing was already an old habit.

The next door was the one I wanted. It put me in a large room that smelled like a lab.

I shut that door behind me, too, and spent a long time just standing there, making sure I wasn't making any noise. Then I broadened the beam of my flash and spread it around the room.

Definitely a laboratory. At this end there were four large work-tables covered with equipment: burners, microscopes, glassine apparatus of all kinds—I couldn't identify half that stuff. I couldn't identify the chemicals ranked along the shelves on this wall or figure out what was in the specimen bottles on the opposite side of the room (What the hell did Paracels need all this for?) But there was one thing I could identify.

A surgical laser.

It was so fancy it made the one in the surgery look like a toy.

When I saw it, something deep down in my chest started to shiver.

And that was only half the room. The other half was something else. When I was done checking over the lab equipment, I scanned the far end, and spotted the cremator.

It was set into the wall like a giant surgical sterilizer, but I knew what it was. I'd seen cremators before. This was just the largest one I'd ever come across. It looked big enough to hold a grizzly. Which was strange, because hunting preserves didn't usually have animals that size. Too expensive to replace.

But almost immediately I saw something stranger. In front of the cremator stood a gurney that looked like a hospital cart. On it was a body, covered with a sheet. From what I could see, it looked like the body of a man.

I didn't run over to it. Instead, I forced myself to locate all the doors into the lab. There were four—two opposite each other at each end of the room. So no matter what I did I was going to have to turn my back on at least one of them.

But there was nothing I could do about that. I went to the door across from me and put my ear to it for a long minute, listening as hard as I knew how, trying to tell if anything was happening on the other side. Then I went to the other two doors and did the same thing. But all I heard was the thudding of my heart. If Sharon's Point was using sound-sensor alarms instead of field scanners, I was in big trouble.

I didn't hear anything. But still my nerves were strung as tight as a cat's as I went over to the gurney. I think I was holding my breath.

Under the sheet I found a dead man. He was naked, and I could see the bullet holes in his chest as plain as day. There were a lot of them. Too many. He looked as if he'd walked into a machine gun. But it must have happened a while ago. His skin was cold, and he was stiff, and there was no blood.

Now I understood why Ushre and Paracels needed a cremator. They couldn't very well send bodies to the next of kin looking like this.

For a minute I just stood there, thinking I was right, Sharon's Point used people instead of animals, people hunting people.

Then all the lights in the lab came on, and I almost collapsed in surprise and panic.

Avid Paracels stood in the doorway where I'd entered the lab. His hand was still on the light switch. He didn't look like he'd even been to bed. He was still wearing his white coat, as if it was the most natural thing in the world for him to be up in his lab at 1 A.M. Well, maybe it was. Somehow that kind of light made him look solider, even more dangerous.

And he wasn't surprised. Not him. He was looking right at me as if we were both keeping some kind of appointment.

For the first couple heartbeats I couldn't seem to think anything except, Well, so much for technology. They have some other kind of alarm system.

Then Paracels started talking. His thin old voice sounded almost smug. "Ushre spotted you right away," he said. "We knew you would come back tonight. You're investigating us."

For some strange reason, that statement made me feel better. My pick hadn't failed me after all. My equipment was still reliable. Maybe I was better adjusted to being a cyborg than I thought. Paracels was obviously unarmed—and I had my blaster. There was no way on God's green earth he could stop me from using it. My pulse actually began to feel like it was getting back to normal.

"So what happens now?" I asked. I was trying for bravado. Special Agents are supposed to be brave. "Are you going to kill me?"

Paracels's mood seemed to change by the second. Now he was bitter again. "I answered that question this morning," he snapped. "I'm a doctor. I don't take lives."

I shrugged, then gestured toward the gurney. "That's probably a real comfort to him." I wanted to goad the good doctor.

But he didn't seem to hear me. Already he was back to smug. "A good specimen." He smirked. "His genes should be very useful."

"He's dead," I said. "What good're dead genes?"

Paracels almost smiled. "Parts of him aren't dead yet. Did you know that? Some parts of him won't die for two more days. After that we'll burn him." The tip of his tongue came out and drew a neat line of saliva around his lips.

Probably that should've warned me. But I was concentrating on him the wrong way. I was watching him as if he was the only thing I had to worry about. I didn't hear the door open behind me at all. All I heard was one last quick step. Then something hit the back of my head and switched off the world.

5

Which just goes to show that being a cyborg isn't everything it's cracked up to be. Cyborgs are in trouble as soon as they do start adjusting to what they are. They don't rely on themselves anymore—they rely on their equipment. Then when they're in a situation where they need something besides a blaster, they don't have it.

Two years ago there wasn't a man or animal that could sneak up behind me. The hunting preserves taught me how to watch my back. The animals didn't know I was on their side, and they were hungry. I had to watch my back to stay alive. Apparently not any more. Now I was Sam Browne, Special–Agent–cyborg–hotshot. As far as I could tell, I was as good as dead.

My hands were taped behind my back, and I was lying on my face in something that used to be mud before it dried, and the sun was slowly cooking me. When I cranked my eyes open, all I could see was brush a few cm. from my nose. A long time seemed to pass before I could get up the strength to focus my eyes and lift my head. Then I saw I was lying on a dirt path that ran through a field of low bushes. Beyond the bushes were trees.

All around me there was a faint smell of blood. My blood. From the back of my head.

Which hurt like a sonofabitch. I put my face back down in the dirt. I would've done some cursing, but I didn't have the strength. I knew what had happened.

Ushre and Paracels had trussed me up and dropped me off in the middle of their preserve. Smelling like blood. They weren't going to kill me—not them. I was just going to be another one of their dead hunters.

Well, at least I was going to find out who was hunting what (or whom) around here.

Minutes passed before I mustered enough energy to find out if my legs were taped, too. They weren't. How very sporting. I wondered if it was Ushre's idea or Paracels'.

That hit on the head must've scrambled my brains (the pain was scrambling them for sure). I spent what felt like ages trying to figure out who was responsible for leaving my legs free, when I should've been pulling myself together. Getting to my feet. Trying to find some water to wash off the blood. Thinking about staying alive. More time passed before I remembered I had a transceiver in my skull. I could call for help.

Help would take time. Probably it wouldn't come fast enough to save me. But I could at least call for it. It would guarantee that Sharon's Point got shut down. Ushre and Paracels would get murder-one—mandatory death sentence. I could at least call.

My tongue felt like a sponge in my mouth, but I concentrated hard, and managed to find the transmission switch. Then I tried to talk. That took longer. I had to swallow several times to work up enough saliva to make a sound. But finally I did it. Out loud I said one of the Bureau's emergency code words.

Nothing happened.

Something was supposed to happen. That word was supposed to trigger the automatic monitors in the tape room. The monitors were supposed to put the duty room on emergency status. Instantly. Inspector Morganstark (or whoever was in charge) was supposed to come running. He was supposed to start talking to me (well, not actually talking—my equipment didn't receive voices. Only a modulated hum. But I knew how to read that hum). My transceiver was supposed to hum.

It didn't.

I waited, and it still didn't. I said my code word again, and it still didn't. I said all the code words, and it still didn't. I swore at it until I ran out of strength. Nothing.

Which told me (when I recovered enough to do more thinking) that my transceiver wasn't working. Wonderful. Maybe that hit on the head had broken it. Or maybe—

I made sure my right hand was behind my left. Then I tongued the switch that was supposed to fire my blaster.

Again nothing.

Twisting my right hand, I used those fingers to probe my left palm. My blaster was intact. The concealing membrane was still in place. The thing should've worked.

I was absolutely as good as dead.

Those bastards (probably Ushre, the electronics engineer) had found out how to turn off my power pack. They had turned me off.

That made a nasty kind of sense. Ushre and Paracels had already cremated one Special Agent. Probably that was where they had gotten their information. Kolcsz's power pack wouldn't have melted. With the thing right there in his hand, Ushre would've had an easy time making a magnetic probe to turn it off. All he had to do was experiment until he got it right.

What didn't make sense was the way I felt about it. Here I was, a disabled cyborg with his hands taped behind him, lying on his face in a hunting preserve that had already killed forty-five people— forty-six counting the man in Paracels's lab—and all of a sudden I began to feel like I knew what to do. I didn't feel turned off: I felt as if I was coming back to life. Strength began coming back into my muscles. My brain was clearing. I was getting ready to move.

I was going to make Ushre and Paracels pay for this.

Those bastards were so goddamn self-confident, they hadn't even bothered to search me. I still had my knife. It was right there—my hands were resting on it.

What did they think the Bureau was going to do when the monitors found out my transceiver was dead? Just sit there on its ass and let Sharon's Point go its merry way?

I started to move, tried to get up. Which was something I should've done a long time ago. Or maybe it wouldn't have made any difference. That didn't matter now. By the time I got to my knees, it was already too late. I was in trouble.

Big trouble.

A rabbit came out of the brush a meter down the path from me. I thought he was a rabbit—he looked like a rabbit. An ordinary long-eared jackrabbit. Male—the males are a lot bigger than the females. Then he didn't look like a rabbit. His jaws were too big; he had the kind of jaws a dog has. His front paws were too broad and strong.

What the hell?

In his jaws he held a hand grenade, carrying it by the ring of the pin.

He didn't waste any time. He put the grenade down on the path and braced his paws on it. With a jerk of his head, he pulled the pin. Then he dashed back into the bushes.

I just kneeled there and stared at the damn thing. For the longest time all I could do was stare at it and think: That's a live grenade. They got it from the Procureton Arsenal.

In the back of my head a desperate voice was screaming: Move it, you sonofabitch!

I moved. Lurched to my feet, took a step toward the grenade, kicked it away from me. It skidded down the path. I didn't wait to see how far it went. I ran about two steps into the brush and threw myself flat. Any cover was better than nothing.

I landed hard, but that didn't matter. One second after I hit the ground, the grenade went off. It made a crumping noise like a demolition ram hitting concrete. Cast-iron fragments went ripping through the brush in all directions.

None of them hit me.

But it wasn't over. There were more explosions. A line of detonations came pounding up the path from where the grenade went off. The fourth one was so close the concussion flipped me over in the brush, and dirt rained on me. There were three more before the blasting stopped.

After that, the air was as quiet as a grave.

I didn't move for a long time. I stayed where I was, trying to act like I was dead and buried. I didn't risk even a twitch until I was sure my smell was covered by all the gelignite in the air. Then I pulled up the back of my shirt and slipped out my knife.

Getting my hands free was awkward, but the serrated edges of the blade helped, and I didn't cut myself more than a little bit. When I had the tape off, I eased up onto my hands and knees. Then I spent more time just listening, listening hard, trying to remember how I used to listen two years ago, before I got in the habit of depending on equipment.

I was in luck. There was a slow breeze. It was blowing past me across the path—which meant anything upwind couldn't smell me, and anything downwind would get too much gelignite to know I was there. So I was covered—sort of.

I crawled forward to take a look at the path.

The line of shallow craters—spaced about a half dozen meters apart—told me what had happened. Antipersonnel mines. A string of them wired together buried in the path. The grenade set one of them off, and they all went up. The nearest one would have killed me if it hadn't been buried so deep. Fortunately the blast went upward instead of out to the sides.

I wiped the sweat out of my eyes and lay down where I was to do a little thinking.

A rabbit that wasn't a rabbit. A genetically altered rabbit, armed with munitions from the Procureton Arsenal.

No wonder Ushre and Paracels raised their own animals—the genes had to be altered when the animal was an embryo. No wonder they had a vet hospital. And a cremator. No wonder they kept their breeding pens secret. No wonder their rates were so high. No wonder they wanted to keep their clientele exclusive.

No wonder they wanted me dead.

All of a sudden, their confidence didn't surprise me any more.

I didn't even consider moving from where I was. I wasn't ready. I wanted more information. I was as sure as hell rabbits weren't the only animals in the Sharon's Point Hunting Preserve. I figured those explosions would bring some of the others to me.

I was right sooner than I expected. By the time I had myself reasonably well hidden in the brush, I heard the soft flop of heavy paws coming down the path. Almost at once, two dogs went trotting by. At least they should've been dogs. They were big brown boxers, and at first glance the only thing unusual about them was they carried sacks slung over their shoulders.

But they stopped at the farthest mine crater, and I got a better look. Their shoulders were too broad and square, and instead of front paws they had hands—chimp hands, except for the strong claws.

They shrugged off their sacks, nosed them open. Took out half a dozen or so mines.

Working together with all the efficiency in the world, they put new mines in the old craters. They wired the mines together and attached the wires to a flat gray box that must have been the arming switch. They hid the wires and the box in the brush along the path (fortunately on the opposite side from me—I didn't want to try to fight them off). Then they filled in the craters, packing them down until just the vaguest discoloration of the dirt gave away where the mines were. When that was done, one of them armed the mines.

A minute later, they went gamboling away through the brush. They were actually playing with each other, jumping and rolling together as they made their way toward the far line of trees.

Fifteen minutes ago they'd tried to kill me. They'd just finished setting a trap to kill someone else. Now they were playing.

Which didn't have anything to do with them, of course. They were just dogs. They had new shoulders and new hands—and probably new brains (setting mines seemed a little bit much for ordinary boxers to me)—but they were just dogs. They didn't know what they were doing.

Ushre and Paracels knew.

All of a sudden, I was tired of being cautious. I was mad, and I didn't want to do any more waiting around. My sense of direction told me those dogs were going the same way I wanted to go: toward the front gate of the preserve. When they were out of sight, I got up into a crouch. I scanned the field to make sure there was nothing around me. Then I dove over the path, somersaulted to my feet, and started to run. Covering the same ground the dogs did. They hadn't been blown up, so I figured I wouldn't be either. Everything ahead of me was upwind, so except for the noise nothing in those trees would know I was coming. I didn't make much noise.

In two minutes, I was into the trees and hiding under a rotten old log.

The air was a lot cooler in the shade, and I spent a little while just recovering from the heat of the sun and letting my eyes get used to the dimmer light. And listening. I couldn't tell much at first because I was breathing so hard, but before long I was able to get my hearing adjusted to the breeze and the woods. After that, I relaxed enough to figure out exactly what I meant to do.

I meant to get at Ushre and Paracels.

Fine. I wanted to do that. There was only one problem. First I had to stay alive.

If I wanted to stay alive, I had to have water. Wash the blood off. If I could smell me this easily, it was a sure bet every animal within fifty meters could, too.

I started hunting for a tree I could climb—a tree tall enough to give me a view out over these woods.

It took me half an hour because I was being so cautious, but finally I found what I needed. A tall straight ash. It didn't have any branches for the first six meters or so, but a tree nearby had fallen into it and stuck there, caught leaning in the lowest branches. By risking my neck, and not thinking too hard about what I was doing, I was able to shinny up that leaning trunk and climb into the ash.

With my left hand the way it was, I didn't have much of a grip, and I learned quickly enough that I wasn't going to be able to climb as high as I wanted. But just when I figured I'd gone about as far as I could go, I got lucky.

I spotted a stream. It was a couple of km. away past a meadow and another line of trees, cutting across between me and the front gate. Looked like exactly what I needed. If I could just get to it.

I didn't waste time worrying. I took a minute to fix the territory in my mind. Then I started back down the trunk.

My ears must've been improving. Before I was halfway to the ground (which I couldn't see because the leaves and branches were so thick), I heard something heading toward me through the trees.

Judging by the sound, whatever it was wasn't in any hurry, just moving across the branches in a leisurely way. But it was coming close. Too close.

I straddled a branch with my back to the trunk and braced my hands on the wood in front of me, and froze. I couldn't reach my knife that way, but I didn't want to. I couldn't picture myself doing any knife-fighting in a tree.

I barely got set in time. Three seconds later, there was a thrashing above me in the next tree over, and then a monkey landed maybe four meters away from me on the same branch.

He was a normal howler monkey—normal for Sharon's Point. Sturdy gray body, pitch-black face with deep gleaming eyes; a good bit bigger and stronger than a chimp. But he had those wide square shoulders, and hands that were too broad. He had a knapsack on his back.

And he was carrying an M-16 by the handle on top of the barrel.

He wasn't looking for me. He was just wandering. He was lonely. Howler monkeys live in packs; in his dumb instinctive way, he was probably looking for company—without knowing what he was looking for. He might've gone right on by without noticing me.

But when he hit the branch, the lurch made me move. Just a few cm.—but that was enough. It caught his attention. I should've had my eyes shut, but it was too late for that now. The howler knew I had eyes—he knew I was alive. In about five seconds he was going to know I smelled like blood.

He took the M-16 in both hands, tucked the stock into his shoulder, wrapped a finger around the trigger.

I stared back at him and didn't move a muscle.

What else could I do? I couldn't reach him—and if I could, I couldn't move fast enough to keep him from pulling the trigger. He'd cut me to pieces before I touched him. I wanted to plead with him, Don't shoot. I'm no threat to you. But he wouldn't understand. He was just a monkey. He would just shoot me.

I was so scared and angry I was afraid I was going to do something stupid. But I didn't. I just stared and didn't move.

The howler was curious. He kept his M-16 aimed at my chest, but he didn't shoot. I could detect no malice or cunning in his face. Slowly he came closer to me. He wanted to see what I was.

He was going to smell my blood soon, but I had to wait. I had to let him get close enough.

He kept coming. From four meters to three. To two. I thought I was going to scream. The muzzle of that rifle was lined up on my chest. It was all I could do to keep from looking at it, keep myself staring straight at the howler without blinking.

One meter.

Very, very slowly, I closed my eyes. See, howler. I'm no threat.

I'm not even afraid. I'm going to sleep. How can you be afraid of me?

But he was going to be afraid of me. He was going to smell my blood.

I counted two heartbeats with my eyes closed. Then I moved.

With my right foot braced on the trunk under me, I swung my left leg hard, kicked it over the top of the branch. I felt a heavy jolt through my knee as I hit the howler.

Right then, he started to fire. I heard the rapid metal stuttering of the M-16 on automatic, heard .22 slugs slashing through the leaves. But I must have knocked him off balance. In that first fraction of a second, none of the slugs got me.

Then my kick carried me off the branch. I was falling.

I went crashing down through the leaves with M-16 fire swarming after me like hornets.

Three or four meters later, a stiff limb caught me across the chest. I saw it just in time, got my arms over it and grabbed it as it hit. That stopped me with a jerk that almost tore my arms off.

I wasn't breathing any more, the impact knocked all the air out of me. But I didn't worry about it. I craned my neck, trying to see what the monkey was doing.

He was right above me on his branch, looking right at me. From there he couldn't have missed me to save his life.

But he wasn't firing. As slowly as if he had all the time in the world, he was taking the clip out of his rifle. He threw it away and reached back into his knapsack to get another one.

If I'd had a handgun or even a blaster, I could have shot him dead. He didn't even seem to know he was in danger, that it was dangerous for him to expose himself like that.

I didn't wait around for him to finish. Instead I swung my legs under the branch and let myself fall again.

This time I got lucky. For a second. My feet landed square on another branch. That steadied me, but I didn't try to stop. I took a running step down onto another branch, then jumped for another one.

That was the end of my luck. I lost my balance and fell. Probably would have broken my leg if I hadn't had those plastene struts along the bones. But I didn't have time to worry about that, either. I wasn't any more than ten meters off the ground now. There was only one branch left between me and a broken back, and it was practically out of reach.

Not quite. I got both hands on it.

But I couldn't grip with my left. The whip of my weight tore my right loose. I landed flat on my back at the base of the tree.

I didn't feel like the fall kicked the air out of me—I couldn't remember the last time I did any breathing anyway. But the impact didn't help my head much. I went blind for a while, and there was a long crashing noise in my ears, as if the only thing I was able to hear, was ever going to hear, was the sound of myself hitting the ground. I felt like I'd landed hard enough to bury myself. But I fought it. I needed air. Needed to see.

That howler probably had me lined up in his sights already.

I fought it.

Got my eyes back first. Felt like hours, but probably didn't take more than five seconds. I wanted to look up into the tree, try to locate the monkey, but something else snagged my attention.

A coughing noise.

It wasn't coming from me. I wasn't breathing at all. It was coming from somewhere off to my left.

I didn't have to turn my head much to look in that direction. It was practically no trouble at all. But right away I wished I hadn't done it.

I saw a brown bear. A big brown bear. He must've been ten meters or more away, and he was down on all fours, but he looked huge. Too huge. I couldn't fight anything like that. I couldn't even breathe.

He was staring at me. Must've seen me fall. Now he was trying to decide what to do. Probably trying to decide whether to claw my throat out or bite my face off. The only reason he hadn't done anything yet was because I wasn't moving.

But I couldn't keep that up. I absolutely couldn't help myself. I needed air. A spasm of carbon-dioxide poisoning clutched my chest, made me twitch. When I finally took a breath, I made a whooping noise I couldn't control.

Which told the bear everything he wanted to know about me. With a roar that might have made me panic if I hadn't already been more dead than alive, he reared up onto his hind legs, and I got a look at what Paracels had done to him.

He had hands instead of forepaws. Paracels certainly liked hands. They were good for handling weapons. The bear's hands were so humanlike I was sure Paracels must have got them from one of the dead hunters. They looked too small for the bear. I couldn't figure out how he was able to walk on them. But of course that wasn't too much of a problem for a bear. They were big enough for what Paracels had in mind.

Against his belly the bear had a furry pouch like a kangaroo's. As he reared up, he reached both hands into his pouch. When he brought them out again, he had an automatic in each fist. A pair of .22 Magnums.

He was going to blow my head off.

There was nothing I could do about it.

I had to do something about it. I didn't want to die. I was too mad to die.

Whatever it was I was going to do, I had about half a second to do it in. The bear hadn't cocked his automatics. It would take him half a second to pull the trigger far enough to get off his first shot—and that one wouldn't be very accurate. After that, the recoil of each shot would cock the gun for him. He'd be able to shoot faster and more accurately.

I flipped to my feet, then jumped backward, putting the tree between him and me.

I was too slow. He was firing before I reached my feet. But his first shots were wild, and after that I was moving. As I jerked backward, one of his bullets licked a shallow furrow across my chest. Then I was behind the tree. A half dozen slugs chewed into the trunk, too fast for me to count them. He had ten rounds in each gun. I was stuck until he had to reload.

Before I had time to even wonder what I was going to do, the howler opened fire.

He was above me, perched on the leaning dead tree. He must've been there when I started to move.

With all that lead flying around, he took aim at the thing that was most dangerous to him and opened up.

Damn near cut the bear in half.

Nothing bothered his aim, and his target was stationary. In three seconds he emptied an entire clip into the bear's guts.

He didn't move from where he was. He looked absolutely tame, like a monkey in a zoo. Nothing could have looked tamer than he did as he sat there taking out his spent clip, throwing it away, reaching into his knapsack for a fresh one.

That was the end of him. His blast had knocked the bear backward until the bear was sitting on the ground with his hind legs stretched out in front of him, looking as human as any animal in the world. He was bleeding to death; he'd be dead in ten seconds. But bears generally are stubborn and bloody-minded, and this one was no exception. Before he died, he raised his guns and blew the howler away.

I didn't spend any time congratulating myself for being alive. All that shooting was going to draw other animals, and I was in no shape to face them. I was bleeding from that bullet furrow, the back of my head, and a half dozen other cuts and scrapes. And the parts of me that weren't bleeding were too bruised to be much good. I turned and shambled away as quietly as I could in the direction of the stream.

I didn't get far. Reaction set in, and I had to hide myself in the best cover I could find and just be sick for a while.

Sick with anger.

I was starting to see the pattern of this preserve. These animals were nothing but cannon fodder. They were as deadly as could be—and at the same time they were so tame they didn't know how to run away. That's right: *tame*. Because of their training.

Genetic alteration wasn't enough. First the animals had to be taught how to use their strange appendages. Then they had to be taught how to use their weapons, and finally they had to be taught not to use their weapons on their trainers or on each other. That mix-up between the bear and the howler was an accident; the bear just happened to be shooting too close to the monkey. They had to be taught not to attack each other every chance they got. Paracels probably boosted their brainpower, but they still had to be taught. Otherwise they'd just butcher each other. Dogs and rabbits, bears and dogs—they don't usually leave each other alone.

With one hand, Paracels gave them guns, mines, grenades; with the other, he took away their instincts for flight, self-preservation, even feeding themselves. They were crippled worse than a cyborg with his power turned off. They were deadly—but they were still crippled. Probably Paracels or Ushre or any of the handlers could walk the preserve end to end without being in any danger.

That was why I was so mad.

Somebody had to stop those bastards.

I wanted that somebody to be me.

I knew how to do it now. I understood what was happening in this preserve. I knew how it worked; I knew how to get out of it. Sharon's Point was unnatural in more ways than one. Maybe I could take advantage of one of those ways. If I could just find what I needed.

If I was going to do it, I had to do it now. Noon was already past, and I had to find what I was looking for before evening. And before some animal hunted me down. I stank of blood.

My muscles were queasy, but I made them carry me. Sweating and trembling, I did my damnedest to sneak through the woods toward the stream without giving myself away.

It wasn't easy, but after what I'd been through, nothing could be easy. I spent a while looking for tracks—and even that was hard. After all the rain, the ground was still soft enough to hold tracks, but I had trouble getting my eyes focused enough to see them. Sweat made all my scrapes and wounds feel like they were on fire.

But the only absolutely miserable trouble I had was crossing the meadow. Never mind the danger of exposing myself out in the open. I was worried about mines. And rabbits with hand grenades. I had to stay low, pick my way with terrible care. I had to keep off bare ground, and grass that was too thin (grass with a mine under it was likely to be thin), and grass that was too thick (rabbits might be hiding there). For a while I didn't think I was ever going to make it.

After that, the outcome was out of my hands. I was attacked again. At the last second, my ears warned me: I heard something cutting across the breeze. I fell to the side—and a hawk went whizzing past where my head had been. I didn't get a very good look at it, but there was something strange about its talons. They looked a lot like fangs.

A hawk with poisoned talons?

It circled above me and poised for another dive, but I didn't wait around for it. A rabbit with a grenade probably couldn't hit a running target. And if I touched a mine, I was better off moving fast—or so I told myself. I ran like hell for the line of trees between me and the stream.

The hawk's next dive was the worst. I misjudged it. If I hadn't tripped, the bird would have had me. But the next time I was more careful. It didn't get within a meter of me.

Then I reached the trees. I stopped there, froze as well as I could and still gasp for breath. After a while the hawk went barking away in frustration.

When I got up the nerve to move again, I scanned the area for animals. Didn't spot any. But on the ground I found what looked like a set of deer tracks. I didn't even try to think about what kind of alterations Paracels might have made in a deer. I didn't want to know. They were like the few tracks I'd seen back in the woods; they came toward me from the left and went away to the right. Downstream.

That was what I wanted to know. If I was wrong, I was dead.

I didn't wait much longer—just long enough to choose where I was going to put my feet. Then I went down to the stream. There was a small pool nearby, and I slid into it until I was completely submerged.

I stayed there for the better part of an hour. Spent a while just soaking—lying in the pool with my face barely out of water—trying to get back my strength. Then with my knife I cut away my clothes wherever I was hurt. But I didn't use the cloth for bandages; I had other ideas. After my wounds had bled clean and the bleeding had stopped, I eased partway out of the water and set about covering myself with mud.

I didn't want to look like a man and smell like blood; I wanted to look and smell like mud. The mud under the banks was just right—it was thick and black, and it dried fast. When I was done, my eyes, mouth, and hands were the only parts of me that weren't caked with mud.

The solution wasn't perfect, but mud was the best camouflage I was likely to find. And it would keep me from bleeding some more, at least for a while. As soon as I felt up to it, I started to work my way downstream along the bank.

My luck held. Nothing was following my track out of the woods. Probably all that blood around the dead bear and monkey was enough to cover me, keep any other animals from recognizing the man-blood smell and nosing around after me. But other than that I was in as much trouble as ever. I wasn't exactly strong on my feet. And I was running out of time. I had to find what I was looking for before evening. Before the animals came down to the stream to drink.

Before feeding time.

I didn't know how far I had to go, or even if I was going in the right direction. And I didn't like being out in the open. So I pushed myself pretty hard until I got out of the meadow. But when the stream ran back into some woods, I had to be more careful. I suppose I should have been grateful I didn't have to make my way through a swamp, but I wasn't. I was too busy trying to watch for everything and still keep going. Half the time I had to fight myself to stay alert. And half the time I had to fight myself to move at all.

But I found what I was looking for in time. For once I was right. It was just exactly where it should have been.

In a clearing in the trees. The woods around it were thick and tall, so it would be hard to spot—except from the air. Paracels and Ushre certainly didn't want their hunters to do what I was doing. The stream ran along one edge. And the bottom had been leveled. So a hovercraft could land.

Except for the landing area, the clearing was practically crowded with feeding troughs of all kinds.

Probably there were several places like this around the preserve. Sharon's Point needed them to survive. The animals were trained not to hunt each other. But that kind of training wouldn't last very long if they got hungry. Animals can't be trained to just let them-selves starve. So Ushre and Paracels had to feed their animals. Regularly. At places like this.

Now the only question remaining was how soon the 'craft would come. It had to come—most of the troughs were empty. But if it came late—if the clearing had time to fill up before it got here— I wouldn't have a chance.

But it wasn't going to do me any good to worry about it. I worked my way around the clearing to where the woods were closest to the landing area. Then I picked a tree with bark about the same color as my mud, sat down against it, and tried to get some rest.

What I got was lucky—one last piece of luck to save my hide. Sunset was still a good quarter of an hour away when I began to hear the big fan of the 'craft whirring in the distance.

I didn't move. I wasn't all that lucky. Some animals were already in the clearing. A big whitetail buck was drinking at the stream, and a hawk was perched on one of the troughs. Out of the corner of my eye I could see two boxers (probably the same two I'd seen before) sitting and waiting, their tongues hanging out, not more than a dozen meters off to my left. Hidden where I was, I was practically invisible. But if I moved, I was finished.

At least there weren't very many of them. Yet.

I almost sighed out loud when the 'craft came skidding past the treetops. Gently it lined itself up and settled down onto the landing area.

Now time was all against me. Every animal in this sector of the preserve had heard the 'craft coming, and most of them would already be on their way to supper. But I couldn't just run down to the 'craft and ask for a ride. If the handler didn't shoot me himself, he'd take off, leaving me to the mercy of the animals. I gripped myself and didn't move.

The handler was taking his own sweet time.

As he moved around in the cockpit, I saw he was wearing a heavy gray jumpsuit. Probably all the handlers—as well as Ushre and Paracels when they worked with the animals—wore the same uniform. It provided good protection, and the animals could recognize it. Furthermore it probably had a characteristic smell the animals had been taught to associate with food and friends. So the man was pretty much safe. The animals weren't going to turn on him.

Finally he started heaving sacks and bales out onto the ground: hay and grain for the deer, chow for the dogs, fruit for the monkeys—things like that. When he was finished emptying his cockpit, he jumped out of the 'craft to put the food in the troughs.

I still waited. I waited until the dogs ran out into the clearing. I waited until the hawk snatched a piece of meat and flew away. I waited until the handler picked up a sack of grain and carried it off toward some of the troughs farthest away from the 'craft (and me).

Then I ran.

The buck saw me right away and jumped back. But the dogs didn't. The man didn't. He was looking at the buck. I was halfway to the 'craft before the dogs spotted me.

After that, it was a race. I had momentum and a headstart; the boxers had speed. They didn't even waste time barking; they just came right for me.

They were too fast. They were going to beat me.

In the last three meters, they were between me and the 'craft. The closest one sprang at me, and the other was right behind.

I ducked to the side, slipped the first dog past my shoulder. I could hear his jaws snap as he went by, but he missed.

The second dog I chopped as hard as I could across the side of the head with the edge of my left fist. The weight of my blaster gave that hand a little extra clout. I must have stunned him, because he fell and was slow getting up.

I saw that out of the corner of my eye. By the time I finished my swing, I was already sprinting toward the 'craft again. It wasn't more than three running steps away. But I could hear the first dog coming at me again. I took one of those steps, then hit the dirt.

The boxer went over and cracked into the bulging side of the 'craft.

Two seconds later, I was in the cockpit.

The handler had a late start, but once he got going, he didn't waste any time. When I landed in the cockpit, he was barely five meters away. I knew how to fly a hovercraft, and he'd made it easy for me—he'd left it idling. All I had to do was rev up the fan and tighten the wind convector until I lifted off. But he was jumping at me by the time I started to rise. He got his hands on the edge of the cockpit. Then I yanked him up into the air.

The jerk took his feet out from under him, so he was just hanging there by his hands.

Just to be sure he'd be safe, I rubbed a hand along the arm of his jumpsuit, then smelled my hand. It smelled like creosote.

I leveled off at about three meters. Before he could heave himself up into the cockpit, I banged his hands a couple times with my heavy left fist. He fell and hit the ground pretty hard.

But a second later he was on his feet and yelling at me. "Stop!" he shouted. "Come back!" He sounded desperate. "You don't know what you're doing!"

"You'll be all right," I shouted back. "You can walk out of here by tomorrow morning. Just don't step on any mines."

"No!" he cried, and for a second he sounded so terrified I almost went back for him. "You don't know Ushre! You don't know what he'll do! He's crazy!"

But I thought I had a pretty good idea what Fritz Ushre was capable of. It didn't surprise me at all to hear someone say he was crazy—even someone who worked for him. And I didn't want the handler along with me. He'd get in my way.

I left him. I gunned the 'craft up over the trees and sent it skimming in the direction of the front gate. Going to give Ushre and Paracels what I owed them.

6

But I didn't let myself think about that. I was mad enough already. I didn't want to get all livid and careless. I wanted to be calm and quick and precise. More dangerous than anything Paracels ever made—or ever even dreamed about making. Because I was doing something that was too important to have room for miscalculations.

Well, important to me, anyway. Probably nobody in the world but me (and Morganstark) gave a rusty damn what was happening at Sharon's Point—just as long as the animals didn't get loose. But that's what Special Agents are for. To care about things like this, so other people don't have to.

But I didn't have to talk myself into anything; I knew what I was going to do. The big thing I had to worry about was the lousy shape I was in. I was giddy with hunger and woozy with fatigue and queasy with pain, and I kept having bad patches where I couldn't seem to make the 'craft fly straight, or even level.

The darkness didn't improve my flying any. The sun went down right after I left the clearing, and by the time I was halfway to the front gate evening had turned into night. I suppose I should've been grateful for the cover: when I finally got to the gate, my bad flying probably wouldn't attract any attention. But I wasn't feeling grateful about much of anything right then. In the dark I had to fly by my instruments, and I wasn't doing a very good job of it. Direction I could handle (sort of), and I already had enough altitude to get me over the hills. But the little green dial that showed the artificial horizon seemed to have a life of its own; it wouldn't sit still long enough for me to get it into focus. I spent the whole trip yawing back and forth like a drunk.

But I made it. My aim wasn't too good (when I finally spotted the bright pink freon bulb at the landing area, it was way the hell off to my left), but it was good enough. I went skidding over there until I was sitting almost on top of the light, but then I took a couple minutes to scan the area before I put the 'craft down.

I suppose what I should've done was not land there at all. I should've just gone until I got some place where I could call the Bureau for help. But I figured if I did that Ushre and Paracels would get away. They'd know something was wrong when their hovercraft didn't come back, and they'd be on the run before the Bureau could do anything about it. Then the Bureau would be hunting them for days—and I'd miss out on the finish of my own assignment. I wasn't about to let that happen.

So I took a good look below me before I landed. Both the other 'craft were there (they must've had shorter feeding runs), but nobody was standing around outside—at least not where I could see them. Most of the windows of the barracks showed light, but the office complex was dark—except for the front office and the laboratory wing.

Ushre and Paracels.

If they stayed where they were, I could go in after them, get them out to the 'craft—take them into St. Louis myself. If I caught them by surprise. And didn't run into anybody else. And didn't crack up trying to fly the 300 km. to St. Louis.

I didn't even worry about it. I put the 'craft down as gently as I could and threw it into idle. Before the fan even had time to slow down, I jumped out of the cockpit and went pelting as fast as I could go toward the front office.

Yanked open the door, jumped inside, shut it behind me.

Stopped.

Fritz Ushre was standing behind the counter. He must have been doing some work with his ac- computer; he had the console in front of him. His face was white, and his little boar eyes were staring at me as if I'd just come back from the dead. He didn't even twitch— he looked paralyzed with surprise and fear.

"Fritz Ushre," I said with my own particular brand of malice, "you're under arrest for murder, attempted murder, and conspiracy." Then, just because it felt good, I went on, "You have the right to remain silent. If you choose to speak, anything you say can and will be used against you in a court of law. You have the right to be represented by an attorney. If you can't afford one—"

He wasn't listening. There was a struggle going on in his face that didn't have anything to do with what I was saying. For once, he looked too surprised to be cunning, too beaten to be malicious. He was trying to fight it, but he wasn't getting anywhere. He was trying to find a way out, a way to get rid of me, save himself, and there wasn't any. Sharon's Point was dead, and he knew it.

Or maybe it wasn't. Maybe there was a way out. All of a sudden the struggle was over. He met my eyes, and the expression on his face was more naked and terrible than anything he'd ever let me see before. It was hunger. And glee.

He looked down. Reached for something under the counter.

I was already moving, throwing myself at him. I got my hands on the edge of the counter, vaulted over it, hit him square in the chest with both heels.

He smacked against the wall behind him, bounced back, stumbled to his knees. I fell beside him. But I was up before he could move. In almost the same movement, I got my knife out and pressed the point against the side of his fat neck. "If you make a sound," I said, panting, "I'll bleed you right here."

He didn't act like he heard me. He was coughing for air. And laughing.

Quickly, I looked around behind the counter to find what he'd been reaching for.

For a second I couldn't figure it out. There was an M-16 lying on a shelf off to one side, but that wasn't it—he hadn't been reaching in that direction.

Then I saw it. A small gray box built into the counter near where he'd been standing. It wasn't much—just a big red button and a little red light. The little red light was on.

Right then, I realized I was hearing something. Something so high-pitched it was almost inaudible. Something keen and carrying.

I'd heard something like it before, but at first I couldn't remember where. Then I had it.

An animal whistle.

It was pitched almost out of the range of human hearing, but probably there wasn't an animal in 10 km. that couldn't hear it. Or didn't know what it meant.

I put my knife away and picked up the M-16. I didn't have time to be scrupulous; I cocked it and pointed it at Ushre's head. "Turn it off," I said.

He was just laughing now. Laughing softly. "You cannot turn it off. Once it has been activated, nothing can stop it."

I got out my knife again, tore the box out of the counter, cut the wires. He was right. The red light went off, but the sound didn't stop.

"What does it do?"

He was absolutely shaking with suppressed hilarity. "Guess!"

I jabbed him with the muzzle of the M-16. "What does it do?"

He didn't stop shaking. But he turned to look at me. His eyes were bright and wild and mad. "You will not shoot me." He almost giggled. "You are not the type."

Well, he was right about that, too. I wasn't even thinking about killing him. I wanted information. I made a huge effort to sound reasonable. "Tell me anyway. I can't stop it, so why not?"

"Ah," he sighed. He liked that idea. "May I stand?"

I let him get to his feet.

"Much better," he said. "Thank you, Mr. Browne."

After that, I don't think I could've stopped him from telling me. He enjoyed it too much. He was manic with glee. Some sharp appetite maybe he didn't even know he had was about to get fed.

"Dr. Paracels may be old and unbalanced," he said, "but he is brilliant in his way. And he has a taste for revenge. He has developed his genetic techniques to the point of precise control.

"As you may know, Mr. Browne, all animals may be conditioned to perform certain actions upon certain signals—even human animals. The more complex the brain of the animal, the more complex the actions which may be conditioned into it—but also the more complex and difficult the conditioning process. For human animals, the difficulty of the process is often prohibitive."

He relished what he was saying so much he was practically slobbering. I wanted to scream with frustration, but I forced the impulse down. I had to hear what he was saying, needed to hear it all.

"Dr. Paracels—bless his retributive old heart—has learned how to increase animal brain capacity enough to make possible a very gratifying level of conditioning without increasing it enough to make conditioning unduly difficult. That provides the basis for the way in which we train our animals. But it serves one other purpose also.

"Each of our animals has been keyed to that sound." He gestured happily at the air. "They have been conditioned to re-spond to that sound in a certain way. With violence, Mr. Browne!" He was bubbling over with laughter. "But not against each other. Oh no—that would never do. They have been conditioned to attack humans, Mr. Browne—to come to the source of the sound and then attack.

"Even our handlers are not immune. This conditioning overrides all other training. Only Dr. Paracels and myself are safe. All our animals have been imprinted with our voices, so that even in their most violent frenzies they will recognize us. And obey us, Mr. Browne. Obey us!"

I was shaking as bad as he was, but for different reasons. "So what?" I demanded. "They can't get past the fence."

"Past the fence?" Ushre was ecastatic. "You fool! The gate is open! It opened automatically when I pressed the button."

So finally I knew what that handler back in the preserve had been so scared about. Ushre was letting the animals out. Out to terrorize the countryside until God knows how many people were killed trying to hunt them down. Or just trying to get away from them. Or even just sitting at home minding their own business.

I had to stop those animals.

With just an M-16? Fat chance!

But I had to try. I was a Special Agent, wasn't I? This was my job. I'd signed up for it of my own free will.

I rammed the muzzle of the M-16 hard into Ushre's stomach. He doubled over. I grabbed his collar and yanked his head up again.

"Listen to me," I said very softly. "I didn't used to be the type to shoot people in cold blood, but I am now. I'm mad enough to do it now. Get moving."

I made him believe me. When I gave him a shove, he went where I wanted him to go. Toward the front door.

He opened it, and we went out together into the night.

I could see the front gates clearly in the light from the landing area. He was absolutely right. They were open.

I was already too late to close them. A dark crowd of animals was already coming out of the preserve. They bristled with weapons. They didn't hurry, didn't make any noise, didn't get in each other's way. And more came over the ridge every second, moving like they were on their way out of Fritz Ushre's private hell. In the darkness they looked practically numberless. For one dizzy second I couldn't believe Ushre and Paracels had had time to engineer so many helpless creatures individually. But of course they'd been working at it for years. Sharon's Point must have been almost completely stocked when they opened for business. And since then they'd had twenty months to alter and raise even more animals.

I had to move fast. I had one gamble left, and if it didn't work I was just going to be the first on a long list of people who were going to die.

I gave Ushre a shove that sent him stumbling forward.

Out in front of that surging crowd. Between them and the road.

Before he could try to get away, I caught up with him, grabbed his elbow, jabbed the M-16 into his ribs. "Now, Mr. Ushre," I said through my teeth. "You're going to tell them to go back. Back through the gates. They'll obey you." When he didn't respond, I gouged him viciously. "Tell them!"

Well, it was a good idea. Worth a try. It might even have worked—if I could've controlled Ushre. But he was out of control. He was crazy for blood now, completely bananas.

"Tell them to go back?" he cried with a laugh. "Are you joking?" There was blood in his voice—blood and power. "These beasts are mine! Mine! My will commands them! They will rain bloodshed upon the country! They will destroy you, and all people like you. I will teach you what hunting truly means, Mr. Browne!" He made my name sound like a deadly insult. "I will teach you to understand death!"

"You'll go first!" I shouted, trying to cut through his madness. "I'll blow you to pieces where you stand."

"You will not!"

He was faster than I expected. Much faster. With one quick swing of his massive arm, he smacked me to the ground.

"Kill him!" he howled at the animals. He was waving his fists as if he was conducting an orchestra of butchery. "Kill them all!"

A monkey near the front of the crowd fired, and all of a sudden Ushre's hell erupted.

All the animals that had clear space in front of them started shooting at once. M-16 and .22 Magnum fire shattered the air; bullets screamed wildly in all directions. The night was full of thunder and death. I couldn't understand why I wasn't being hit.

Then I saw why.

Two thin beams of ruby-red light were slashing back and forth across the front of that dark surge of animals. The animals weren't shooting at me. They were firing back at those beams.

Laser cannon!

I spotted one of them in the woods off to one side of the landing area. The other was blazing away from a window of the barracks.

They were cutting the animals to shreds. Flesh and blood can't stand up against laser cannon, no matter what kind of genes it has. Monkeys and bears were throwing sheets of lead back at the beams, but they were in each other's way, and most of their shooting was wild. And the people operating the cannon were shielded. It was just slaughter, that's all.

Because the animals couldn't run away. They didn't know how. They were conditioned. They reminded me of a tame dog that can't even try to avoid an angry master. But instead of cringing they were shooting.

The outcome wasn't any kind of sure thing. The animals were getting cut down by the dozens—but all they needed was a few hand grenades, or maybe a couple mines in the right places, and that would be the end of the cannon. And the dogs, for one, didn't have to be told what to do. Already they were trying to get through the fire with mines in their jaws. The lasers had to draw in their aim to get the dogs, and that gave the other animals time to spread out, get out of direct range of the lasers.

It was going to be a long, bloody battle. And I was lying in the dirt right in the middle of it. I didn't know how I was going to live through it.

I don't know how Ushre lasted even that long. He was on his

feet, wasn't even trying to avoid getting hit. But nothing touched him. There must've been a charm of madness on his life. Roaring and laughing, he was on his way to the hovercraft. A minute later he climbed into the one I had so conveniently left idling.

I wanted to run after him, but I didn't get the chance. Before I could move, a rabbit went scrambling past and practically hit me in the face with a live grenade.

I didn't stop to think about it. I didn't have time to ask myself what I was doing. I didn't want to ask. All those dogs and deer and rabbits and God knows what else were getting butchered, and I'd already gone more than a little bit crazy myself.

I picked up the grenade and threw it. Watched it land beside Ushre in the cockpit of the craft.

Blow him apart.

The 'craft would've gone up in flames if it hadn't been built around a power pack like the one that wasn't doing me any good.

I just turned my back on it.

The next minute, a man came running out of the barracks. He dodged frantically toward me, firing his blaster in front of him as he ran. Then he landed on his stomach beside me.

Morganstark.

"You all right?" he panted. He had to stop blasting to talk, but he started up again right away.

"Yes!" I shouted to make myself heard. "Where did you come from?"

"Your transceiver went off!" he shouted back. "Did you think I was going to just sit on my hands and wait for your death certificate?" He fired a couple bursts, then added, "We've got the handlers tied up in the barracks, but there's one missing. Who was that you just blew up?"

I didn't tell him. I didn't have time. I didn't want Paracels to get away.

What I wanted was to tell Morganstark to stop the killing. I was going wild, seeing all those animals die. But I didn't say anything about it. What choice did Morganstark have? Let Paracels' fine creations go and wreak havoc around the countryside? No, I was going to have to live with all this blood. It was my doing as much as anybody else's. If I'd done my job right, Ushre would never have gotten a chance to push that button. If I'd killed him right away.

Or if I hadn't confronted him at all. If I'd let that handler back in the preserve tell me what he was afraid of.

"Get those gates shut!" I yelled at Morganstark. "I'm going after Paracels!"

He didn't have a chance to stop me. I was already on my feet, running and dodging toward the office door.

I took the M-16 with me. I thought it was about time Dr. Avid Paracels had one of these things pointed at him.

7

I don't know how I made it. I was moving low and fast—I wasn't very easy to see, much less hit. And I had only about twenty meters to go. But the air was alive with fire. Bullets were ripping all around me. Morganstark and his men were answering with lasers and blasters. Ushre must not have been the only one with a charm on him. Five seconds later, I dove through the open doorway, and there wasn't a mark on me. Nothing new, anyway.

Inside the complex, I didn't slow down. It was a sure thing Paracels knew what was happening—he could hear the noise if nothing else. So he'd be trying to make some kind of escape. I had to stop him before he got out into the night. He was the only one left who could stop the slaughter.

But I was probably too late. He'd had plenty of time to disappear; it wouldn't take much at night in these hills. I ran like a crazy man down the corridor toward the surgery—like I wasn't exhausted and hurt and sick, and didn't even know what fear was. Slammed into the clinic, scanned it. But Paracels wasn't there. I went on, hunting for a way into the lab wing.

A couple of corridors took me in the right direction. Then I was in one of those spots where I had several doors to choose from and no way to tell which was right. Again. But now I was doing things by instinct—things I couldn't have done if I'd been thinking about them. I knew where I was in the building and had a relative idea where the lab was. I went straight to one of the doors, stopped. Touched the knob carefully.

It was unlocked.

I threw it open and stormed in.

He was there.

I'd come in through a door near the cremator. He was across the room from me, standing beside the lab tables. He didn't look like he'd even changed his clothes since last night—he didn't look like he had enough life in him to make the effort. In the bright white lights he looked like death. He should not have even been able to stand up, looking like that. But he was standing up. He was moving around. He wasn't hurrying, but he wasn't wasting any time, either. He was packing lab equipment into a big black satchel.

He glanced at me when I came in, but he didn't stop what he was doing. Taking everything he could fit in his bag.

I had the M-16 tucked under my right elbow and braced with my left hand. My index finger was on the trigger. Not the best shooting position, but I wasn't likely to miss at this range.

"They're getting butchered," I said. My voice shook, but I couldn't help it. "You're going to stop it. You're going to tell me how to shut down that goddamn whistle. Then you're going to go out there with me, and you're going to order them back into the preserve."

Paracels glanced at me again, but didn't stop what he was doing.

"You're going to do it *now*!"

He almost smiled. "Or else?" Every time I saw him he seemed to have a different voice. Now he sounded calm and confident, like a man who'd finally arrived at a victory he'd been working toward for years, and he was mocking me.

"Or else," I hissed at him, trying to make him feel my anger, "I'll drag you out there and let them shoot you themselves."

"I don't think so." I wasn't making any kind of dent in him. He surprised me when he went on. "But part of that I was going to do anyway. I don't want too many of my animals killed." He moved to the far wall, flipped something that looked like a light switch. All at once, the high-pitched pressure of the whistles burst like a bubble and was gone.

Then he really did smile—a grin that looked as if he'd learned it from Ushre. "Ushre probably told you it couldn't be shut off. And you believed him." He shook his head. "He wanted to make it that way. But I made him put a switch in here. He isn't very farsighted."

"Wasn't," I said. I don't know why. I didn't have any intention of bandying words with Dr. Avid Paracels. But something changed for me when the whistle stopped. I lost a lot of my urgency. Now the animals would stop coming, and Morganstark would be able to get the gates closed. Soon the killing would be over. All at once I realized how tired I was. I hurt everywhere.

And there was something else. Something about the good doctor didn't fit. I had a loaded M-16 aimed right at him. He didn't have any business being so sure of himself. I said, "He's dead. I killed him." Trying to shake his confidence.

It didn't work. He had something going for him I didn't know about—something made him immune to me. All he did was shrug and say, "I'm not surprised. He wasn't very stable."

He was so calm about it I wanted to start shooting at him. But I didn't. I didn't want to kill him. I wanted to make him talk. It took a real effort, but I asked him as casually as I could, "Did you know what you were getting into when you started doing business with him?"

"Did I know?" He snorted. "I counted on it. I knew I could handle him. He was perfect for me. He offered me exactly what I was looking for—a chance to do some research." For an instant there was something in his eyes that almost looked like a spark of life. "And a chance to pay a few debts."

"The genetic riots," I said. "You lost your job."

"I lost my career!" All of a sudden he was mad, furious. "I lost my whole future! My life! I was on my way to things you couldn't even imagine. Recombinant DNA was just the beginning, just the first step. By now I would have been able to synthesize genes. I would've been making supermen! Think about it. Geniuses smart enough to run the country decently for a change. Smart enough to crack the speed of light. Smart enough to create life. A whole generation of people that were immune to disease. People who could adapt to whatever changes in food or climate the future holds. Astronauts who didn't need pressure suits. I could have done it!"

"But there were riots," I said softly.

"They should have been put down. The government should have shot anybody who objected. What I was doing was too important.

"But they didn't. They blamed the riots on me. They said I violated the sanctity of life. They sent me out in disgrace. By the time they were finished, I couldn't get a legitimate research grant to save my life."

"That's why you want revenge," I said. Keep talking, Paracels. Tell me what I need to know.

"Retribution." He loved the sound of that word. "When I'm done, they're going to beg me to let them give me whatever I want."

I tried to steer him where I wanted him to go. "How're you going to accomplish that? So far all you've done is kill a few hunters. That isn't exactly going to topple the government."

"Ah"—he grinned again—"but this is just the beginning. In about two minutes, I'm going to leave here. They won't be able to find me—they won't know where I've gone. By the time they find out, I'll be ready for them."

I shook my head. "I don't understand."

"Of course you don't understand!" He was triumphant. "You spent the whole day in my preserve and you still don't understand. You aren't able to understand."

I was afraid he was going to stop then, but he didn't. He was too full of victory. "Tell me, cyborg"—the way he said *cyborg* was savage—"did you happen to notice that all the animals you saw out there are male?"

I nodded dumbly. I didn't have the vaguest idea what he was getting at.

"They're all male. Ushre wanted me to use females, too—he wanted the animals to breed. But I told him that the animals I make are sterile—that grafting new genes onto them makes them sterile. And I told him the males would be more aggressive if they didn't have mates. I knew how to handle him. He believed me.

"Ah, you're all fools! I was just planning ahead—planning for what's happening right now. The animals I make aren't sterile. In fact, they're genetically dominant. Most of them will reproduce themselves three times out of four."

He paused, playing his speech for effect. Then he said, "Right now, all the animals in my breeding pens are female. I have hundreds of them. And there's a tunnel that runs from this building to the preserve.

"I'm going to take all those females and go out into the preserve. Nobody will suspect—nobody will ever think I've done such a thing. They won't look for me there. And once the gates are shut,

I'll have time. Nobody will know what to do with my animals. Humanitarians'll want to save them—they'll probably even feed them. Scientists'll want to study them. Nobody will want to just kill them off. Even if they want to, they won't know how. Time will pass. Time for my animals to breed. To breed, cyborg! Soon I'll have an army of them. And then I'll give you revenge that'll make the genetic riots look like recreation!"

That was it, then. That was why he was so triumphant. And his scheme just might work—for a while, anyway. Probably wouldn't change the course of history, but a lot more than just forty-six hunters would get killed.

I was gripping the M-16 so hard my hands trembled. But my voice was steady. I didn't have any doubt or hesitation left to make me sound uncertain. "First you're going to have to kill me."

"I'm a doctor," he said. He was looking straight at me. "*I* won't have to kill you."

With the tip of his tongue, he made a small gesture around his lips.

He almost got me for the second time. It was just instinct that warned me—I didn't hear anything behind me, didn't know I was in any danger. But I moved. Spun where I was, whipped the M-16 around.

I couldn't have messed it up any better if I'd been practicing for weeks. My turn slapped the barrel of the M-16 into the palm of a hand as big as my face. Black hairy fingers as strong as my whole arm gripped the rifle, ripped it away from me. Another arm clubbed me across the chest so hard I almost did a flip in the air. When I hit the floor, I skidded until I whacked into the leg of the nearest table.

I climbed back to my feet, then had to catch myself on the table to keep from falling. My head was reeling like a sonofabitch—the room wouldn't stand still. For a minute I couldn't focus my eyes.

"I call him Cerberus." Paracels smirked. "He's been with me for a long time.

Cerberus. What fun. With an effort that almost split my skull, I ground my eyeballs into focus, forced myself to look at whatever it was.

"He's the last thing I created before they kicked me out. When I saw what was going to happen, I risked everything on one last experiment. I took the embryo with me and built incubators for it myself. I raised him with my own hands from the beginning."

That must've been what hit me the last time I was here. I'd been assuming it was Ushre, but it must've been this thing all along. It was too quiet and fast to have been Ushre.

Basically, it was a gorilla. It had the fangs, the black fur, the ape face, the long arms. But it wasn't like any gorilla I'd ever met before. For one thing, it was more than two meters tall.

"You see the improvements I made," Paracels went on. I didn't think he could stop. He'd gone past the point where he could've stopped. "He stands upright naturally—I adjusted his spine, his hips, his legs. His thighs and calves are longer than normal, which gives him increased speed and agility on the ground.

"But I've done much more than that." He was starting to sound like Ushre. "By altering the structure of his brain, I've improved his intelligence, reflexes, dexterity, his ability to do what I teach him to do. And he is immensely strong."

That I could see for myself. Right there in front of me, that damn ape took the M-16 in one hand and hit it against the wall. Wrecked the rifle. And took a chunk out of the concrete.

"In a sense, it's a shame we turned you off, cyborg. The contest might've proved interesting—an artificial man against an improved animal. But of course the outcome would've been the same. Cerberus is quick enough to dodge your blaster and strong enough to withstand it. He's more than an animal. You're less than a human being."

It was coming for me slowly. Its eyes looked so vicious I almost believed it was coming slowly just to make me more scared. I backed away, put a couple of tables between us. But Paracels moved too—didn't let me get closer to him. I could hardly keep from screaming, Morganstark! But Morganstark wasn't going to rescue me. I could still hear shooting. He wasn't likely to come in after me until he was finished outside and the gates were closed. He couldn't very well run the risk of letting any of those animals go free.

Paracels was watching me, enjoying himself. "That's the one thing I can't understand, cyborg." I wanted to yell at him to shut up, but he went on maliciously, "I can't understand why society tolerates, even approves of mechanical monstrosities like you, but won't bear biological improvements like Cerberus. What's so sacred about biology? Recombinant DNA research has unlimited potential. You're just a weapon. And not a very good one."

I couldn't stand it. I had to answer him somehow.

"There's just one difference," I gritted. "I chose. Nobody did this to me when I was just an embryo."

Paracels laughed.

A weapon—I had to have a weapon. I couldn't picture myself making much of an impression on that thing with just a knife. I scanned the room, hunted up and down the tables, while I backed away. But I couldn't find anything. Just lab equipment. Most of it was too heavy for me to even lift. And I couldn't do anything with all the chemicals around the lab. I didn't know anything about chemicals.

Paracels couldn't seem to stop laughing.

Goddamn it, Browne! Think!

Then I had it.

Ushre had turned off my power pack. That meant he'd built a certain kind of magnetic probe. If that probe was still around, I could turn myself back on.

Frantically, I started hunting for it.

I knew what to look for. A field generator, a small field generator, something no bigger than a fist. It didn't have to be strong, it had to be specific; it had to make exactly the right magnetic shape to key my power pack. It had to have three antenna as small as tines set close together in exactly the right pattern. I knew what that pattern looked like.

But Paracels's ape wasn't giving me time to search carefully. It wasn't coming slowly anymore. I had to concentrate to stay away from it, keep at least a couple of tables between us. Any minute now it was going to jump at me, and then I was going to be dead. Maybe the generator wasn't even here.

I reached for my knife. I was going to try to get Paracels anyway, at least take care of him before that thing finished me off.

But then I spotted it.

Lying on a table right in front of the gorilla.

"All right, Cerberus," Paracels said. "We can't wait any longer. Kill him now."

The ape threw himself across the tables at me so fast I almost didn't see it coming.

But Paracels had warned me. I was already moving. As the gorilla came over the tables, I ducked and went under them.

I jumped up past the table I wanted, grabbing at the generator. I was in too much of a hurry: I fumbled it for a second. Then I got my right hand on it. Found the switch, activated it. Now all I had to do was touch those tines to the center of my chest.

The ape crashed into me, and everything went blank. At first I thought I'd broken my spine; there was an iron bar of pain across my back just under my shoulder blades. But then my eyes cleared, and I saw the gorilla's teeth right in front of my face. It had its arms around me. It was crushing me.

My left arm was free. But my right was caught between me and the ape. I couldn't lift the generator.

I couldn't reach the ape's eyes from that angle, so I just stuck my left hand in its mouth and tried to jam it down its throat.

The ape gagged for a second, then started to bite my hand off.

I could hear the bones breaking, and there was a metallic noise that sounded like my blaster cracking.

But while it gagged, the ape eased its grip on my chest. Just a fraction, just a few millimeters. But that was all I needed. I was desperate. I dragged the generator upward between us, upward, closer to the center of my chest.

There was blood running all over the ape's jaw. I wanted to scream, but I couldn't—I had my tongue jammed against the switches in my teeth. I just dragged, dragged, with every gram of force in my body.

Then the tines touched my sternum.

The blaster was damaged. But it went off. Blew the gorilla's head to pieces.

Along with most of my hand.

Then I was lying on top of the ape. I wanted to just lie there, put my head down and sleep, but I wasn't finished. My job wasn't finished. I still had Paracels to worry about.

Somehow I got to my feet.

He was still there. He was at one of the tables, fussing with a piece of equipment. I stared at him for the longest time before I realized he was trying to do something to the surgical laser. He was trying to get it free of its mounting. So he could aim it at me.

Strange snuffling noises were coming out of his mouth. It sounded like he was crying.

I didn't care. I was past caring. I didn't have any sentimentality left. I took my knife out and threw it at him. Watched it stick itself halfway to the hilt in the side of his neck.

Then I sat down. I had to force myself to take off my belt and use it for a tourniquet on my left arm. It didn't seem to be worth the effort, but I did it anyway.

Some time later (or maybe it was right away—I don't know) Morganstark came into the lab. First he said, "We got the gates shut. That'll hold them—for a while, anyway."

Then he said, "Jesus Christ! What happened to you?"

There was movement around me. Then he said, "Well, there's one consolation, anyway." (Was he checking my tourniquet? No, he was trying to put some kind of bandage on my mangled hand.) "If you don't have a hand, they can build a laser into your forearm. Line it up between the bones—make it good and solid. You'll be as good as new. Better. They'll make you the most powerful Special Agent in the Division."

I said, "The hell they will." Probably I was going to pass out. "The hell they will."

UNWORTHY OF · THE ANGEL

"Let no man be unworthy of the Angel who stands over him."
—UNKNOWN

. . . AND STUMBLED WHEN MY FEET SEEMED TO COME DOWN on the sidewalk out of nowhere. The heat was like walking into a wall; for a moment, I couldn't find my balance. Then I bumped into somebody; that kept me from falling. But he was a tall man in an expensive suit, certain and pitiless, and as he recoiled his expression said plainly that people like me shouldn't be allowed out on the streets.

I retreated until I could brace my back against the hard glass of a display window and tried to take hold of myself. It was always like this; I was completely disoriented—a piece of cork carried down the river. Everything seemed to be melting from one place to another. Back and forth in front of me, people with bitten expressions hurried, chasing disaster. In the street, too many cars snarled and blared at each other, blaming everything except themselves. The buildings seemed to go up for miles into a sky as heavy as a lid. They looked elaborate and hollow, like crypts.

And the heat— I couldn't see the sun, but it was up there somewhere, in the first half of the morning, hidden by humidity and filth. Breathing was like inhaling hot oil. I had no idea where I was; but wherever it was, it needed rain.

Maybe I didn't belong here. I prayed for that. The people who flicked glances at me didn't want what they saw. I was wearing a gray overcoat streaked with dust, spotted and stained. Except for a pair of ratty shoes, splitting at the seams, and my clammy pants, the coat was all I had on. My face felt like I'd spent the night in a pile of trash. But if I had, I couldn't remember. Without hope, I put my hands in all my pockets, but they were empty. I didn't have a scrap of identification or money to make things easier. My only hope was that everything still seemed to be melting. Maybe it would melt into something else, and I would be saved.

But while I fought the air and the heat and prayed, Please, God, not again, the entire street sprang into focus without warning. The sensation snatched my weight off the glass, and I turned in time to see a young woman emerge from the massive building that hulked beside the storefront where I stood.

She was dressed with the plainness of somebody who didn't have any choice—the white blouse gone dingy with use, the skirt fraying at the hem. Her fine hair, which deserved better, was efficiently tied at the back of her neck. Slim and pale, too pale, blinking at the heat, she moved along the sidewalk in front of the store. Her steps were faintly unsteady, as if she were worn out by the burden she carried.

She held a handkerchief to her face like a woman who wanted to disguise the fact that she was still crying.

She made my heart clench with panic. While she passed in front of me, too absorbed in her distress to notice me or anyone else, I thought she was the reason I was here.

But after that first spasm of panic, I followed her. She seemed to leave waves of urgency on either side, and I was pulled along in her wake.

The crowd slowed me down. I didn't catch up with her until she reached the corner of the block and stopped to wait for the light to change. Some people pushed out into the street anyway; cars screamed at them until they squeezed back onto the sidewalk. Everybody was in a hurry, but not for joy. The tension and the heat daunted me. I wanted to hold back—wanted to wait until she found her way to a more private place. But she was as distinct as an appeal in front of me, a figure etched in need. And I was only afraid.

Carefully, almost timidly, I reached out and put my hand on her arm.

Startled, she turned toward me; her eyes were wide and white, flinching. For an instant, her protective hand with the handkerchief dropped from the center of her face, and I caught a glimpse of what she was hiding.

It wasn't grief. It was blood.

It was vivid and fatal, stark with implications. But I was still too confused to recognize what it meant.

As she saw what I looked like, her fright receded. Under other circumstances, her face might have been soft with pity. I could tell right away that she wasn't accustomed to being so lost in her own needs. But now they drove her, and she didn't know what to do with me.

Trying to smile through my dirty whiskers, I said as steadily as I could, "Let me help you."

But as soon as I said it, I knew I was lying. She wasn't the reason I was here.

The realization paralyzed me for a moment. If she'd brushed me off right then, there would have been nothing I could do about it. She wasn't the reason—? Then why had I felt such a shock of importance when she came out to the street? Why did her nosebleed—which really didn't look very serious—seem so fatal to me? While I fumbled with questions, she could have simply walked away from me.

But she was near the limit of her courage. She was practically frantic for any kind of assistance or comfort. But my appearance was against me. As she clutched her handkerchief to her nose again, she murmured in surprise and hopelessness, "What're you talking about?"

That was all the grace I needed. She was too vulnerable to turn her back on any offer, even from a man who looked like me. But I could see that she was so fragile now because she had been so brave for so long. And she was the kind of woman who didn't turn her back. That gave me something to go on.

"Help is the circumference of need," I said. "You wouldn't be feeling like this if there was nothing anybody could do about it. Otherwise the human race would have committed suicide two days after Adam and Eve left the Garden."

I had her attention now, but she didn't know what to make of me. She wasn't really listening to herself as she murmured, "You're wrong." She was just groping. "I mean your quote. Not help. Reason. 'Reason is the circumference of energy.' Blake said that."

I didn't know who Blake was, but that didn't matter. She'd given me permission—enough permission, anyway, to get me started. I was still holding her arm, and I didn't intend to let her go until I knew why I was here—what I had to do with her.

Looking around for inspiration, I saw we were standing in front of a coffee shop. Through its long glass window, I saw that it was nearly empty; most of its patrons had gone looking for whatever they called salvation. I turned back to the woman and gestured toward the shop. "I'll let you buy me some coffee if you'll tell me what's going on."

She was in so much trouble that she understood me. Instead of asking me to explain myself, she protested, "I can't. I've got to go to work. I'm already late."

Sometimes it didn't pay to be too careful. Bluntly, I said, "You can't do that, either. You're still bleeding."

At that, her eyes widened; she was like an animal in a trap. She hadn't thought as far ahead as work. She had come out onto the sidewalk without one idea of what she was going to do. "Reese—" she began, then stopped to explain, "My brother." She looked miserable. "He doesn't like me to come home when he's working. It's too important. I didn't even tell him I was going to the doctor." Abruptly, she bit herself still, distrusting the impulse or instinct that drove her to say such things to a total stranger.

Knots of people continued to thrust past us, but now their vehemence didn't touch me. I hardly felt the heat. I was locked to this woman who needed me, even though I was almost sure she wasn't the one I was meant to help. Still smiling, I asked, "What did the doctor say?"

She was too baffled to refuse the question. "He didn't understand it. He said I shouldn't be bleeding. He wanted to put me in the hospital. For observation."

"But you won't go," I said at once.

"I can't." Her whisper was nearly a cry. "Reese's show is tomorrow. His first big show. He's been living for this all his life. And he has so much to do. To get ready. If I went to the hospital, I'd have to call him. Interrupt—. He'd have to come to the hospital."

Now I had her. When the need is strong enough—and when I've been given enough permission—I can make myself obeyed. I let go of her arm and held out my hand. "Let me see that handkerchief."

Dumbly, as if she were astonished at herself, she lowered her hand and give me the damp cloth.

It wasn't heavily soaked; the flow from her nose was slow. That was why she was able to even consider the possibility of going to work. But her red pain was as explicit as a wail in my hand. I watched a new bead of blood gather in one of her nostrils, and it told me a host of things I was not going to be able to explain to her. The depth of her peril and innocence sent a jolt through me that nearly made me fold at the knees. I knew now that she was not the person I had been sent here to help. But she was the reason. Oh, she was the *reason*, the victim whose blood cried out for intervention. Sweet Christ, how had she let this be done to her?

But then I saw the way she held her head up while her blood trickled to her upper lip. In her eyes, I caught a flash of the kind of courage and love that got people into trouble because it didn't count the cost. And I saw something else, too—a hint that on some level, intuitively, perhaps even unconsciously, she understood what was happening to her. Naturally she refused to go to the hospital. No hospital could help her.

I gave the handkerchief back to her gently, though inside I was trembling with anger. The sun beat down on us. "You don't need a doctor," I said as calmly as I could. "You need to buy me some coffee and tell me what's going on."

She still hesitated. I could hardly blame her. Why should she want to sit around in a public place with a handkerchief held to her nose? But something about me had reached her, and it wasn't my brief burst of authority. Her eyes went down my coat to my shoes; when they came back up, they were softer. Behind her hand, she smiled faintly. "You look like you could use it."

She was referring to the coffee; but it was her story I intended to use.

She led the way into the coffee shop and toward one of the booths; she even told the petulant waiter what we wanted. I appreciated that. I really had no idea where I was. In fact, I didn't even know what coffee was. But sometimes knowledge comes to me when I need it. I didn't even blink as the waiter dropped heavy cups in front of us, sloshing hot, black liquid onto the table. Instead, I concentrated everything I had on my companion.

When I asked her, she said her name was Kristen Dona. Following a hint I hadn't heard anybody give me, I looked at her left hand and made sure she wasn't wearing a wedding ring. Then I said to get her started, "Your brother's name is Reese. This has something to do with him."

"Oh, no," she said quickly. Too quickly. "How could it?" She wasn't lying: she was just telling me what she wanted to believe. I shrugged. There was no need to argue with her. Instead, I let the hints lead me. "He's a big part of your life," I said, as if we were talking about the weather. "Tell me about him."

"Well—" She didn't know where to begin. "He's a sculptor. He has a show tomorrow—I told you that. His first big show. After all these years."

I studied her closely. "But you're not happy about it."

"Of course I am!" She was righteously indignant. And under that, she was afraid. "He's worked so hard...! He's a good sculptor. Maybe even a great one. But it isn't exactly easy. It's not like being a writer—he can't just go to a publisher and have them print a hundred thousand copies of his work for two ninety-five. He has to have a place where people who want to spend money on art can come and see what he does. And he has to charge a lot because each piece costs him so much time and effort. So a lot of people have to see each piece before he can sell one. That means he has to have shows. In a gallery. This is his first real chance."

For a moment, she was talking so hotly that she forgot to cover her nose. A drop of blood left a mark like a welt across her lip.

Then she felt the drop and scrubbed at it with her handkerchief. "Oh, damn!" she muttered. The cloth was slowly becoming sodden. Suddenly her mouth twisted and her eyes were full of tears. She put her other hand over her face. "His first *real* chance. I'm so scared."

I didn't ask her *why*. I didn't want to hurry her. Instead, I asked, "What changed?"

Her shoulders knotted. But my question must have sounded safe to her. Gradually, some of her tension eased. "What do you mean?"

"He's been a sculptor for a long time." I did my best to sound reasonable, like a friend of her brother's. "But this is his first big show. What's different now? What's changed?"

The waiter ignored us, too bored to bother with customers who only wanted coffee. Numbly, Kristen took another handkerchief out of her purse, raised the fresh cloth to her nose; the other one went back into her purse. I already knew I was no friend of her brother's.

"He met a gallery owner." She sounded tired and sad. "Mortice Root. He calls his gallery The Root Cellar, but it's really an old brownstone mansion over on 49th. Reese went there to see him when the gallery first opened, two weeks ago. He said he was going to beg.... He's become so bitter. Most of the time, the people who run galleries won't even look at his work. I think he's been begging for years."

The idea made her defensive. "Failure does that to people. You work your heart out, but nothing in heaven or hell can force the people who control *access* to care about you. Gallery owners and agents can make or break you because they determine whether you get to show your work or not. You never even get to find out whether there's anything in your work that can touch or move or inspire people, no matter how hard you try, unless you can convince some owner he'll make a lot of money out of you."

She was defending Reese from an accusation I hadn't made. Begging was easy to understand; anybody who was hurt badly enough could do it. She was doing it herself—but she didn't realize it.

Or maybe she did. She drank some of her coffee and changed her tone. "But Mr. Root took him on," she said almost brightly. "He saw Reese's talent right away. He gave Reese a good contract and an advance. Reese has been working like a demon, getting ready, making new pieces. He's finally getting the chance he deserves."

The chance he deserves. I heard echoes in that—suggestions she hadn't intended. And she hadn't really answered my question. But now I had another one that was more important to me.

"Two weeks ago," I said. "Kristen, how long has your nose been bleeding?"

She stared at me while the forced animation drained out of her face.

"Two weeks now, wouldn't you say?" I held her frightened eyes. "Off and on at first, so you didn't take it seriously? But now it's constant? If it weren't so slow, you'd choke yourself when you went to sleep at night?"

I'd gone too far. All at once, she stopped looking at me. She dropped her handkerchief, opened her purse, took out money and scattered it on the table. Then she covered her face again. "I've got to go," she said into her hand. "Reese hates being interrupted, but maybe there's something I can do to help him get ready for tomorrow."

She started to leave. And I stopped her, just like that. Suddenly, she couldn't take herself away from me. A servant can sometimes wield the strength of his Lord.

I wanted to tell her she'd already given Reese more help than she could afford. But I didn't. I wasn't here to pronounce judgment. I didn't have that right. When I had her sitting in front of me again, I said, "You still haven't told me what changed."

Now she couldn't evade me, couldn't pretend she didn't understand. Slowly, she told me what had happened.

Mortice Root had liked Reese's talent—had praised it effusively—but he hadn't actually liked Reese's work. Too polite, he said. Too reasonable. Aesthetically perfect, emotionally boring. He urged Reese to "open up"—dig down into the energy of his fears and dreams, apply his great skill and talent to darker, more "honest" work. And he supplied Reese with new materials. Until then, Reese had worked in ordinary clay or wax, making castings of his figures only when he and Kristen were able to afford the caster's price. But Root had given Reese a special, black clay which gleamed like a river under a swollen moon. An ideal material, easy to work when it was damp, but finished when it dried, without need for firing or sealer or glaze—as hard and heavy as stone.

And as her brother's hands had worked that clay, Kristen's fear had grown out of it. His new pieces were indeed darker, images which chilled her heart. She used to love his work. Now she hated it.

I could have stopped then. I had enough to go on. And she wasn't the one I'd been sent to help; that was obvious. Maybe I should have stopped.

But I wanted to know more. That was my fault: I was forever trying to swim against the current. After all, the impulse to "open up"—to do darker, more "honest" work—was hardly evil. But the truth was, I was more interested in Kristen than Reese. Her eyes were full of supplication and abashment. She felt she had betrayed her brother, not so much by talking about him as by the simple fact that her attitude toward his work had changed. And she was still in such need—

Instead of stopping, I took up another of the hints she hadn't given me. Quietly, I asked, "How long have you been supporting him?"

She was past being surprised now, but her eyes didn't leave my face. "Close to ten years," she answered obediently.

"That must have been hard on you."

"Oh, no," she said at once. "Not at all. I've been happy to do it." She was too loyal to say anything else. Here she was, with her life escaping from her—and she insisted she hadn't suffered. Her bravery made the backs of my eyes burn.

But I required honesty. After a while, the way I was looking at her made her say, "I don't really love my job. I work over in the garment district. I put in hems. After a few years"—she tried to sound self-deprecating and humorous—"it gets a little boring. And there's nobody I can talk to." Her tone suggested a deep gulf of loneliness. "But it's been worth it," she insisted. "I don't have any talent of my own. Supporting Reese gives me something to believe in. I make what he does possible."

I couldn't argue with that. She had made the whole situation possible. Grimly, I kept my mouth shut and waited for her to go on.

"The hard part," she admitted finally, "was watching him grow bitter." Tears started up in her eyes again, but she blinked them back. "All that failure—year after year—" She dropped her gaze; she couldn't bear to look at me and say such things. "He didn't have anybody else to take it out on."

That thought made me want to grind my teeth. She believed in him—and he took it out on her. She could have left him in any number of ways: gotten married, simply packed her bags, anything. But he probably wasn't even aware of the depth of her refusal to abandon him. He simply went on using her.

My own fear was gone now; I was too angry to be afraid. But I held it down. No matter how I felt, she wasn't the person I was here to defend. So I forced myself to sound positively casual as I said, "I'd like to meet him."

In spite of everything, she was still capable of being taken aback.

"You want me to—?" She stared at me. "I couldn't!" She wasn't appalled; she was trying not to give in to a hope that must have seemed insane to her. "He hates being interrupted. He'd be furious." She scanned the table, hunting for excuses. "You haven't finished your coffee."

I nearly laughed out loud. I wasn't here for her—and yet she did wonderful things for me. Suddenly, I decided that it was all worth the cost. Smiling broadly, I said, "I didn't say I needed coffee. I said you needed to buy it for me."

Involuntarily, the corners of her mouth quirked upward. Even with the handkerchief clutched to her face, she looked like a different person. After all she had endured, she was still a long way from being beaten. "Be serious," she said, trying to sound serious. "I can't take you home with me. I don't even know what to call you."

"If you take me with you," I responded, "you won't have to call me."

This time, I didn't need help to reach her; I just needed to go on smiling.

But what I was doing made sweat run down my spine. I didn't want to see her hurt any more. But there was nothing I could do to protect her.

The walk to the place where she and her brother lived seemed long and cruel in the heat. There were fewer cars and crowds around us now—most of the city's people had reached their destinations for the day—and thick, hot light glared at us from long aisles of pale concrete. At the same time, the buildings impacted on either side of us grew older, shabbier, became the homes of ordinary men and women rather than of money. Children played in the street, shrieking and running as if their souls were on fire. Derelicts shambled here and there, not so much lost to grace as inured by alcohol and ruin, benumbed by their own particular innocence. Several of the structures we passed had had their eyes blown out.

Then we arrived in front of a high, flat edifice indistinguishable from its surroundings except by the fact that most of its windows were intact. Kristen grimaced at it apologetically. "Actually," she said, "we could live better than this. But we save as much money as we can for Reese's work." She seemed to have forgotten that I looked worse than her apartment building did. Almost defiantly, she added, "Now we'll be able to do better."

That depended on what she called *better*. I was sure Mortice Root had no end of money. But I didn't say so.

However, she was still worried about how Reese would react to us. "Are you sure you want to do this?" she asked. "He isn't going to be on his good behavior."

I nodded and smiled; I didn't want her to see how scared and angry I was. "Don't worry about me. If he's rude, I can always offer him some constructive criticism."

"Oh, terrific," she responded, at once sarcastic and relieved, sourly amused. "He just *loves* constructive criticism."

She was hardly aware of her own bravery as she led me into the building.

The hall with the mail slots and the manager's apartment was dimly lit by one naked bulb. It should have felt cooler, but the heat inside was fierce. The stairs up to the fourth floor felt like a climb in a steambath. Maybe it was a blessing after all that I didn't have a shirt on under my coat. I was sweating so hard that my shoes felt slick and unreliable against my soles, as if every step I took was somehow untrustworthy.

When Kristen stopped at the door of her apartment, she needed both hands to fumble in her purse for the key. With her face uncovered, I saw that her nosebleed was getting worse.

Despite the way her hands shook, she got the door open. After finding a clean handkerchief, she ushered me inside, calling as she did so, "Reese! I'm home!"

The first room—it would've been the living room in anybody else's apartment—was larger than I'd expected; and it implied other rooms I couldn't see—bedrooms, a kitchen, a studio. The look of dingyness and unlove was part of the ancient wallpaper and warped baseboards, the sagging ceiling, not the result of carelessness; the place was scrupulously kempt. And the entire space was organized to display Reese's sculptures.

Set on packing crates and endtables, stacks of bricks, makeshift pedestals, old steamer trunks, they nearly filled the room. A fair number of them were cast; but most were clay, some fired, some not. And without exception they looked starkly out of place in that room. They were everything the apartment wasn't—finely done,

247

idealistic, painless. It was as if Reese had left all his failure and bitterness and capacity for rage in the walls, sloughing it away from his work so that his art was kind and clean.

And static. It would have looked inert if he'd had less talent. Busts and madonnas stared with eyes that held neither fear nor hope. Children that never laughed or cried were hugged in the arms of blind women. A horse in one corner should have been prancing, but it was simply frozen. His bitterness he took out on his sister. His failures reduced him to begging. But his sculptures held no emotion at all.

They gave me an unexpected lift of hope. Not because they were static, but because he was capable of so much restraint. If reason was the circumference of energy, then he was already halfway to being a great artist. He had reason down pat.

Which was all the more surprising because he was obviously not a reasonable man. He came bristling into the room in answer to Kristen's call, and he'd already started to shout at her before he saw I was there.

At once, he stopped; he stared at me. "Who the hell is *this*?" he rasped without looking at Kristen. I could feel the force of his intensity from where I stood. His face was as acute as a hawk's, whetted by the hunger and energy of a predator. But the dark stains of weariness and strain under his eyes made him look more feverish than fierce. All of a sudden I thought, Only two weeks to get a show ready. An entire show's worth of new pieces in only two weeks. Because of course he wasn't going to display any of the work I could see here. He was only going to show what he'd made out of the new, black clay Mortice Root had given him. And he'd worn himself ragged. In a sense, his intensity wasn't directed at me personally: it was just a fact of his personality. He did everything extremely. In his own way, he was as desperate as his sister. Maybe I should have felt sorry for him.

But he didn't give me much chance. Before I could say anything, he wheeled on Kristen. "It isn't bad enough you have to keep interrupting me," he snarled. "You have to bring trash in here, too. Where did you find him—the Salvation Army? Haven't you figured out yet that I'm *busy*?"

I wanted to intervene; but she didn't need that kind of protection.

Over her handkerchief, her eyes echoed a hint of her brother's fire. He took his bitterness out on her because she allowed him to, not because she was defenseless. Her voice held a bite of anger as she said, "He offered to help me."

If I hadn't been there, he might have listened to her; but his fever made him rash. "*Help* you?" he snapped. "This bum?" He looked at me again. "He couldn't help himself to another drink. And what do you need help...?"

"*Reese.*" This time, she got his attention. "I went to the doctor this morning."

"What?" For an instant, he blinked at her as if he couldn't understand. "The doctor?" The idea that something was wrong with her hit him hard. I could see his knees trying to fold under him. "You aren't sick. What do you need a doctor for?"

Deliberately, she lowered her hand, exposing the red sheen darkening to crust on her upper lip, the blood swelling in her nostrils. He gaped as if the sight nauseated him. Then he shook his head in denial. Abruptly, he sagged to the edge of a trunk that held two of his sculptures. "Damn it to hell," he breathed weakly. "Don't scare me like that. It's just a nosebleed. You've had it for weeks."

Kristen gave me a look of vindication; she seemed to think Reese had just showed how much he cared about her. But I wasn't so sure. I could think of plenty of selfish reasons for his reaction.

Either way, it was my turn to say something. I could have used some inspiration right then—just a little grace to help me find my way. My emotions were tangled up with Kristen; my attitude toward Reese was all wrong. I didn't know how to reach him. But no inspiration was provided.

Swallowing bile, I made an effort to sound confident. "Actually," I said, "I can be more help than you realize. That's the one advantage life has over art. There's more to it than meets the eye."

I was on the wrong track already; a halfwit could have done better. Reese raised his head to look at me, and the outrage in his eyes was as plain as a chisel. "That's wonderful," he said straight at me. "A bum *and* a critic."

Kristen's face was tight with dismay. She knew exactly what would happen if I kept going.

So did I. I wasn't stupid. But I was already sure I didn't really want to help Reese. I wanted somebody a little more worthy.

Anyway, I couldn't stop. His eyes were absolutely daring me to go on.

"Root's right," I said. Now I didn't have any trouble sounding as calm as a saint. "You know that. What you've been doing"—I gestured around the room—"is too controlled. Impersonal. You've got all the skill in the world, but you haven't put your heart into it.

"But I don't think he's been giving you very good advice. He's got you going to the opposite extreme. That's just another dead end. You need a balance. Control and passion. Control alone has been destroying you. Passion alone—"

Right there, I almost said it: passion alone will destroy your sister. That's the kind of bargain you're making. All it costs you is your soul.

But I didn't get the chance. Reese slapped his hand down on the trunk with a sound like a shot. One of his pieces tilted; it would have fallen if Kristen hadn't caught it. But he didn't see that. He jerked to his feet. Over his shoulder, he said to her, "You've been talking to this tramp about me." The words came out like lead.

She didn't answer. There was no defense against his accusation. To catch the sculpture, she'd had to use both hands, and her touch left a red smudge on the clay.

But he didn't seem to expect an answer. He was facing me with fever bright in his eyes. In the same heavy tone, he said, "It's your fault, isn't it. She wouldn't do that to me—tell a total stranger what a failure I've been—if you hadn't pried it out of her.

"Well, let me tell *you* something. Root owns a gallery. He has *power*." He spat the word as if he loathed it. "I have to listen to him. From you I don't have to take this kind of manure."

Which was true, of course. I was a fool, as well as being useless. In simple chagrin I tried to stop or at least deflect what was coming.

"You're right," I said. "I've got no business trying to tell you what to do. But I can still help you. Just listen to me. I—"

"No," he retorted. "You listen. I've spent ten years of my life feeling the way you look. Now I've got a chance to do better. You don't know anything I could possibly want to hear. I've *been* there."

Still without looking at his sister, he said, "Kristen, tell him to leave."

She didn't have any choice. I'd botched everything past the point where there was anything she could do to save it. Reese would just rage at her if she refused—and what would that accomplish? I watched all the anger and hope drain out of her, and I wanted to fight back; but I didn't have any choice, either. She said in a beaten voice, "I think you'd better leave now," and I had to leave. I was no use to anybody without permission; I could not stay when she told me to go.

I didn't have the heart to squeeze in a last appeal on my way out. I didn't have any more hope than she did. I studied her face as I moved to the door, not because I thought she might change her mind, but because I wanted to memorize her, so that if she went on down this road and was lost in the end there would be at least one man left who remembered. But she didn't meet my eyes. And when I stepped out of the apartment, Reese slammed the door behind me so hard the floor shook.

The force of his rejection almost made me fall to my knees.

In spite of that, I didn't give up. I didn't know where I was or how I got here; I was lucky to know why I was here at all. And I would never remember. Where I was before I was here was as blank as a wall across the past. When the river took me someplace else, I wasn't going to be able to give Kristen Dona the bare courtesy of remembering her.

That was a blessing, of a sort. But it was also the reason I didn't give up. Since I didn't have any past or future, the present was my only chance.

When I was sure the world wasn't going to melt around me and change into something else, I went down the stairs, walked out into the pressure of the sun, and tried to think of some other way to fight for Kristen's life and Reese's soul.

After all, I had no right to give up hope on Reese. He'd been a failure for ten years. And I'd seen the way the people of this city looked at me. Even the derelicts had contempt in their eyes, including me in the way they despised themselves. I ought to be able to understand what humiliation could do to someone who tried harder than he knew how and still failed.

But I couldn't think of any way to fight it. Not without permission. Without permission, I couldn't even tell him his sister was in mortal danger.

The sun stayed nearly hidden behind its haze of humidity and dirt, but its brutality was increasing. Noon wasn't far away; the walk here had used up the middle of the morning. Heatwaves shimmered off the pavement. An abandoned car with no wheels leaned against the curb like a cripple. Somebody had gone down the street and knocked over all the trashcans, scattering garbage like wasted lives. Somewhere there had to be something I could do to redeem myself. But when I prayed for help, I didn't get it.

After a while, I found myself staring as if I were about to go blind at a street sign at the corner of the block. A long time seemed to pass before I registered that the sign said, "21st St."

Kristen had said that Root's gallery, The Root Cellar, was "over on 49th."

I didn't know the city; but I could at least count. I went around the block and located 20th. Then I changed directions and started working my way up through the numbers.

It was a long hike. I passed through sections that were worse than where Kristen and Reese lived and ones that were better. I had a small scare when the numbers were interrupted, but after several blocks they took up where they'd left off. The sun kept leaning on me, trying to grind me into the pavement, and the air made my chest hurt.

And when I reached 49th, I didn't know which way to turn. Sweating, I stopped at the intersection and looked around. 49th seemed to stretch to the ends of the world in both directions. Anything was possible; The Root Cellar might be anywhere. I was in some kind of business district—49th was lined with prosperity— and the sidewalks were crowded again. But all the people moved as if nothing except fatigue or stubbornness and the heat kept them from running for their lives. I tried several times to stop one of them to ask directions; but it was like trying to change the course of the river. I got glares and muttered curses, but no help.

That was hard to forgive. But forgiveness wasn't my job. My job was to find some way to help Reese Dona. So I tried some outright begging. And when begging failed, I simply let the press of the crowds start me moving the same way they were going.

With my luck, this was exactly the wrong direction. But I couldn't think of any good reason to turn around, so I kept walking, studying the buildings for any sign of a brownstone mansion and muttering darkly against all those myths about how God answers prayer.

Ten blocks later, I recanted. I came to a store that filled the entire block and went up into the sky for at least thirty floors; and in front of it stood my answer. He was a scrawny old man in a dingy gray uniform with red epaulets and red stitching on his cap; boredom or patience glazed his eyes. He was tending an iron pot that hung from a rickety tripod. With the studious intention of a halfwit, he rang a handbell to attract people's attention.

The stitching on his cap said, "Salvation Army."

I went right up to him and asked where The Root Cellar was.

He blinked at me as if I were part of the heat and the haze. "Mission's that way." He nodded in the direction I was going. "49th and Grand."

"Thanks, anyway," I said. I was glad to be able to give the old man a genuine smile. "That isn't what I need. I need to find The Root Cellar. It's an art gallery. Supposed to be somewhere on 49th."

He went on blinking at me until I started to think maybe he was deaf. Then, abruptly, he seemed to arrive at some kind of recognition. Abandoning his post, he turned and entered the store. Through the glass, I watched him go to a box like half a booth that hung on one wall. He found a large yellow book under the box, opened it, and flipped the pages back and forth for a while.

Nodding at whatever he found, he came back out to me.

"Down that way," he said, indicating the direction I'd come from "About thirty blocks. Number 840."

Suddenly, my heart lifted. I closed my eyes for a moment to give thanks. Then I looked again at the man who'd rescued me. "If I had any money," I said, "I'd give it to you."

"If you had any money," he replied as if he knew who I was, "I wouldn't take it. Go with God."

I said, "I will," and started retracing my way up 49th.

I felt a world better. But I also had a growing sense of urgency. The longer I walked, the worse it got. The day was getting away from me—and this day was the only one I had. Reese's show was tomorrow. Then Mortice Root would've fulfilled his part of the bargain. And the price would have to be paid. I was sweating so hard my filthy old coat stuck to my back; but I forced myself to walk as fast as the fleeing crowds.

After a while, the people began to disappear from the sidewalks again and the traffic thinned. Then the business district came to an end, and I found myself in a slum so ruined and hopeless I had to grit my teeth to keep up my courage. I felt hostile eyes watching me from behind broken windows and gaping entrances. But I was protected, either by daylight or by the way I looked.

Then the neighborhood began to improve. The slum became close-built houses, clinging to dignity. The houses moved apart from each other, giving themselves more room to breathe. Trees appeared in the yards, even in the sidewalk. Lawns pushed the houses back from the street, and each house seemed to be more ornate than the one beside it. I would have thought they were homes, but most of them had discreet signs indicating they were places of business. Several of them were shops that sold antiques. One held a law firm. A stockbroker occupied a place the size of a temple. I decided that this was where people came to do their shopping and business when they were too rich to associate with their fellow human beings.

And there it was—a brownstone mansion as elaborate as any I'd seen. It was large and square, three stories tall, with a colonnaded entryway and a glass-domed structure that might have been a greenhouse down the length of one side. The mailbox on the front porch was neatly numbered, 840. And when I went up the walk to the porch, I saw a brass plaque on the door with words engraved on it:

THE ROOT CELLAR

a private gallery

Mortice Root

At the sight, my chest constricted as if I'd never done this before. But I'd already lost too much time; I didn't waste any more of it hesitating. I pressed a small button beside the door and listened to chimes ringing faintly inside the house as if Mortice Root had a cathedral in his basement.

For a while, nothing happened. Then the door opened, and I felt a flow of cold air from inside, followed by a man in a guard's uniform, with a gun holstered on his hip and a badge that said, "Nationwide Security," on his chest. As he looked out at me, what he saw astonished him; not many of Root's patrons looked like I did. Then his face closed like a shutter. "Are you out of your mind?" he growled. "We don't give handouts here. Get lost."

In response, I produced my sweetest smile. "Fortunately, I don't want a handout. I want to talk to Mortice Root."

He stared at me. "What in hell makes you think Mr. Root wants to talk to you?"

"Ask him and find out," I replied. "Tell him I'm here to argue about Reese Dona."

He would have slammed the door in my face; but a hint of authority came back to me, and he couldn't do it. For a few moments, he gaped at me as if he were choking. Then he muttered, "Wait here," and escaped back into the house. As he closed the door, the cool air breathing outward was cut off.

"Well, naturally," I murmured to the sodden heat, trying to keep myself on the bold side of dread. "The people who come here to spend their money can't be expected to just stand around and sweat."

The sound of voices came dimly through the door. But I hadn't heard the guard walk away, and I didn't hear anybody coming toward me. So I still wasn't quite ready when the door swung open again and Mortice Root stood in front of me with a cold breeze washing unnaturally past his shoulders.

We recognized each other right away; and he grinned like a wolf. But I couldn't match him. I was staggered. I hadn't expected him to be so *powerful.*

He didn't look powerful. He looked as rich as Solomon—smooth, substantial, glib—as if he could buy and sell the people who came here to give him their money. From the tips of his gleaming shoes past the expanse of his distinctively styled suit to the clean confidence of his shaven jowls, he was everything I wasn't. But those things only gave him worldly significance; they didn't make him powerful. His true strength was hidden behind the bland unction of his demeanor. It showed only in his grin, in the slight, avid bulging of his eyes, in the wisps of hair that stood out like hints of energy on either side of his bald crown.

His gaze made me fell grimy and rather pathetic.

He studied me for a moment. Then, with perfectly cruel kindness, he said, "Come in, come in. You must be sweltering out there. It's much nicer in here."

He was that sure of himself.

But I was willing to accept permission, even from him. Before he could reconsider, I stepped past him into the hallway.

As I looked around, cold came swirling up my back, turning my sweat chill. At the end of this short, deeply carpeted hall, Root's mansion opened into an immense foyer nearly as high as the building itself. Two mezzanines joined by broad stairways of carved wood circled the walls; daylight shone downward from a skylight in the center of the ceiling. A glance showed me that paintings were displayed around the mezzanines, while the foyer itself held sculptures and carvings decorously set on white pedestals. I couldn't see anything that looked like Reese Dona's work.

At my elbow, Root said, "I believe you came to argue with me?" He was as smooth as oil.

I felt foolish and awkward beside him, but I faced him as squarely as I could. "Maybe 'contend' would be a better word."

"As you say." He chuckled in a way that somehow suggested both good humor and malice. "I look forward to it." Then he touched my arm, gestured me toward one side of the foyer. "But let me show you what he's doing these days. Perhaps you'll change your mind."

For no good reason, I said, "You know better than that." But I went with him.

A long, wide passage took us to the glass-domed structure I'd taken to be a greenhouse. Maybe it was originally built for that; but Root had converted it, and I had to admit it made an effective gallery—well-lit, spacious, and comfortable. In spite of all that glass, the air stayed cool, almost chill.

Here I saw Reese's new work for the first time.

"Impressive, aren't they," Root purred. He was mocking me.

But what he was doing to Reese was worse.

There were at least twenty of them, with room for a handful more—attractively set in niches along one wall, proudly positioned on special pediments, cunningly juxtaposed in corners so that they showed each other off. It was clear that any artist would find an opportunity like this hard to resist.

But all the pieces were black.

Reese had completely changed his subject matter. Madonnas and children had been replaced by gargoyles and twisted visions of the damned. Glimpses of nightmare leered from their niches. Pain writhed on display, as if it had become an object of ridicule. In a corner of the room, a ghoul devoured one infant while another strove urgently to scream and failed.

And each of these new images was alive with precisely the kind of vitality his earlier work lacked. He had captured his visceral terrors in the act of pouncing at him.

As sculptures, they were admirable; maybe even more than that. He had achieved some kind of breakthrough here, tapped into sources of energy he'd always been unable or unwilling to touch. All he needed now was balance.

But there was more to these pieces than just skill and energy. There was also blackness.

Root's clay.

Kristen was right. This clay looked like dark water under the light of an evil moon, like marl mixed with blood until the mud congealed. And the more I studied what I saw, the more these grotesque and brutal images gave the impression of growing from the clay itself rather than from the independent mind of the artist. They were not Reese's fears and dreams refined by art; they were horrors he found in the clay when his hands touched it. The real strength, the passion of these pieces, came from the material Root supplied, not from Reese. No wonder he had become so hollow-eyed and ragged. He was struggling desperately to control the consequences of his bargain. Trying to prove to himself he wasn't doing the wrong thing.

For a moment, I felt a touch of genuine pity for him. But it didn't last. Maybe deep down in his soul he was afraid of what he was doing and what it meant. But he was still doing it. And he was paying for the chance to do such strong work with his sister's life.

Softly, my opponent said, "It appears you don't approve. I'm so sorry. But I'm afraid there's really nothing you can do about it. The artists of this world are uniquely vulnerable. They wish to create beauty, and the world cares for nothing but money. Even the cattle who will buy these"—he gave the room a dismissive flick of the hand—"trivial pieces hold the artist in contempt." He turned his wolf-grin toward me again. "Failure makes fertile ground."

I couldn't pretend that wasn't true; so I asked bitterly, "Are you really going to keep your end of the bargain? Are you really going to sell this stuff?"

"Oh, assuredly," he replied. "At least until the sister dies. To-morrow. Perhaps the day after." He chuckled happily. "Then I suspect I'll find myself too busy with other, more promising artists to spend time on Reese Dona."

I felt him glance at me, gauging my helplessness. Then he went on unctuously, "Come, now, my friend. Why glare so thunderously? Surely you realize that he has been using her in precisely this manner for years. I've merely actualized the true state of their relationship. But perhaps you're too innocent to grasp how deeply he resents her. It is the nature of beggars to resent those who give them gifts. He resents *me*." At that, Root laughed outright. He was not a man who gave gifts to anybody. "I assure you that her present plight is of his own choice and making."

"No," I said, more out of stubbornness than conviction. "He just doesn't understand what's happening."

Root shrugged. "Do you think so? No matter. The point, as you must recognize, is that we have nothing to contend *for*. The issue has already been decided."

I didn't say anything. I wasn't as glib as he was. And anyway I was afraid he was right.

While I stood there and chewed over all the things I wasn't able to do, I heard doors opening and closing somewhere in the distance. The heavy carpeting absorbed footsteps; but it wasn't long before Reese came striding into the greenhouse. He was so tight with eagerness or suppressed fear he looked like he was about to snap. As usual, he didn't even see me when he first came into the room.

"I've got the rest of the pieces," he said to Root. "They're in a truck out back. I think you'll like—"

Then my presence registered on him. He stopped with a jerk, stared at me as if I'd come back from the dead. "What're *you* doing here?" he demanded. At once, he turned back to Root. "What is *he* doing here?"

Root's confidence was a complete insult. "Reese," he sighed, "I'm afraid that this—gentleman?—believes that I should not show your work tomorrow."

For a moment, Reese was too astonished to be angry. His mouth actually hung open while he looked at me. But I was furious enough for both of us. With one sentence, Root had made my position impossible. I couldn't think of a single thing to say now that would change the outcome.

Still, I had to try. While Reese's surprise built up into outrage, I said as if I weren't swearing like a madman inside, "There are two sides to everything. You've heard his. You really ought to listen to mine."

He closed his mouth, locked his teeth together. His glare was wild enough to hurt.

"Mortice Root owes you a little honesty," I said while I had the chance. "He should have told you long ago that he's planning to drop you after tomorrow."

The sheer pettiness of what I was saying made me cringe, and Root simply laughed. I should have known better than to try to fight him on his own level. Now he didn't need to answer me at all.

In any case, my jibe made no impression on Reese. He gritted, "I don't care about that," like a man who couldn't or wouldn't understand. "This is what I care about." He gestured frantically around the room. *"This.* My work."

He took a couple of steps toward me, and his voice shook with the effort he made to keep from shouting. "I don't know who you are—or why you think I'm any of your business. I don't care about that, either. You've heard Kristen's side. Now you're going to hear mine."

In a small way, I was grateful he didn't accuse me of turning his sister against him.

"She doesn't like the work I'm doing now. No, worse than that. She doesn't mind the work. She doesn't like the *clay.*" He gave a laugh like an echo of Root's. But he didn't have Root's confidence and power; he only sounded bitter, sarcastic, and afraid. "She tries to tell me she approves of me, but I can read her face like a book.

"Well, let me tell you something." He poked a trembling finger at my chest. "With my show tomorrow, I'm alive for the first time in ten years. I'm alive *here.* Art exists to communicate. It isn't worth manure if it doesn't communicate, and it can't communicate if somebody doesn't look at it. It's that simple. The only time an artist is alive is when somebody looks at his work. And if enough people look, he can live forever.

"I've been sterile for ten years because I haven't had one other soul to look at my work." He was so wrapped up in what he was saying, I don't think he even noticed how completely he dismissed his sister. "Now I am alive. If it only lasts for one more day, it'll still be something nobody can take away from me. If I have to work in black clay to get that, who cares? That's just something I didn't know about myself—about how my imagination works. I never had the chance to try black clay before.

"But now—" He couldn't keep his voice from rising like a cry. "Now I'm alive. *Here.* If you want to take that away from me, you're worse than trash. You're evil."

Mortice Root was smiling like a saint.

For a moment, I had to look away. The fear behind the passion in Reese's eyes was more than I could stand. "I'm sorry," I murmured. What else could I say? I regretted everything. He needed me desperately, and I kept failing him. And he placed so little value on his sister. With a private groan, I forced myself to face him again.

"I thought it was work that brought artists to life. Not shows. I thought the work was worth doing whether anybody looked at it or not. Why else did you keep at it for ten years?"

But I was still making the same mistake, still trying to reach him through his art. And now I'd definitely said something he couldn't afford to hear or understand. With a jerky movement like a puppet, he threw up his hands. "I don't have time for this," he snapped. "I've got five more pieces to set up." Then, suddenly, he was yelling at me. "And I don't give one lousy damn what you think!" Somehow, I'd hit a nerve. "I want you to go away. I want you to leave me alone! Get out of here and *leave me alone!*"

I didn't have any choice. As soon as he told me to go, I turned toward the door. But I was desperate myself now. Knotting my fists, I held myself where I was. Urgently—so urgently that I could hardly separate the words—I breathed at him, "Have you looked at Kristen recently? Really looked? Haven't you seen what's happening to her? You—"

Root stopped me. He had that power. Reese had told me to go.

Root simply raised his hand, and his strength hit me in the chest like a fist. My tongue was clamped to the roof of my mouth. My voice choked in my throat. For one moment while I staggered, the greenhouse turned in a complete circle, and I thought I was going to be thrown out of the world.

But I wasn't. A couple of heartbeats later, I got my balance back. Helpless to do anything else, I left the greenhouse.

As I crossed the foyer toward the front door, Reese shouted after me, "And stay away from my sister!"

Until I closed the door, I could hear Mortice Root chuckling with pleasure.

Dear God! I prayed. Let me decide. Just this once. He isn't worth it.

But I didn't have the right.

On the other hand, I didn't have to stay away from Kristen. That was up to her; Reese didn't have any say in the matter.

I made myself walk slowly until I was out of sight of The Root Cellar, just in case someone was watching. Then I started to run.

It was the middle of the afternoon, and the heat just kept getting worse. After the cool of Root's mansion, the outside air felt like glue against my face. Sweat oozed into my eyes, stuck my coat to my back, itched maliciously in my dirty whiskers. The sunlight looked liked it was congealing on the walks and streets. Grimly, I thought if this city didn't get some rain soon it would start to burn.

And yet I wanted today to last, despite the heat. I would happily have caused the sun to stand still. I did not want to have to face Mortice Root and Reese Dona again after dark. But I would have to deal with that possibility when it came up. First I had to get Kristen's help. And to do that, I had to reach her.

The city did its best to hinder me. I left Root's neighborhood easily enough; but when I entered the slums, I started having problems. I guess a running man dressed in nothing but an overcoat, a pair of pants, and sidesplit shoes looked like too much fun to miss. Gangs of kids seemed to materialize out of the ruined buildings to get in my way.

They should have known better. They were predators themselves, and I was on a hunt of my own; when they saw the danger in my eyes, they backed down. Some of them threw bottles and trash at my back, but that didn't matter.

Then the sidewalks became more and more crowded as the slum faded behind me. People stepped in front of me, jostled me off my stride, swore angrily at me as I tried to run past. I had to slow down just to keep myself out of trouble. And all the lights were against me. At every corner, I had to wait and wait while mobs hemmed me in, instinctively blocking the path of anyone who wanted to get ahead of them. I felt like I was up against an active enemy. The city was rising to defend its own.

By the time I reached the street I needed to take me over to 21st, I felt so ragged and wild I wanted to shake my fists at the sky and demand some kind of assistance or relief. But if God couldn't see how much trouble I was in, He didn't deserve what I was trying to do in His name. So I did the best I could—running in spurts, walking when I had to, risking the streets whenever I saw a break in the traffic. Finally I made it. Trembling, I reached the building where Reese and Kristen had their apartment.

Inside, it was as hot as an oven, baking its inhabitants to death. But here at least there was nobody in my way, and I took the stairs two and three at a time to the fourth floor. The lightbulb over the landing was out, but I didn't have any trouble finding the door I needed.

I pounded on it with my fist. Pounded again. Didn't hear anything. Hammered at the wood a third time.

"Kristen!" I shouted. I didn't care how frantic I sounded. "Let me in! I've got to talk to you!"

Then I heard a small, faint noise through the panels. She must have been right on the other side of the door. Weakly, she said, "Go away."

"Kristen!" Her dismissal left a welt of panic across my heart. I put my mouth to the crack of the door to make her hear me. "Reese needs help. If he doesn't get it, you're not going to survive. He doesn't even realize he's sacrificing you."

After a moment, the lock clicked, and the door opened.

I went in.

The apartment was dark. She'd turned off all the lights. When she closed the door behind me, I couldn't see a thing. I had to stand still so I wouldn't bump into Reese's sculptures.

"Kristen," I said, half pleading, half commanding. "Turn on a light."

Her reply was a whisper of misery. "You don't want to see me."

She sounded so beaten I almost gave up hope. Quietly, I said, "Please."

She couldn't refuse. She needed me too badly. I felt her move past me in the dark. Then the overhead lights clicked on, and I saw her.

I shouldn't have been shocked—I knew what to expect—but that didn't help. The sight of her went into me like a knife.

She was wearing only a terrycloth bathrobe. That made sense; she'd been poor for a long time and didn't want to ruin her good clothes. The collar of her robe was soaked with blood.

Her nosebleed was worse.

And delicate red streams ran steadily from both her ears.

Sticky trails marked her lips and chin, the front of her throat, the sides of her neck. She'd given up trying to keep herself clean. Why should she bother? She was bleeding to death, and she knew it.

Involuntarily, I went to her and put my arms around her.

She leaned against me. I was all she had left. Into my shoulder, she said as if she were on the verge of tears, "I can't help him anymore. I've tried and tried. I don't know what else to do."

She stood there quivering; and I held her and stroked her hair and let her blood soak into my coat. I didn't have any other way to comfort her.

But her time was running out, just like Reese's. The longer I waited, the weaker she would be. As soon as she became a little steadier, I lowered my arms and stepped back. In spite of the way I looked, I wanted her to be able to see what I was.

"He doesn't need that kind of help now," I said softly, willing her to believe me. Not the kind you've been giving him for ten years. "Not anymore. He needs me. That's why I'm here.

"But I have to have permission." I wanted to cry at her, You've been letting him do this to you for ten years! None of this would've happened to you if you hadn't allowed it! But I kept that protest to myself. "He keeps sending me away, and I have to go. I don't have any choice. I can't do anything without permission.

"It's really that simple." God, make her believe me! "I need somebody with me who wants me to be there. I need you to go back to The Root Cellar with me. Even Root won't be able to get rid of me if you want me to stay.

"Kristen." I moved closer to her again, put my hands in the blood on her cheek, on the side of her neck. "I'll find some way to save him. If you're there to give me permission."

She didn't look at me; she didn't seem to have the courage to raise her eyes. But after a moment I felt the clear touch of grace. She believed me—when I didn't have any particular reason to believe myself. Softly, she said, "I can't go like this. Give me a minute to change my clothes."

She still didn't look at me. But when she turned to leave the room, I saw determination mustering in the corners of her eyes.

I breathed a prayer of long-overdue thanks. She intended to fight.

I waited for her with fear beating in my bones. And when she returned—dressed in her dingy blouse and fraying skirt, with a towel wrapped around her neck to catch the blood—and announced that she was ready to go, I faltered. She looked so wan and frail—already weak and unnaturally pale from loss of blood. I felt sure she wasn't going to be able to walk all the way to The Root Cellar.

Carefully, I asked her if there was any other way we could get where we were going. But she shrugged the question aside. She and Reese had never owned a car, and he'd taken what little money was available in order to rent a truck to take his last pieces to the gallery.

Groaning a silent appeal for help, I held her arm to give her what support I could. Together, we left the apartment, went down the old stairs and out to the street.

I felt a new sting of dread when I saw that the sun was setting. For all my efforts to hurry, I'd taken too much time. Now I would have to contend with Mortice Root at night.

Twilight and darkness brought no relief from the heat. The city had spent all day absorbing the pressure of the sun; now the walks and buildings, every stretch of cement seemed to emit fire like the sides of a furnace. The air felt thick and ominous—as charged with intention as a thunderstorm, but trapped somehow, prevented from release, tense with suffering.

It sucked the strength out of Kristen with every breath. Before we'd gone five blocks, she was leaning most of her weight on me. That was frightening, not because she was more than I could bear, but because she seemed to weigh so little. Her substance was bleeding away. In the garish and unreliable light of the streetlamps, shop windows, and signs, only the dark marks on her face and neck appeared real.

But we were given one blessing: the city itself left us alone. It had done its part by delaying me earlier. We passed through crowds and traffic, past gutted tenements and stalking gangs, as if we didn't deserve to be noticed anymore.

Kristen didn't complain, and I didn't let her stumble. One by one, we covered the blocks. When she wanted to rest, we put our backs to the hot walls and leaned against them until she was ready to go on.

During that whole long, slow creep through the pitiless dark, she only spoke to me once. While we were resting again, sometime after we turned on 49th, she said quietly, "I still don't know your name."

We were committed to each other; I owed her the truth. "I don't either," I said. Behind the wall of the past, any number of things were hidden from me.

She seemed to accept that. Or maybe she just didn't have enough strength left to worry about both Reese and me. She rested a little while longer. Then we started walking again.

At last we left the last slum behind and made our slow, frail approach to The Root Cellar. Between streetlights I looked for the moon, but it wasn't able to show through the clenched haze. I was sweating like a frightened animal. But Kristen might have been immune to the heat. All she did was lean on me and walk and bleed.

I didn't know what to expect at Root's mansion. Trouble of some kind. An entire squadron of security guards. Minor demons lurking in the bushes around the front porch. Or an empty building, deserted for the night. But the place wasn't deserted. All the rest of the mansion was dark; the greenhouse burned with light. Reese wasn't able to leave his pieces alone before his show. And none of the agents that Root might have used against us appeared. He was that sure of himself.

On the other hand, the front door was locked with a variety of bolts and wires.

But Kristen was breathing sharply, urgently. Fear and desire and determination made her as feverish as her brother; she wanted me to take her inside, to Reese's defense. And she'd lost a dangerous amount of blood. She wasn't going to be able to stay on her feet much longer. I took hold of the door, and it opened without a sound. Cool air poured out at us, as concentrated as a moan of anguish.

We went in.

The foyer was dark. But a wash of light from the cracks of the greenhouse doors showed us our way. The carpet muffled our feet. Except for her ragged breathing and my frightened heart, we were as silent as spirits.

But as we got near the greenhouse, I couldn't keep quiet anymore. I was too scared.

I caused the doors to burst open with a crash that shook the walls. At the same time, I tried to charge forward.

The brilliance of the gallery seemed to explode in my face. For an instant, I was dazzled.

And I was stopped. The light felt as solid as the wall that cut me off from the past.

Almost at once, my vision cleared, and I saw Mortice Root and Reese Dona. They were alone in the room, standing in front of a sculpture I hadn't seen earlier—the biggest piece here. Reese must have brought it in his rented truck. It was a wild, swept-winged, malignant bird of prey, its beak wide in a cry of fury. One of its clawed feet was curled like a fist. The other was gripped deep into a man's chest. Agony stretched the man's face.

At least Reese had the decency to be surprised. Root wasn't. He faced us and grinned.

Reese gaped dismay at Kristen and me for one moment. Then, with a wrench like an act of violence, he turned his back. His shoulders hunched; his arms clamped over his stomach. "I told you to go away." His voice sounded like he was strangling. "I told you to leave her alone."

The light seemed to blow against me like a wind. Like the current of the river that carried me away, taking me from place to place without past and without future, hope. And it was rising. It held me in the doorway; I couldn't move through it.

"You are a fool," Root said to me. His voice rode the light as if he were shouting. "You have been denied. You cannot enter here."

He was so strong that I was already half turned to leave when Kristen saved me.

As pale as ash, she stood beside me. Fresh blood from her nose and ears marked her skin. The towel around her neck was sodden and terrible. She looked too weak to keep standing. Yet she matched her capacity for desperation against Reese's need.

"No," she said in the teeth of the light and Root's grin. "He can stay. I want him here."

I jerked myself toward Reese again.

Ferocity came at me like a cataract; but I stood against it. I had Kristen's permission. That had to be enough.

"Look at her!" I croaked at his back. "She's your sister! *Look* at her!"

He didn't seem to hear me at all. He was hunched over himself in front of his work. "Go away," he breathed weakly, as if he were talking to himself. "I can't stand it. Just go away."

Gritting prayers between my teeth like curses, I lowered my head, called up every ache and fragment of strength I had left, and took one step into the greenhouse.

Reese fell to his knees as if I'd broken the only string that held him upright.

At the same time, the bird of prey poised above him moved.

Its wings beat downward. Its talons clenched. The heart of its victim burst in his chest.

From his clay throat came a brief, hoarse wail of pain.

Driven by urgency, I took two more steps through the intense pressure walled against me.

And all the pieces displayed in the greenhouse started to move.

Tormented statuettes fell from their niches, cracked open, and cried out. Gargoyles mewed hideously. The mouths of victims gaped open and whined. In a few swift moments, the air was full of muffled shrieks and screams.

Through the pain, the fierce current forcing me away from Reese, and the horror, I heard Mortice Root start to laugh.

If Kristen had failed me then, I would have been finished. But in some way she had made herself blind and deaf to what was happening. Her entire soul was focused on one object—help for her brother—and she willed me forward with all the passion she had learned in ten years of self-sacrifice. She was prepared to spend the last of her life here for Reese's sake.

She made it possible for me to keep going.

Black anguish rose like a current at me. And the force of the light mounted. I felt it ripping at my skin. It was as hot as the hunger ravening for Reese's heart.

Yet I took two more steps.

And two more.

And reached him.

He still knelt under the wingspread of the nightmare bird he had created. The light didn't hurt him; he didn't feel it at all. He was on his knees because he simply couldn't stand. He gripped his arms over his heart to keep himself from howling.

There I noticed something I should have recognized earlier. He had sculpted a man for his bird of prey to attack, not a woman. I could see the figure clearly enough now to realize that Reese had given the man his own features. Here, at least, he had shaped one of his own terrors rather than merely bringing out the darkness of Mortice Root's clay.

After that, nothing else mattered. I didn't feel the pain or the pressure; ferocity and dismay lost their power.

I knelt in front of Reese, took hold of his shoulders, and hugged him like a child. "Just look at her," I breathed into his ear. "She's your sister. You don't have to do this to her."

She stood across the room from me with her eyes closed and her determination gripped in her small fists.

From under her eyelids, stark blood streamed down her cheeks.

"Look at her!" I pleaded. "I can help you. Just *look*."

In the end, he didn't look at her. He didn't need to. He knew what was happening.

Suddenly, he wrenched out of my embrace. His arms flung me aside. He raised his head, and one lorn wail corded his throat:

"Kristen!"

268

Root's laughter stopped as if it'd been cut down with an axe.

That cry was all I needed. It came right from Reese's heart, too pure to be denied. It was permission, and I took it.

I rose to my feet, easily now, easily. All the things that stood in my way made no difference. Transformed, I faced Mortice Root across the swelling force of his malice. All his confidence was gone to panic.

Slowly, I raised my arms.

Beams of white sprouted from my palms, clean white almost silver. It wasn't fire or light in any worldly sense; but it blazed over my head like light, ran down my arms like fire. It took my coat and pants, even my shoes, away from me in flames. Then it wrapped me in the robes of God until all my body burned.

Root tried to scream, but his voice didn't make any sound.

Towering white-silver, I reached up into the storm-dammed sky and brought down a blast that staggered the entire mansion to its foundations. Crashing past glass and frame and light fixtures, a bolt that might have been lightning took hold of Root from head to foot. For an instant, the gallery's lights failed. Everything turned black except for Root's horror etched against darkness and the blast that bore him away.

When the lights came back on, the danger was gone from the greenhouse. All the crying and the pain and the pressure were gone. Only the sculptures themselves remained.

They were slumped and ruined, like melted wax.

Outside, rain began to rattle against the glass of the greenhouse.

Later, I went looking for some clothes; I couldn't very well go around naked. After a while, I located a suite of private rooms at the back of the building. But everything I found there belonged to Root. His personal stink had soaked right into the fabric. I hated the idea of putting his things on my skin when I'd just been burned clean. But I had to wear something. In disgust, I took one of his rich shirts and a pair of pants. That was my punishment for having been so eager to judge Reese Dona.

Back in the greenhouse, I found him sitting on the floor with Kristen's head cradled in his lap. He was stroking the soft hair at her temples and grieving to himself. For the time being, at least, I was sure his grief had nothing to do with his ruined work.

Kristen was fast asleep, exhausted by exertion and loss of blood. But I could see that she was going to be all right. Her bleeding had stopped completely. And Reese had already cleaned some of the stains from her face and neck.

Rain thundered against the ceiling of the greenhouse; jagged lines of lightning scrawled the heavens. But all the glass was intact, and the storm stayed outside, where it belonged. From the safety of shelter, the downpour felt comforting.

And the manufactured cool of the building had wiped out most of Root's unnatural heat. That was comforting, too.

It was time for me to go.

But I didn't want to leave Reese like this. I couldn't do anything about the regret that was going to dog him for the rest of his life. But I wanted to try.

The river was calling for me. Abruptly, as if I thought he was in any shape to hear me, I said, "What you did here—the work you did for Root—wasn't wrong. Don't blame yourself for that. You just went too far. You need to find the balance. Reason and energy." Need and help. "There's no limit to what you can do, if you just keep your balance."

He didn't answer. Maybe he wasn't listening to me at all. But after a moment he bent over Kristen and kissed her forehead.

That was enough. I had to go. Some of the details of the greenhouse were already starting to melt.

My bare feet didn't make any sound as I left the room, crossed the foyer, and went out into...

THE CONQUEROR WORM

And much of Madness, and more of Sin,
And Horror the soul of the plot.
—EDGAR ALLAN POE

BEFORE HE REALIZED WHAT HE WAS DOING, HE SWUNG THE knife.

The home of Creel and Vi Sump. The living room.

Her real name is Violet, but everyone calls her Vi. They've been married for two years now, and she isn't blooming.

Their home is modest but comfortable. Creel has a good job with his company, but he isn't moving up. In the living room, some of the furnishings are better than the space they occupy. A good stereo contrasts with the state of the wallpaper. The arrangement of the furniture shows a certain amount of frustration: there's no way to set the armchairs and sofa so that people who sit on them can't see the waterspots in the ceiling. The flowers in the vase on the endtable are real, but they look plastic. At night, the lights leave shadows at odd places around the room.

They were out late at a large party where acquaintances, business associates, and strangers drank a lot. As Creel unlocked the front door and came into the living room ahead of Vi, he looked more than ever like a rumpled bear. Whisky made the usual dullness of his eyes seem baleful. Behind him, Vi resembled a flower in the process of becoming a wasp.

"I don't care," he said, moving directly to the sideboard to get himself another drink. "I wish you wouldn't do it."

She sat down on the sofa, took off her shoes. "God, I'm tired."

"If you aren't interested in anything else," he said, "think about me. I have to work with most of those people. Half of them can fire me if they want to. You're affecting my job."

"We've had this conversation before," she said. "We've had it eight times this month." A vague movement in one of the shadows across the room turned her head toward the corner. "What was *that*?"

"What was what?"

"I saw something move. Over there in the corner. Don't tell me we've got mice."

"I didn't see anything. We haven't got mice. And I don't care how many times we've had this conversation. I want you to stop."

She stared into the corner for a moment. Then she leaned back on the sofa. "I can't stop. I'm not *doing* anything."

"The hell you're not doing anything." He took a drink and refilled his glass. "If you were after him any harder, you'd have your hand in his pants."

"That's not true."

"You think nobody sees what you're doing. You act like you're alone. But you're not. Everybody at that whole damn party was watching you. The way you flirt—"

"I wasn't flirting. I was just talking to him."

"The way you *flirt*, you ought to have the decency to be embarrassed."

"Oh, go to bed. I'm too tired for this."

"Is it because he's a vice-president? Do you think that's going to make him better in bed? Or do you just like the status of playing around with a vice-president?"

"I wasn't *flirting* with him. I swear to God, there's something the matter with you. We were just talking. You know—moving our mouths so that words could come out. He was a literature major in college. We have something in common. We've read the same books. Remember *books*? Those things with ideas and stories printed in them? All you ever talk about is football—and how somebody at the company has it in for you—and how the latest secretary doesn't wear a bra. Sometimes I think I'm the last literate person left alive."

She raised her head to look at him. Then she sighed, "Why do I even bother? You're not listening to me."

"You're right," he said. "There *is* something in the corner. I saw it move."

They both stared at the corner. After a moment, a centipede scuttled out into the light.

It looked slimy and malicious, and it waved its antennae hungrily. It was nearly ten inches long. Its thick legs seemed to ripple as it shot across the rug. Then it stopped to scan its surroundings. Creel and Vi could see its mandibles chewing expectantly as it flexed its poison claws. It had entered the house to escape the cold, dry night outside—and to hunt for food.

She wasn't the kind of woman who screamed easily; but she hopped up onto the sofa to get her bare feet away from the floor. "Good God," she whispered. "Creel, look at that. Don't let it come any closer."

He leaped at the centipede and tried to stamp one of his heavy shoes down on it. But it moved so fast that he didn't come close to it. Neither of them saw where it went.

"It's under the sofa," he said. "Get off of there."

She obeyed without question. Wincing, she jumped out into the middle of the rug.

As soon as she was out of the way, he heaved the sofa onto its back.

The centipede wasn't there.

"The poison isn't fatal," Vi said. "One of the kids in the neighborhood got stung last week. Her mother told me all about it. It's like getting a bad bee-sting."

Creel didn't listen to her. He lifted the entire sofa into the air so that he could see more of the floor. But the centipede was gone.

He dropped the sofa back onto its legs, knocking over the end-table, spilling the flowers. "Where did that bastard go?"

They hunted around the room for several minutes without leaving the protection of the light. Then he went and got himself another drink. His hands were shaking.

She said, "I wasn't flirting."

He looked at her. "Then it's something worse. You're already sleeping with him. You must've been making plans for the next time you get together."

"I'm going to bed," she said. "I don't have to put up with this. You're disgusting."

He finished his drink and refilled his glass from the nearest bottle.

* * *

The Sumps' game-room.

This room is the real reason why Creel bought this house over Vi's objections: he wanted a house with a game-room. The money which could have replaced the wallpaper and fixed the ceiling of the living room has been spent here. The room contains a full-size pooltable with all the trimmings, a long, imitation leather couch along one wall, and a wet-bar. But the light here isn't any better than in the living room because the fixtures are focused on the pooltable. Even the wet-bar is so ill-lit that its users have to guess what they're doing.

When he isn't working, traveling for his company, or watching football with his buddies, Creel spends a lot of time here.

After Vi went to bed, Creel came into the gameroom. First he went to the wet-bar and refilled his glass. Then he racked up the balls and broke so violently that the cueball sailed off the table. It made a dull, thudding noise as it bounced on the spongy linoleum.

"Fuck," he said, lumbering after the ball. The liquor he had consumed showed in the way he moved but not in his speech. He sounded sober.

Bracing himself with his custom-made cuestick, he bent to pick up the ball. Before he put it back on the table, Vi entered the room. She hadn't changed her clothes for bed, but she had put her shoes back on. She scrutinized the shadows around the floor and under the table before she looked at Creel.

He said, "I thought you were going to bed."

"I can't leave it like this," she said tiredly. "It hurts too much."

"What do you want from me?" he said. "Approval?"

She glared at him.

He didn't stop. "That would be terrific for you. If I approved, you wouldn't have anything else to worry about. The only problem would be, most of the bastards I introduce you to are married. Their wives might be a little more normal. They might give you some trouble."

She bit her lip and went on glaring at him.

"But I don't see why you should worry about that. If those women aren't as understanding as I am, that's their tough luck. As long as I approve, right? There's no reason why you shouldn't screw anybody you want."

"Are you finished?"

"Hell, there's no reason why you shouldn't screw *all* of them. I mean, as long as I approve. Why waste it?"

"Damn it, are you *finished*?"

"There's only one thing I don't understand. If you're so hot for sex, how come you don't want to screw me?"

"That's not true."

He blinked at her through a haze of alcohol. "What's not true? You're not hot for sex? Or you do want to screw me? Don't make me laugh."

"Creel, what's the matter with you? I don't understand any of this. You didn't used to be like this. You weren't like this when we were dating. You weren't like this when we got married. What's happened to you?"

For a minute, he didn't say anything. He went back to the edge of the pooltable, where he'd left his drink. But with his cue in one hand and the ball in the other, he didn't have a hand free. Carefully, he set his stick down on the table.

After he finished his drink, he said, "You changed."

"*I* changed? *You're* the one who's acting crazy. All I did was talk to some company vice-president about *books*."

"No, I'm not," he said. His knuckles were white around the cueball. "You think I'm stupid. Because I wasn't a literature major in college. Maybe that's what changed. When we got married, you didn't think I was stupid. But now you do. You think I'm too stupid to notice the difference."

"What difference is that?"

"You never want to have sex with me anymore."

"Oh, for God's sake," she said. "We had sex the day before yesterday."

He looked straight at her. "But you didn't want to. I can tell. You never *want* to."

"What do you mean, you can tell?"

"You make a lot of excuses."

"I do not."

"And when we do have sex, you don't pay any attention to me.

You're always somewhere else. Thinking about something else. You're always thinking about somebody else."

"But that's *normal*," she said. "Everybody does it. Everybody fantasizes during sex. *You* fantasize during sex. That's what makes it fun."

At first, she didn't see the centipede as it wriggled out from under the pooltable, its antennae searching for her legs. But then she happened to glance downward.

"Creel!"

The centipede started toward her. She jumped back, out of the way.

Creel threw the cueball with all his strength. It made a dent in the lineoleum beside the centipede, then crashed into the side of the wet-bar.

The centipede went for Vi. It was so fast that she couldn't get away from it. As its segments caught the light, they gleamed poisonously.

Creel snatched his cuestick off the table and hammered at the centipede. Again, he missed. But flying splinters of wood made the centipede turn and shoot in the other direction. It disappeared under the couch.

"Get it," she panted.

He shook the pieces of his cue at her. "I'll tell you what I fantasize. I fantasize that you *like* having sex with me. You fantasize that I'm somebody else." Then he wrenched the couch away from the wall, brandishing his weapons.

"So would you," she retorted, "if you had to sleep with a sensitive, considerate, imaginative *animal* like you."

As she left the room, she slammed the door behind her.

Shoving the furniture bodily from side to side, he continued hunting for the centipede.

The bedroom.

This room expresses Vi as much as the limitations of the house permit. The bed is really too big for the space available, but at least it has an elaborate brass headstead and footboard. The sheets and pillowcases match the bedspread, which is decorated with white flowers on a blue background. Unfortunately, Creel's weight makes the bed sag. The closet doors are warped and can't be closed.

There's an overhead light, but Vi never uses it. She relies on a pair of goose-necked Tiffany reading lamps. As a result, the bed seems to be surrounded by gloom in all directions.

Creel sat on the bed and watched the bathroom door. His back was bowed. His right fist gripped the neck of a bottle of tequila, but he wasn't drinking.

The bathroom door was closed. He appeared to be staring at himself in the full-length mirror attached to it. A strip of fluorescent light showed past the bottom of the door. He could see Vi's shadow as she moved around in the bathroom.

He stared at the door for several minutes, but she was taking her time. Finally, he shifted the bottle to his left hand.

"I never understand what you *do* in there."

Through the door, she said, "I'm waiting for you to pass out so I can go to sleep in peace."

He looked offended. "Well, I'm not going to pass out. I never pass out. You might as well give up."

Abruptly, the door opened. She snapped off the bathroom light and stood in the darkened doorway, facing him. She was dressed for bed in a nightie that would have made her look desirable if she had wished to look desirable.

"What do you want now?" she said. "Are you finished wrecking the gameroom already?"

"I was trying to kill that centipede. The one that scared you so badly."

"I wasn't scared—just startled. It's only a centipede. Did you get it?"

"No."

"You're too slow. You'll have to call an exterminator."

"Damn the exterminator," he said slowly. "*Fuck* the exterminator. Fuck the centipede. I can take care of my own problems. Why did you call me that?"

"Call you what?"

He didn't look at her. "An animal." Then he did. "I've never lifted a finger to hurt you."

She moved past him to the bed and propped the pillows up against the brass bedstead. Sitting on the bed, she curled her legs under her and leaned back against the pillows.

"I know," she said. "I didn't mean it the way it sounded. I was just mad."

He frowned. "You didn't mean it the way it sounded. How nice. That makes me feel a whole lot better. What in hell *did* you mean?"

"I hope you realize you're not making this any easier."

"It isn't easy for *me*. Do you think I like sitting here begging my own wife to tell me why I'm not good enough for her?"

"Actually," she said, "I think you do like it. This way, you get to feel like a victim."

He raised his bottle until the tequila caught the light. He peered into the golden liquid for a moment, then transferred the bottle back to his right hand. But he didn't say anything.

"All right," she said after a while. "You treat me like you don't care what I think or how I feel."

"I do it the way I know how," he protested. "If it feels good for me, it's supposed to feel good for you."

"I'm not just talking about sex. I'm talking about the way you treat me. The way you talk to me. The way you assume I have to like everything you like and can't like anything you don't like. The way you think my whole life is supposed to revolve around you."

"Then why did you marry me? Did it take you two years to find out you don't really want to be my wife?"

She stretched her legs out in front of her. Her nightie covered them to the knees. "I married you because I loved you. Not because I want to be treated like an object for the rest of my natural life. I need friends. People I can share things with. People who care what I'm thinking. I almost went to grad school because I wanted to study Baudelaire. We've been married for two years, and you still don't know who Baudelaire is. The only people I ever meet are your drinking buddies. Or the people who work for your company."

He started to say something, but she kept going. "And I need freedom. I need to make my own decisions—my own choices. I need to have my own life."

Again, he tried to say something.

"And I need to be cherished. You use me like I'm less interesting than your precious poolcue."

"It's broken," he said flatly.

"I know it's broken," she said. "I don't care. This is more important. I'm more important."

In the same tone, he said, "You said you loved me. You don't love me anymore."

"God, you're dense. *Think* about it. What on earth do you ever do to make me feel like *you* love *me*?"

He shifted the bottle to his left hand again. "You've been sleeping around. You probably screw every sonofabitch you can get into the sack. That's why you don't love me anymore. They probably do all kinds of dirty things to you I don't do. And you're hooked on it. You're bored with me because I'm just not exciting enough."

She dropped her arms onto the pillows beside her. "Creel, that's *sick*. You're *sick*."

Disturbed by her movement, the centipede crawled out between the pillows onto her left arm. It waved its poison claws while it tasted her skin with its antennae, looking for the best place to bite in.

This time, she did scream. Wildly, she flung up her arm. The centipede was thrown into the air.

It hit the ceiling and came down on her bare leg.

It was angry now. Its thick legs swarmed to take hold of her and attack.

With his free hand, he struck a backhand blow down the length of her leg that slapped the centipede off her.

As the centipede hit the wall, he pitched his bottle at it, trying to smash it. But it had already vanished into the gloom around the bed. A shower of glass and tequila covered the bedspread.

She bounced off the bed, hid behind him. "I can't take any more of this. I'm leaving."

"It's only a centipede," he panted as he wrenched the brass frame off the foot of the bed. Holding the frame in one hand for a club, he braced his other arm under the bed and heaved it off its legs. He looked strong enough to crush one centipede. "What're you afraid of?"

"I'm afraid of you. I'm afraid of the way your mind works."

As he turned the bed over, he knocked down one of the Tiffany lamps. The room became even darker. When he flipped on the overhead light, he couldn't see the centipede anywhere.

The whole room stank of tequila.

* * *

The living room again.

The sofa sits where Creel left it. The endtable lies on its side, surrounded by wilting flowers. The water from the vase has left a stain that looks like another shadow on the rug. But in other ways the room is unchanged. The lights are on. Their brightness emphasizes all the places they don't reach.

Creel and Vi are there. He sits in one of the armchairs and watches her while she rummages around in a large closet that opens into the room. She is hunting for things to take with her and a suitcase to carry them in. She is wearing a shapeless dress with no belt. For some reason, it makes her look younger. He seems more awkward than usual without a drink in his hands.

"I get the impression you're enjoying this," he said.

"Of course," she said. "You've been right about everything else. Why shouldn't you be right now? I haven't had so much fun since I dislocated my knee in high school."

"How about our wedding night? That was one of the highlights of your life."

She stopped what she was doing to glare at him. "If you keep this up, I'm going to puke right here in front of you."

"You made me feel like a complete shit."

"Right again. You're absolutely brilliant tonight."

"Well, you look like you're enjoying yourself. I haven't seen you this excited for years. You've probably been hunting for a chance to do this ever since you first started sleeping around."

She threw a vanity case across the room and went on rummaging through the closet.

"I'm curious about that first time," he said. "Did he seduce you? I bet you're the one who seduced him. I bet you begged him into bed so he could teach you all the dirty tricks he knew."

"Shut up," she muttered from inside the closet. "Just shut up. I'm not listening."

"Then you found out he was too normal for you. All he wanted was a straight screw. So you dropped the poor bastard and went looking for something fancier. By now, you must be pretty good at talking men into your panties."

She came out of the closet holding one of his old baseball bats.

"Damn you, Creel. If you don't stop this, so help me God, I'm going to beat your putrid brains out."

He laughed humorlessly. "You can't do that. They don't punish infidelity, but they'll put you in jail for killing your husband."

Slamming the bat back into the closet, she returned to her search.

He couldn't take his eyes off her. Every time she came out of the closet, he studied everything she did. After a while, he said, "You shouldn't let a centipede upset you like this."

She ignored him.

"I can take care of it," he went on. "I've never let anything hurt you. I know I keep missing it. I've let you down. But I'll take care of it. I'll call an exterminator in the morning. Hell, I'll call ten exterminators. You don't have to go."

She continued ignoring him.

For a minute, he covered his face with his hands. Then he dropped them into his lap. His expression changed.

"Or we can keep it for a pet. We can train it to wake us up in the morning. Bring in the paper. Make coffee. We won't need an alarm clock anymore."

She lugged a large suitcase out of the closet. Swinging it onto the sofa, she opened it and began stuffing things into it.

He said, "We can call him Baudelaire."

She looked nauseated.

"Baudelaire the Butler. He can meet people at the door for us. Answer the phone. Make the beds. As long as we don't let him get the wrong idea, he can probably help you choose what you're going to wear.

"No, I've got a better idea. You can wear *him*. Put him around your neck and use him for a ruff. He'll be the latest thing in sexy clothes. Then you'll be able to get fucked as much as you want."

Biting her lip to keep from crying, Vi went back into the closet to get a sweater off one of the upper shelves.

When she pulled the sweater down from the shelf, the centipede landed on the top of her head.

Her instictive flinch carried her out into the room. Creel had a perfect view of what was happening as the centipede dropped to her shoulder and squirmed inside the collar of her dress.

She froze. All the blood drained out of her face. Her eyes stared wildly.

"Creel," she breathed. "Oh my God. Help me."

The shape of the centipede showed through her dress as it crawled over her breasts.

"*Creel.*"

At the sight, he heaved himself out of his armchair and sprang toward her. Then he jerked to a stop.

"I can't hit it," he said. "I'll hurt you. It'll sting you. If I try to lift your dress to get at it, it might sting you."

She couldn't speak. The sensation of the centipede creeping across her skin paralyzed her.

For a moment, he looked completely helpless. "I don't know what to do." His hands were empty.

Suddenly, his face lit up.

"I'll get a knife."

Turning, he ran out of the room toward the kitchen.

Vi squeezed her eyes shut and clenched her fists. Whimpering sounds came between her lips, but she didn't move.

Slowly, the centipede crossed her belly. Its antennae explored her navel. All the rest of her body flinched, but she kept the muscles of her stomach rigid.

Then the centipede found the warm place between her legs.

For some reason, it didn't stop. It crawled onto her left thigh and continued downward.

She opened her eyes and watched as the centipede showed itself below the hem of her dress.

Searching her skin every inch of the way, the centipede crept down her shin to her ankle. There it stopped until she looked like she wasn't going to be able to keep herself from screaming. Then it moved again.

As soon as it reached the floor, she jumped away from it. She let herself scream, but she didn't let that slow her down. As fast as she could, she dashed to the front door, threw it open, and left the house.

The centipede was in no hurry. It looked ready and confident as its thick legs carried it under the sofa.

A second later, Creel came back from the kitchen. He carried a carving knife with a long, wicked blade.

"Vi?" he shouted. "Vi?"

Then he saw the open door.

At once, a snarl twisted his face. "You bastard," he whispered. "Oh you *bastard*. Now you've done it to me."

He dropped into a crouch. His eyes searched the rug. He held the knife poised in front of him.

"I'm going to get you for this. I'm going to find you. You can bet I'm going to find you. And when I do, I'm going to cut you to pieces. I'm going to cut you into little, tiny pieces. I'm going to cut all your legs off, one at a time. Then I'm going to flush you down the disposal."

Stalking around behind the sofa, he reached the place where the endtable lay on its side, surrounded by dead flowers.

"You utter bastard. She was my wife."

But he didn't see the centipede. It was hiding in the dark water-stain beside the vase. He nearly stepped on it.

In a flash, it shot onto his shoe and disappeared up the leg of his pants.

He didn't know the centipede had him until he felt it climb over his knee.

Looking down, he saw the long bulge in his pants work its way toward his groin.

Before he realized what he was doing—

SER VISAL'S TALE

THE PROSPECT OF A TALE FROM SER VISAL DREW US AS A flame draws moths, though only the most timid goodwoman—or the most rigorous Templeman—would claim that there was any danger in stories. And we were young, the sons of men of station throughout the region. Naturally, we scoffed at danger. The thought that we might hear something profane or even blasphemous—something that would never cross our hearing in the Temple or in the bosoms of our generally cautious families—only made the attraction more compelling. When the inns reopened between nones and vespers, we gathered, as eager as boys, in the public room of the Hound and Whip and opened our purses to provide Ser Visal with the lubrication his tongue required. The keeper of the Hound and Whip had the particular virtue of being as deaf as iron; he responded only to the vibrations he felt when we stamped our boots upon the boards, and he served us whatever wines God or inattention advised. For our part, we made certain that there were no tattlers among us in the public room before we urged Ser Visal to begin.

"Disorderly louts!" he responded, glaring around at us with a vexation which we knew to be feigned. He relished our enthusiasm for his stories. "Our God is a God of order. Confusion is abominable. Good King Traktus himself worships in the Temple of God. Twice a day he meets with High Templeman Crossus Hught to study and pray, that Heaven may defend us from evil. Have you nothing better to do with your time than to gaggle around me like puppies and loosen a fat old man's tongue with wine?"

One of our fellows giggled unfortunately at this brief jape of the Temple's teachings. But an elbow in the ribs silenced him before Ser Visal was diverted into a lecture on piety. He was prone to such digressions, perhaps thinking that they would whet our attention for his stories—and we dared not interrupt him, for fear that he would grow vexed in truth and refuse to continue. He demanded a rapt audience, and we sought to satisfy him.

Ser Quest Visal was indeed *a fat old man*—as fat as a porker, with eyes squeezed almost to popping in the heavy flesh of his face, arms that appeared to stuff his sleeves like sausages, and fingers as thick and pale as pastries. His grizzled hair straggled like a beldame's. Careless shaving left his jowls speckled with whiskers. Though he sat in the corner of the hearth—the warmest spot in the Hound and Whip—he wore two robes over his clothing, with the result that sweat ran from his brows as from an overlathered horse. Yet every gesture of his hands beyond his frilled cuffs held us, and every word he uttered was remembered. We were familiar with his storytelling.

He had returned to town after an absence of some days. In fact, it was rumored that he had fled to his estates immediately following the unprecedented—and unexplained—turmoil which had resulted from the most recent sitting of the judica. It was known to all that the judica had assembled to pass judgment upon a suspected witch, but no judgment had been announced. The disruption of the sitting had been followed by a rough and bitter search of the town, such as only the Templemen had the power and determination to pursue. Since then, the mood had been one of anger. Men who did not like the implied distrust of the search were further irked by the righteous frustration of the searchers. And finally—a development piquant to us all—no accounts of the judica, no high condemnations of witchcraft, no exhortations to shun for our souls the fires of damnation had been issued from the pulpits of the Temple. Instead, we had heard read out for the first time in our lives a writ of excommunication.

Its object had been Dom Sen Peralt.

You are cut off, the Templemen had thundered or crowed, according to their natures, *cut off root and trunk, branch and leaf, cut off from God and Temple, Heaven and hope. You are shunned by all men, blighted by all love. The sun will not warm your face. Shade will not cool your brow. Water and food will give you no sustenance. You are cursed in your mind and in your heart, in your blood and in your loins. Your loves will die, and your offspring will wither, and all that you have touched will be destroyed. This is the will of God.*

We knew that Ser Visal—like every other man of his rank—had attended the judica. And we prayed that he would reveal what had happened.

"Disorderly louts," he repeated, wiping wine from his chins. "Impious lovers of freedom and romance, which seduce souls to perdition." If his words were to be believed, he had always been one of the staunchest supporters of the Templemen. And surely none of us had ever heard him accused of courage. Yet we did not take his admonitions seriously. His voice had a special quaver which he used only to protest his devotion, and his eyes appeared to bulge with astonishment at what he heard himself say. "Well, attend me for your hope of Heaven. I will instruct you."

We settled ourselves on the long wooden benches of the Hound and Whip, hunched over the wide, planked tables, and listened.

"Boys are fools all," he began, and his fat fingers waggled at us. "I include you, every one. Fools! Lovers of dreams and freedom. And I count every man who has not set aside such toys a boy, whatever his age. You will learn better from me. I will lesson you in order and justice, in the folly of human passion against God's Temple and God's judgment. Your fathers will thank me for it." Without looking at any of us in particular, he remarked, "My flagon is empty."

Several of us stamped our feet. The son of Dom Tahl scattered coins onto the table. In response, the keeper brought a small cask of an unusually drinkable canary wine and left it for us to deal with as we saw fit.

Refreshed by a long draught, Ser Visal set down his flagon and sighed. "Boys and fools," he said, "surely none will deny that life has been much improved since good King Traktus became concerned for his salvation and turned to the Temple of God—and to High Templeman Crossus Hught—for spiritual assistance. The Templemen have become the right hand of the King as well as of God, and our lives are cleansed and straitened and made wiser thereby. Consider our prior state. Young whelps such as yourselves, Domsons and Sersons all, spent their lives riotously while their sires plotted for advantage or land. Farmers priced their produce as they chose and grew fat. Merchants wandered from town to town, spreading gossip and dissension with their wares. Gypsies and carnivals flourished upon credulity wherever it was found. The poor lined the streets as beggars, and when they died they were not left in the mud as they deserved, but were rather buried at public expense. Minstrels purveyed lies of heroism and great deeds, of thrones to be won in faraway lands, of adventures and dreams. Goodwomen who should have tended hearths and spinning left their homes to command shops and crops and men. And there were witches—

"The Temple has taught us that there are witches. We have learned to see the evil of a flashing glance"—Ser Visal rolled his eyes in mimicry—"the touch of a white hand, the smile of an unveiled face. We have learned that some women possess power to disorder men's minds as they disorder life, doing things which cannot be done and imposing their wills on those around them, weaving damnation and all foul perversion. For this reason we have the judica, to hunt that evil and root it out. So, good louts, you will hardly credit that there was once a time when some men and perhaps a few goodwomen did not believe in witches.

Yet witches there were." He rubbed his hands through the sweat on his brow, then flicked his fingers negligently, as though aping a holy sign for our silent amusement. "This is excellent canary." The candles of the inn were new and bright because there were no windows, and the dancing flames made his eyes appear to stare from his face. "Witches, indeed. They lived quietly among the dark woods, or secretly in barrows which few could find beneath the hedgerows, or openly with the gypsies and the minstrels. And woe to any man who went near them with his heart unguarded by righteousness, for they were strange and powerful and lovely as only evil can be, and that man would never again look upon his own goodwoman or his promised maid with quite the same—shall we say, quite the same enthusiasm?"

On the word, his plump lips twisted into a sardonic expression. But before we could laugh, he raised his gaze to the smoke-stained ceiling and went on devoutly, "Praise the Temple of God that the danger is no longer what it was! Oh, some witches yet live. Some have fled where men cannot follow. And some have learned to pass in covert among us, concealing their powers. But forewarned is forearmed. And most witches have gone to judgment and the hot iron of the judica, destroyed by Temple zealotry. Many of them, you puppies—more than you imagine. So many, it is astonishing that we are able to live without them—gone to feed the cauldron with their bones and their sins and their terrible cries. And"—he lowered his voice portentiously—"not one of them innocent. Not *one*. The judica has condemned every creature with a slim leg and a pert breast which the Templemen have brought for judgment."

He paused to refill his flagon and toss off another draught, then said, "Of course, I have not mentioned the many other amendments which good King Traktus has imposed upon our lives at the counsel of the High Templeman. Prices and merchants have been wisely regulated. Carnivals where such louts as you are were led into folly have been banned, on pain of slavery. And slavery itself—!

"It is an admirable institution, is it not? At one stroke, we are rid of all miscreants—the poor, the idle, the wicked—we are pro-vided with cheap service which any honest tradesman or farmer or man of station may afford, and the coffers of the Temple of God are enriched, to the benefit of our immortal souls, for by the King's edict all the fees of the slavers are shared with the Templemen. An *admirable* institution.

"So you see, my eager young gallants, it is not surprising that the tale of Dom Peralt began with a slave and ended with a witch."

At that, we all stiffened. Our attention grew even sharper, if that were possible. The sound of excommunication was in our ears. This story was precisely the one we most wished to hear.

Ser Visal smiled at the effect of his announcement. Then—per-haps recollecting that it was unwise to smile on any subject asso-ciated with the disfavor of the Temple—he frowned and slapped a fat hand to the table. "Be warned, whelps! This is not the tale of daring and passion you expect. It is sordid and foolish, and I tell it to caution you, so that you will be wiser than mad Dom Peralt, who was nothing more than a boy some few years older than yourselves."

But we were not daunted. We watched Ser Visal brightly, our breathing thick with anticipation in our chests. And slowly his face appeared to refold itself to lines of sadness. His gaze receded, as though he were now seeing the past rather than the public room of the Hound and Whip. We knew that look. If we did not interrupt him now, he would tell his story.

"Dom Sen Peralt," he sighed. "I knew his father. The old Dom was a goodly man, as all agreed—perhaps somewhat too little concerned for the state of the public weal, somewhat too much immersed in the private affairs of his estates and dependents, but hale of heart and whole of mind nonetheless. And grown like a tree!" The memory made Ser Visal chuckle voluminously within his robes. "An oak of a man. He bore no weapons; the threat of his fist was as good as a broadsword." Then he relapsed to sadness. "And many folk flourished under the shade of his care. He was more interested in the commonest babe born in the farthest cottage on his lands than in all the affairs of kings and counselors. A goodly man, greatly grieved in his passing.

"By ill chance, however, young Sen Peralt's mother died during his babyhood, and the old Dom was too occupied elsewhere to attend closely to the rearing of his son. He trusted, I believe, that a decent heart would be inherited—and that his example would supply what his attention did not. In young Sen's early youth, his father had no cause to complain. But as the boy came toward manhood, he fell among ill companions"—Ser Visal gave us a glare—"shiftless whelps and roisterers such as yourselves, Serson Nason Lew and Domson Beau Frane chief among them, and he discovered the pleasures of folly. The old Dom was not a man to enforce his will upon others, and he knew not how to intervene. To his sorrow, his son become a tremendous gallant, dedicated to wine and min-strelsy and compliant women. Sen Peralt's brawls became matters of legend. I shudder to think of the inns he wrecked, the virgins he—"

Abruptly, Ser Visal stopped. "You are too young to understand virgins," he said severely. "Refill my flagon."

But when he had replaced some of the fluid he sweated away, he resumed his tale. "Unfortunately, the old Dom died while helping one of his farmers clear a field of boulders. In his mourning, the new Dom was consoled as he had been entertained by his boon companions, Serson Lew and Domson Frane. I will say of him that he gave fit respect to his father. But when he had taken upon himself his father's station, he showed no inclination to follow his father's path. He did not altogether neglect his duties. And he took no slaves, as his father had taken none. But the greater part of his time

was spent in carouse, defying both the advice of his father's friends"—
Ser Visal's expression suggested that he had given Dom Peralt hogs-
heads of good advice—and had helped him drink them—"and the
strict attention of the Templemen. He was a scandal in the region,
though doubtless you louts admired him. Templeman Knarll himself
let it be known that sermons would soon be preached against Dom
Peralt from every pulpit within a day's ride, if young Sen did not
begin to take better care of his salvation. It was, said Templeman
Knarll, precisely to protect good people from such sins that the
Temple of God had become so rigorous."

Ser Visal shrugged his round shoulders. "And it was precisely in
this state of ill grace that Dom Peralt came to town on slaving day.

"You are familiar with slaving day. It is most instructive—*most*
instructive. A lesson to us all. There in the marketplace gather the
slavers to sell their wares—and the Templemen to collect their fees.
The streets are thick with mud, as rank as sewers, and pickpockets
work happily among the crowds, and merchants hawk all manner
of commodities, and every townsman comes to consider what may
be bought. It is as near to festivity as the Temple of God permits.
Goodwomen remain in their homes, but jades wear their brightest
colors, and gallants preen, and money seeps everywhere from hand
to hand, more subtle than the mud but not less tainted." Perhaps
we saw anger in Ser Visal's eyes—or perhaps he was simply spinning the mood of his story. "And amid it all are the new slaves for
purchase.

"They are chained to each other like cattle, hardly able to lift
their fetters for exhaustion or hunger, and dressed as much in muck
as in rags. In their eyes—when their eyes are open and their heads
raised—are every kind of hate and fear and despair, but no love.
I have seen children of no more than four summers manacled to
known molesters of children—and the parents bound elsewhere
for their debts, helpless. I have seen the sons of impoverished farmers coupled by iron to desperate whores. I have seen innocent travelers pleading for release from the slavers' quotas. Their filth and
degradation exemplify all the evils which have brought slavery among
us. The Templemen accompany them, garnering fees from the slavers—and so the world is cleansed. *Most* instructive. Learn its lesson
well, puppies."

With one long pull, Ser Visal emptied his flagon, then glowered at us as though he were outraged. But almost at once the flesh swelled around his eyes, and he smiled humorlessly.

"To slaving day," he said, "came Dom Sen Peralt and his two cohorts in debauch, Domson Frane and Serson Lew.

"He had not the full size of his father, but still he was *large* of frame, and neither wine nor feast had softened the edges of his strength. He bore his head high, as if he were of regal birth. The black curls which crowned his head gleamed darkly. His gaze shone in the sunlight. His stride was strong, immune to the mud sucking at his boots. His fine mouth above his chin showed a bemused contempt for all the human ruin enchained around him. And his comrades slogged at his side, struggling to match him and appearing only foolish.

"Do I make him seem grand?" asked Ser Visal acidly. "He was as drunk as a tinker. Only the prospect of more drink kept him on his feet. If he had tripped, he might have lain face down in the mud and been trampled without noticing it."

At once, however, our instructor reverted to piety. "But God's will was otherwise. Before Dom Peralt had crossed the marketplace to the inn he sought, he was accosted by a man nearly as large as himself—by Growt, most feared of the slavers.

"It is said of Growt—but such tales are told everywhere, especially among boys. Well, my puppies, the tales are true. Growt is feared because he asks no questions concerning those he hales into slavery. If the Templemen desire a man or woman punished, they merely give the name to Growt. If a miller comes to loathe his goodwoman's shrewish tongue, he gives her name to Growt. If a usurer covets the property of a debtor, he gives the name to Growt. And when he has not enough commissions to fill his quota, Growt takes minstrels and travelers and gypsies where he finds them.

"Now among slavers, as in the Temple of God, such men as Dom Peralt are looked upon with resentment—and perhaps also with fear—because they take no slaves. Their wealth is denied to those who most merit it. And on this slaving day Growt's resentment had grown beyond its usual blackness. His wares were in little demand. It will not surprise you that innocent travelers and shrewish goodwomen are not always docile slaves. Growt's wares were rendered suspect by his means of obtaining them. Therefore it was in no mood of good fellowship that he set himself in the way of Dom Sen Peralt.

"Burly as a bear, but entirely hairless from the knob of his pate to the tops of his toes, and dressed in his slavers' leathers, he was a formidable obstacle to be found in any man's path, were the man drunk or sober. But he was not content merely to bar Dom Peralt's way. When the young Dom neared him, Growt thrust out an arm as heavy as an axletree and jolted Dom Peralt in his tracks.

"It appeared momentarily that Dom Peralt would go sprawling at the feet of Growt's slaves. But he regained his balance. Young Nason and Beau Frane gaped at Growt as if he had been translated from the nether regions to appall them. Indeed, he was blackened and dirty enough to be a fiend—but of course he was not, being about the Temple's business. Arms akimbo, he stood his ground and awaited Dom Peralt's reaction.

"Hauling himself upright, Dom Peralt turned a smile upon Growt. For a moment, he seemed to study this barrier—though in truth he was hardly able to focus his eyes for drink. Then he said in a friendly manner, 'Slaver, you stand between me and a flagon of ripe sack. Already it languishes for me, and I mean to relieve it of its longing.' His cohorts giggled at this. 'Do not hinder me,' Dom Peralt concluded, 'in my errand of mercy.' To which Domson Frane, the bolder of the two, added, 'You mustn't hinder him, no, you mustn't. Hinderance makes him bilious.'

"'Your pardon,' replied Growt with admirable insincerity. 'Buy a slave, and I will let you pass.'

"Dom Peralt blinked in response, his smile unaltered. 'A slave?' he asked, betraying the impairment of his wits. 'You wish me to buy a slave? Heinous custom. Why should I buy a slave?'

"Growt had the trick of appearing to bristle with menace instead of hair. 'You insult me, Dom,' he answered. 'I do the work of the Temple of God. It is not heinous. And I do not *wish* you to buy a slave. I *mean* you to buy a slave.'

"Sunlight or some other gleam kindled in Dom Peralt's eyes. 'You are mistaken, slaver,' he said affably. 'I have not insulted you. It is not possible to insult you.'

"Growt glowered. Again, his great arm jabbed Dom Peralt, nearly depriving him of balance. Serson Lew retreated a step. Beau Frane looked to his leader for some hint of what was to be done. But

Growt ignored those whelps as he would ignore you. 'Nevertheless,' he repeated, 'I mean you to buy a slave.' As Dom Peralt steadied himself, the slaver gestured toward his wares. 'I have young ones and old ones. I have women with open legs and men with strong backs. I have skilled laborers and dumb cattle. I even have one'—his mouth leered, but his eyes did not—'who will tune a lute—and a song with it—if you know the way to twist his thumbs.' Then, abruptly, his manner changed, and he used the voice which kept his charges cowering by day and pliant by night. *'Buy one.'*

"Again, Dom Peralt contrived to regain his bearing. On his lips was the smile which made maidens blush and caused women some weakness in their knees. He paid no regard to his companions, though Nason Lew whispered for retreat and young Beau silently urged fight. To Growt, he said sweetly, 'Now it is I who must ask your pardon. The cries of lorn sack from yonder inn are piteous, filling my ears. I fear I have been remiss in my attention—I did not hear you clearly. Will you be so kind as to repeat? I believe you began by begging my pardon. Continue from there.'

"Well, he had audacity. That I will say for him. But a playful mood was on him. In any other mind, he might simply have put his fist to Growt's face and chanced the outcome. And *that*, you louts, would have gone hard for him. He was roundly drunk—and Growt was not notably scrupulous in the use of his hands. But it is commonly said that God watches over drunkards; and so Dom Peralt sought contest with his sodden wits rather than with his equally sodden strength.

"For his part, however, Growt had no wit. He replied with a growl which bared what remained of his rotten teeth. Grabbing at the front of Dom Peralt's fine jacket, he wrenched young Sen from his feet to his knees in the mud. There Growt bent him backward and demanded softly, 'Buy a slave.'

"A crowd had gathered. Witnesses abounded, all hungry for excitement. In their hearts, most of the townspeople would have cheered for Dom Peralt to rise up and repay some of Growt's great debt of grief. But there were Templemen present, watching and wary for sins to be punished—and so most of the spectators kept the nature of their eagerness to themselves. Serson Lew hopped from one foot to the other, wanting to run. And his fellow had come to be of a similar mind. They were accustomed to observe Dom Peralt's brawls and applaud them, not to participate in them. No one considered intervention.

"For all his follies, however, Dom Peralt had been formed in another mold. On his knees in muck, and nearly falling backward under the pressure of Growt's grasp, he betrayed no whit of consternation. His smile remained sweetly upon his lips—his gaze did not waver from Growt's. 'Buy a slave?' he said, articulating carefully through his drunkenness. 'Splendid idea. Why have I never done so before? Truly, my own thoughtlessness astonishes me. I am in your debt, slaver. I will buy a slave at once.'

"This nonplussed Growt. He sensed Dom Peralt's sport, but could not fathom it. Clearly, the slaver wished to grind Dom Peralt's smile into the mud. But how could he do so, when Dom Peralt had just offered to meet his demand? 'Do not toy with me,' he snarled, attempting to recapture his menace. 'Buy a slave.'

" 'But of course,' replied Dom Peralt. 'I said the same myself. Just now, as I recall. A splendid idea. Altogether splendid. Did I say that also?' There was laughter in his eyes, but none in his voice.

"Growt's whole face twisted as he strove to guess young Sen's game. Bending over him, he hissed, 'One of mine—or I will break your back where you kneel.'

"Dom Peralt flung his arms wide in a gesture of appeal. 'Slaver, you wound me. I have not deserved this doubt. I cannot deny that I am young and thoughtless. But none accuse me of ingratitude. You have awakened me to my error. What other wares should I consider, except yours?' In a subtle way, his tone turned harder as he spoke. But his smile belied all hint of anger. 'However,' he continued reasonably, 'you must allow me to rise. I cannot inspect your merchandise from here.'

"Growt was snared and knew it. Titterings and chuckles arose from the crowd, galling him—but he was compelled by his own demand to release Dom Peralt's jacket and stand back. He did so with a muttered curse and a black look that stilled some of the mirth of the onlookers. Then he pointed to the nearest chained line and said harshly, 'There. Choose.' And he named a price which was twice what any of his prisoners was worth.

"But Dom Peralt was a match for Growt's ill grace, and his sport had only begun. 'I thank you slaver,' he said with a glance at the slaves. Instead of moving to make selection, he drew a linen handkerchief from his sleeve. With the slow care of the drunken, he wiped the clots of mud from his breeches and boots. While Growt fretted and waited furiously, young Sen made a great show of cleaning himself. Then, when Growt was nearly frustrated enough to strike him again, he tossed his handkerchief aside and swayed toward the slaves.

"They were an unprepossessing lot—as you have perhaps seen on other occasions. Filth and poor food and fear had deprived them of their charms. To be frank, those charms might once have been substantial, considering the sources from which Growt obtained his merchandise. But where other slavers naturally attempted to put the best face possible upon their wares, Growt reveled in demonstrating the extent to which men and women created in God's image might be degraded. Dom Peralt could not keep a frown from his face as he surveyed his choices.

"Domson Frane and Serson Lew watched him with the honest astonishment of too much wine, as unable as Growt to fathom Dom Peralt's game. They did not fear that their leader would abandon his principles. What did they know of principles? *Their* fathers had slaves. Perhaps they owned slaves themselves. Doubtless they considered Dom Peralt's former refusals a harmless affectation—part of the jesting and fun of his company. No, they feared only that his reputation for courage would be tarnished, thus diminishing his stature—and theirs—in the eyes of other young roisterers like yourselves.

"Similarly the other onlookers. They did not wish Dom Peralt to fight for his beliefs—if he had any. They wished him to fight because they feared Growt. Only the Templemen felt otherwise. For the most part, Dom Peralt was surrounded by disappointment as he contemplated his selection.

"But he was blind and deaf to all concerns except his own, and his concern was to make his choice. Or perhaps it was simply to keep himself from falling on his face. Resisting unsteadiness, he moved along the chained line, stopping here before a girl still too young to live without her mother, there before a man so old that he could hardly lift his manacles—and yet he made no choice. One cynic among the townspeople offered wagers as to whether Dom

Peralt would succeed at picking out a slave and paying before he lapsed into unconsciousness.

"Perhaps therefore it is open to question whether God watches over drunkards. Instead of lapsing into unconsciousness, Dom Peralt found a young woman locked to the chain between two battered fellows who had the look of dispossessed farmers. That she was young could be discerned through the grime. And the tatters which remained of her raiment suggested that she had lived for some time among gypsies—as guest, not gypsy herself, for her blue eyes and the shape of her face lacked the swart sullenness of that kind. But nothing of beauty survived the treatment she had received. A swollen cheek and blood showed that some teeth had been knocked from her jaw. Even the shade of her hair could not be determined through the muck. Oh, she was unsavory. Faugh! I know not what attracted Dom Peralt to her. Her wrists were gouged and infected from the efforts she had made to twist free of her fetters. Only her eyes—Their blue was startling in her smudged and beaten face. They suggested that she was better acquainted with anger than with fear.

"Dom Peralt roused himself as if he had dozed while studying her. With a nod, he said, 'This one. I want her.' Then he turned to Growt, and his smile was resumed. 'Hear you, slaver? I want this one.'

"Growt grinned and glowered because he had triumphed—and did not like the taste of Dom Peralt's manner, which deprived this triumph of the salt Growt preferred. Sourly, he named his price again. It was twice what he had already demanded.

"Still in all the sum was a trifle to a man with Dom Peralt's properties. From his purse he fumbled out coins which approximated the amount of Growt's price and tossed them to the slaver. So unsteady was young Sen now that Growt could not claim insult in the way the coins were thrown so that he could not catch them all. Anger corded his neck as he retrieved his earnings from the mud, but he had no choice left. Even the Templemen would not smile on him if he harmed a purchaser of his wares. Snarling and vicious, he went to unlock Dom Peralt's selection from the chains.

"When the clasp was undone and the chain dropped from the manacles, a peculiar shudder ran through the woman, as if a weight had been lifted from her soul. Perhaps there were tears amid the grime on her cheeks. Stepping forward, she raised her ironbound wrists to Dom Peralt, dumbly asking that he have those fetters removed as well.

"Whenever he met her gaze, his smile failed him. 'Free her wrists,' he commanded Growt. 'I want her arms free.' A sharp edge had entered his voice. To disguise it, he pretended a jest. 'Have no fear that she will escape me.'

"Cursing continuously under his breath, Growt complied. From a pouch at his belt, he took a chisel of hardened iron—from among his tools, a hammer and a rude anvil. He was not gentle, but he did nothing which might be protested—nothing which would require even the justice of the Templemen to compel the return of some portion of the price for damaged merchandise—as he set first one wrist and then the other against the anvil and struck away the manacles. The task finished, however, he could not resist thrusting the slave so that she stumbled at Dom Peralt, staining his clothes with her filth. She trembled against him as though the removal of the iron had made her feverish.

"'There,' growled the slaver. 'She is yours. Another rape or two, and she will be well suited to you.'

"'No,' replied Dom Peralt. His smile was restored, and his eyes laughed as his game ended. Setting the woman away from him, he turned to Growt and gave the slaver a mocking bow. 'She is free. I want no slaves. I have purchased her, and now I set her free. It is my right. *Hear you?*" he demanded of the crowd, his witnesses— a shout perhaps of pleasure, perhaps of concealed outrage. *'I set her free!'*

"That was his triumph over Growt the slaver. Heed me well, you louts—and learn. Thus passes the romance of the world. To the dismay of his cohorts—and the great glee of the crowd—his eyes rolled back in his head and he toppled into the mud.

"When anyone thought to look toward the woman he had freed— well, she was gone. Before so many onlookers, she disappeared as if she were merely mist and dream. No sign of her remained but her fetters lying at Dom Peralt's feet.

"Are you blind? My flagon is empty."

Abashed by our negligence, we stamped our feet, shoveled coins from our purses. This time, the keeper saw fit to bring us a wine which God had intended to be malmsey but which man had reduced to something approaching vinegar. Ser Visal, however, quaffed it without protest. Sweat poured from him so profusely that the collar of his outer robe had turned dark and the shoulders were spotted. He, too, had a look of fever about him. While he drank, we held our breath and prayed in silence that he would not cease his tale.

For a moment, his pale, plump hands trembled on the flagon. Wine dribbled from the corners of his mouth to diversify the stains on his robe. But slowly the drink—rank though it was—appeared to ease or mask his discomfort. He refilled his flagon and drank again, spilling less. When at last he looked around at us once more, his bulging eyes had a whetted aspect, a sharpness which might have been mockery or cunning.

"So much"—he snapped his fingers, a fat, popping sound— "for the gallantry of Dom Sen Peralt. A grand figure, is he not? Face down and drunken in the mud, having risked himself in sport with a man who might have taken a hammer to his thick skull—altogether worthy of your emulation. I am pleased to see that I have your attention. Perhaps you will learn something which will do you credit. Have I spoken to you concerning witches?"

We nodded, hoping to deflect him from a digression. But he ignored us. "It is said," he mused, "in the stories that goodwomen tell around their hearths of a winter's evening that iron is the bane of all witches. A witch's power is over flesh and plant, and with both she works many things which the Templemen abominate— but iron blocks her strength, reducing her to mortal helplessness. This, my puppies, chances to be true. Every witch brought before the judica comes with her wrists bound in iron, and none escape. Escape would surely be without difficulty for a woman capable of turning the minds of the men around her, causing them to see in her place the goodwoman who mothered them or married them, the daughter of their loins—or perhaps to see no woman at all, but only a chamber full of men gathered about a cauldron of molten metal to no purpose. But that does not transpire, though the women haled before the judica are never innocent. Their wrists are manacled, and so they are seen to be what they are, witches deprived of power. Thus the efficacy of iron is proven."

Ser Visal drank again, then looked at us and smiled. "When Dom Sen Peralt awakened from his stupor, he found himself in a windowless cell on a pallet of foul straw. The walls were of blocked granite—the door, barred iron. He was alone except for the light of one small tallow candle and the scurrying sound of rats.

"This was no little surprise to him, as you may perhaps imagine"—Ser Visal grinned sardonically—"and in his fuddled state he was slow to comprehend it. He was afire with thirst, and his first thought was for wine to quench the burning—his second, for water if he could not have wine. Lurching up from the pallet, he blundered from wall to wall of the cell as though it were the public room of an inn and shouted for the keeper to attend him until the pain of effort threatened to split his skull. But he was young and hale, and when he had rested a few moments he became conscious that it was cold stone to which his face was pressed, rather than honest planking. Still he did not understand. Slowly, however, he mastered himself enough to grasp the meaning of the single candle left burning in the center of the earthen floor—and of the barred door.

"His head hurt horridly. His tongue was a dry sponge in his mouth, and the back of his throat was hot with acid. Rats came sniffing about his boots, but he ignored the vermin. He stood with his back to the stone while his mind turned like a rusted and squalling millwheel. Then he went back to the pallet, seated himself there, folded his arms about his knees, and strove to will the pain from his head.

"Much time passed, but he endured it as though he were stoic, sitting upon the pallet and moving only to fend away the rats. I have said—have I not?—that he had wit. Despite his debauched state, he employed that wit to some purpose. Rather than ranting about the cell and howling from the door and expending himself wildly, he attempted instead to clear his mind and conserve his strength.

"Gradually, his hurt eased, but his thirst did not. At last, he left the pallet and searched the dark corners of the cell, hoping to find that his captors possessed humanity enough to have left him some water. But they had not. Outwardly calm—and inwardly raging, both with thirst and with other passions—he resumed his seat and his waiting.

"Without a window, he had no measure for the time. The hour-bells were not audible. But he was familiar enough with drink to estimate the duration of his unconsciousness. Eventually, he judged that vespers and compline had rung and passed. Despite his thirst, which grew upon him like a rage, he set himself to endure the night as well as he was able.

"But his captors were accustomed to darkness, and they came for him when he did not expect them. He heard the striding of boots outside his cell. In such cases, men hope unreasonably. It was with great difficulty that he refrained from springing to the door and croaking for help. He possessed himself upon the pallet, however, and shortly a key groaned in the lock of his cell. Armed guards entered. They bore with them a writing desk lit by several candles and a chair, which they set facing their prisoner. Then they withdrew to the walls on either side of the door, so that Dom Peralt would be prevented from either violence or escape.

"Into the cell came Templeman Knarll himself, highest of all servants of the Temple of God in this region.

"He wore his formal robes, which were customarily reserved for the pulpit of the Temple. Resplendent in white surplice and gold chasuble, symbolizing Heavenly purity and worldly power, he would have appeared impressive if— Well, Templeman Knarll is known to you. He is a devout and searching man, worthy of admiration." Ser Visal employed his pious tone to good effect. "He is not to be mocked for his appearance. That he has the form of a toad and the face of a hedgehog is the will of the Almighty—surely not of Templeman Knarll. Nevertheless, it is not to be wondered at that he has little patience for those better made by their Creator than he.

"Without a glance at Dom Peralt, he seated himself at the desk, produced parchment, quill, and ink, and began to write.

"As he listened to the scratching of Templeman Knarll's pen, Dom Peralt had opportunity to inquire what he had done to expose himself to the Temple's anger—and the King's justice. He was surely imprisoned in the Temporal Office of the Temple of God, where crimes both physical and spiritual were perse—that is to say, *prose*cuted since good King Traktus joined hands with High Templeman Crossus Hught. But for what reason? Doubtless any of you would have asked that question, were you brave enough to address Templeman Knarll before gaining his permission to speak. Dom Peralt was formed in another mold. He allowed his spiritual father a few moments' silence. Then he said as clearly as his parched throat permitted, 'Templeman, I thirst. I must have water.'

"Templeman Knarll raised his head and scowled—no comforting sight. Releasing his pen, he began to read aloud what he had written. 'Dom Sen Peralt, son of'—and so on, on such-and-such date, in the following place—'by authority of the Temple of God, and of His Royal Highness'—as you might imagine"—Ser Visal waggled his plump fingers as though conducting music—" 'you are adjured on your soul, and in the sight of God, to answer the questions put to you herewith.'

"But young Sen had not given Templeman Knarll the courtesy of rising to his feet, and his reply was similarly respectful. 'Have done, Templeman,' he interposed. 'I will answer your questions. I will pay whatever price you require for absolution. But I must have water. Slake my thirst, and I will give you no cause to complain of me.' He was a fool, as I have said.

" 'You misunderstand your plight,' replied Templeman Knarll. He was angered, but too certain of his power to give way to vexation. 'First you will satisfy me. Then perhaps I will grant you water—or vinegar, if I see fit. For the sake of your soul, I will have no pity on your poor flesh.' Glancing at the parchment before him, he said formally, 'Dom Sen Peralt, you are a carouser and a wastrel, a source of sin and shame to the Temple of God and the community of believers. But such faults may be forgiven, if they are fully and abjectly repented. The crime of which you are accused knows no absolution. It is an offense against Heaven and must be cleansed with blood. That blood will be yours rather than another's, if you fail to answer me truthfully and contritely.

" 'Dom Peralt, for how long have you been in consort with the witch Thamala?'

"During his wait, Dom Peralt had readied himself for many things—but he was not prepared for *that* accusation. In astonishment, he demanded, '*Who?*'

" 'For how long,' Templeman Knarll repeated heavily, 'have you been in consort with the witch Thamala?'

" 'No,' muttered young Sen. 'No.' He now had some glimmering of his true plight—and yet he could not understand it at all. In something akin to panic, he stumbled to his feet and steadied himself against the wall, swallowing at the taste of brimstone in his dry mouth. 'I know nothing of witches.' Fervidly, he gathered his strength. 'I do not consort with witches. I have never met one. If I did, I would shun her. You err with me, Templeman.'

"Templeman Knarll's regard did not waver. 'Denial is foolish—and dangerous,' he replied. 'Innumerable witnesses will attest that you freed her of your own will, when she was ironbound and helpless. That was not the act of one who knows nothing of witches. It was the act of a man who saw his debauched lover in peril and sought to free her, so that he would not be deprived of the evil for which he had bartered his soul.'

"Hungry, thirst-ravaged, and frightened, Dom Peralt could not stifle his trembling. Yet he held his gaze firm. 'I repeat. I do not consort with witches. I have never met one. You have been gulled with lies, Templeman.'

"'Lies!' snorted Templeman Knarll. 'You are glib, Dom Peralt. Do you deny that of all the slaves proffered by the slaver Growt you chose none other than the witch Thamala? Do you deny that you willingly paid an exorbitant price for her? Do you deny that you commanded the iron struck from her wrists? Do you deny,' concluded the Templeman, chewing upon each word, 'that you set her free?'

"Dom Peralt stared at his interrogator and for a moment had no answer. He had wit, as I have said—he was not blind to the gulf yawning at his feet. Oh, he was young and strong and cocksure, not much prone to the fears which bedevil those of weaker flesh. But he was not faulty of mind. So he did not protest that he had purchased and freed that woman merely upon a whim, to mock Growt. Instead, he said carefully, 'It appears that I must make some defense. Questions occur to me, Templeman.'

"'Do not think to play with me,' snapped Templeman Knarll. 'I am not come here to answer your questions. You will answer mine—and feel gratitude that I deign to ask them.'

"'If this Thamala was a witch,' insisted Dom Peralt, 'why was she not haled before the judica rather than granted to Growt for sale? Is it the custom of Templemen to sell proven witches as merchandise, in order to trap and damn the innocent man who makes purchase?'

"Young whelps, it is well that the Temple of God is served by able men such as Templeman Knarll rather than by ignorant louts such as yourselves. He also is not blind. He saw that this question was one which he must answer. It would be asked again before the judica, when Dom Peralt was brought for judgment—and the men of land and station and power there would not look kindly upon an affirmative reply. Restraining his ire, Templeman Knarll responded, 'Thamala was not known to be a witch. She was merely a finding of Growt's, nothing more. And he took her asleep in a camp of gypsies, where she was in hiding from the justice of the Temple. His iron blocked her wiles before she had opportunity to employ them. Therefore he was unaware of her—and did not report her. Had she been known to us, we would have taken her from him at once, to protect the innocent.'

"At this, Dom Peralt bowed. 'Your integrity relieves me greatly,' he said. 'It does, however, inspire another question. By what means have you now determined that this Thamala was indeed a witch? Have you taken her captive? Has the judica already pronounced judgment upon her?'

"From this unseemly inquiry Templeman Knarll stepped back. Dom Peralt's second question did not appear as dangerous as his first. 'I caution you,' said the Templeman. 'I will have no more of your insolence. It is in my power to deprive you of water until your flesh screams for it, if I choose. For how long have you been in consort—?'

"Dom Peralt made no movement which might attract the force of the guards. He stood against the stone, his hands still at his sides—no threat in him. Yet he interrupted Templeman Knarll in a voice which caused that worthy to flinch as though he had been struck. 'Have you named this Thamala a witch merely because I set her free?'

"Provoked to fury, the Templeman pounded a fist on the top of his writing desk, so that the candleflames wavered and danced and his eyes echoed the fires of damnation. 'She *vanished*!' he roared. 'No Godly goodwoman simply disappears before townspeople and Templemen—but your consort did! With her foul power, she veiled her flight from all around her. And that was *witnessed*! It was witnessed by *Templemen*!' By degrees, he regained his composure. 'You freed her,' he said in a tone at once soft and venomous. '*You.* Of all the slaves offered you, you chose her and freed her—her and no other. I notice you do not protest your innocence. Why her, Dom Peralt? Why her and no other?'

"Dom Peralt smiled as well as the growing anguish of his thirst permitted. 'You say that she has vanished, and you have not recaptured her. Therefore you cannot present her as evidence of my wrong-doing to the judica. You have no case against me, Templeman.'

"Templeman Knarll did not blink or turn aside. Why should he permit this degraded youth to anger him? His power was sure. More softly still, he repeated, 'Why her and no other?'

"But Dom Peralt also did not turn aside. His smile in no way softened the hardness in his eyes. 'When I looked at her,' he answered, 'I saw that her spirit was greater than her fear. Though she was enslaved—and enslaved by Growt!—she was not cowed. For that reason, I chose her.' Then he said again, 'Templeman, you have no case against me.'

"Abruptly, Templeman Knarll stood from his chair. With great care, he set aside his quill, stopped his inkpot, then gathered up his sheets of parchment and tucked them away within the sleeve of his surplice. As he did so, he said, 'Dom Sen Peralt, you are an impious wretch, careless of your soul, and a hazard to all who love salvation. Praise God, the Temple is stronger. And we who serve the will of Heaven will never permit such as you to disorder our good work. If you think to defy me, you are a fool. I will return to question you when thirst has lessened your haughtiness somewhat.

"'Understand me well,' he continued as he moved to the door. 'By the word of the Temple, you are bound—and by the word of the Temple, your bones will burn in molten iron if you refuse to answer me. Tell me how you came into the company of this witch— how she wove her wiles upon you—and how we may find her again, recapture her so that her evil can be destroyed—and you will be spared from agony if not from death. Hear you? The Temple is *stronger* than you. You have no escape. Your soul is in our care, whether you are determined for Heaven or Hell, and we will wrest you from evil at any cost. You are bound to us as all are bound, from the meanest slave to King Traktus himself, and *we will rule our own*. Think upon it and recant.'

"A stirring speech," Ser Visal commented after a fresh draught of that vile malmsey. "You would do well to heed it. But I regret to say that Dom Peralt was not swayed by such chaff. Perverse man, he faced Templeman Knarll as he had earlier faced Growt the slaver and was not abashed.

"'I think not,' he said. 'For the most part, the folk under your rule are cattle, and so you misjudge all others. But to condemn me you must try me before the judica—and the judica is composed of men like myself, men of my own station. Do you believe they will pass judgment upon me? They will not dare. For the safety of their own skins, they will not dare. You have no case against me,' he said for the third time. 'And if any Dom or Ser may be sent to the cauldron on such a pretext, then none of their lives are secure. They will not permit it.'

" 'They will not be asked to permit it,' replied Templeman Knarll almost mildly. 'Before the judica sits, I will obtain your confession. Thirst and pain, Dom Peralt. I will obtain all the answers I require. In simple mercy for a confessed consort of witches, the judica will condemn you—and all your insolence will avail you nothing.'

"This Dom Peralt chose to ignore. His thirst was already severe, and he did not wish to consider its consequences. 'Further,' he continued as if Templeman Knarll had not spoken, 'my friends will support me. Serson Nason Lew and Domson Beau Frane will testify that I have no knowledge of witches. Especially they will testify that I had never beheld the woman Thamala until I purchased her—and that I purchased her while drunk—*and* that I did so only under Growt's bullying, so that he would not break my skull. It is plain that I will be freed. You will know how you are feared if no one of the judica laughs in your face.'

"But Templeman Knarll was no longer to be baited. He gestured the guards to retrieve his writing desk and chair. As they obeyed, he said, 'Your friends have already spoken.' Now he did not trouble to meet Dom Peralt's gaze. 'They understand the error of their ways and are prepared to be truthful. They will testify that frequently you left them at night, to go they knew not where. But always when you returned you bore the marks of blood and debauch upon your person. And always when you returned you proposed some new revel, prank, or crime, each more degrading and vile than the one before. They will testify that they have long suspected your involvement with witchcraft—and that only their fear of you impelled them to hold their tongues until now.

" 'Dom Peralt, I advise confession.' Brusquely, Templeman Knarll waved the guards from the cell. He stood aside in the passage as the door was locked. Then through the bars he concluded, 'You will earn a kinder death.'

"Without further word, he strode away. The boots of his escort knelled upon the hard earth as they departed.

"*'Whoresons!'* Dom Peralt shouted after them—and had the satisfaction of hearing his anger echo from the walls. But the echoes faded rapidly, and he was left alone.

"Doubtless," said Ser Visal abruptly, disdaining transition, "you are all agog with curiosity concerning the witch Thamala." There he misjudged us—or judged us better than we knew. For the moment, we were not concerned with Thamala at all. Our first thought was a righteous indignation that Dom Peralt had been betrayed by his trusted friends. What manner of men were they, to be so spineless? *We* would have been braver. But then we thought again. At one time or another, all of us had tasted the severity of the Temple in small ways, and from our cradles we had learned an abiding fear of Templemen. Their authority ruled our lives. Would any of us truly have defied them to champion a friend who had fallen under their disfavor? If we were honest, we admitted that we had doubt of ourselves.

Therefore we felt Dom Peralt's plight the more poignantly. Imprisoned by Templemen, intended for torture and death—and betrayed by his friends! How had he borne it? Alone and without hope, how had he borne it?

But Ser Visal told his tales in his own way, and he chose to misinterpret our avid attention. Bracing his hands upon the table, he shifted his weight to settle his hams more comfortably. Then he leaned again into the warmth of the hearth. "Well," he continued, "there is little I can profitably relate to you. All witches conceal their homes, parentage, and skill, striving in that way to preserve themselves from the cauldron of the judica. I may say of her only that her mother was also a witch—and unlucky, unable to elude the grasp of the Templemen. In bitter flight because she could not aid her mother—for were not her mother's wrists bound in iron, proof against witchery?—Thamala turned to the gypsies for sanctuary. And there she indeed found safety for a time. But at last some trifling display of witchcraft concerning a young man and a girl incurred the hostility of the crone who ruled the band. Jealous of her authority, that old beldame made occasion to drug Thamala's food and sell her, helpless, to Growt.

"As for her escape when Dom Peralt had freed her—an ordinary woman might have crept away to safety, avoiding the notice of the townspeople. Their attention was elsewhere—upon Dom Peralt's fall into the mire. But the Templemen are more vigilant. Suspicious of him for his carousing, his refusal of slaves, his scorn toward the Temple, they would not have failed to watch the woman he freed, hoping that she would provide them opportunity against him. Thamala would not have escaped them without employing the evil of her wiles.

"Yet she was safe. That was the thought with which Dom Peralt consoled his thirst and his fear. I do not credit him with any selfless concern for her person. He had freed her only on a whim, to spite Growt the slaver, not for love or conviction. But in this matter, he reflected, her safety was his. Though it was an uncertain hope at best, it enabled him to master the anger of his betrayal. After his first outrage, a number of regrettably sacrilegious oaths, and a time of tense pacing, he found some comfort in the knowledge that the case against him was composed entirely of inference and malice. Lacking Thamala, the Templemen lacked the sure evidence which would compel the judica to enact judgment. And if it were not compelled, the judica might think better of the precedent it was asked to establish—a precedent potentially dangerous to all its members.

"With that hope, Dom Peralt urged himself to conserve his strength. An undertaste of vinegar lurked in the wine of his reasoning. If a confession were wrung from him, by whatever coercions the Templemen chose, then no evidence would be required to consign him to the cauldron. It was utterly necessary that he keep up his courage, husband his resources.

"I assure you—though I doubt you fully understand me—that this was not easily done. To remain calm alone in a hard and rat-infested cell is certainly difficult. To remain calm in the face of unjust accusation and betrayal would test the patience of a saint. But thirst is a terrible thing, destructive to the self-possession of its victims." Ser Visal snatched up his flagon and drank deeply as though to ward away the mere thought of true thirst. "Before midnight, Dom Peralt began to doubt that his resolve would hold.

"In due time, it occurred to him to wonder whether the blood of rats were fit for human drink."

His eyes squeezed and glittering in the flesh of his face, Ser Visal cast a glance around the public room, then said with unexpected sanctimony, "Perhaps it would have been well for his immortal soul if he had been driven to that extremity. But what is done may not be undone. It is the will of Heaven—not to be questioned. Midnight was well gone by Dom Peralt's reckoning when he was startled to hear a key labor once again in the lock of the door. And he was more than startled when the door opened, admitting the witch Thamala to his cell."

Though our astonishment was plain, Ser Visal appeared to take no pleasure in it. For the moment, his story held him as it did us, and he did not note our reaction.

"The witch Thamala," he repeated softly. "She had made shift to bathe herself and obtain clean clothing, so that she little resembled the begrimed wretch he had freed. Her bruises and swellings had alread begun to heal, allowing the beauty of her face to show itself. Her hair was a soft and generous brown, a color which invites the touch of a man's hand. In simple justice, she should have been unrecognizable. But Dom Peralt stared and stared at her and could not be mistaken.

"She entered the cell as if it were free of access to all. No hue arose behind her—no guard came to watch what she did. As she had once vanished, so she now reappeared.

"In her hands, she bore the iron ring, as large around as a fist, from which jangled the keys of the jailer. But when she had ascertained that it was indeed Dom Peralt who sat, dumbfounded, before her, she cast the ring from her, spurning that metal as though its touch burned her. Then she knelt before him, so that her gaze met and studied his.

"What she saw satisfied her. Placing her hands on his arms where they folded across his knees, she said, 'Come. We must flee this dire place.' A smile touched her lips. 'Even with my aid, the guards will not sleep forever. Come.'

"Dom Peralt stared at her and did not respond. He felt that he had somehow fallen into drunkenness again—his wits refused to function. That she had come here, he thought stupidly. A witch. Had come here. It required understanding, but he had none to give. Her gaze called him down the road to his soul's ruin, and he could not understand.

"Some of his plight she was able to see for herself. After a moment, she released one hand from his arm and raised it to his temple. Her fingertips stroked the tight skin there, where the pulse of his life beat—and—

"Faugh!" Ser Visal muttered. "A murraine upon you all. Words will not convey it. Such things defy utterance. She touched her fingers to his temple, and his thirst was gone. Impossible! Yet it was true. In an instant, all that pain left him. And the relief was sweet! Surely even such louts as you are may grasp that the relief was sweet.

"But its sweetness came to Dom Peralt commingled with flavors of horror. Some wit returned to him at last. He grabbed at Thamala's wrist, pulled her hand from his temple. 'Why are you here?' he demanded in his dismay.

"His grip hurt her iron-scored skin, and she did not like the look of his consternation. But she answered him bravely. 'To free you, as you freed me. For all its faults, life remains desirable. Come.' Gently, she attempted to tug him out of his amazement.

"She was unprepared for violence. He flung her from him, so that she sprawled among the rats. Heaving himself up from the pallet, he crouched on his feet, ready to spring after her. As she regained her legs—more lithe and strong of movement than Growt's treatment of her would have augured—he panted at her, 'Witch! *Why are you here?*'

"'Witch, is it?' she replied. 'I know that tone. I had expected better of you, Dom Sen Peralt.' Straightening her hair with her fingers, she faced him angrily. 'Well, be answered. I am indebted to you for my freedom—and I pay my debts. I have come to give you that which you gave me.'

"Too horrified to realize that now it was she who did not understand, he raged at her—but softly, softly, so that the guards would not be roused. 'You damn me,' he hissed. 'There is no debt. Your freedom was only a matter of a few coins. A paltry sum. Trivial. I could make a hundred such purchases and not feel the price. Your freedom cost me *nothing*. And you damn me for it.'

"'No,' she retorted. She had been much abused in recent days, and her temper was somewhat short. 'This I will not endure.' Power curled in her fingers as she raised her hands against him. 'Murder and treachery have become the constant lot of my kind, and I accept

those things as well as I am able. At the least, I have turned my
back on revenge. But insult I do *not* accept—not while I am still
able to defend myself. If there are evil and damnation here, they
are *your* doing, not mine.

"'We whom you call witches commit no crimes. We desire only
to live in peace among the leas and woodlands that we love—and
to expand our knowledge of the weaving of true dreams—and to
barter our help for the simple necessities we lack. And for that we
are *slaughtered*. You and your precious Templemen abhor us because we are free in spirit—and because we possess knowledge
which you are too cowardly to share.'

"Dom Peralt sought to interrupt her indignation, but she did not
permit him. 'Do you believe,' she continued, 'that I need only wave
my hands to steal clothes and cleansing and access to your cell from
anyone I choose? No! The first I obtained honestly, healing the
walleye of a child and the abcessed teeth of a goodwoman in trade.
And for my appearance here—by good fortune, the outer street
was deserted. But two guards hold the door of this building. Scribes
labor at desks everywhere, lettering indictments. Four more guards
dice with the jailer, thinking themselves secret. Three Templemen
confer together nearby. And between that chamber and this, six
guards more. For all of them, *all*, I spin the dreams which enable
them to believe they have not seen me. No harm to them—but
women like myself have gone mad under such strains.

"'Heed me well, you who despise the aid of witches. I pay my
debts. But you will accompany me without insult, or I will cramp
the tongue in your mouth until it chokes you.'

"Here at last Dom Peralt's wit caught up with him. By a great
effort, he reined his growing frenzy. Under careful control, he rose
from his crouch, straightened his back. 'Your pardon,' he said, his
voice at once hard-edged and quiet. 'I meant no insult. When I
bought your freedom, I cared not what you were. I care not now.
And I believe that you have come here honestly, intending to help
me.' Then his urgency returned, too strong to be stifled. 'But you
know not what you do. Whatever is done now, you have damned
me. The escape you offer must be seen as the work of witchcraft.
No other explanation will occur to the minds of the Templemen.
Therefore they will hound us until I falter, lacking your powers—

and my life will be forfeit upon the spot. Or we will be taken in the attempt, and your involvement will give proof of my guilt, dooming me without defense to the cauldron.'

"Now she saw the import of his fear. Her anger fell away. Dismay softened her face. But he was not done. The vision of his plight drove him. 'While you remained free, there was hope for me. The Templemen might harm and harass me, but they could not procure the judgment of the judica without evidence—without you, without proof of your witchery, without demonstration of complicity between us.' For the moment, he believed that Templeman Knarll would never wrest a confession from him. 'My friends who speak against me would alter what they say, when they were given time to see that they would imperil their own fathers by witnessing falsely. I had hope.

"'It is gone. You give the Templemen the demonstration they desire. Your freedom truly cost me nothing more than discomfort and inconvenience. Your help costs me my life.'

"There he stopped. I have said that he was not blind. How could he close his eyes to the bitter grief which welled up in her at his words? As grim as talons, her hands covered her face. Her shoulders stretched the fabric of her blouse, knotting to restrain sobs. She had been *much* abused—too much to be endured. Helpless and alone, her mother had been taken to the cauldron, and Thamala had fled for her life. The gypsies had betrayed her to Growt. And Growt's record of rapes and beatings," commented Ser Visal mordantly, "would daunt a lesser man. Her sufferings transcend your imaginations, whelps. And now the one act of kindness she had received she repaid with ill. You are taught, all of you, I do not doubt, that women weep easily and often, for any reason. But I tell you, it is no small matter when such a woman as Thamala weeps. She was at once fierce and pitiable to behold, and the sight would have touched a harder heart than Dom Peralt's.

"But while he stood there like a lout, shuffling his feet in shame and groping desperately to conceive some new hope for them both, she returned to herself. The pity went out of her—the fierceness remained. Meeting his gaze, not as a woman who wished for counsel, but as one who desired to know his mind, she asked, 'What would you have me do?'

"Dom Peralt was a young man—a youth and a fool, as I have

said. But he was growing older swiftly. The thought of what he might expect from the tender mercies of Templeman Knarll came to him with some force, but he put it aside. Swallowing his fear, he replied, 'Escape. Relock the door, return the keys. Preserve your freedom. Ignorant that you have come here, the Templemen will remain without evidence. Eventually, I will be released.'

"Perhaps she was unaccustomed to such answers. For a long moment, her clear eyes searched him. Then she asked softly, 'Do you believe that?'

"In response, he made shift to appear certain and resolute. 'Yes.'

"She shook her head. 'No. You think it. You reason it. But you do not believe it.' Briefly, a shadow of her own fear showed in her face—a face not formed for fear. But she took a deep, shuddering breath and dismissed what she felt. Her arms hung at her sides, the strength gone from them. Yet there was strength enough in her voice. 'I pay my debts,' she said. 'Summon the guards.'

"He gaped at her. If he had spoken, he would have protested that she had lost her wits. The Templemen would bind her over to the judica for certain and terrible death—after they had tortured her enough to sate them. But he was too astonished to reply at once. Mad—she was unquestionably mad.

"'You will capture me,' she continued. The look in her eyes was bleak and dire. 'You will deliver me to the Templemen. That will ascertain your innocence. You will be freed.'

"Thinking her mad, Dom Peralt sought to reason with her. 'It will not be believed. You are a witch. I have no means to capture you. The Templemen will suspect some trick. They will believe that we have agreed together to obtain my release—so that I may in turn contrive to rescue you. The fact that you came to me will damn us both.'

"For an instant, thought furrowed her brow. She glanced toward the keys which she had thrown to the floor. Then she shrugged. 'You will slip the key-ring over my wrists. That will give you means. If I am held powerless, none will doubt that you have captured me.' Her loathing for the touch of cold iron was evident, but she did not let it sway her. 'My debt will be paid.'"

Ser Visal coughed, cleared his throat, drank. Sitting slumped in his chair, he resumed with a sigh, "Ah, the strange courage of witches. She put Dom Peralt to the test in a way which humbled

Templeman Knarll's threats. He saw at once that her plan would succeed. Some lie would be required to account for her presence in the cell, but the evidence of iron held about her wrists by his own hand would defeat all suspicion. He would be freed. And she— why, she would go to the doom which God demands of all witches. Though he was young and debauched, he understood that his soul hung in the balance here. If he captured her, he would be saved.

"It was not in him. He had purchased her freedom with a few coins. She meant to purchase his with her life. The simple injustice of it was more than he could stomach.

"'No,' he replied, though his head reeled with fear and his guts knotted sickly. 'I will not. There is no debt. Do you hear me? I deny that there is any debt. I did not buy your freedom. You were evilly used—whatever the Temple teaches. With a few coins, I merely restored what was yours by birth and decency. And the blame of my plight does not fall to you. It is on my head. I was too drunk to do what any sane man would have done—to take you with me and release you only when you might better profit from your freedom. I *will not* accept the sacrifice of your life in so small a cause.'

"Thamala waited until he was done. Then she said, 'You are brave, Dom Sen Peralt.' Her tone suggested both mockery and respect. 'But no coin measures the value I place upon my life. How do you intend to prevent me?'

"For his pride—if for no other reason—he attempted to match her. 'I need do nothing,' he said, 'nothing other than wait. When next the guards come to this cell, they will find us together—and then we will both be undone.' He smiled wryly through his fear. 'To avert that outcome—so that your life will be preserved, and I will be able to hope—you will depart before the guards come, relocking the door after you to protect my protestations of innocence. Of what worth is my life,' he concluded, 'if it may only be saved by your death?'

"The witch shook her head again. 'You are mistaken,' she said. 'The world has need of such men.' For no evident reason, her voice now seemed to come to him from a great distance. The candlelight blurred, as if his eyes were failing. 'Therefore,' she uttered in a tone which could not be refused, 'it will be necessary for you to dream.'

"Then the flame of the candle shrank away, and the cell's darkness closed over his head. He heard nothing beyond the promise she had made, at once fierce and gentle. 'I pay my debts.'

"But in the dream...

"Faugh!" spat Ser Visal. "Dream, indeed. *Witchcraft*. With her wiles, she deprived him of will and choice. *Faugh!*" Hawking up phlegm, he grabbed for his flagon and drank. But he did not stop his tale. Despite his apparent indignation, he sounded weak and in some way frightened as he said, "I shudder for his soul. In the dream he was not himself.

"In the dream, he raised his voice and shouted lustily for the guards. He kicked the door so that it rang against the wall. He shouted again. Then he went to the key-ring.

"She held her hands behind her back for him, but they would not both fit through the ring. No matter—one sufficed. With iron closed about any part of her, she was caught.

"At that moment, he felt that he began to awaken. But still the dream persisted. He could not break free of it. He could only watch with the taste of horror in his mouth as guards came to the cell at a run and he called out to them, saying, 'Here is the witch Templeman Knarll seeks. She sought to seduce me to her foul ends, but I have captured her with iron,' and Thamala made pretense of struggling against him while he clasped the ring over her wrist.

"He did not return to himself entirely until the Templemen had taken her from him, to bind her with surer fetters, and Templeman Knarll had grudgingly granted his release. Then he found that there were tears in his eyes, and they would not be stanched, for the deed was done, and he could not now afford to cry out in anger or protest.

"I must have more wine."

The candles had begun to wane, a reminder that afternoon was on its way to evening and all of us were required by our God-fearing families—and by Temple curfew—to be in our homes before vespers rang. But none of us thought of such things. For a long moment, none of us thought to stamp our feet and produce money so that the keeper would bring more wine. We were held. All our attention was centered on Ser Visal. He appeared oddly shrunken in the fading candlelight, his eyes glazed by what he saw in his mind, his stubbled cheeks ashen and sagging from the bones of his skull. At another time—during another tale—we might have nudged each other and winked, thinking in silent laughter that the heat of the hearth made him melt, that his fat flesh was composed of nothing but tallow and wine, which he sweated away. But not now. We were held. And he seemed hardly to be aware of us.

There was one thought in all our minds. *He is afraid. This tale is dangerous, and he fears to tell it.*

Nevertheless, he soon restored a sense of our duties. Without forewarning, he crashed his flagon down upon the tabletop and bellowed, "Are you deaf? I must have more wine!"—a mere croak of his normal roar, but enough to startle us from our stupefaction. Hastily, we labored the boards with our boots. From our purses, we dredged up coin for another cask. The keeper responded without interest or hurry, as if when he had lost his hearing all other questions had been answered for him. Upon this occasion, he produced a cask of liquid which only a Templeman who did not drink would have called wine. It smelled of cattle and tasted as if it had been fermented by wringing the moisture from Ser Visal's sodden robe. Yet we made no protest—we cared only that he should finish his tale. And he showed his disfavor only by frowning as he tossed two measures of the vile stuff past his avid lips and began on a third.

Despite its faults, however, the drink amended his appearance somewhat. In his piggish eyes, a dull smoldering glower hinted at angers he did not choose to explain. Yet he smiled, and his voice took on its particular quaver of piety as he resumed.

"In an age of remarkable institutions," he said, "and outstanding men, when the Temple of God gives us order, morality, and slavery, and a figure such as High Templeman Crossus Hught aids in the management of the kingdom, the judica is especially worthy of note. Founded upon the highest principles, for the highest purpose—to defend the innocent and the honorable from evils which would otherwise deprive them of Heaven—the judica has prosecuted the sinners haled before it—primarily witches—with unflagging rigor. For lesser crimes, men and women are sold into slavery, their property confiscated, their homes burned. But for witchcraft and all its abominations, only one punishment is deemed just—the cauldron.

"You have not seen that black pot, or the chamber which holds it. None who do not belong are admitted there. And I wager that your fathers have not spoken of it, just as they have not told you the outcome of Thamala's judgment. Such things are too holy and severe to be discussed lightly.

"It is a high chamber, and round, housed in the same Temporal Office where malefactors are imprisoned. From tiered seats circling the walls, Templemen and judges look down on two doors—one heavily barred and timbered to prevent escape to the outside, the other opening to the guards and passages of the Temporal Office— and on the cauldron itself.

"It resembles an immense stewpot in which three or four men— or I alone—might stand comfortably. But its victims find little comfort there. Somewhat precariously balanced, I fear, upon its bricks, it sits over a kiln in the floor, in which the fire is never permitted to fade, and it is full to its middle with bubbling iron, melted for the doom of witches. The pot itself does not melt only because its sides have been hardened with alloys. The heat is tremendous! Its victims feel its force as they are questioned and judged, and it causes them to sweat in terror.

"From the floor to the rim on one side rises a ramp of masonry. There the evil are led when they have been judged. For a moment or two, they are suspended over the cauldron, so that they may have opportunity to repent and pray, perhaps—or to name those who consort with them. Then, when they have screamed enough, they are let drop."

Ser Visal drank again, urgently, and refilled his flagon. But almost at once he continued, "As is right and fitting, the judica is led by Templemen. The spiritual welfare of the kingdom is in their care. But to that august body also belongs each Dom and Ser of the region, every man of station. It is they who pronounce the judgment when the Templemen have produced the evidence and searched the witnesses. And these men of station do not—I may say, *dare* not— fail of attendance. The calling of their duty is too high. And the consequences of failure may not be contemplated calmly.

"The more so in the present case. The matter of Thamala was of unusual importance, offering especially bold evidence of witchery—so bold as to make all virtuous souls tremble—and touching as it did upon the honor of a high family. That was rare. In all the years that I have attended the judica, I do not remember a similar case. It is generally true that those who consort with witches come from among the poor and unenlightened. For that reason, as I am sure you have heard, High Templeman Crossus Hught himself elected to preside over Thamala's judgment.

"It is rumored—I know not why—that Templeman Knarll made a special appeal for the presence of good King Traktus' counselor. That is of no importance. The judica was delayed several days to permit the High Templeman to settle his affairs and make the journey—also a matter of no importance. The point I wish you to grasp is that this judica transcended all others in authority and significance.

"Do you understand me, puppies? Are your minds clear enough for thought? *This* judica was one which Dom Peralt was required to attend. By virtue of his new station—and of the High Templeman's presence—he had no choice. The woman who had purchased his life with her own would be consigned to the cauldron, and he was required to assist in the judgment.

"This, of course, he understood. Perhaps he understood it from the moment when Thamala first proposed to save his life with hers." Ser Visal's sanctimony had given way to muffled sarcasm. "He was young and gallant, and he had something of a reputation for boldness, which he prized. And yet a woman whom he had not known for the total of an hour repaid a debt which had cost him nothing by sacrificing everything. When at last Templeman Knarll released him from the Temporal Office, Dom Peralt went back to his estates in mortal shame to await the sitting of the judica.

"In shame? you ask. Why in shame?" Ser Visal glared around at us. It became increasingly difficult to distinguish between his piety and his sarcasm. "For no good reason. The woman was a *witch*, offensive to God and Temple. If she chose to do one honorable thing before she died, perhaps her soul would be the better for it. And I repeat that he had not known her for the total of an hour. He knew nothing about her at all, except her power.

"Yet he *was* shamed. His skin burned with it, and his heart ached. Every twist of his thoughts squeezed sweat from his brow. It was a cauldron more subtle than iron, but no less compulsory. Hiding himself within the walls of his manor, he drank wine by the barrel to slake the fire—but it only burned higher. All about him were reminders of his father, that strong and just man who had filled his life with care for those dependent upon him—memories which gave young Sen no ease. In desperation, he turned from strong wine to clear water and became sober, hoping that cold reason would succeed where besottedness failed. But the flame did not subside. He consulted those who still named themselves his friends—not young Beau Frane and Serson Lew, I assure you, but older heads and wiser—and obtained no relief. He attempted every solace but one, the strict comfort of the Temple. All failed him, as all things human and prone to sin must fail. His shame would not be quenched. One thought tormented him: *it was not just.* He had purchased Thamala with a few coins—his father's earnings, not his own. It was not just.

"In due time, word was brought to him that the High Templeman had arrived, and that therefore the judica would meet upon the morrow. According to custom, the sitting would commence promptly at the third hour, so that the remainder of the day would be purified by its labors. Again he searched his conscience and consulted his friends. Then he returned a somewhat terse message to Templeman Knarll, saying that he would surely attend the judica, as God and duty required of him.

"That night"—Ser Visal had turned his glower to the tabletop, avoiding our rapt eyes—"the slaver Growt was put out of work with two broken legs. And the next morning, Dom Sen Peralt was among the first to enter the chamber of the judica after the ringing of the time.

"He and your fathers engaged in no idle conversation upon such a solemn occasion. In silence, they entered the chamber and took their proper seats—Dom Peralt and those of like station around the middle tiers, men of lesser rank above them, near the walls. In silence, they awaited the coming of the Templemen. Dom Peralt bore himself gravely, his eyes downcast with a humility new to him. But the cauldron's heat flushed his face. This was not a place in which any man sat at ease. The sound of the fire was loud in the stillness, as was the closing of the bolts as the outer door was sealed, so that no rescue of the witch might be attempted.

"There was some small delay. Then the inner doors were opened, and the Templemen entered.

"All were clad in the black cassocks which signalized the dark work they meant to do, the wrestling with evil—black contrasted only by the scarlet ropes knotted at their waists and the strict pallor of their faces. All appeared as dour as the day of God's doom. Half a score of those who served under Templeman Knarll's jurisdiction took their seats around the lowest tier. After them came Templeman Knarll himself, bearing in his hands the iron crozier of his office— and looking more than ever like a creature born in a swamp. And when he had assumed his place, he was followed by High Templeman Crossus Hught.

"Though he was similarly black-clad, the High Templeman did not need the golden miter which he carried in the crook of his arm to distinguish him from the other servants of the Temple. He was tall, strong despite his years, and commanding. Much of his authority was in his eyes, which seemed to have no color at all. Indeed, at first glance his face itself appeared to have no color. His thin, close-cropped hair was white—his skin, pale with the translucence of old age. Upon nearer inspection, however, a faint red hue could be seen, for every blood vessel was visible beneath the skin, as distinct as madness—I mean, of course, that purity of mind which the sinful world might term madness, but which is in truth the most exalted devotion to God. Seeing him, it was at last possible to understand his importance to good King Traktus. He was not a man who would be easily refused.

"As he entered, the Templemen began to chant the appropriate orisons against evil. But no special homage was demanded by the High Templeman. Here judgment was in the hands of the men of station, not of the Temple—though the guidance and authority of the Templemen were properly plain to all. When High Templeman Crossus Hught had assumed his place—he and Templeman Knarll stood opposite each other on either side of the ramp leading up to the lip of the cauldron—he joined the chanting, his colorless gaze fixed upon Heaven. 'God damn all witches. Punish all presumption. Preserve the purity of the Temple.' If I were able, I would recite each prayer for your edification. It is a fault of mine—which I rue daily—that I have no memory for such holy things.

"During the chants, Dom Peralt bore himself as a man who had sworn a great oath that he would not fidget. Rather, he watched the door as we all did, awaiting the arrival of the prisoners.

"Did I say prisoners? Well, we had assumed that the witch would not be brought to judgment without company. The Templemen had had several days in which to question her—and it was a rare woman who could not be persuaded by righteous interrogation to name consorts or other witches. But when the prayers were ended, and Templeman Knarll called for Thamala to be brought into the chamber, she was alone.

"Two guards bore her between them, supporting her because she was hardly able to stand. They took her to the foot of the ramp and left her there, withdrawing from the chamber and closing the doors after them. Somehow, she remained on her feet. Iron manacles still clasped her wrists behind her. The guards had positioned her with her back to the cauldron—perhaps deliberately—so that she faced Dom Peralt. But she did not meet his brief glance. Weakly, she turned so that her doom was directly before her, as though she wished to see it for what it was and prepare herself to meet it.

"But Dom Peralt did not need a long look to see what the Templemen had done to her. Her hair was torn and ragged, leaving bloody patches upon her scalp and giving her a frenzied aspect. One eye was closed with swelling—the other, raw and aggrieved. Indeed, all her face had been beaten to a new shape. Dirt and hunger outlined the bruises. Her clothing had been torn in various places—some of them indecent—and through the rents showed wounds and welts. Blood crusted her fetters. Plainly, her evil was stronger than her flesh, for how else was it possible for her to keep her feet—or to gaze upon the cauldron without terror?

"Yet she had given no other name to her questioners. The Templemen had not succeeded at wringing the answers they desired from her. As he looked at the places where blood caked her clothing to her back, Dom Peralt began to smile—the same smile with which he had faced Growt's bullying.

"At once, High Templeman Crossus Hught snapped, '*You.*' His voice struck like the cut of a whip through the cauldron's heat and the silence. All eyes sprang to him. With his long arm, he pointed his miter straight at Dom Peralt's face. 'Why do you smile?'

"'That is Dom Sen Peralt,' whispered Templeman Knarll to his temporal lord. 'The same who bought and freed the witch.'

"The High Templeman ignored Templeman Knarll. He seemed

to know by Divine inspiration whom he addressed. His miter did not waver. 'Are you,' he demanded, 'amused by the plight of wickedness in the hands of the Temple of God?'

"Dom Peralt—fool that he was—shook his head, but his smile remained.

"'You have been familiar with this foul woman,' pursued Crossus Hught. 'Now you betray her, and you smile because you think to escape her fate. Evil is weak against the will of Heaven for many reasons, but most because it knows no virtue except treachery. So the very demons sacrifice each other, to procure their own safety. Do not think that we who serve the Temple are blind.'

"Dom Peralt lowered his eyes, bowing his head so that his smile would be less plain. 'Your pardon, High Templeman,' he said softly. His voice conveyed a tremor which might have been fear. 'I mean nothing unseemly. I smile only at the thought of justice.'

"'Justice, is it?' returned the High Templeman. Abruptly, he settled his miter once again in the crook of his arm. 'You do not appear to be a man who is much concerned for such pure matters. If you care for justice, why have you not set foot in the Temple of God from the day of the witch's capture to this, seeking remission for your mortal faults from the justice of Heaven?'

"When Dom Peralt raised his eyes again, they were full of darkness, and his smile was gone. With elaborate care, he replied, 'In the matter of the witch Thamala I have committed no fault. Before this last slaving day, I had never seen her. I purchased her because the slaver Growt demanded it of me. I chose her from among all his slaves because she caught my whim. And for that same whim I set her free. I had no knowledge of her evil.' With more wisdom than I had credited to him, he refrained from claiming that the Templemen had imprisoned him unjustly. Instead, he said, 'When she came to me in my cell, I snared her and delivered her to the Templemen, fulfilling my duty to both God and man.

"'High Templeman,' he concluded in a tone which might have been mistaken for humility, 'will you declare here, before the judica, that I must repent what I have done?'

"*That* was foolish. A child could have warned Dom Peralt that such men as Crossus Hught are not notoriously forgiving of wit in others. But the High Templeman had no present recourse but to ignore that wit. Turning from Dom Peralt, he said stiffly to Templeman Knarll, 'Let us commence.'

"Sighing between battered lips, the witch Thamala sank to her knees. Were it not sacrilege to consider her honorable, one might have thought that she retained strength enough—in spirit, if not in body—to care what happened to Dom Peralt.

"Templeman Knarll glowered his disfavor at her. Perhaps now he regretted the impulse which had led him to request the High Templeman's attendance. Thamala had resisted his most searching interrogations. Her reticence—like Dom Peralt's affrontery—did not speak well for Templeman Knarll's stewardship over the region. There was a particular grimness in his voice as he began the ceremonies of the judica.

"First he welcomed us to the performance of our duty. He asked for the names of any men of our station who were not present. Then he charged us to adjudge the heinous crime of witchcraft strictly, according to the will of Heaven, for the safety of our own souls. Faugh! It is well that the Temple is served by abler men than I. My fat head will not hold half the proper admonitions. Templeman Knarll's memory, however, did not fail. And that was well for him. He did not wish to appear foolish before High Templeman Crossus Hught.

"After the appropriate invocations, he proceeded to deliver the Temple's formal accusation against the witch Thamala. 'It is charged'—or some such phrase—'that you have abandoned the teachings of Heaven. That you have consorted with witches, participating in their most foul practices. That you have studied witchcraft, knowing it to be evil—a defiance of God and His Temple.' A fulsome list, truly. It was plain that Thamala had never drawn a breath which was not deliberate and mortal sin. But that, of course, was merely the ritual accusation cited against all witches. A listing of Thamala's particular evils followed. 'That you have lived among gypsies, the outcast of Heaven. That you have worked your abominable wiles upon them, whose souls have no defense.' And so on. Such an impressive recital would justly have won confession from the first mother of all witches.

"Certainly we were impressed. Experienced as we were with the judica and its work, we were still impressed. It is an impressive thing to hear a helpless woman damned in every item of her life, every corner of her soul. For good reason, no one accused by the Temple has ever been found innocent.

"Dom Peralt listened attentively, his eyes on Templeman Knarll's face, his smile faintly upon his lips. But he appeared unmoved, as though his innocence were complete. And Thamala remained on her knees and showed no reaction, as though she were deaf to what was being said against her.

"But when Templeman Knarll came to his conclusion and asked of her, 'What do you say to these things?' she gave him an answer. With great difficulty because of her weakness—and because her hands were bound with iron at her back—she rose to her feet. On her face was a look of strange yearning, as though she wished as keenly as love for the strength to mount the ramp at once and cast herself into the cauldron, before she could be condemned. In a voice hardly audible around the highest tier, she replied, 'You have murdered my mother and all who held her dear. Now you mean to murder me. Do it and have done. God in His Heaven gazes down upon you with abhorrence.'

"'Vile wretch!' snarled Templeman Knarll, raising his hand to strike her. But High Templeman Crossus Hught snapped at once, 'Hold! Here she may say whatever she will. Her words purify the judica of doubt and false pity.' Then he turned toward Thamala and touched his miter to her shoulder.

"Dumbly, she gazed at him as though he had power to command her. Bending his look of madness over her, he said softly, almost fondly, 'Woman, you are my daughter in the spirit. The care of your immortal soul is my duty and my great treasure. You believe that we mean to deal with you harshly—and perhaps by mortal standards we *are* harsh. But there is God's love for you in what we do. By the standards of Heaven, only the harsh mortification of the flesh may hope to free the soul. The sufferings of your body will soon end. But the sufferings of your soul—Ah, your soul cries out for forgiveness, though you do not heed it.

"'Woman, you say that we have murdered your mother. What was she, that the judica required her death?'

"Thamala did not reply. Crossus Hught seemed to hold her eyes so that she could not turn away. But she did not speak.

"In response, his manner became more stern. 'If you confess

humbly and repent your life, there is hope of Heaven's smile. But if you harden your heart, the torment which awaits your soul will make child's play of your present pain.' Had I been in her place, I would have admitted to all that he desired. Truly! Though I sat in the highest tier and had no part of her crimes, I could hardly hold my tongue. 'Your mother met her death,' he continued, 'because she pursued the fiendish power of witchcraft. Knowing her fate— the fate which God wills for all evil—why did you choose the way of witchery for yourself? Did you wish to revenge yourself upon those who judged her? Or did you love the lascivious ill of witches?'

"Still she made no answer. Around the chamber, strong, good men sweated in the heat of the cauldron—and in plain dread of what they witnessed—but she was not swayed. The bruises and swellings on her face distorted her expression, so that it could not be read. But her eyes held life yet, and they were not cowed by Crossus Hught.

"For a moment, he glanced around the chamber. Perhaps he wished to see that we judged her silence as it deserved. His colorless gaze rested briefly on Dom Peralt. Then he returned his attention to Thamala.

"Setting the end of his miter to her cheek, he pressed her to face the cauldron. Standing at the foot of the ramp below the pot, she could not see its contents. But the fire in the kiln made a steady roaring, and at intervals the molten iron could be heard to bubble.

"'There is your doom, witch,' said the High Templeman. 'Look for hope and mercy there, not from me. You will find that the agony is terrible. But it will be brief. A moment's anguish—a few screams. Nothing more. The agony of your soul will endure. Fiercer than any physical hurt, it will go on and on without let, and you will never escape. Only by confession and repentence may you hope to ameliorate the fire which awaits you.

"'Answer but one question, and God may be moved to hear you. Thamala, why did you enter the cell of Dom Sen Peralt when he had set you free? Was he not your paramour in witchcraft? Did you not attempt to rescue him because you had need of him, in love and in power?' Crossus Hught's voice had become a lash again, cutting at her. 'And did he not betray you in an effort to save himself, snaring you for the judica because he feared to risk his life in flight with you?'

"In the chamber, the silence of the judica became intense. The High Templeman had found his way around Dom Peralt's protestations of innocence. Now with one word Thamala could damn Dom Peralt, and nothing that he might say in his own defense would save him. He sat rigidly, heedless of the sweat standing on his brow. A greater fool might have made objections, but he had wit enough to avoid that pitfall. Clenching his silence between his teeth, he watched Thamala's blood-crusted back and waited. We all watched and waited, knowing that if Dom Peralt could be thus implicated in witchery none of us would ever again be safe. At last we saw why High Templeman Crossus Hught had accepted Templeman Knarll's invitation. Here the High Templeman sought to extend his power into new territory.

"And Thamala did answer. Facing the cauldron with Crossus Hught's miter jabbed against her bruises, she said in tight outrage, 'Do you never wonder how witches breed? You murder us and murder us—and yet we endure. But there are no male witches. We must seduce men to beget children upon us, so that we will continue.

"'When Dom Peralt purchased me, I saw that he was strong and goodly—a fit man to father a child. Therefore I sought to rescue him, thinking that he would find me desirable. But he did not. In his eyes, I was evil, and he spurned me.'

"Thus she paid her debt. Damning herself, she defeated the accusation against Dom Peralt.

"For a moment, an appearance of consternation reigned over the judica as your fathers disguised their relief with surprise and indignation. High Templeman Crossus Hught's face grew red, his blood enflamed by the failure of his ploy. Perhaps he saw a vision of good King Traktus's reaction when our monarch learned that the High Templeman had attempted to embroil an innocent Dom in the judgment of a witch. Dom Peralt's jaws knotted with the effort he made to suppress what he felt.

"'Godless wretch!' cried Templeman Knarll. With the end of his crozier, he struck Thamala so that she fell to the stone. 'Will you utter falsehood in the teeth of doom?' He had good reason for his dismay. Whatever chagrin afflicted the High Templeman because of this failure would be visited doubly upon Templeman Knarll. But his eyes—and Crossus Hught's—watched Dom Peralt avidly.

"That snare Dom Peralt also avoided. By no movement or expression or word did he betray any concern for the witch. Let all her bones be broken there before him, and let her be damned! Raising his head, he said in a loud voice, 'Praise be to God and the justice of the Temple! I am vindicated!'

"The glare which High Templeman Crossus Hught fixed upon Dom Peralt was murderous and wild. The blood beat so furiously beneath his pale skin that we feared a seizure, but there remained nothing that he could do. Not one of us would now vote death upon Dom Peralt. If the High Templeman persisted, he would appear to have lost his reason. And that report must surely damage him in the eyes of good King Traktus. Therefore he put the best face possible upon his defeat. Trembling in voice and limb, he turned his back toward Dom Peralt and addressed the judica.

" 'It is our work to judge and punish evil,' he said. 'An accusation of witchcraft has soiled the good name of Dom Sen Peralt'—he cast a dire glance at Templeman Knarll, who appeared to shrink under it like a depleted wineskin—'and that accusation has been found false. In this the high purpose of the judica shows itself, winnowing the honest from the ill. For this was the judica instituted, so that the innocent would be spared when the guilty are adjudged.

" 'But this woman is condemned out of her own mouth.' As he spoke, his passion rose. 'Out of her own mouth! She admits herself the daughter of a witch. She admits herself vulnerable to the judgment of the judica, and she offends Heaven by naming that judgment murder. She admits her intent to seduce Dom Peralt, so that she might breed her evil! She refuses repentence. She denies the just interrogation of the judica. And to this must be added that she entered Dom Peralt's cell when none but a witch might do so, bypassing the guards with her wiles.

" 'No other evidence is required.'

"When he chose to unleash it, his voice was indeed an admirable instrument—at once clarion and cutting. By such men, even Kings may be daunted. 'It remains to us,' he continued, 'to consider who we are and why we are here by the will of Heaven. We are the spiritual servants of the Temple of God and the temporal servants of our estates and towns and peoples. To us belongs the duty to protect and purify what we serve. We give the world order! Around us lurk fiends and darknesses of every kind—demons of seduction, souls that know not God, terrifying powers. Threatened by such perils, no honorable man or devout goodwoman may set foot from home without fear. At any moment, any good thing may be devoured in evil. Only *we*—we who serve God in spirit and in body—only we stem the world's ill.

"'To do so, we must acknowledge that pity and forgiveness are in God's hands, not ours. They are too high for us. We cannot ask whether this crime or that may be let pass. On our souls, we cannot! We can only call evil by its true name and consign it to fire, as the will of Heaven demands.

"'The name of the evil which we are called upon to judge this day is witchcraft, *witchcraft*! The woman Thamala is a *witch*, self-confessed and abominable, defiant of all things holy. And no ordinary witch! So cunning is her malice that she nearly dragged down an innocent young man with her.' As I have said, the High Templeman put the best face possible upon his defeat. Thamala had risen again to her knees. New blood seeped from the wounds which Templeman Knarll had opened on her back. But Crossus Hught had already dispensed with pity and forgiveness. 'Men of the judica,' he concluded, 'the judgment is yours. What is your word?'

"For a moment, your fathers remained mute under the High Templeman's gaze—not doubting what their word would be, of course, but wondering who would be the first to speak it. By virtue of his years and his great wealth, Dom Tahl often took precedence. But upon this occasion both Ser Lew and Dom Frane had cause to stand forward, if for no other reason than simple gratitude that their sons had not been called to give evidence against Dom Peralt. Had I wished to call attention to myself, I might have spoken. Thamala's guilt was certainly plain to me. It was awkward for Crossus Hught that no man sprang up at once to offer verdict.

"But the moment was short—too short to do more than gall the High Templeman. Then Dom Peralt stood slowly from his seat.

"'High Templeman,' he said, 'no word is required here but mine. All have heard the witch's confessions. But only I have experienced her seductions. Only I have felt her foul power. *My* judgment is sufficient to doom her.' As he spoke, Thamala bowed her head, but gave no other sign that she heard him. 'And I proclaim that she is the most evil of all witches, deserving of excruciation and death.' His voice had the sound of a man who had been truly humbled.

"His gaze, however, did not waver from Crossus Hught's hot

glower. 'High Templeman,' he continued, 'if you will permit it, I will give her to the cauldron myself. Her vileness has besmirched me, and I wish to aid in her punishment. By so doing, I hope to cleanse her touch from my soul.'

"At this, High Templeman Crossus Hught studied Dom Peralt narrowly. He did not know what to make of the young man's offer. It has always been the Templemen themselves who cast witches to the cauldron. But almost at once he saw the benefit to himself. Thus far, the tale of this judica did not promise to augment his stature with good King Traktus. But if he could report that the honor of a reckless young Dom had been questioned by an over-zealous subordinate—and that he, Crossus Hught, had determined the young man's innocence during the judica—and that the young man had been allowed to deliver the witch to death himself, thereby restoring his good repute beyond all doubt—why, then the High Templeman would have no reason to fear that he might lose by the tale.

"But he was too wise to sanction such a breach of custom without encouragement. Holding Dom Peralt's gaze, he asked softly, 'Men of the judica, what say you to this?'

"Dom Frane and Ser Lew responded instantly, 'Permit him!' It could be seen in their faces that they did not mean to deal gently with their offspring when the judica was done.

"Other men promptly added their voices. Every proof of Dom Peralt's innocence secured their own safety further. In moments, the will of the judges was plain.

"The High Templeman nodded gravely, but betrayed no satisfaction. 'Very well,' he said to Dom Peralt. 'The deed is yours. Her death will indeed go far to cleanse your soul.'

"It would have been seemly if Dom Peralt had spoken a word of thanks or obeisance to the High Templeman. But perhaps the solemn duty he had undertaken confused his sense of fitness. Or perhaps he was serious now as he had not been before the slaver Growt, and so did not see the wit in thanking Crossus Hught. He glanced once around the upper tiers of the chamber, then left his seat to approach the witch Thamala.

"She had not moved from her knees. When he set his hand to her shoulder, she stiffened as if expecting to be struck again. But she did not resist him. She had reconciled herself to death. As he lifted her, she assisted him as well as she could.

"In the heat of the kiln and the molten iron, with all the eyes of the judica upon them, they climbed the ramp toward the rim of the cauldron.

"Starved and beaten as she was, she had no strength for the ascent. The reflected glow of the metal showed fiercely upon her swellings and bruises. Dom Peralt was compelled to support her, one arm around her back, one hand on her shoulder. For that reason, he did not resemble a man who intended to hurl her into agony when they gained the head of the ramp.

"At the rim of the cauldron, they halted. She leaned, half stumbling, toward the terrible heat, as though he had already thrust her to fall. But he caught her back. A smile made savage by the direct radiance of the iron twisted his mouth. He gazed into her face— but she would not raise her eyes. He was her slayer, and she had chosen this death to pay her debts.

"Roughly, he turned her away from him. His hands clamped her sore shoulders. If she had tried to struggle—even if she had been healthy—she could not have escaped his young strength. Her head hanging weakly, she did not struggle.

"'Thamala,' he said in a voice which we all heard, 'you are doomed. This I do for justice.'"

Ser Visal lifted his flagon to his lips—and lowered it without drinking. "My puppies," he said slowly, "you will not be more surprised than your fathers were by what transpired." Several of the candles had failed, and the dimmer light seemed to give his face a grim intensity, almost a keenness, as though he were not as fat and soft as he appeared. "As you may imagine, the attention of every man in the chamber was fixed upon Dom Peralt and the witch. None who witnessed the event were able to account for what they saw.

"From somewhere about the tiers, a goatskin full of water was hurled into the cauldron. Striking the molten iron, it burst with such an eruption of steam and noise that the onlookers ducked their heads. High Templeman Crossus Hught and Templeman Knarll recoiled against each other. The cauldron and the head of the ramp were obscured from view.

"When the vapor cleared—before any Templeman could call out—Dom Peralt and Thamala became visible again. She lay on her side on the ramp, her manacles held against the stone. In one hand, he gripped a hammer which he had worn hidden under his belt—in the other, a hardened chisel that he had borrowed from Growt. As the judica watched in astonishment and horror, he struck the iron from Thamala's left wrist.

"Templeman Knarll gaped to shout, but Crossus Hught was quicker. 'Guards!' he thundered. 'Treachery! Beware of witchcraft! *Guards!*' A thrust of his thin arm impelled Templeman Knarll toward the ramp.

"Nevertheless, Dom Peralt might have succeeded in his attempt. Only a moment was required. But he was inexperienced with Growt's tools. His first blow was luckier than he deserved—his second, unluckier. As he swung the hammer, the chisel slipped from the manacle. Striking the stone, it twisted from his grasp, skidded away, and fell to the floor beside the kiln.

"At that moment, the inner doors crashed open. A company of guards charged into the chamber, waving their swords—ready to butcher a whole host of helpless witches and weaponless young fools. Templemen dove into the tiers to clear the path of the guards.

"Dom Peralt did not hesitate. At the last, his wit—or his bravado—did not fail him. Pulling Thamala with him, he jumped after the fallen chisel.

"But when he had regained the tool, he made no effort to use it. Rather, he gave it to Thamala and thrust her to the floor. He had no time to break her remaining fetter. The guards were too near.

"To counter that threat, he did what no sane man would have done, regardless of his courage. He put his shoulder to the side of the cauldron and pushed."

Ser Visal wiped the sweat from his face, scrubbed his hands on the front of his robe. His eyes stared amazement at remembered visions. "It was plain to all in the chamber," he said softly. "Every man of the judica witnessed it. And no wonder that we fear to speak of it now! We saw the pressure of his great frame against the iron. We saw his clothing take fire from the heat. We smelled his flesh as it burned. We heard the howl wrung from him in hideous pain.

"And we saw the brick which held the cauldron upright crumble.

"After that"—Ser Visal threw up his hands—"chaos. The cauldron tilted and fell, pouring molten iron at the guards. In instant panic, they did their utmost to avoid that liquid agony. Some sprang to safety among the seats. Others were hurt only by the spattering droplets. But a few were too slow. They lost feet and limbs before they were pulled free.

"Amid the shouts and screams and confusion, only a few of us saw that Dom Peralt retained consciousness, despite his tremendous hurt. Thamala held the chisel against her manacle as he raised the hammer and brought it down with his last strength.

"She had been tortured and starved for days, reduced to such frailty that she could hardly stand. But she did not fail him. As the iron fell from her waist, she called up her power—and both she and Dom Peralt seemed to vanish as though they had ceased to exist.

"A moment later, all the wood of the outer doors burst from the hinges and bolts.

"At once, the High Templeman roared, 'They flee!' Brandishing his miter like a club, he sent every guard and Templeman within reach chasing outward in a rush. And we followed, half thinking that we might yet recapture the witch and her rescuer, half desiring only to escape the pain and ruin of the judica.

"But Dom Peralt and Thamala were gone."

Abruptly, Ser Visal tossed down the dregs of the bitter wine and thumped his flagon to the table. "The rest you know," he said brusquely. In a surge of flesh and robes, he gained his feet. "The witch and her consort were not found. A great search was made, and many men and goodwomen were offended by it. A writ of excommunication was read against Dom Peralt. But no sign of him or the witch was found.

"The breaking of the outer door was a ruse, of course. Neither he nor Thamala had the strength for flight. They remained in the judica, and she kept them from being seen, until the chamber was left empty. Then they made their way to whatever means of escape he had prepared for them.

"That is enough. Vespers will be rung soon. You must go." Balancing his bulk on his stout legs, Ser Visal started toward the door.

Consternation stopped our mouths. He was not done—surely he was not done? There was so much we wished to know. Yet he was on his way to the door without a backward glance.

The son of Dom Tahl, however, was accustomed to leadership among us, and he spoke when the rest of us could not. "Ser Visal, how do you know all this?" Was there a hint of warning in his voice—a threat? Perhaps he meant to tell his father what he had heard. "How do you know what ruses Dom Peralt and the witch used?"

Ser Visal turned. In the failing light, the gaze he cast toward Domson Thal appeared furtive, frightened. "It needs no great wit," he replied with an effort of blandness. "I have heard that the injured guards are recovering remarkably well. Without exception, they suffer less than expected—and heal more rapidly. And some admit that they felt a beneficent influence while they waited for succor." He shrugged his mounded shoulders. "Witches are known to be healers."

Domson Tahl frowned and nodded. But at once he asked, "And how do you know what Dom Peralt and the witch said to each other in his cell?"

Bulging in his fat cheeks, Ser Visal's eyes shifted among us warily. Still slick with sweat, his skin had a pasty color. Twice he opened his thick lips and closed them again, gaping like a fish. Some of us nudged Domson Thal warningly. Others clenched their fists. We wanted no harm to come to Ser Visal for the things he had revealed to us. But at last he swallowed his fear and accepted the full risk of his tale.

"Do you louts have minds of stone?" he retorted acidly. "Who do you suppose threw the goatskin of water into the cauldron?"

Turning on his heel, he left the Hound and Whip.

We followed him out into the dusty street and the evening. Some of us staggered a little from the wine we had consumed, but drink had no effect on Ser Visal. He was as steady on his feet as a sack of grain as he walked away.

ABOUT THE AUTHOR

Born in 1947 in Cleveland, Ohio, Stephen R. Donaldson graduated from the College of Wooster (Ohio) in 1968, served two years as a conscientious objector doing hospital work in Akron, then attended Kent State University where he received his M.A. in English in 1971. He made his publishing debut in 1977 with the first Covenant trilogy; shortly thereafter, he was named best New Writer of the Year and given the prestigious John W. Campbell Award. The bestselling fantasy series continued in *The Second Chronicles of Thomas Covenant*, which was completed in 1983 with the publication of *White Gold Wielder*. Donaldson now lives in New Mexico.